THE HAUNTER OF THE THRESHOLD

EDWARD LEE

deadite press

deadite press

DEADITE PRESS
205 NE BRYANT
PORTLAND, OR 97217
www.DEADITEPRESS.com

AN ERASERHEAD PRESS COMPANY
www.ERASERHEADPRESS.com

ISBN: 1-936383-11-X

"The Haunter of the Threshold" first appeared as a limited edition hardback by Infernal House in 2009.

Copyright © 2010 by Edward Lee

Cover art copyright © 2010 Alan M. Clark
www.alanmclark.com

All rights reserved. No part of this book may be reproduced or transmitted in any form or by any means, electronic or mechanical, including photocopying, recording, or by any information storage and retrieval system, without the written consent of the publisher, except where permitted by law.

Printed in the USA.

For Brian McNaughton.
Rest in peace.

ACKNOWLEDGMENTS: Wendy Brewer, Bob Strauss, Larry & Shane, Ken Arneson, Christine Morgan, Chrisperridas, jonah, Steve Vernon, Tree705, vampduster, Rob Johns, Morleyisozzy, Miss Wellington, Ogreblood, bsaenz24, Bob Taylor, liquidnoose, and many, many others.

Author's Note

I must preamble, as authors often do. THE HAUNTER OF THE THRESHOLD is a sequel—more than likely a damnable one—to what is arguably H.P. Lovecraft's last story in earnest, the brilliant "The Haunter of the Dark"—which is probably my favorite of his stories. ("He," "The Rats in the Walls," "The Hound," and "The Dreams in the Witch-House" are among my other favorites, though almost all of the Master's non-Dunsanian works I hold a very high regard for.) Many of you have read "The Haunter of the Dark," but it was probably none-too-recently; therefore, I urge you to re-read it before embarking on my effort, and rediscover its macabre wonder and phantasmal genius. And those of you who have never read HPL's final masterpiece, please do so now. It is easily procured via public domain sites online, such as: www.psy-q.ch/lovecraft/html/

As you can see, I've dedicated this book to the late, great award-winning novelist Brian McNaughton. Though I never met Brian, I corresponded with him actively in the early '80s (he claimed I was his first "fan" letter not related to his porn books). His horror novels *Satan's Love Child*, *Satan's Mistress*, and *Satan's Seductress* were of a paramount influence. (By the way, those weren't his titles, they were the publisher's! The publisher was Carlyle Communications.) Though some will easily object, I contend that never has Lovecraft's ground-breaking Mythos been so entertainingly redefined in contemporary terms than in these three wonderful books. Revised versions have been re-issued under new titles, though I prefer the originals, and I urge you to seek them out. They're available quite inexpensively from used dealers.

Lastly, I want to thank you, for having enough faith in whatever talents I may have to buy this book. I hope you enjoy it. And may God and H.P. Lovecraft forgive me.

—*Edward Lee*

PROLOGUE

NEPTUNE, NEW JERSEY

It must have been some imp of the perverse that led Wally Gilman to the fly-specked and cigarette-smoke-tinged windows every night. He even remembered that line—"imp of the perverse"—from a Poe story he'd read as a child. (Or perhaps it was another author . . .) Why it occurred to him now (with his penis out!) and why something close to a literary allusion might thrust itself into his darkest introspections . . . he had not the alacrity to cerebrate; lo, he was a fairly unmotivated night-watchmen, not a delver into symbology. He was something else, too: a hopeless voyeur—hence the evidence not only of his exposed and desperately erect penis but also the dried ghost-crust-tracks below this and every window of the motel.

It was a penultimate fleabag *dump* called the McNaughton-Regency Motel that had employed Gilman for so long, though the word "regency," in truth, figured not at all into any aspect of the establishment. The L-shaped hovel sat near a bluff above the coast road and all its well-heeled beach hotels below—just past the exit off the turnpike. The $39-per-night rate told all. Wayfarers came here, not businessmen, and the lower-crust, not tourists and vacationers. Truckers pulled in often as well, which explained the periodic tenancy of prostitutes. Regardless of the nature of the occupants, Gilman had spied upon many a sex act through the dingy windows, and he'd done so with much gusto, exuberance, and satisfaction. He'd watched college choo-choo trains, "Roofie" parties, bachelor parties, "youporn.com" parties, crack-whore tricks, generic one-night stands, and much, much else. Best of all, he got *paid* to perceive this cornucopia of visual delights whilst slaking himself by hand. *I have the BEST job in the world,* Wally mused on a regular basis. For the entirety of his employ, though, no single guest had ever stayed more than a week.

Until now.

The woman in No. 18. *She's been here two months,* he figured, peering in through the gap in the tattered curtains. And a strange situation it was. The woman was pregnant, and, shit, she'd looked fit to drop way back when she'd checked in, yet here she sat, staring at the television night after night, doing absolutely nothing. To Wally's knowledge, she'd yet to even set foot out of the room.

But she was a looker and that's all he cared about–eye-candy and then some. She sat around the room naked *all the time,* and even though her stomach stuck out like a skin-covered basketball, she didn't have a whole lot of fat going on like lots of women once they'd been knocked up awhile. There was something . . . just *something* . . .

The realization was revelatory to Wally Gilman. With the advent of this woman, he came to the conclusion that he must have some kinky "thing" for pregnant chicks. Something about the *fullness* of her, that big alabaster-white belly sticking out like it meant business, all stretched tight; that big beautiful almost black plot of hair between her legs; and—

Those tits, he thought now as he did most every night since she'd arrived. They were big as proverbial cantaloupes, with nipples the size of beer-can rims. Wally was pushing sixty now but even the mere thought of those breasts, at any time of the day or night, got him hard and oozing.

He was done in a minute, imagining her spraddled before him and offering that delectable pink twist of flesh in the middle of her bush. *Shit,* he thought, huffing. His frantic climax pumped yet another milky line below the window sill. When he looked at it, and then looked at all the other dried-up lines in proximity, he thought, *I wonder how just how much cum I've shot on that wall . . .*

Indeed.

He'd never stolen a peek onto the sheet at the check-in desk to discern her name; asking questions of the dried-apricot-faced night-clerk Miss Tilton was something he'd never done. Why bring attention to himself? There were no worries that Miss Tilton might stealthily check up on him during his "rounds" because the sucked-dry, withered stick of an old biddy had a walker. Took her ten minutes just to hobble from the front door to the desk. And though Mr. McNaughton, the owner, had never checked up on Wally, either, the cognizant security officer knew he mustn't take this luxury for granted. Wally had likely masturbated at these windows thousands of times over the years, but he always kept an ear out. *Shit, if I got caught?* The ensuing embarrassment would be inexpugnable.

Back to the woman, though, the woman in No. 18. He could only guess that she was from New Hampshire because every Friday at midnight, some rube-looking redneck dude in a pickup truck stopped by to bring her food, take out the previous week's garbage, and presumably pay the next week's rent. It was all canned food he brought her, and when he came, he scarcely said a word to her. She just smiled kind of dopily at him as he went about his business; she either lay on the bed or sat in the beaten recliner all big-titted and sassy, rubbing her bloated stomach. At any rate, this dude's truck had New Hampshire plates. He was a lean but well-muscled redneck, one long-accustomed to hard manual labor; they were all over the place. The only oddity was the very uncharacteristic ring on his hand: a chunky red stone, a little smaller than a marble maybe. It looked downright silly on a working-class 'neck if you asked Wally.

Most times the dude helped himself to a little midnight delight once he'd discharged his duties. Blowjobs, mainly, and once he'd stroked off on her big, beautiful, wobbly tits. A few other times he'd positioned her on hands and knees and cornholed her. It was all very perfunctory and silent. And when he was done, he left.

Weird, not that Wally was complaining.

Weirder, though, was just a few days ago when, for the first time since she'd checked in, the woman had received additional visitors. This time the pickup truck dude had brought four more rough-and-tumble-looking men, and one woman on the fat side. Wally had peered in evermore keenly at the unusual scene–penis in hand, of course–and witnessed something he couldn't quite explain.

The four men and one woman had stood in line before the pregnant gal, who'd sat in the recliner with her knees hooked over the chair's arms. The hassle was the chair's back faced the window through which Wally secretly peered. *It's fuckin' up my view!* he'd raged in thought, but those were the breaks for a voyeur, eh? You couldn't have it all, all the time.

He'd watched nonetheless. From that flawed vantage point, he saw each newcomer kneel between the pregnant chick's legs and lower their faces. *They're all eating her out,* Wally had reasoned. When they were done, they all left at the same time.

The strangeness begged the question: Why would four dudes and an over-the-hill fat woman come here to simply go down on a pregnant chick and then leave?

Off the wall . . .

Crickets tremoloed; the moon shimmered. Wally's private

business was done for the night but when he turned to get back to his rounds—

He locked up in his tracks.

Shit!

Footsteps came crunching around the corner. Wally stood with his eyes peeled open as the back-lit figure stepped into view.

It's Mr. McNaughton! Fuck! Did he see me jerking off?

Wally snapped on his flashlight.

"Hey, Wal. What'cha doin' back here?" came the familiar but not-terribly-welcome voice.

Wally's adrenalin dropped; he snapped off the flash. It was not Mr. McNaughton, it was Joe Sargent, the stoop-shouldered wise-acre who drove the Route 428 bus. He stopped by at night sometimes to shoot the shit.

"Hey, Joe," came Wally's relieved greeting. "You scared the bejesus out of me."

"How come you're back *here?*" Joe strode up. His face looked weird; it was kind of flat, and he had eyes that seemed too big.

"I was . . . making sure . . . the windows are all secure."

Joe sniggered. "Yeah, and if I had a square dick-hole, I could piss dice." Joe peered into the window and smiled. "Ooo, leggo my preggo!" he said of the pregnant chick who now lay asleep and spread-eagled on the bed. Joe elbowed Wally. "What'cha think? Think she's a virgin?" and then he laughed.

"Shhh! You'll wake her up!"

"Aw, that knocked-up mama's sound asleep." The bus driver peered more intently. "Man, you could plant fuckin' cabbage in all that pussy hair, huh? And would you get a *load* of them *tits?*"

Wally could hardly disagree.

"Yeah. Man," Joe muttered, still peeping. His fingers caged his crotch and squeezed, an action that Wally pretended *not* to see.

Then Joe pulled down his zipper.

"Come on, Joe," Wally griped.

Joe frowned. "What?" He pointed to the window sill and chuckled. "It ain't like you don't."

I guess he's got a point, Wally admitted.

But Joe had scarcely been pumping ten seconds before engine noise alerted them both.

"Fuck!"

"Someone just pulled into the motel!" Wally whispered. "Put your cock back in your pants, man!"

Inside, the pregnant woman came awake at the noise. For one terrifying moment, she looked at the window with a suspicious squint, but then her eyes darted to the motel room door.

When the door opened, six people walked in, led by the original rube.

"Him again," Wally whispered.

"What do you mean?"

"Usually he comes every Friday night by himself, but last time he brought five others with him. And they-and they . . ."

Joe glowered. "Yeah?"

"They all went down on the pregnant chick."

Joe couldn't have been more amused. "You're shitting me!"

"Nope–er, at least I think that's what they were doing. She was sitting with her back to the window so I couldn't see everything."

"But they fucked her, too, right? Or got blowjobs?"

"Naw. They each ate her pussy for a minute and then left. Oh, and one of 'em was a woman." Then Wally pointed. "But these ain't the same people."

This time the rube had brought three men and two women, all of the same low-scale blue-collar cast. But unlike that first occasion, the pregnant woman remained on the bed, hitching her ass to the mattress edge, and then she pulled her knees up. The position puffed her pubis out like a hair-covered tart.

"Now watch," Wally whispered. "Here they go . . ."

A beer-bellied guy in a wife-beater T-shirt was the first to kneel between the woman's legs. The vantage point was much better this time, for Wally could see the action directly. He could also see . . .

How do you like that?

The man in the wife-beater wore a ring just like the original rube: a marble-sized scarlet stone.

"This is gonna be great!" Joe whispered and grinned. "A pussy-eating party on a pregnant girl!" Joe had his cock right back out and in his hand, ready to go.

With great intensity, then, they both stared. Neither of them were the least bit aware that someone was standing right behind them.

1

PROVIDENCE, RHODE ISLAND
TWO MONTHS PREVIOUS

Just as you begin to urinate, the bearded man with the gun lopes into the bathroom.

The pistol goes *click!* and is immediately pressed to your head. Shock bulges your eyes; shock freezes your nerves; shock cuts off the stream of your urine.

"Don't scream," the intruder advises. "Don't fight. Do everything I tell you. Do you understand?"

Your throat wobbles once, then you gasp out, "Yes, but, please, don't—"

The pistol barrel ticks right against your teeth. "And don't talk. I'm not kidding."

The voice sounds dry, slightly muffled, like someone speaking through a scarf. In this instantaneous and utterly unprepared-for horror, you're able to note no details regarding his physical characteristics, race, or attire. All you noticed was the beard when he'd loped right into the bathroom an instant after you'd sat down on the toilet. After that, you see nothing more than the pistol: large and black, and its oddly extended barrel.

"Now," he orders. "Finish pissing."

The command astonishes you, but rather than protesting, you close your eyes, take a deep breath, and *push.*

Nothing comes out.

"I-I'm sorry. I'm just too nervous—"

His hand blurs, and *cracks* you across the face.

"Concentrate," issues the cool monotone. "And lean forward with your hands on your knees. And arch your back."

Your teeth chatter, but in spite of your terror, you do as commanded, while your mind ticks back to the moments before this event barged into the middle of your unassuming life . . .

You'd walked home from campus just as the sun was setting. You felt tired yet fulfilled because you know you're getting the hang of teaching. In your apartment you lock the door behind you at once—there have been rapes just off campus—and you kick off your shoes and strip in the middle of the room, reveling in the gracious stun of cool air after escaping the heat and humidity outside. It's the cool air which constricts your nipples and covers you with delightful gooseflesh. *God, I have to pee,* you think, striding to the bathroom. At once your image is captured in the bathroom mirror and you stop to appraise your reflection.

You *hate* your hair, the unruly red frizz which can only be managed by tying it back behind your head; on any other woman it would become a silken ponytail but on you, it looks like a bristle brush. Yes, you hate your hair and its queer ox-blood-red color, yet everyone else, men and women alike, seem to find it fascinating. Your wedge of pubic hair matches the color, and puffs out in abundance. Shaving or waxing seems all the rage these days, especially with women your age, yet you know you'll never do that, as if the existence of your pubic hair proves something—a ludicrous thought.

You hate your frame too—you think you're too skinny—and you hate the barely perceptible freckles which cover you from head to foot. Like your hair, everyone else finds them fascinating, or "Exotic," several men have said.

But now was not the time to contemplate your self-image: your bladder feels fit to burst, so just as you move to sit on the toilet, a sparkle in the mirror stops you.

It's the cross glittering.

Your father gave it to you long ago, when you at least in part believed in what it symbolized. *How can I now, though?* you wonder, feeling suddenly tainted . . . Your father's last phone message reverberates in your mind: "Please, come back to church. Come back to God. It's where you belong, honey . . . ," so similar to so many other messages which you never had the nerve to answer.

This was when you sat on the toilet and began to urinate, after which the bearded man with the gun waltzed in . . .

"And spread your legs—yeah, like that," he says. "Shit, I love that big red bush. And put your feet back a little too. Push up off the balls of your feet."

Mind-numb, you obey the inexplicable commands.

"It's the image—understand? The image of the pose. I want that image while you're pissing. I need to *see* the pee coming out . . ."

He's crazy, you think.

"Now. Finish pissing. If you don't, then I'll—"

If I don't . . . he'll kill me, you know.

You concentrate, reclosing your eyes. You think of a garden hose cranked all the way open. You think of lawn sprinkler. You think of broken water pipes.

"Come on."

Out it comes, then, the glittering cascade. You can feel the warm void race out of you as if it's escaping this terrible predicament that you cannot escape yourself. Likewise, you hear the near-musical sound of it tinkling down into the toilet water.

"Good. Now, with one hand, play with my cock."

You hitch when you reopen your eyes. He'd already gotten it out, and there it hangs—so suddenly—right in your face. It's limp but fat, with a collar of wrinkled skin. Wiry hairs stick out all around it, as if disgorged through the zipper. You begin to knead it with your fingertips, then—perhaps out of instinct—you incline forward, opening your mouth.

"What are you doing?"

"I . . . Don't you want me to—"

"If I wanted you to suck it, I would have said so. *Play* with it, but just with that hand. The other one stays on your knee. And pull the balls out and play with those too."

You dig into the opened zipper, then gingerly extract his testicles. You cup them, squeeze a few times ever so gently, then let your hand coruscate around their hot, meaty weight. You smell soap, and even in the midst of this atrocious crime think: *At least he washed first. How do you like that? A hygienic rapist . . .*

But that's what this is, beyond a doubt. A rape. *You always hear about it on the news or read it in the paper,* you reflect. *It's always something that happens to someone else . . . But now it's happening to me.*

"Good. Now stand up."

You'd emptied your bladder without realizing it, and when you look again you notice that his penis is fully erect and beating noticeably, well more than average size.

Smack!

You whine at this next smack across your face. "What did I *do?*"

"I said stand up," and then his hand lands in your hair and pulls, yanking you to your feet. Your face buzzes from the slaps, and your scalp aches.

"Open the medicine cabinet."

You watch your shock-wide eyes and moist face slide away as you open the mirrored door.

"Let's see," he says to himself. "There, the Vaseline. Take the top off and put the jar on the floor, then sit back on the toilet."

What on earth . . . , yet you do so, but when you look back up for his next command, all you see is his bobbing erection.

"With your right hand, keep stroking my cock, and with your left hand take the rubber out of my right pocket."

Rubber? You find the packet, and feel now with your other hand that his penis is even harder. When you squeeze it, it doesn't give at all.

"Now put the rubber on my cock," he says, the gun still hovering around your face. "And do it right." A chuckle. "You've probably never even *seen* a rubber before. What I hear is you let all those students of yours fuck you bareback."

When you glare at him—

Smack!

—you get another, harder crack across the face. The impact stifles you this time, you reel a moment, then fumble frantically to remove the condom and roll it down over his penis.

Now it looks alien as it throbs before your eyes. It looks like something cooked and packaged. At this moment, that's what the whole world is: this rapist's erection sheathed in latex.

"Hands and knees," he tells you, and when you assume the position as ordered, he continues, "Turn your head to the right, then put your cheek to the floor," and after you obey, "Stick your fingers in the Vaseline jar and pull out a glob. Rub it all over your asshole, and when you're done doing that, I want you to reach back and pull your butt apart."

Your heart hammers. When you're finished . . .

"Ugh!"

He'd already kneed up behind you and slammed his penis in. The abrupt pressure startles you. Your assailant wastes no time; he's pistoning in and out of you quite quickly, drawing the corona all the way out with each stroke, only to plunge it immediately back in. After but ten strokes, you tighten your rectum—you've tended to enjoy anal sex with lovers, and constricting your anus was something you'd read in *Cosmo* to increase the man's pleasure. It makes sense, doesn't it? To *please* this rapist, for if you don't he'll only be more liable to kill you. So you tighten it as hard as you can—

The man moans, and immediately steps up his pace. You feel his testicles slapping your vagina. Then—

He grunts, hitches, the strokes retard and eventually stop. Moments later, you feel his penis begin to deflate inside you.

This is when you make your most grave mistake.

You chuckle.

"Funny?" he snaps. "What's funny?" and then you squeal as he grabs your hair again and hauls you to your feet. "What? I came fast, so that's *funny?*"

"No, no," you sob.

He slams you so hard against the bathroom door, all your wind goes out. You see him put the gun down, but in the tense paralysis that companions your impact with the door, you can't even think much less commence in a defensive move. Stars burst before your eyes . . .

"Let's see how funny *this* is," and then something goes around your neck, and in the buzz of your terror you realize what it is: the sash from your robe.

You gasp, tears pouring now. "I wasn't—I wasn't laughing, I swear–"

Crack!

Another slap to the face. "Yes, you were. You were laughing at me for coming fast. Well, fuck it, I was gonna let you go, but I think I'll just hang you instead."

It's almost with an expertise that he loops the sash over the hook on the door. You can't help but deduce, *He's done this before.* Your breath barely returns when both of his hands pull down on the other end of the sash.

The makeshift noose tightens as you rise and your feet leave the bathroom's cool tile. Your fingers fly to relieve the noose but it's too tight. Your face begins to swell.

You hear his words now like something muttered in a fish bowl: "Yeah, I guess I'll just hang you, since you're not gonna be a good girl."

Your bare heels pound the door. You're kicking, however, uselessly, for your *life,* and somehow you manage to force words through the noose constricting your throat: "I'll be a good girl, I'll be a good girl—"

Thunk!

He lets the sash go and you collapse to the floor.

The near-strangulation leaves you more disoriented than your worst drunk. Equilibrium is long gone, you're propped on the floor like a lone survivor on a raft rocking in high seas. There's a drone in your head that sounds, somehow, evil, and you know that's what this is: the coal-black evil of lust, perversity, and mental illness dropped like a depth charge into the middle of your life. He grabs the stout brush of hair banded behind your head and shakes it. "Don't pass out. We're not done. Look up here," and you squeal again when he gives your hair a hard twist.

"Take the rubber off. Grab it by the end with your thumb and forefinger and then—listen!—upend it over the toilet. Let the cum fall out of it into the toilet."

The evil drone is fading all too slowly. Your cognizance struggles to understand him. When you see his crotch in your face, you smell your own excrement wafting off it: a rich, fresh funk. Your hands shake when you carefully slip the condom off and empty its contents into the toilet.

"Now . . ." His voice is back to the cool, calm monotone. "Eat the cum out of the toilet."

Dizzily, you look up at him. Your lips tremble as if to speak, but then the pistol is shoved into your face again.

"The thing on the end of my gun is called a chambered sound-suppressor," he tells you. "You know, a silencer? Like in the movies? The gun's loaded with sub-sonic ammunition. If I squeeze this trigger, there'll be no noise. No one will hear the sound. Do you understand?"

Wobbling on your knees, you gulp, manage to nod, then lower your face into the toilet.

It is an act completely subconscious, however, when your hand flies up to your chest to hold back the cross, so it will not depend into the water.

You see the sperm floating there, the milk-white coagulation. You think of a piece of twist pasta. Only now do you remember that after you urinated you didn't flush, so not only will you have to eat his sperm, but you'll have to eat it out of toilet water tinted by your own piss. You stick your lips out like fish lips, lower more, and suck.

You get it on your first try, slurping the lump into your mouth and swallowing.

When you lift your head out, he bends over to inspect. "Hmm. Good," he says in more of the same cool voice, but then it is with his most aggressive violence yet that he grabs your throat and hurls you into the bathtub. Your elbows, knees, and head all *thunk* against the inside of the tub.

"Put the stopper in the drain," he orders. His penis is still hanging out, withered as if exhausted, and wriggling as he speaks, "then lay on your back."

You don't even attempt to understand. The pain in various areas throbs when you turn around in the cramped tub and incline yourself. For one second, you dare to look up. You see him there, standing, gun hovering.

Feebly, you whimper, "I—I'm on my back now . . ."

"I can see that. Just be quiet. Now pull your knees back to your shoulders, all the way back as far as you can."

Here is another unwitting opportunity to please him. From first grade to twelfth you were a gymnast. Your nimble physique, spry form, and double-jointedness left you perfect for this mode of athleticism. With almost no effort, you bring your knees back and slip them fully behind your shoulders.

"Wow, that's cool," he remarks.

But then he begins urinating on you.

You tense in the contorted position; the initial stream hits your belly with such force, it stings. Then he rakes it across your nipples, and they constrict. His urine feels piping hot. You seethe through your teeth when he zigzags the stream back down your belly, then roves it up and down over your vaginal groove. He seems to be trying to piss *into* you from a distance.

"The reason I had you stopper the tub is because I don't want it going down the drain," he says, half-focused on his task. "When I'm done pissing, you're going to drink it. *You're* the drain. Get it?"

I'm the drain, you think.

But what will come after that?

You're being showered on. Your flesh is someone's yard being sprinkled, and you writhe beneath it all.

"Put your hand between your legs and open your pussy . . ."

When you do, the stream begins to separate the folds of your vagina.

"Now masturbate," he says next.

The word, oddly, *clunks* in your head.

"You heard me." A bit more gruff. "Masturbate."

Again, the word *clunks.* It's like a bad chord tainting competent music.

"You deaf? Masturbate! Masturbate while I'm pissing on you!"

The last *clunk,* then the muse shatters like safety glass. *You've got to be kidding me!* you think, and then you unlock your knees from behind your shoulders, slouch up, and eye him with a sigh and look of either disgust or grievous disappointment.

"Damn it, Ashton!" you yell. "That's not in the script! You messed it all up again!"

The stream of urine dwindles. The intruder pulls off the false beard and goes, "Huh?"

It was done. Just like that. The build-up had been near-perfect, but then he had to go and wreck it all. *I didn't even get to come,* she griped to herself.

Hazel Greene hopped up in the tub and yanked the stopper chain. A dull vehemence beat headache-like behind her eyes as she cranked on the shower.

"I followed the script!" insisted the "rapist," who was actually Hazel's boyfriend–er, her *semi*-boyfriend, she thought of him as–a grad student named Ashton Clark.

"You screwed up the *words,* Ashton." She twirled in the shower spray, plunged her face in, then began to lather up with this neat body wash she'd found that smelled like blueberry muffins. "The words, the words, the words."

Ashton stared at her.

Hazel shook her head, which was now an aura of bubbles. "Ashton, a rapist would never say *masturbate.* He'd say 'frig yourself, bitch,' or 'Play with your pussy' or 'finger your snatch'. Something like that."

"Oh for shit's sake!" Ashton flung the dollar-store beard in the waste can, put his penis back in his pants, washed his hands, and stormed out of the room.

Oops, Hazel thought.

After she'd dried off, she traipsed into the living room, wearing only panties covered with orange Smiley Face bats and a towel wrapped about her head. With a cat-grin she came up behind him in the chair and began to rub his shoulders. "Ashton, I'm sorry. I didn't mean to criticize you–"

"Oh, no, not at all," came the obvious sarcasm as he looked coldly at the TV. "I feel like such a loser that I didn't get your precious *script* right again."

"I over-reacted," she whined, "I'm *sorry.* You were really getting me into it—I thought it would be the best ever, but then—"

"I said the wrong words," he finished with a smirk. "Christ, the things I do for women. Makes me wonder about myself; I must be co-dependent or something. Next you'll be wanting me to take acting lessons, just so you can have a better time."

"You seemed to have a good time," Hazel almost snapped back. "You came, didn't you?"

"Hazel, I had to force myself." He laughed sardonically. "I had to think about doing you missionary-style. Shit, what ever happened to the good ole slow comfortable screw, huh? I guess people just don't do that anymore, do they? It's blasé. I guess I'm just not *hip* 'cos I'm not into all this sexual perversion and deviation stuff."

Now Hazel pouted. "It's just a game, Ashton. Lots of couples do it. It's just innocent role-playing."

He gawped at her. "Hazel, Dungeons and Dragons is role-playing. Choking a woman and pissing on her in order to fulfill her addiction to rape-fantasies is something else altogether."

He just doesn't understand, Hazel thought. *He'll get over it.* "But this time it was really intense. Maybe *I'm* the one who should be an actor. I really was able to assume the mind-set of a rape victim. Never once did I—"

"Wait, wait," he said holding his hand up as a commercial ended. "I want to hear this. It's more about that guy who survived the Mother's Day Storm."

Him again, Hazel thought. *Frank's friend.* She sat on the edge of Ashton's chair and began to pat her hair dry. What the news had dubbed the Mother's Day Storm was still mystifying the meteorological and scientific community. It happened two months ago, shortly before dawn; the entire downtown area of St. Petersburg, Florida, had been ravaged by what the National Oceanic and Atmospheric Administration and National Hurricane Center had determined to be some manner of fluke storm activity, something described as a spontaneous confined array of multiple-vortex tornados. 2,900 people had died, with several times that injured, making it the country's worst natural disaster since the San Francisco Earthquake in 1906. This man that Ashton was watching had been the only survivor from the "ground zero" point, where all of the vortexes had apparently touched down. Billions of dollars of damage had been done, several "storm-proof" high-rises had actually collapsed while dozens more had blown out all their windows and had their entire contents sucked out. Occupied apartment complexes were flattened, and even the famous St. Petersburg Pier was torn from its steel-and-cement moorings and broken into chunks. A harrowing tragedy, yes, but like many young people, Hazel regarded it with a distanced detachment. Indeed, like rape, hurricanes, tornados, tidal waves, etc., were things that only happened to other people.

"There he is," Ashton said of the picture flashed on the national news, news: that of a fiftyish man with solemn, intelligent eyes and a gray-touched goatee. "Wilmarth. Did you know he taught here?"

"Yes, Ashton," Hazel droned, bored already. *I guess I should have more compassion,* she realized of her aloofness, *like my father always said.* "Didn't I tell you? Frank Barlow knew him very well."

"Frank–oh, you mean, Professor Barlow, the head of the geometry department?"

"Yeah. Sonia's fiancé."

Ashton smirked, like he always did whenever Hazel referred to her best friend, Professor Sonia Heald, by her first name. "Yeah, the fastest way to earn the title of fiancé is to knock a woman up."

Hazel slapped him—not quite as hard as she would've liked–on the shoulder. She changed the subject's tangent, jabbing her finger at the TV. "So, what? The guy died a few days ago, right? Was he murdered?"

"Maybe if you'd stop talking, we could find out," and then Ashton turned the volume up. A blond newscaster who looked more suited for Hooters employment was informing: "—hours ago when the Belknap County Coroner's Office ruled suicide as

Professor Henry Wilmarth's official cause of death. Wilmarth, a professor in high-standing at Providence, Rhode Island's Brown University, was found dead on his property four nights ago. Local police initially believed that Wilmarth had been murdered, as his lodgings were found ransacked upon the discovery of his body. Today, however, we know that Professor Wilmarth took his own life by hanging himself. Wilmarth miraculously survived last May's massive multiple-vortex tornado system which killed nearly 3000 residents in a fifteen-minute period and damaged or demolished a several-square-mile perimeter of the city of St. Petersburg. Shortly before sunrise on May 12, Wilmarth had been sitting on a bench in a park-area known as Mirror Lake, and witnessed the entire storm from all directions. He'd undergone treatment for shock immediately afterward, and later, trauma therapy." Now the screen showed an aerial of "ground zero." Trees were uprooted, buildings either crushed or roofless, car-sized chunks of rubble lay scattered everywhere save for a modest circle of land near a pond. A graphic arrow appeared on the screen, pointing to that circle, with the legend, WILMARTH'S POSITION DURING THE STORM.

"Good God," Ashton gasped. "Every time they show this, it looks worse. It looks like Berlin after the Allied bomber offensive."

"All but that little area where Professor Wilmarth was sitting," Hazel remarked with fading attention. "Talk about lucky . . ."

The newscaster went on, "Wilmarth commented very little about his eye witnessing the storm, only to say, 'It wasn't a tornado cluster. Of that I'm certain . . .'"

More shots of the city's destruction flashed. "Experts at the U.S. Meteorological Center estimate that the destructive energy released in these several square miles may have equaled all of the force combined during the April, 1974, Super Outbreak that tore through 13 states from Ohio to North Carolina, produced 148 twisters, and killed over 300 people."

"All that power," Ashton muttered, "packed into just a couple square miles . . ."

"It's too depressing," Hazel complained and switched it off. "And they show it over and over again. I don't know why they do that. Like Katrina, and the tsunami several years ago."

"Hazel, how can the daughter of a Christian minister be so apathetic? It was a tragic event. It'll take years to repair all that damage," Ashton said.

"I'm not denying that! I just don't understand why they have to show it over and over. It's like the media's rubbing our faces in it. Christ, it happened months ago."

But Ashton was still reflecting upon the event itself. "Can you imagine what would've happened it if had lasted for fifteen hours instead of fifteen minutes?"

Hazel chose *not* to imagine. "But I wonder what Wilmarth meant when he said it wasn't really tornados?"

"Who knows . . . After sitting through all that? And being right in the middle of it, and somehow being the only survivor? Just the shock of it all probably fried his brain crispier than a bag of pork rinds."

At last a question occurred to Hazel, not that it mattered much. "What was he doing in Florida anyway?"

"Vacation, I guess," Ashton said. "He only retired from Brown a year or two ago. Hell, why don't you ask Frank Barlow? You're going to *see* him this week, aren't you?"

Hazel smirked. She didn't like the way he said that. "I'm not going on this road trip to see *him.* I'm riding up with Sonia, to keep her company."

"*Sonia,*" he emphasized. "You mean *Professor* Heald."

"She's my boss, Ashton, and my best friend—"

Ashton was beginning to develop a permanent frown. "You're twenty-two, Hazel. She's thirty-five. Twenty-two-year olds don't have *best friends* who're thirty-five. It's weird."

It's not weird, Hazel confessed to herself. *It's just that I'm in love . . . "* Let me get this straight. Is it *Frank Barlow* you're jealous of, or *Sonia?*"

He made a grim chuckle under his breath and got up. "With *my* karma? It's probably both."

She could've spit . . . but then how disingenuous would *that* have been? She didn't feel bad about being an overly sexualized woman, but she did feel bad about keeping things from Ashton. In truth, she'd had a sexual dalliance with Sonia last winter, and one with Frank Barlow before that. *None of them can ever know about the other,* she fretted. "Don't be so uptight all the time," she said after Ashton. "The only one I'm sleeping with is you."

"*Sleeping* with?" he questioned, and now the cynicism was really pouring out. "Is that what we do?" He meandered over to some bookshelves and grimaced at the titles along the top row. *Understanding Chronic Female Paraphilia,* one read. *Ideas of Reference and Sexual Aberrancy. The Modern Rape-Fantasy Complex.*

"Jesus," Ashton muttered.

"It's just fetish stuff, Ashton," she complained, because she knew what he was thinking.

He raised a high brow at her. "I think some of your interests go *beyond* fetishism, Hazel. Hell, you *know* they do, otherwise you wouldn't have gone to those counselors."

"That was before you and I were dating, and—shit—I wish I'd never told you about it now. It's like you're throwing it in my face."

"I'm just confused . . ."

"I have sexual desires that are different from most women, Ashton. That's all. Why can't you accept that? The only reason I went to counselors in the first place was to find out if I was sick, which I'm *not.*"

"I never said you were—"

"No, but that's what you imply." She leveled her eyes on him. "That's what you think: I'm *sick.* I'm fucked up in the head."

"I do not."

"I'm only twenty-two years old and I'm already working on my doctorate," she pressed on, maybe to give him a little pay back. "Do *sick* people do that? How many 'fucked up in the head' *twenty-two year olds* already have their masters? Oh, and by the way, you're *how* old? Twenty-*six?* And still working on yours?"

Ashton laughed. "I never said I was smarter than you, Hazel. But your idea of fun and games can really get over the top. I don't know how to–what's the word? I don't know how to *reckon* it. I don't know how to assess our relationship sometimes."

Hazel's shoulders and pert bare breasts slumped at the same time. "Ashton, you know you're not supposed to use the R-word. We've discussed this over and over. We're lovers, that's all. We're friends, and what's wrong with that? I'm not looking for a *relationship* now—

not the kind you're talking about." She drifted to the window, only half-noticing the Providence's stately financial district, the School of Design, and the fringes of the college whose lights were just flicking on as dusk arrived. Headlamps beat like glitter down Fulton Street, and the bay looked like something molten as the sun sank. "Things are better when they're not complicated, right?"

"But I love you," he replied.

This is not going well. Why are men so needy? "You're kidding me, Ashton. The R-word *and* the L-word in the same day!"

He pulled his t-shirt back on, which read HARRY WAS RIGHT. THE CELLAR WAS THE SAFEST PLACE. Hazel had never known what that meant, and had never asked. *Because I'm not interested in HIM. I'm only interested in what he does for ME.* This she knew too well and usually felt guilty.

"I can't help how I feel," came his next blank remark. He put the pistol back in a box that read REPLICA SIG P-226. When he put the box up on the shelf he noticed Hazel's answering machine blinking. "You've got a message."

"I'm sure it's just my father again."

"Aren't you going to call him back?"

The question exasperated her. "Yeah, later, Ashton. What's it to you?" but, again, she knew what he was thinking in his ever-tailspinning paranoia. *He thinks it's some guy who called, some guy I'm fucking behind his back.* "Here, listen, since you're so interested," she griped and hit the play button:

"Hazel, honey, it's me, your father. Please call me, I haven't talked to you in weeks, and I'm worried." A pause. "God wants you back, and He always will. So, please. Come back. Come back to church . . ."

The message ended.

"Not a bad idea, huh?" Ashton said.

"What?"

"It might do you some good, going back to church, I mean."

She couldn't resist. "You have a big credibility problem. Here's a guy who just held me at gunpoint and made me eat his *cum* out of the toilet, telling me I need to go to church."

His teeth ground, and he growled, "I only do that nutty sicko stuff because it's what *you* want!"

"Jeez, Ashton, I was only joking. You set yourself up, you know."

"You ain't kidding." He flung his book bag over his shoulder. "But if you don't believe in God, why do you wear that cross?"

Do I believe in God? she asked herself. The question made her feel withered. "Maybe I'm just into iconography, Ashton. Did you ever think of that?"

"Ask a silly question . . ." He looked utterly defeated as he gazed at her. "I have to go now."

"Don't you want to go to dinner? We could drive out to Cagliastro's Fry House." she objected. "It's my last night."

"Yeah, before your *road trip* with your best friend—"

"Sonia's my best female friend, and you're my best male friend," she amended.

"Great. I have to go to the Hay and study tonight. But have fun on your trip." He headed for the door. "Where exactly is this campground you're going to?"

"It's in central New Hampshire, near some town called Laconia."

Ashton turned very slowly to re-face her.

"Why are you looking at me like I just said 'Rosebud?'"

"Didn't you say you and Sonia were driving up there to meet her fiancé, Frank Barlow?"

"Yeah. He's been up there a few days. We're going hiking and nature-trailing. So?"

"To a campground near *Laconia,* New Hampshire?"

"Yeah . . ."

"And Frank Barlow was friends with Professor Henry Wilmarth."

Hazel's lips pursed. "Yes, Ashton! So what?"

"That's where Henry Wilmarth committed suicide," Ashton augmented. "It said so on the news. He committed suicide at a campground near *Laconia, New Hampshire.*"

Finally the words sunk in. Hazel's green eyes glittered in bewilderment. "How . . . odd."

Ashton flapped it off. "Just a coincidence. I'm sure there are a thousand campgrounds up there. Couldn't possibly be the same one . . ."

2

Hazel dreamed of faceless men gang-raping her in what appeared to be a barn. Though she'd never actually *been* in a barn, ever in her life, this had to be one because she saw bales of hay, racks of tools, wagons with harnesses as if to be drawn by horses, plows, etc. Wooden ladders led to upper lofts above crisscrossing rafters, and stacked on platforms sat more bales of hay. The men were dressed in Colonial garb: brass-buckle boots, billow-sleeved tunics, rough-fabric trousers with rope belts, and they all wore three-pointed hats; but, as aforementioned, they had no faces. Neither did they speak; in fact, the dream—the nightmare—existed in dead silence.

She was nude and covered with scratches; when her profuse sweat ran into the long, thin cuts, her skin sang in pain. The men all stood round watching, their uncircumcised penises hanging from the fronts of the pants like dirty, fleshy snouts. One held her from behind, pinioning her elbows together so extremely that her breasts thrust right out and her spine arched back like a bow. Another stepped up and began to lay his open palm across her face time and time again, dozens of times, then dozens more until her cheek throbbed and she could see nothing but a dizzied tulle of sparkles. When the blows had all but rendered her senseless she was lain down in the straw and a man on each ankle wish-boned her legs. A third kept his boot-sole vising her throat so she couldn't squirm. One by one and in grueling, silent slowness they raped her, each dirty "snout" sliding into her over-lubricated sex, in and out until, at the precise moment before crisis, each was promptly withdrawn to ejaculate copiously upon her belly and bosom.

At the end of this first round, Hazel lay enslimed and shimmering. Some minutes passed, then round two commenced. Her ankles were pulled over her head, to essentially fold her in half, and then the process repeated itself, only this time it was her rectum that was routed; here, though, the ejaculations were not externalized but instead pumped deep into her bowel. When they'd all finished, she was held in that same position . . . and round three began.

Oh my God, is that a . . .

Two men led in a large, mangy field dog that was immediately positioned over her. The animal needed little goading before the glistening pink bone slid out of its penile sheath and got to the task of steady fornication. Hazel felt cross-eyed as it desperately humped, yet in the middle of the process one man dragged a cotton sack over her head and then—

Whiiiiiizzzzzzz

—the sack grew saturated. Hazel knew that one of them had urinated on the sack, and the sequent moisture made it nearly impossible to breathe through the fabric. Meanwhile, the dog humped on and on, that pink bone darting in and out, and as Hazel's consciousness began fading to black, she thought, *They're going to smother me to death while I'm being fucked by a dog,* and it was during the instant that this thought crossed her mind, her loins began to quake in a series of powerful orgasmic spasms. Every muscle in her body drew taut from the cannonade of gusting pleasure . . .

Moments before she would surely suffocate, the sack was yanked off her head. She sucked in breath while at the same time sensing the dog's hot, watery release. Hazel sighed from the exhausting satisfaction.

Suddenly the men's voices could be heard, like a mute button being switched off. "Keep her devil's slit upward, brothers. It mustn't spill out."

"T'is no transgression to defile one who blasphemes against God."

"Christian soldiers, let's be about it! String her up!"

Pulleys keened after loops were slipped around her ankles and she was suddenly being hoisted upside-down in the air.

"This ungodly harlot needs to die full of the cur's jism . . ."

The ropes were tied off, leaving Hazel suspended. Upside-down, she watched the men leave the barn, but even in the horror of this trauma, every nerve still buzzed from the delicious orgasm.

"Hazel, my child," came a soft, echoic voice.

It had come from above. Squinting, she looked up into the loft-platforms past the network of rafters. From the lower lofts, squashed, indescribable faces peered down, fang-mouthed, snake-tongued, and gibbering in delight at what had been done to her. *Demons,* she thought, because some of them had horns in their heads.

"Hazel, I adjure you . . ."

It was from the highest loft that the clement voice issued, and it was not the face of a demon she saw speaking to her. It was a long-haired, bearded man whose eyes radiated a strange and pristine *peace.*

"Hazel, child of God. Come back. I adjure you."

Save me, she thought and reached up to him, but as she did so, the cross hanging about her neck slipped off her head and fell to the dirt below.

Hazel woke up as if at a pistol shot, and after a moment of shifting awareness, she covered her face with her hands and thought, *Sick, sick, sick . . .*

Then she jerked up in bed and shuddered.

"I'm sick," she whispered aloud, and when she did so she glimpsed her reflection in the mirror above the dresser and thought of *The Scream* by Edvard Munch. *If any other woman had a dream like that, they'd throw up,* she thought. *But me? I'm turned on like a light.* It was bleak times like this that Hazel realized no amount of rationalization or liberal shrink-talk could sway the truth. Last night when she'd snidely told Ashton that she wasn't sick, just highly sexualized, she knew she was lying. She was obsessed—*titillated*—by fantasies of defilement, debasement, and all manner of rape. *It's not right. It's all I think about . . .*

Well, not quite *all.*

I think about Sonia, too. A lot. And these thoughts carried with them no taint of the rough and seamy fantasies that so occupied her id. Somehow, Sonia was the floodgate. Hazel's secret love for the older woman burned so acutely that her subconscious punished her in the knowledge that that love could never be returned. Her love for Sonia Heald couldn't have been more crystalline, nor more beautiful . . . but then the floodgates opened like a sewer line piped directly into the midst of her soul. *If I can't have Sonia, then fate force-feeds me filth,* she knew.

Why?

She deliberately blanked her mind as she readied herself, then dressed in shorts, a tank top, and fluorescent-orange flipflops. This was the only time of the year when such flimsy apparel was a comfortable bet in New England. Her Salvador Dali clock—a melting dial—read two minutes to seven in the morning. She grabbed her bags and rushed out of the off-campus apartment; she'd scarcely set foot in the parking lot when Sonia beeped and pulled up in her brand-new silver Prius.

"Hi, Hazel," said the pretty, near-black-haired woman in the driver's window. "You're right on time, as always."

I love you, Hazel thought, staring with her bags hanging off her arms. She could've wept.

"Get out," Hazel directed. "Let me drive."

"Oh, I can drive—"

"You should just *relax* and enjoy the scenery. The doctor told you to relax." Hazel threw her bags in the back, then opened the driver's door.

"Hazel, you don't need to pamper me. I'm perfectly capable of driving–"

Hazel giggled. "You'll be uncomfortable. Come on, look. Your stomach barely fits behind the wheel."

Sonia looked down at her gravidity, then raised her brows. Only an inch of space existed between the bottom of the wheel and her belly. "Well . . ."

"Women who're nine months pregnant shouldn't be driving on six-hour road trips."

"I'm *eight* months pregnant, Hazel, and it's only a *three*-hour drive."

"Come on. Out."

Sonia, with more than a little difficulty, swiveled her legs out of the footwell, then let Hazel take her hand and help her to her feet. *Ashton says I'm more like a guy visually,* Hazel mused. *And I guess he's right.* When Sonia leaned over to rise, her thinly bra'd breasts slid half out of the v-cut of her summer dress. Hazel's eyes targeted the fleshy, white valley without forethought. She wanted to plunge her face into the warm abundance of mammarian flesh. She wanted to lick the valley . . .

"Up you go," she said when Sonia got fully to her feet.

Sonia stood five-eight—six inches taller than Hazel—and impeccably postured for a woman late in term. Even before she'd become pregnant, she'd always been robust-bodied, not overweight: exorbitant curves; wide hips; strong, well-toned legs; and a high, full bosom. A "brick shit-house" men would call her, whereas they called Hazel a "spinner." *Luxurious* was the word Hazel would use to best describe her friend's physique. Even in her pregnancy, she'd not gained undue weight. The mere sight of Sonia's body made Hazel want to melt. *I'm like a teenaged boy looking at a centerfold of Pam Anderson.*

The angles of Sonia's face would make a model jealous, and there was something about her creamy, white-white skin that just seemed flawless. It glowed in the healthiest luster, while the thick, straight hair put a black frame around the beaming face.

Ice-blue eyes blinked over a beaming smile. "What's wrong?"

"Wrong?" Hazel snapped out of it. "Nothing, I was . . ."

A scolding half-smile. "Never mind! Just help me in."

Hazel knew that *Sonia* knew . . .

Once they were belted in, Hazel got on the road, happy to be taking a break from the college and the hot summer session.

"It's sweet of you to drive," Sonia said. "But when you get tired, just say so, and I'll take over."

"Forget it." The university's main gate shrank in the rearview. "This'll be a lot of fun. I *need* a long drive to clear my head."

"Oh, yeah?"

"Sure. I just graded forty term papers on the elements of Naturalism in Henrik Ibsen's *The Master-Builder*."

"You're the one who wants to be an English professor. *The Wild Duck's* better, anyway." Sonia eyed her. "But that's not *really* what you want to clear your head of. Hazel, I can always tell."

I'll bet you can. "Guy Stuff, then. Ashton thinks I'm a perv. It's starting to bother me."

"Like they say, 'Can't live with 'em, can't put 'em out with the garbage.' If he truly loves you, he'll view your kinkiness not as perversity but as sexual diversity, as *uniqueness*."

But it IS perversity, Hazel thought, remembering the noxious yet ecstatic dream. "I don't really want him to love me, anyway. He'll wind up getting hurt, and I'd feel bad about that."

"Ah, someone else on the horizon, then . . ."

Hazel remained silent for a long pause. "I just want to forget about men during this trip. Pretend they don't exist."

"That might not be too easy. Frank'll be joining us tomorrow."

"Tomorrow? I thought he was there now."

"Not at the cabin. He's out camping and hiking."

Hazel tried not to let the sudden inner-exhilaration show. *If he won't be there till tomorrow . . . then Sonia and I'll be alone together tonight.* "I haven't camped since Girl Scouts—hated it."

"Hazel!" Sonia squealed. "*You* were a Girl Scout?"

"Well, yeah."

"I just can't picture that . . ."

Yeah, but I can picture you. In bed. With me, Hazel teased herself with the thought. *Just like last December . . .* "And I was a *terrible* Girl Scout too."

Sonia grinned. "In what way?"

"I . . . ," but then Hazel caught herself. *I can't possibly tell her that.* "Smoking cigarettes and stuff," she lied. "Smuggling dirty romance novels." In truth, though, at twelve years old, Hazel had seduced several of the other girls. She'd shown them how to masturbate, she'd demonstrated cunnilingus. *My God, if I'd been caught . . . If they'd told my father . . .* She shivered.

"I don't know why," Sonia remarked. Breeze from the window tossed her perfect black hair around, "but I was trying to think of that word the other day, after the three-fifteen class. You'd already left—"

"What word?"

"The word that you always mention, that the counselor applied to you. Not fetishism, but . . ."

"Paraphilia," Hazel informed. "The direction of sexual interest towards objects, non-coital sex acts, or sexual stimulation under unconventional circumstances. It's a bit more complex than fetishism; it's more compulsive, or so they say. But 'non-obstructive paraphilia' is what I have, so it's not considered clinical and therefore not a *syndrome* that requires therapy."

"Non-obstructive?" Sonia questioned.

"It's like the difference between someone who drinks too much socially and a clinical alcoholic. An alcoholic is controlled by booze. It *obstructs* his ability to function at work and maintain an operable social and domestic life. Eventually the alcohol addiction costs him his job, family, friends, finances, and all that. But in non-obstructive paraphilia, people still function successfully. That's me," but even as Hazel rendered the explanation she knew she was being less than truthful. She functioned "normally," and was successful in her assistant teaching post, but deep-down her obsessions periodically boiled over into something nearly aberrant. She *knew* this. It even got to the point that she was so uncomfortable and ashamed of some of her obsessions that she eventually downplayed them to the short-lived therapist last year. *I was too afraid she'd give me a clinical diagnosis . . .*

"But, Sonia, why on earth would you be thinking of that?"

Sonia's smile constricted like someone admitting to something they weren't too proud of. "But you said paraphilia is rare among women?"

"Yeah, very rare–believe me, I've read as much about it as most shrinks. Paraphilia affects ninety-five percent men, and five percent women." Hazel shot a reproving frown. "Now answer my question."

Sonia sighed. "Well I've got one too, then, that's all I meant."

The comment strangely sped Hazel's heart. "What?"

"I don't want to say!"

"Bullshit!" Hazel raised her voice. "I've told you all my groaty stuff! That's not fair!"

"It's just a . . . visual thing, well . . . sort of."

"Sonia, if you don't tell me, I'm gonna pull over and leave you on the road, pregnant or not!"

"All right . . ." the older woman conceded. "You know that new transfer student from Marquette—our five-fifteen, Tuesday, Thursday? George something."

"George Cucker," Hazel said. "I guess he's okay looking. What, you have fantasies about *him?*"

"There's something about his build and face, I guess," Sonia admitted, "but the other day before he left class, he asked me something about *Gatsby*—God, I hate that book, Fitzgerald was so overrated—but after he left, I had the weirdest idea: I fantasized that I was in bed with him, and while he was asleep, I was feeling him up and, well, jerking him off. All while he was asleep."

Hazel laughed.

"But that doesn't qualify as a paraphilia, does it?"

"Oh, yes it does," Hazel assured. "It's called somnophilia."

"You're kidding me. There's a *term* for it?"

"Sure. You wouldn't believe some of the paraphilic labels. Klismaphilia: sexual arousal from receiving an enema."

"No way! There are people like that?"

"Yep. Oh, and here's a keeper: Agalmatophilia, sexual attraction to statues or mannequins."

Sonia squealed.

"But I don't get the George Cucker thing," Hazel went on. "He's kind of a dolt, isn't he?"

"I guess, but he had how do I say this without sounding crude?"

"Just say it!" Hazel cracked.

"He must be endowed because he had a really big crotch-bulge."

"I *love* it! Not only are you a somnophiliac, you're also a macrogenitagliac! Arousal to large male sex organs."

"Well, come on, every woman has that," Sonia supposed.

"Not really. Some women—*micro*genitagliacs are turned on by guys with small penises. And then there's endovulvism: men who're attracted to girls with overly large vaginal folds."

Sonia's mouth hung open in disbelief.

"And I hate to tell you this," Hazel kept pedantizing, "There's also lactaphily—"

"Attraction to lactating women?"

Hazel nodded. "And—are you ready? Cyesolagnia: men turned on by *pregnant* women."

"Oh, that's good to know!"

Hazel leaned over, lowering her voice. "Can I ask a personal question?"

Sonia's face scrinched. "I don't know!" she laughed. "This conversation is getting pretty gritty!"

"Since you're now a confirmed somnophiliac . . . do you ever jerk Frank off in his sleep?"

"I'm not telling!"

"Of course, you have," Hazel felt sure. "And there's nothing wrong with that. Everybody's got some little sexual quirk. At least you're not an *idrophrodiac.*"

"Hazel, I *don't* want to know–"

"Someone who's aroused by the smell of unwashed genitals."

"Shut up! No more!" Sonia's laughter pealed. "We're *changing* the subject!"

It was too funny. "Since you *are* my boss, I guess I can go along with that." She'd already turned off onto the Providence outer loop and was suddenly navigating the small car amid rows of weaving traffic. "Wait a minute! Which way to New Hampshire? I've never been there."

"This exit here, get on I-95 north. It's a shame you've never been to New Hampshire. The place is absolutely *beautiful.*"

Hazel caught the ramp. "It's the *Granite* state, isn't it? Granite doesn't appeal to me."

"Eighty-percent of the state is under forest cover, and wait'll you see the lakes region, where we're going. I've never been to the cabin, but I've driven through many times. You've never seen the Great Outdoors like this."

"But . . . Laconia," Hazel wondered. "Isn't that a ritzy lakefront area full of rich snobs with multi-million-dollar yachts?"

"Yes, but we're going west of there, to a place called"—Sonia pulled her Mapquest sheets out of her purse. "Bosset's Way. Frank says it's like Hooterville New England-style."

"*Hooter*ville? Sounds like a guy-place: lots of women with big breasts."

"No! Didn't you ever watch *Petticoat Junction* when you were little?" Sonia rolled her eyes through a pause. "Oh, of course not. You're too young."

"I guess so." Hazel put the car on cruise-control. Deep down she brimmed with an obscure expiation. *See, I'm not the only one with sexual kinks. Even Sonia's got one* . . .

Or was this simply more rationalization?

It summoned every effort not to take side-glances at Sonia, who sat contentedly in the passenger seat, reading over school notes. Her sturdy legs crossed at the ankles, the heavy but firm bosom jiggling minutely atop the life-filled belly. Hazel's lip trembled in the hijacking fantasy: they stood together, nude, caressing each other, their hands exploring every inch of the other's body. Hazel dribbled baby oil into her hands, then adoringly glazed Sonia's skin with it, gently kneading the swollen breasts, smoothing the oil over the even more swollen abdomen, then the arms, legs, and back, until Sonia shined like a beautiful human gem . . .

"Are you day-dreaming?" Sonia asked with some alarm. Hazel's muse had distracted her to the extent that the tires crossed the shoulder's outer line. She righted it at once, thinking, *Pay attention!* "Sorry. I'm just happy to—" she wanted to say how happy she was to be with Sonia, but that wouldn't do. "I'm happy to be getting out of town. I still have papers to grade from our classics class, but it'll just be so nice to do it in a log cabin in the middle of the woods instead of my dreary little apartment."

"Couldn't agree more," Sonia said. "It's not a *log* cabin, though. It's called a slant cabin. Frank showed me pictures; it looks pretty cool–very Henry David Thoreau, so English junkies like us will appreciate it more. And the water supply comes from a real underground spring."

"Sounds pretty rustic." Hazel's ponderings lengthened. "There *is* electricity, isn't there?"

"Oh, sure. It's not *total* boondocks."

"What compelled Frank to rent this particular cabin just for a mid-summer break?"

"Nothing," Sonia said. "The cabin is owned by Professor Henry Wilmarth. I told you he and Frank were colleagues, right?"

Professor Henry . . . Hazel's eyes held on the road.

"Or I should say, the cabin *was* owned by him," Sonia corrected.

"I remember talking to him a few times. The man who committed suicide a few days ago," Hazel droned.

"Last Saturday night to be exact. I'm sure you've seen stuff about him on the news since last May."

The man who walked out of ground-zero of the Mother's Day Storm. "This is too much of a coincidence, Sonia. Just last night, when they said on the news his official cause of death was suicide, Ashton couldn't believe it when I told him where we were going. We thought it was just a fluke that his place of death was in the same vicinity to where you and I were going."

Sonia tossed her head. "I didn't think it necessary to tell you *all* the details." She errantly touched Hazel's bare shoulder. "Then you might not have come along."

The comment ambushed Hazel. *She was thinking of ME. She really wanted ME to go with her* . . .

"Wilmarth and Frank were working together on some side project for years," Sonia said. "Originally Frank's father was working on it too."

"Frank's father?"

"Yeah, he'd known Wilmarth long before Frank met him. But several years ago, Frank's father got some disease and lost his sight."

"Oh, that's too bad."

"But, anyway, that's why Frank invited us up. Wilmarth had a lot of papers stored at the cabin, so Frank's collecting it all. The gross part is Wilmarth was pretty deliberate in his intentions. See, early last week he asked Frank to come up to work on some stuff, he told

Frank to arrive on Sunday."

"But you said Wilmarth killed himself Saturday," Hazel remembered.

"Yeah. So it's pretty clear Wilmarth orchestrated the invitation only to make sure that his body was discovered promptly. It was Frank who found it."

Hazel ground her teeth. "Oh, that *is* gross."

"Must've been quite a shock. Frank walked in there thinking he was going to see his old friend, but his old friend was dead."

"Wait a minute," the idea flashed in Hazel's head. "So you're telling me that Henry Wilmarth killed himself in the same cabin we're going to be staying in?"

Sonia nodded with some reluctance. "I . . . guess I should've told you that too—"

Hazel was astonished. "Yeah, well, maybe that might've been nice!"

"But then you wouldn't have come . . ."

Yes, I would've, Hazel knew.

"You're a teaching assistant at an Ivy League college, Hazel," Sonia justified her neglect with information. She cast Hazel another beaming grin. "You don't believe in ghosts, do you?"

"No! But at least tell me he didn't off himself in the bed *I'll* be sleeping in!"

Sonia laughed light-heartedly. "No. He hanged himself. In his den. If anyone needs to be concerned about ghosts, it's Frank 'cos the den's where all Wilmarth's papers are."

Great. I'm staying in a cabin out in the boondocks where a guy croaked! Hazel liked surprises of a *sexual* nature but not surprises such as this. However, her irritation melted away when Sonia, next, patted Hazel's knee, and assured, "We're going to have a lot of fun, just you wait."

"Oh, I'm fine," Hazel said.

"And Frank says there are some neat, out-of-the-way places to eat. Authentic regional cuisine."

"Oh, granite burgers, right?"

"Don't be a smart ass."

"Actually, I pretty much eat anything," Hazel said. "When I eat rock crabs or lobster, I even eat the guts."

"Thanks for sharing that with me," Sonia said and made a face.

"When I was in junior high, my father took me to Phoenix—he had some kind of minister's convention—and I ate roasted iguana, and—yes—it tasted like chicken."

"Yuck. Cold-blooded animals should be in a terrarium, not on the dinner table."

Yeah, I eat anything, all right, Hazel's dirty thoughts kicked in. *And I'd sell my soul to eat YOU,* but then the cross about her neck seemed to heat up as if in outrage. *My soul?* She could've laughed. *Who am I kidding? With the shit in my head, and all the sins I've committed, my soul's worth about a buck. In Monopoly money.*

Exits for Framingham, Waltham, and Boston swooshed by on the overhead green road signs; even in this little time, they'd already penetrated Massachusetts. Suddenly Hazel felt a pang of despair. Time tended to fly when she was enjoying herself, and she feared this trip would be over before she knew it. It would be the most time she'd spent with Sonia in the two years she'd known her. *She MUST know I have feelings for her. I KNOW she does.* Hazel could only hope that circumstance—and perhaps a little attraction on Sonia's part–might leave the older woman with her guard down. *Just one night, just one hour . . . Please . . .*

Her mind was running circles again; it always did when her obsessions encroached. *Find something to talk about!* She fished for small-talk ideas, then settled for, "You said Frank and Wilmarth were working on a side project?"

"Yes, for years, along with Frank's dad."

"What kind of project?"

"Just boring math shit. They're all eggheads. In fact, a long time ago, Frank's father was the dean of Princeton's school for applied mathematics."

"Wow. I guess Frank inherited dear ole dad's smarts."

Sonia giggled. "And his looks, too. One time I saw an old picture of his father and he was the spitting image of Errol Flynn."

"Errol . . . . Oh, is he the guy with the mullet on *American Idol?*"

Sonia stared. "You really are a kid, Hazel. But I guess that's my point: smarts *and* looks run in the family. It's funny, the thing I'm most attracted to in Frank is his personality, but it also helps that he's handsome as hell."

Hazel kept her hands steady on the wheel. She knew she had to say something in response but she also knew how careful she must be. *She'd hate me if she ever found out*... "Personality? I don't really know him that well but, yeah, sure, he's got a good personality."

Several moments of silence followed, which seemed strange, but when Hazel glanced over she noticed Sonia grinning at her some more, only the grin was widening to the point she feared her friend was about to burst out laughing.

"Sonia, why are you grinning at me?"

"Oh, nothing. I shouldn't play with you like that."

"*What?*"

"Oh for goodness sake, Hazel. Whenever you and I are talking and Frank's name comes up, you act like you're on pins and needles. It's *okay.*"

Dread began to slide into Hazel's spirit.

"I *know* about your little get-it-on session with Frank last summer," Sonia added.

Now it felt like ice-water had flooded Hazel's gut. She gulped, then suddenly had tears in her eyes. "You—you *do?*"

"Yes, honey, and don't worry." Another pat on the knee. "It's okay."

"I . . . I—Oh, Jesus, Sonia!"

Sonia laughed. "He told me about that the day after it happened."

Hazel was still trembling at the jolt. Suddenly she bubbled over with the need to confess. "I'm sorry! It was the night when the drama department did *Lear,* and I got drunk, remember, and–"

"Yes, Hazel, I remember. And I got tired and left early and made Frank promise to drive you home—"

"And—and—Holy fuck, Sonia! I didn't mean to, and it was mostly my doing 'cos I was so crocked! And—damn it—I've felt like such a shit ever since but—but—but . . . you *knew* all along?"

"Yes. It's no big deal."

Hazel was practically apoplectic. "You're my best friend and I fucked your fiancé, and you're not *mad?*"

"Not at all."

"I can't believe you're still speaking to me!"

Sonia put her arm about Hazel's shoulder, then gave her a peck on the cheek. "Honey, I'm a liberal college professor and so is Frank. We both know that humans are human and sometimes people falter when their inhibitions are down. Jealousy doesn't *exist* in my relationship with Frank. So there's no need for you to get all weird anymore whenever the topic of Frank comes up."

Hazel looked fretfully over. "But he doesn't know about—"

"About the little fun-session you and I had last winter after the faculty Christmas party? Of *course* he does."

My God . . . It took Hazel several moments to come to grips with this eruption of information. "Sonia, I swear, I never meant to deceive you–you're *very* important to me!"

"And you're important to me too, Hazel," Sonia said more like a mother calming down a child.

Hazel felt desperate that Sonia believe her. "The only reason I didn't tell you was because, because I know how much you love him and I thought if I told you, then it would ruin everything for both of you."

"You were sweet to think that," Sonia passed it off. "But just forget about it all now—"

"But-but, you know, we didn't really even *do* much," Hazel continued to stammer. "We-we didn't really even have sex, er, intercourse, I mean. We just—"

"Relax!" Sonia laughed. "He told me all the gory details."

Hazel gulped again.

"Frank and I have done open-sex stuff before, and we probably will again." Now Sonia was checking her lashes in the flip-down mirror. "It's just a matter of acknowledging the human sex drive and the need for periodic diversity; it's proof that he and I are *secure* in our relationship. But now that I've told you—please—stop acting all stressed whenever the topic of Frank comes up. Everything's cool."

Hazel felt herself deflating in relief as she drove on. *Thank God, thank God, thank God* . . . Though her assignation with Frank would rank low on the Richter Scale of cheating, Hazel had always felt horribly about it, for her inebriation had been what stoked him. Once he'd driven her back to her apartment, she'd more falsely than truthfully claimed to be too drunk to undress. Would Frank help her? "Well, all right." Once she'd been naked, he managed several double-takes at her body. The excitement of exhibiting herself gorged her nipples, which had a way of plumping up more profoundly than most women. Frank had been trying to slip her nightgown over her head when her hand had found his crotch and begun to rub. "Come on, Hazel. What are you doing?" but by the time he'd gotten around to making the objection, she'd already pulled his cock out and had finagled it erect. She'd tossed the nightgown aside, sitting on the bed's edge, and whispered, "Just let me suck you off. All I wanna do is taste your cum."

"I . . . ," Frank had responded—then he was in her mouth. The excitement sucked Hazel's belly in; she had to knead her privates with her hand while her lips tightly slid back and forth over Frank's sensitive penile flesh. Each time she drew back, she tasted that delectable viscid saltiness of his pre-cum. Eventually she coaxed him prone on the bed.

In a near-69 position, she continued to suck with an unforgiving slowness; she wanted him *pining* to come. Alternately she took her mouth off the slick shaft to suck each testis. Evidently Frank hadn't felt right about making his own oral reciprocation but it had been of his own volition to grab the plainly visible vibrator off the nightstand and play the buzzing tip over, first, her majora, then her clitoris. She'd let that subconscious sewer open in her mind, then imagined him pissing right through his erection into her mouth. That idea alone had trebled her yearning, and it trebled again when her mind's eye saw him cracking her hard across the face with an open palm. She almost came when she pretended he was fucking her outright, then, and simultaneously reducing blood-flow to her brain by clamping his hands about her throat, but it wasn't until she shifted the image from him to Sonia that her climax unreeled. She'd merely dreamed of kissing her, and that's when the orgasm crested and exploded. His cock popped out of her mouth as she cringed in the girding spasms of pleasure, her pussy suddenly beating like a frantic heart as her back arched and her toes curled and she squealed until the sensations ebbed. Then she limpened, lying back inert, and grinned at him. When he rubbed his corona against her lips, seeking re-entry, she grinned all the more and shook her head. "I'm not going to. I wanna see you do it yourself."

"What!"

"You heard me. The only way you're coming now is to do it yourself."

"Why you little cock-tease *bitch,*" but that was the reaction she wanted. It was with adamance that he bolted up, straddled her stomach, and began to masturbate. The fingers of his free hand twisted a nipple until pain spiraled, and when she said, "You don't have the *balls* to choke me," that same hand clamped onto her throat and squeezed harder than she thought he'd dare, and it didn't let go until her vision had half-dimmed. He bucked, then the first bolt of his ejaculant landed in a diagonal line across her breasts. When she shot her mouth open wide, he leaned over and let the rest fall right in. She idled the lump slowly on her tongue, then let it slide into her belly with a gulp. Once swallowed, the warm mass seemed to throb and even grow warmer, absurdly, as if it approved of its new home.

"You wanted to taste it," he said, still mad from being manipulated, "Well, there you go," then he squeezed out a final bead and smeared it over her lips.

"That was fun," she slurred, "but a *real* man would lick off the rest." She slid her finger across the line of sperm that lay across her breasts.

"Yeah, that'll be happening," came his snide reply as he packed his penis back in his pants and pulled up the zipper.

"Well, then," she asked, "what do you think of this?" and she leaned over, took the spoon out of an empty coffee cup, then meticulously scooped up the remaining semen. Frank stared, agape, as she sucked the spoon clean.

"What are you doing teaching in the English Department?" he questioned. "You should be in porn."

"Naw," she murmured. "This is more fun, but you know . . . If you were a *real* man, you'd piss on me now."

Frank burst out laughing.

"Come on," she cooed. "You're ticked off I wouldn't finish blowing you, so here's your chance for revenge. Deep down, all men want to piss on women. I read that somewhere. It's your remnant caveman genes kicking in. Come on, Frank, don't be a pussy. Piss all over me. You know you want to."

Frank was honking laughter now. "Hazel, do yourself a BIG favor. Avoid alcohol at all costs. It turns you into a whory nitwit. And you might want to go to sleep now. You and Sonia have an eight o'clock class to teach and, believe me, you'll be packing a mighty hangover."

He headed for the door, still chuckling. She grinned at him through slitted eyes, her cheek resting against a pillow. She raised one leg to arrogantly display her red-muffed sex and said, "Thanks for taking me to *King Lear* . . ."

Frank laughed some more and said, "You're a loony." "So?" she replied. Then he left, chuckling away . . .

In Hazel's Me-Generation mentality, inducing a man to masturbate on her wasn't nearly as severe a breach as intercourse or oral sex to completion. Nevertheless, when she woke the next morning, she couldn't have felt more despicable. Sonia was her great Secret Love and her closest friend. *What kind of FRIEND does that make me?* Now, as she drove along the steadily curving road, getting farther and farther away from city-life and closer and closer to the cradle of nature, Hazel's relief washed over her. Anyone else would've ended the friendship immediately, for having been so outrageously betrayed. If *that* had happened . . .

I might not even want to live anymore, she considered.

"Unhook me here, will you?" Sonia's request summoned Hazel out of the memory. Sonia was leaning forward as best she could, trying but failing to disconnect her bra-clasp. "I swear my boobs get bigger every day. This bra's killing me."

"They're making milk, they're getting ready," Hazel said. She reached over and unsnapped the clasp.

"Ah," Sonia gusted. "That's better. They definitely need a break, and *I* definitely need to get bigger bras."

"They'll be even bigger when you're due."

"Christ, I hope not." Sonia cupped them a moment with her hands, to unrest them from the bra.

"You're going to breast-feed, I hope."

"Of course."

"They say the longer you breast-feed, the stronger your child's immune system will be."

"I feel like I've got enough milk in these to breast-feed *ten* kids, Hazel. Jeez . . ."

Breast-feed ME, Hazel mused. Her sex actually twitched when she imagined herself sucking milk from one of Sonia's nipples. She would suck and suck and suck. What would the milk taste like? And what would it feel like to Sonia as the suction pulled it out of her?

Oh, God, I'm so fucked up in the head . . . "If you don't mind my asking . . . Is it safe for pregnant women to continue having normal and regular intercourse?"

Sonia rolled her eyes. "Hazel, is that *all* that's ever on your mind? Sex?"

You don't know the half of it. "Come on. Answer the question."

Sonia's shoulders slumped. "Normally, a woman can have intercourse throughout her term, but wouldn't you know it? Not me."

"Why?"

"Risk factors increase the chances of complications. One, I'm over thirty, and two, my side has a family history of miscarriage and premature birth. So my doctor nixed intercourse for the entirety of the pregnancy."

"Bummer," Hazel said. "But I'm sure you two have found plenty of ways to work around that."

She blushed gently. "Let's just say that Frank gives an amazing oratory."

When Sonia's dash-mounted cellphone rang, she peeked at the caller ID. "It's Frank!" Her face seemed illumined. "I'm putting it on speaker . . . Hi, honey! We're on the road now. God, I really miss you."

Hazel smirked.

"I miss you too, baby," Frank replied, his voice scratchy over the reception. "When will you be at the cabin?"

"A little more than two hours, maybe less. Hazel's driving."

"Hi, Hazel," Frank said.

Hazel slowed down when she noticed she was doing 85. "Hi, Frank. Keeping the nature trails hot for us?"

"You bet. And the camping's great. This is my second night out. It's so beautiful out in these woods. After Henry's funeral, I took off, haven't been back to the cabin yet, but hope to meet you there tomorrow morning or afternoon."

"Don't get too cocky out in the wild, James Fenimore Cooper," Sonia urged.

"Natty Bumpo, you ain't," Hazel laughed.

"Don't worry. I'm pretty impressed with myself for pushing forty. I've hiked almost all the way up the summit, and there's no trails at all. I'm kind of blazing my own."

"What's the summit?" Hazel asked.

"You'll see when you get to the cabin. Just look west. It's called Whipple's Peak, a thousand feet up. It's all covered up with woodland, but there's this fascinating gorge that cuts right in the middle of it."

"Frank!" Sonia complained. "Are you crazy? You're a geometry teacher, not a mountain climber!"

"It's nothing, honey," the voice insisted. "And it's really getting me to appreciate nature."

"You're there to go over Henry Wilmarth's effects! Not climb mountains and sleep in the woods, where there're bears and snakes and—"

"Relax. Henry's papers are in order for now—all that's left is probate. And Whipple's Peak isn't even a true mountain, but in a sense, it's still part of Henry's work."

"A mountain?" Hazel questioned, "or summit or whatever it is?"

"Yeah, supposedly there's a cottage at the top. Henry and my father found it over a decade ago, and I want to see it."

"A cottage," Sonia sputtered. "Of all the things . . ."

"They called it the Gray Cottage. Henry probably has some old papers in the place, which I'd need to see," Frank continued. "The whole thing's kind of curious."

"Just do me a favor, Frank!" Sonia furthered her grievance. "Come down from there right now!"

"Tomorrow, like I said. I've almost found it, and I can't stop after coming this far." The noises crackled over the line. "And, honey, I've found out more since we last talked. When I got here Sunday—I've told you this part–the first thing I see is Henry's body. He'd killed himself the night before."

"But I thought the cabin was ransacked," Hazel remembered. "Couldn't someone have murdered him and made it *look* like suicide?"

"Nope. It's true, someone went through the place looking for something, but they didn't touch Henry's wallet which was full of credit cards and cash. And, besides, Henry left a suicide note: a note specifically for me."

Something about the way he'd said that gave Hazel a chill.

"It was right on the desk in his study. It read something like: *My dear friend Frank: if you're reading this, then I am already dead,* and some other stuff. But at the bottom was a phone number he wanted me to call."

"A phone number?" Sonia asked, not happy with any of this. "Whose?"

"I'll get to that. First thing I did was call the authorities. First the county sheriff's department came out, followed by an ambulance, which transported Henry's body to the morgue at Laconia General."

"Frank!" Sonia yelled. "What was the number?"

"It was a lawyer, in Laconia," Frank said. "So I called him, told him what happened, and then he told me he had urgent papers for me, in the event of Henry's death. Next day, I got Henry's death report and took it to the lawyer, and-and . . . well, here's the shocker."

Hazel and Sonia looked at each other.

"Henry's last will and testament left his estate to me," Frank said.

"You're kidding!" Sonia gasped.

"No. He left me the cabin and the ten acres of land it's on, for one thing. That could be worth a lot of money, but he also left me the fifty grand in his checking account, plus some stocks and certificates. The lawyer's not sure exactly how much it's all worth, but it's at least another couple hundred grand."

What a guy, Hazel thought.

Sonia had her hand to her chest. "I'd say it's wonderful but of course, not under these circumstances. Still, what a shock."

"You're telling me," Frank said. "I don't inherit anything until the will's out of probate, but I honestly can't see Henry owing people a lot of money. Whatever it's all worth, I'll finally be able to get my father out of that shit-hole assisted living place in Concord and move him into something primo."

Sonia was stunned. "Oh, Frank, I don't know what to say."

"I know. It sucks to have a family friend die in order to make out like a bandit. I'm more pissed off than anything. I'm pissed off that he killed himself."

"It was probably something that had been brewing in him for a long time," Hazel offered. "That's the modus for most suicidals."

"Not in this case, I don't think so. It's all that damn storm. He never recovered from that. Dad talked to him a few times since May, said that Henry wasn't himself anymore."

"It's understandable," Sonia reasoned.

"Sure," Hazel added. "He goes to Florida for a vacation and winds up witnessing one of America's worst natural disasters."

Sonia: "And *surviving* when so many others were killed. That would damage anyone's psyche."

Another pause on the line, then Frank said, "But there was one more thing that Henry left me through the lawyer: instructions."

"To finish his work, the side project you, he, and your father were working on," Sonia said.

"No, no, that's what he told me on the phone when he invited me up, but remember, that was ulterior, just to get me up there. The instructions said he wants me to *destroy* all of his papers and files. He said the theory is unworkable, and he didn't want it ever released to the public because he'd be regarded as a crackpot."

"How strange," Sonia said. "It was something you were working on for years."

"For me, yes, it was years, but for Henry and my father it was decades," Frank said.

Hazel had to ask, "What exactly was the nature of the work?"

"Non-Euclidean geometric patterns, but—" Frank chuckled. "You girls are lit-heads. It'd be useless for me to explain."

Sonia didn't have a clue. "Non-Euclid . . ."

"I may be a lit-head, Frank," Hazel admitted, "and a great many men I've dated think of me as something else that rhymes with that, but I took enough math to know that *all* geometry is Euclidean. It has to be 'cos Euclid invented it."

"Did he really *invent* it, Hazel?" Frank queried, "or was he merely the first to understand the measurability of angles, planes, and points well enough to give it a name? Did mathematics exist before someone contemplated the equation one plus one equals two? Did plasma-physics exist a half-million years ago when the only proto-humans were awkward primates who didn't have the sense even to use sticks for tools?"

Sonia and Hazel stared through a pause.

Frank began to spout, "Sure, the hypothesis of non-Euclideanism is considered gimcrackery, but only because it relies on *assumptions* that can't disprove Euclid's Ten Elements and all the laws of geometry that followed them. But in our theory—well, it's mostly Henry's—we've all but proved the existence of *inconstancy* between stable angles, planes, and points."

"Huh?" Hazel asked.

"He's on a roll now," Sonia said. "But *you* asked for it."

"This inconsistency is generated by *identifying* certain sequences of angular degrees that, when properly aggregated, come together to form a *manipulable* configuration. In other words, that configuration changes *without* changing."

Sonia sighed. "Frank. Enough."

"In other words *constancy* and *in*constancy become one in the same. A forty-five degree angle can assume a state of fictility—"

"Oh, sure, we know what that means!" Sonia exclaimed.

"—and, hence, widen to forty-*six* degrees while the original forty-five remains constant."

"Frank," Sonia said, "don't run your cell battery down."

"But what's the ultimate point of the theory?" Hazel asked.

"I'm glad you asked that, since *lit-heads* would never be able to understand without delimitating into layman's terms. The ultimate point is essentially infinite. What we're talking about here is the *malleability* of the unmalleable, Hazel. The tenets of Non-Euclideanism have the potential to produce unlimited energy. They could transpose objects of unequal weight and mass between two points of vast distance. They could prolapse *gravity.* They could elevate an object the size of the Great Pyramid into outer space with an energy cost of *zero.* They could convert the top eighth of an inch of water in the Atlantic into enough hydrogen to provide the entire world with a decade's worth of electricity, for *nothing.*"

"Frank," Sonia said, "We have to go now, but we'll see you tomorrow!"

"To me it sounds like pie in the sky," Hazel said. "It's like cold fusion. Sure, it would be great to achieve nuclear temperatures without a nuclear source, but if it's even possible, the initial energy expenditure would be more than the energy produced."

"Hazel!" Frank shrilled. "You're catching on!"

"Frank, seriously. Let me ask you something–"

Sonia groaned. "Hazel, honey, please don't."

"Between you, your father, and Henry Wilmarth, who's the smartest?"

Frank didn't hesitate. "Henry, beyond a doubt. He's a genius. When he was alive he understood geometric thesis better than anyone in the country."

"So, logically, if the smartest of the trio has determined that the theory can't work, then what's the most rational conclusion?"

A sigh over the line. "I know, that the theory is indeed unworkable. But you don't understand how exciting this was for us. I even called my dad and asked him what I should do."

"What did he say?" Sonia asked with a frown.

"He told me to respect Henry's wishes and destroy all the work.

I mean, I *will* do that, I have to. He left me his entire estate and only asked one thing in return, I *have* to do it." The cell connection drifted. "I *do* have to check this cottage and see what he's got in there, that's all. Bear with me."

Sonia began to whine, "But, Frank, I don't *like* the idea of you gallivanting around on a mountain—"

"It's just a minor geographical summit, honey."

"Whatever! I need you to come down *now.* I *need* you. Tonight! And you . . . you *know* what I mean . . ."

"This is just a wild guess," Hazel laughed, "but I think she means oral sex, Frank."

"Oh, ah, of course!" Frank blurted. "Believe me, honey, there'll be plenty of that tomorrow, and plenty of the, uh, other kind once junior's seen the light of day."

Sonia slapped Hazel on the arm; Hazel only laughed.

"And by the way, how's junior doing?" Frank asked.

"Kicking away as usual," Sonia replied, rubbing her belly. "I really do think it's going to be a boy, and one with a penchant for soccer."

"Perfect! Look, girls, I'm going to get back to my trail-blazing, so drive safe and I'll see you tomorrow. And have fun at the cabin. I'll call you tonight around nine to see how it's going."

"Be careful up there," Sonia pleaded once more. "And don't forget, I love you."

"I love you too—a shitload."

"How romantic!" Hazel squealed.

When the farewells were finished, Sonia ended the call, a tear in her eye.

"He'll be fine," Hazel assured. "Men pushing forty get on an adventure kick. Don't worry."

"*Fuck* adventure," Sonia made the rare profanity. "He shouldn't be climbing mountains and mucking about in the woods. There's *snakes,* for God's sake."

"Don't worry! If a snake comes along, Frank'll bore it to death motor-mouthing about geometry," Hazel offered.

That got a smile out of Sonia.

"And since you won't be with him tonight," Hazel added without thinking, "I've got a three-set of vibrating love-clips, if you want to borrow them. They're *great.*" She grinned. "I'll even put them on for you."

Sonia laughed, astonished. "Hazel, please . . . Just drive . . ."

Two hours later, the turnpikes' monotonous panorama of asphalt, concrete, and flurries of cars had lapse-dissolved into one of plush foliage, hundred-foot-tall trees, and shaded, curving forest roads. Everything was so deliriously green that Hazel had to catch her breath. *I need to get out of the city more,* she thought. She'd never been the outdoorsy type but suddenly being in the midst of all this wildlife, she felt bereft, as though she'd been missing out on something important for so long.

"It's so beautiful," Sonia observed, eyes wide on the scenery pouring past her window. "And it's so cool we're driving on a road called the Daniel Webster Highway."

"Only English majors could appreciate that," Hazel remarked. "But Benet's story still pisses me off."

"*Why?* It's a wonderful story!"

Hazel flapped her hand. "It's a ripoff of Washington Irving's 'The Devil and Tom Walker.'"

"It's a variation on a theme, Hazel. Not plagiarism."

"And the asshole wins the Pulitzer!"

"If it's a ripoff of Irving, dear, then Irving's tale is a ripoff of Goethe."

"In which case, Goethe's *Faust* was a ripoff of Christopher Marlowe, so there."

"Fitzgerald said it best, I'm afraid. 'Minor writers borrow, great writers steal.'"

Hazel's eyes thinned. "You sure that was Fitzgerald and not Wodehouse? Or—no!—Samuel Johnson."

"Who cares? We're almost there!"

Once they passed the turnoff for Laconia, they veered down a wooden fork and suddenly felt as though the forest were swallowing them. First they passed a deer-crossing sign, then another sign read, WELCOME TO BOSSET'S WAY. POPULATION: TOO FEW TO COUNT.

"I love it!" Sonia exclaimed.

"Yeah, and get a load of *this* place . . ."

Hazel slowed to an idle by a long, single-storied tavern constructed from planks of withered timber. The place seemed shoved back into the forest. BOSSET'S WAY WOODLAND TAVERN, read a rickety sign. Mostly pickup trucks filled the dirt-paved lot. As they looked on, an older pickup truck with odd rounded fenders parked, and from it stepped an imposing man well-over six feet. Shaggy, cropped brown hair crowned a head which sat on shoulders that seemed a yard wide; muscles bulged through a sweat-streaked gray T-shirt, and tight, faded jeans looked about to split from the pillar-like legs that filled them.

"I guess that's what you call a woodsman," Sonia commented.

"Would you *look* at that Paul-Bunyan-looking muscle-rack!" Hazel enthused. "I'd do him in a *heartbeat!*"

Sonia looked outraged. "He's literally twice your size, Hazel. He'd split you in two."

"Shit. I'd take his business till he couldn't see straight. He'd be crawling home to his mommy, I'd fuck him so hard . . ."

"Hazel, sometimes you really are too crude. You talk like a guy. And, besides, you should be ashamed of yourself. You've got a boyfriend."

Hazel smirked. "He's a *casual* boyfriend. I'm not married, you know–" She winked. "Or engaged."

"Well maybe you should be. It might clean up your mouth *and* your mind. Honestly, you talk about sex more than any woman I've ever met. You absolutely *dwell* on it, and it's not healthy."

You think I don't know that? Hazel thought in a sudden despair. *I'm NOT healthy. And my only cure is YOU . . .* "Hey, I'm allowed to daydream, aren't I? And don't tell me you don't."

"I don't need to. I've very *into* Frank. He's everything I've ever wanted sexually."

"Great, but you fantasize *sometimes,* for Pete's sake. Everybody does."

Sonia reluctantly tilted her head. "Well, of course, sometimes, sure. But not very often."

"Thank you."

Next, they both noticed another sign: FRESH FISH, MUSSELS, GAME - THURSDAY NIGHT - FISH-FED PORK ALL-U-CAN-EAT!

"Fish-fed pork?" Hazel questioned. "That sounds interesting."

Sonia winced and mouthed *Yuck.*

"There's your *regional* cuisine," Hazel said, "but that's fine with me. I like trying new things."

"Hazel, they've probably got moose on the menu!"

"Like it or not," Hazel insisted, "we're going to be eating in that place soon. We'd be silly not to just for the sake of sensibility."

"Whatever you say," Sonia murmured, but then she looked for some reassurance into her purse and smiled at a box of Pop Tarts.

BOSSET'S WAY LANE, read the next sign. Sonia was following the Mapquest directions when she blurted, "Take a left here!"

A slight incline took them deeper into the woods, then the road gave over to runneled dirt. After pulling round a deeply shaded cul-de-sac, Hazel stopped.

They both stared at a dark-planked cabin. Its slat-shingled roof slanted sharply upward. Crude wooden shutters flanked painfully narrow windows, while darker wooden planks comprised the front door. Most of the edifice had been overcome by ivy and the rearward trees, to the extent that it seemed an outgrowth of the woods, that or a foreign object it wished to expel.

"Is that it?" Hazel asked, puzzled.

Sonia pointed to a cumbersome metal mailbox. WILMARTH, H., it read in hardware-store stick-on letters. "I guess this is the place."

Hazel excitedly jumped out of the car. In spite of the shade, a dense humidity enveloped her. Aside from above the cul-de-sac, no sky was visible due to the tree-cover, and most of the trees—white pine, she thought—were at least a hundred feet high. Only from one precise vantage point could she actually see beyond the all-pervading trees: a narrow lane over open space that followed the property's slight inclination and showed a wedge of open fields, the edge of a significant lake, and what looked like it might be a town.

"Oh my God, it's so hot and muggy!" Sonia moaned when she struggled out.

"It's like a rain-forest effect," Hazel supposed. She offered Sonia a hand. "All these trees are so high and close together they seal out any breezes. The summer heat makes the moisture condense and rise, but it's got no place to go." But Hazel didn't mind a bit. To her—being a life-long New Englander—heat and humidity was a treat after the nine months per year of cold weather. It made her feel vibrant, prickling with youth.

Sonia pointed in horror. "And what-what-WHAT . . . is *that?*"

"I haven't seen one of those since Girl Scouts!" Hazel delighted of the narrow shack off to the cabin's side.

"That's not a—"

"It's a good old fashioned outhouse, Sonia. With all our education, with all our intelligence, our college degrees, our sophistication, and our quest for knowledge, *this* is what it's all led to. We get to shit in a hole in the ground."

"Oh my *God . . .*"

"And that must be the runoff from the spring," Hazel noted of the obtrusive lengths of gutter-pipe which branched out of the cabin's foundation; they veered into a small ravine at the wood's edge. "There's probably a storage keg or spring barrel inside. Tubing behind the house leads from the spring to the house, and the overflow runs down the gutter into the woods. Even in the winter, the water won't freeze 'cos it's always moving."

"Peachy!" Sonia snapped, still appalled by the outhouse.

"And now that I think of it . . ." Hazel began to approach the outhouse. Was it so old it was actually *leaning?* "After three hours on the road, this girl's got to take a mean tinkle."

"So do I , but-but . . . not in *there!*"

"I didn't know you were such a princess," Hazel chuckled and swung open the latrine's wooden door.

Not too bad. She expected more of an odor, but then she remembered how little this receptacle had been used. Frank had only been here a few days, and before that there'd only been Henry Wilmarth off and on. She eyed the crude hole cut in the wooden bench that sufficed for a toilet seat. *Mostly . . . dead man's shit down there,* came the coarse thought. The door swung shut, leaving only a malformed beam of light coming in through the cliched, sickle-moon-shaped hole in the wall. She dropped her shorts and sat down, waited a moment, then her bladder began to void. She listened, and her brow popped up at the lengthy string of seconds that ticked by before she heard the stream finally hit bottom.

She chuckled at an absurd notion: as she sat there, a hand reached up from the waste pit and cupped her pubis. Then another notion: she looked down into the pie-wedge between her legs and saw a face gazing raptly upward . . .

Idiotic! she thought, laughing to herself.

But it didn't take long for these fleeting notions to trigger something else: fantasies. Not *typical* fantasies.

Hazel's fantasies—

—with a great *Crack!* the outhouse door is torn from its hinges. You freeze where you sit, staring up in horror at the enormous silhouette now standing in the doorway. When your jaw drops to scream, your breath stays in your chest and no sound comes out. It's a wide-shouldered, column-legged man with shaggy hair who's stepped in as you remain sitting helplessly with your shorts down. *The man from the tavern!* you realize. The one Sonia had called the "woodsman," because that's what he looks like: a mass of sculptured human muscle and dense brawn, so tall he has to duck to enter. His intent is clearly premeditated, for his penis is already out of his opened jeans—limp but lengthy, and *fat*—hanging there like a raw pork loin. When he sees the fear in your eyes, the penis begins to fill with blood and rise in increments. When you try to lunge past him—

Thunk!

—his ham-hock-sized fist snatches you by the hair and bangs the side of your head against the wall. The heavy, head-spinning daze drops you to the floor. Your feet are lifted up and your shorts are pulled off. Then you hear another *Crack!* and when your vision clears, you notice that this behemoth has torn the "bench" out of its mounts, nails and all, leaving a rectangular hole full of malodorous darkness. His hand grabs your hair again and hauls you to your knees.

Finally, he speaks, in a voice like wet mush. "Do everything I tell you or I'll dislocate your hips and drop you down there. You'll die in shit, which is what you deserve." Fingers fat as hot dogs pluck the tiny cross around your neck and snap it off.

Dizzy, you gaze up. The violence has hardened his penis to something the length and width of a cucumber, with a maroon glans like a baby apple. The tiny piss-slit shimmers with drool.

"Open my pants and pull out my nuts."

Your hands shake, reaching forward, then dig in . . . *Oh my God,* you think as you lift the scrotum out . . .

It's not human, it can't be. In the sun-threaded darkness, you see that you're holding a hot, fleshy mass that is not characterized by two testes; instead it's more like a bunch of grapes sheathed by skin.

Each individual "grape" is easily discerned beneath the vein-webbed covering.

All the while, the stout, slightly lopsided erection throbs in your face.

"Put lots of spit on my cock," the slopping-like voice orders next.

You make the mistake of saying, "Whuh—what?" and the human monster works his fingers to either side of your trachea. You shudder on your knees, tongue sticking out; it seems like he's trying to wretch out your throat, and what's worse is the ease with which he's doing so.

At last, you hack, "I'll do it! I'll do anything you say!"

The fingers retreat and all at once you're leaning forward, spewing saliva all over his cock.

"More. On the knob."

Your fear, by now, has sucked so much gummy sweat through your pores. You're stifled by the heat, and *terrified* because it's so difficult to summon saliva. You suck frantically at the insides of your cheeks, and just as his hand moves back to your throat, you're able to release a sufficient amount of spit on the corona.

There is no hesitation when his hands hook under your clammy armpits and you're lifted of the floor. Your back *slams* against the wall.

The slush-voice: "Pull your knees up."

You obey the order instantly, and an instant after that his spit-slickened, flabbergastingly large cock bumps into the egress of your sex, then *pushes*. You feel the channel spread so wide it hurts. When the erection slips in to its entire length, your teeth clack together. Your vagina has easily accommodated many large penises but never—*never*—one *this* large.

"Are you scared?" he gushes.

"Yes!" you sob.

"But you really *like* this. This is what you *really* want. An ungodly cunt like you?"

The cock drags in and out of you as his pelvis pumps with a machine-like rhythm. It begets a wet clicking sound. You swear you can feel the end of it up about where your navel is.

"You should've done like your daddy said," the slush-voice remarks next, and begins to splatter laughter.

You scream, then, loud as a train whistle when you finally look at his face.

It's not the woodsman–oh, no. The face is upside-down: an eye on either cheek, a toothy mouth and fat lips on the forehead. His ears are pointed.

"The devil told me all about you . . ."

It's your shriek that sparks his orgasm. You can feel it pumping into you, one warm eddy after another. Sicker and sicker you feel, though, as you notice the next distinction: this does not feel like semen shooting into you, it feels more like your vaginal canal is being filled with something unhumanly thicker, like warm marmalade.

The mouth on the man's—or the *thing's*—forehead smiles in a complex satisfaction. "That should fix ya up," his voice splatters, and, again—

Thunk!

—he throws you down to the floor.

It is with more uncontemplatable revulsion that you notice his great scrotal sack is now deflated, as though each of the "grapes" has emptied . . .

Into me, you realize.

The excess oozes from your sex, and it does, indeed, look like marmalade but slightly cloudy and flecked with tiny black things that remind you of whole peppercorns.

"Won't take long now." Your monstrous assailant stuffs the mass of spent genitals back into his jeans. "See, I'm an ectogenically transfected Shoggoth, but you can't know what that means. I've got about ten percent. It changes ya; they like to *change* things from what they're supposed to be . . ."

The words spin in your head. *Shoggoth. Transfected. Ectogenic*. . . They mean nothing. But now your sweat begins to *pour* . . .

"I wish they'd'a changed me all the way to an attendant but they ain't gonna. I ain't smart enough . . . Shit . . ."

You start to shiver, and—

"None'a this nine-month shit. When a gal gets a pussy full'a Shoggoth cum, it don't take but a minute or two . . ."

—and your belly begins to *swell.* The image of an air pump filling a beach ball comes to mind; the pressure is so great, your back is slammed to the floor, and then you notice that your breasts are swelling as well, filling with inhuman milk as something abominable grows in your belly. Your navel pops inside out, and then you groan in rising pain.

"See how fast? Ain't that sumpthin'?"

In only seconds more, your baby bump is larger than Sonia's.

"Time for that critter to come out," the man slushes. "*Push.* Push it *out.*"

You tighten your muscles and push—

—and scream from the prod of pain.

"Lemme help," the thing offers. He places the workboot on your belly and begins to slowly push down. Water splats out as the pressure breaks a membrane; you shriek.

The boot levers down some more.

"Theeeeeere it is," he gutters. You feel your sex stretch, then waves of pain make you convulse as you feel something wriggly slide out of you.

You hear a baby wail.

"Hey there, little buster," says the man-monster's upside-down mouth. The eyes on his cheeks look at you. "It's a boy."

He picks it up.

Your own eyes flick first to the gleaming baby's face and mid-section, which appear normal. It's pudgy-faced, cuddly, cute even, but then a scream fires when you see that its arms and legs are writhing tentacles. And the baby's face? Normal?

Not quite.

Its mouth is a pale, whitish-pink sucker the size of an espresso cup.

The baby's malignant father places the infant at your bosom, whereupon the sucker immediately finds a distended nipple and begins to suck . . .

"There. Mommy'n her little 'un." He hoists you up; you feel the atrocious afterbirth hanging like a tail between your legs. As the tiny creature siphons milk from your sodden tit, the father's voice slops, "You're right. This is just a dream, but a dream ain't nothin' but a bunch of shit from your own head. What ya gotta understand is that, here? In this place? The shit from your own head mixes with the shit out there . . ."

Out there, you recite the words, limp in his arms. The baby has already drained one breast, so the sucker hunts for the other nipple.

"When all your milk's drunk up, it'll drink your blood," you're notified. "Now I'm gonna go out there and fuck that pregnant one. You wouldn't *believe* what Shoggoth cum'll do to a gal already knocked up. It's a piece of work . . ."

The upside-down mouth lowers to yours and kisses you ever so gently.

"But the dude weren't lyin', just so ya know. Euclid's Ten Elements are all wrong. Constant angles are pliable. *Fictile* . . ."

"What?" you gibber.

"And one last thing." Slush runs from the corners of his mouth. "Find the stone . . . and you'll be rewarded," and then you scream as he drops you and your atrocious baby into the excrement pit—

"Hazel!" the shrill voice cracks. "Jesus, how long does it take you to pee!"

Hazel roused from the evil vision as if slapped in the face. *Holy shit, where did THAT come from?* She dripped sweat, still sitting on the crude hole in the board. "Uh, coming!" she shouted back.

Shorts pulled up, she flew from the outhouse. The look on her face no doubt signaled her nauseousness.

"What's wrong with you?" Sonia asked, leaning against the car fender. "You're all flushed and prickly."

"I . . . That outhouse is hotter than a pizza oven," was all Hazel could think to say. The vision or daydream or whatever it was—the *daymare*—confounded her, and as she strode away from the outhouse, she instinctively threw glances back over her shoulder. It was nothing new for lewd and even sick fantasies to sneak up on her when she least expected it, but this?

Unbelievable . . .

She regained her stolen breath. When Sonia reached into the trunk for their bags, Hazel slapped her hands and pushed her away. "You're pregnant, remember? Ready to drop? Pregnant women don't haul suitcases."

"I don't need a nurse maid!"

"Don't argue. Open the house; *I'll* get the bags." In spite of her lithe frame, Hazel managed both large suitcases and both of their laptops in one trip. Sonia had left the front door half open; when Hazel stepped up on the wooden veranda, she couldn't help but stare at the peculiar door knocker: a face of dulled brass showing wide empty eyes but no nose or mouth. For whatever reason, the featureless face gave her an odd shiver.

"Oh my God it's hotter in here than outside!" Sonia squealed from within.

Hazel crossed the threshold into annoying heat, then flinched. "You're not kidding." She dropped the bags and rushed to open each window. "Hopefully we'll get a cross-breeze," but then she deflated when the air remained stagnant. "Sonia, find the lights."

"I'm *trying!*"

Hazel heard switches flick, then, finally, the long broad front room filled with light. "At least they're going green," Sonia remarked of the spiraling high-efficiency bulbs which hung bare from cords in the rafters. "Christ, this place looks like *Bonanza*."

"What?"

"Never mind. I keep forgetting. You're too young."

Great. But now the air inside began to circulate and, hence, cool down. Several ceiling fans had turned on as well.

Hazel at least found the place interesting. This main room comprised most of the house; dark paneling covered the walls, while wooden planks like those on the exterior formed the floor, only these were sealed with a shiny shellac. No paintings hung on any wall, and there was nothing in the way of carpeting, not even a throw rug.

"Fuck," Sonia blurted.

"You've really come full circle," Hazel said, amused. "You were the gung-ho one. But big deal? The place is primitive, sure, but it'll be an adventure."

"Oh, for God's sake, Hazel." Sonia tramped around the great room. There was a high, queen-sized bed in one corner. "There aren't even any bedrooms. *This* is the bedroom."

Built for efficiency, Hazel figured. A half-decent sectional couch sat in a half circle before a large flat-screen. In front of it sat a coffee table full of trade journals about mathematics. Hazel picked one up and frowned. *The American Journal of Geometric Theory.* She couldn't imagine anything more boring.

"And I guess this is the kitchen," she said next, finding the rear of the room lined with cupboards over a butcher-block counter, a small refrigerator, and a microwave. Pots and pans hung from pegs in the wall. "Primitive, but it'll do." She patted a large wood stove. "And I guess this is the range. I have a feeling we'll be eating out a lot."

Sonia suspiciously ran her hand over shelves and table tops. "It's clean, at any rate." Her head tilted abruptly. "Wait——what's that sound?"

Water trickling, Hazel noticed. "I was right—a spring barrel." At the far end of the kitchen stood, not a wooden barrel, but a plastic open-topped keg full of crystal-clear water. An input tube trickled water, while the outflow exited through another tube. "This is how they did it in Colonial days."

"I'm thrilled."

Hazel dipped a tin cup into the water, and took a long drink. "Oh, Sonia! It's delicious and almost ice-cold!"

Sonia took a sip and had to agree but then a look of sheer horror crossed her face. "Wait a minute!"

"What's wrong?"

"Where's the shower!"

Good question. Hazel went on the hunt; all the while Sonia shrilly griped behind her, "I don't care how hot it is, Hazel, I *cannot* take a bath or shower in water that cold! Please tell me there's some sort of water heater!"

Three narrow doors lined the east wall. They looked like closet doors but when Hazel entered the first one, "Here it is. And, wow, things just get more and more primitive."

Sonia peered in behind her, viewing a tiny wood-planked room with an even tinier window. A metal tub with a drain sufficed for the "shower floor," and hanging above it was a simple shower head and a pump handle on the wall.

Sonia was outraged. "We have to *pump* the shower water?"

"It seems so, but—we're in luck." Hazel leaned over a small apparatus on the floor which, via tubes, existed between a modest water reservoir and the shower head. "Here's your hot water heater."

Sonia sighed, a hand to her belly. "Thank God for small favors."

More and more, Hazel speculated that this might be more fun than she'd thought. When she opened the second door she found merely a ladder. "What's this? An attic?"

"Oh, Frank mentioned there was an access to the roof."

"We can star gaze and sunbathe nude!"

Sonia seemed less enthusiastic. "*You* can star gaze and sun bathe nude. Can you see me climbing up that? My giant stomach probably wouldn't even fit through the trapdoor. Frank said the only reason it's there is to make it easier to clear the gutters in the spring."

But Hazel had already shot up the metal-runged ladder. When

she pushed open the trapdoor she could see right down the front road to the open fields. "Oh, this is cool!"

"Come down from there!" ordered Sonia's voice. "You could fall."

Hazel really did want to come up here some time and take some pictures; the higher vantage point offered a better view of the lake's edge and the town. But when she scooted back down the ladder, Sonia wasn't there. For a split-second, she felt a prick of alarm. "Sonia? Where are you?"

"In here . . ."

The third narrow door stood open. "Ah, Henry Wilmarth's study," Hazel said upon entering. It was the only area of the house that appeared normal: a computer, a desk, several bookshelves, a radio.

Sonia was curiously inspecting some papers on the desk. Her expression had deadened.

"What did you find?"

"Pretty dark stuff," Sonia remarked. "It's the suicide note that Henry left for Frank."

It struck Hazel only now that she was standing in the room where Professor Henry Wilmarth had ended his life. Instead of a chill, she felt something akin to a hot-flash. She peeked over Sonia's shoulder and read the tight, concisely formed handwriting:

My dear friend Frank: If you're reading this, then I am already dead. My decease via my own hand is an action I cannot and will not fully explain; I only hope that you and your father Thurnston can understand. I think the world of you both, and was edified by our stimulating research over the years. I apologize after the fact for the spurious manner in which I lured you here, for, now, I'm sure it's occurred to you why I did so. No suicidal person wishes to be found weeks or months after the fact. Forgive me and, again, comprehend me.

Since that calamitous storm in St. Petersburg last May, I've grown quite ill mentally. My spirit feels soiled. I wander these woods, motiveless and desultory, with sleepless eyes and an utter absence of vitality. It's beyond description, my friend. The ghosts of all those dead from the storm follow me everywhere, figuratively speaking, of course. I often wonder of late: is it my afflicted mind or the cabin itself that has so drastically soured my dreams and tainted my thoughts?

Were I not a man of erudition, I think I'd be more inclined to say the latter—though I know this cannot be so. A man's mind can get sick, not a man's house. Nevertheless, my symptoms can only be clinical by this point. My dreams have turned ghastly indeed, tinged by a grotesque carnality unlike anything ponderable. Sometimes, even—I swear—people (or things like *people) make utterances in my dreams that reveal information which I verify later. This is impossible, I know, and I can only fear what you may be thinking. In all, it's just more proof of the enervation of my mind.*

Please arrange for the disposal of my pitiable body; I'm all too sorry to have to leave it to you in this way. My warmest regards for your father, and take care and be well,

Sincerely,

Henry

P.S.—But you're not off the hook this easily! Call the number at the bottom for further instructions that I hope are not too inconvenient.

"The lawyer's number, in town," Hazel recalled.

"Good luck making anything out of this." Sonia handed her the next piece of paper. It had been archaically closed with sealing wax and a brand reading, H.W., the seal now broken, of course. Hazel's eyes poured over it . . .

No doubt, Frank, you've now been informed by my attorney that my estate all goes to you. I hope it will assist your and your father's future, you especially, with a child coming. In return, however, I submit to you my final requests . . .

1) I've delved too deeply into the guts of our research, Frank—for more than a generation. Like proverbial rabbits, we've been chasing a carrot on a stick. Ah, but what dreams we had, eh? Nevertheless, my most recent findings indicate without revocation the falsehood of Non-Euclidics. It doesn't work, Frank. It's an impossibility. So, please, waste no more of your time pursuing this golden calf. I've apprised your father likewise, and he agrees. If this theory were to make its way into our academic channels, my name would be posthumously lambasted. You're young and still full of vigor, Frank, but you must see this my way. Our research, ultimately, can never be functional. So put it out of your mind and return to more productive studies. Moreover, I must ask you with much urgency to destroy all traces of our theory. Destroy all of my papers in this cabin, and delete all my computer files. Do this, Frank, please. Any intellectual legacy I may have will be tainted with ridicule if you don't. The only reason I haven't destroyed it all myself is due to a grievous lack of energy on my part, which I can only suspect is a symptom of severe depression.

2) In years past, before your dear father's affliction, you've heard our references to the Gray Cottage. This, too, is a sullied place, quite dangerous, and, also, quite useless. Please, never go there, Frank. Never try to find it. It's a fool's errand—

"The cottage Frank mentioned on the phone," Hazel uttered. "Wilmarth asked Frank *not* to go there—"

"And said it's *dangerous,*" Sonia augmented. "Frank must be *trying* to give me a heart attack."

–for hundreds of years, this execrable place went unnoticed. Therefore, I'm asking you to mention it to no one, and let it return to its anonymity. You'd likely not be able to find it anyway so just . . . appease me, Frank. Don't try to find it.

3) Likewise, don't try to find the ST. I've disposed of it irretrievably. It's a phony augur, so, like the cottage, forget about it . . .

"The *ST?*" Hazel asked. "What's that?"

"Got no idea," Sonia smirked. "Wilmarth must not've known Frank's character very well. You tell Frank *not* to do something, that only increases the chances of him *doing* it."

"Just like a man."

—I've disposed of it so completely I have every confidence it will never be found. My final rummagings of research revealed the unserviceability of the ST and, attendantly, the entire theory. That dismal ST, Frank. It's a jonah, the mathematician's graven image. Like the Devil, it is a Great Deceiver that solicits us to follow lies. Please don't insult my memory, Frank.

Forget that goddamned stone ever existed.

Hazel folded the paper up, her head misted in confusion. *That goddamned STONE?* The marauder in her ghastly outhouse fantasy had said something about a *stone,* hadn't he? He'd also made references that could be traced back to what Frank had said over the phone, but those references were obviously re-filtered through the fantasy via her subconscious.

But Frank never mentioned anything about a STONE during his phone conversation, did he?

Hazel winced out of a shudder.

"Frank just burns me up sometimes," Sonia fumed, pacing the small room. "Not only is he disregarding Henry's last wishes, he's trying to find some ridiculous *cottage* that's hundreds of years old and probably ready to fall in. With my luck it'll fall in on his *head* and I'll be a widow before I'm even married!"

"He'll probably never even find the place, Sonia," Hazel suggested. "There's whole square miles of tree coverage all the way up that summit—you saw it. But I'd love to know what this *stone* is, this *ST.*"

"I could care less. And he's going to be real sorry he's pulling this stunt." Sonia's hands tightened to fists. "No oral sex for him, just you watch."

Hazel laughed. "Oh, give him a break. He's just out on a camping trip. The poor guy sits in an office ninety-nine percent of the time."

"Stop sticking up for him!" Sonia barked. "He's making me a nervous wreck. How would you feel if Ashton decided to go *mountain climbing* while you had to sit in some ridiculous non-air-conditioned cabin while you were *pregnant* with his kid?"

Hazel smiled, then looked around. "Check this out," and from atop a bookshelf she retrieved some sort of decorative metal box, five or so inches long, and four high.

"Jewelry box?" Sonia wondered.

"Maybe, but . . ." At once, Hazel noted the foremost oddity. "It's uneven. See?" She pointed out the box's slightly unparallel lines. "Pretty funky—a style thing, I guess."

Sonia squinted. "It's not *gold,* is it?"

Hazel tapped the side with a fingernail. "I don't think so." It was a yellowish metal but too dark for gold; however, it didn't look like bronze or brass, either. "Flavescent" was the only word she could think to describe its unique hue. Both women seemed to stare fixedly at it, like some captivating totem.

"What interesting engravings," Sonia observed next.

Hazel wouldn't have called them *interesting.* "More like unsettling . . ." Peculiar glyphs and characters like less-than and greater-than signs had been etched very faintly all about the object. Atop the lid, and centered on each slightly uneven side, were just-as-faint bas reliefs which seemed to depict some obscure figure whose details she could not quite make out. Hazel couldn't understand why the figure unnerved her.

"Open it," Sonia said.

Hazel paused, then raised the off-kilter lid with a fingernail.

An egg-shaped metal band had been fixed by tiny struts within the box. Hazel couldn't imagine what purpose it served. "There goes the jewelry box theory."

"What's the band for? To put something on it?"

Hazel reclosed the lid. Objectively she viewed the box with insignificance, yet something . . .

Something about it . . .

—made her queasy. A vertigo crossed her eyes when she looked harder at the barely visible engravings—mostly shapes like V's on their sides—and she thought it almost seemed as though the little angles were minutely opening and closing. *I'm just tired,* she thought, but then her squint sharpened: she was looking at the etched figure on the lid. Her stomach hitched.

For a moment the figure looked bulb-headed, with a trail of tentacles draped below.

Another fatigue-born mirage. *Tentacles,* the word lolled in her head. Her mind had simply made her think that, based on the horrific baby from her daymare in the outhouse.

"Put it back," Sonia said with a look of distaste. "Don't know why but I don't like it. Suddenly it looks creepy."

"Yeah." Hazel shoved the box back into its shelf. "Maybe it's morbidity on my part but . . . didn't you say Henry killed himself in *this* room?"

"Um-hmm."

Then they both looked up at the study's only overhead rafter. "That must be it," Hazel said. But at the same time Sonia happened to glance in the small waste can by the desk. She jumped back as if startled, pointing down with a frown.

"Now I'm *really* going to kick his butt," she said.

Hazel peered into the waste can. It contained a length of stout rope.

"Thanks a lot, Frank, for leaving the hangman's noose in the *house!*" Sonia added.

"You're really squeamish all of a sudden." Hazel had to chuckle.

"Squeamish *and* bitchy. Christ, my stomach's sticking out like a beer keg while the father of my child is out playing Lewis and Clark, and now I get to look at the friggin' *rope* that Henry killed himself with. Frank really can be an inconsiderate dick sometimes."

"He's just absent-minded—"

"Don't stick up for him!"

"–but you're right, a grade-A dick."

"That's better."

"Look, I'm starving, so let's—"

"We have Pop Tarts," reminded Sonia.

Hazel scowled. "You've got a baby growing inside you, Sonia. He or she deserves better than Pop Tarts. So go get ready. We're going to the Bosset's Tavern or whatever it's called."

"You just want to cozy up to the woodsman," Sonia said, nodding knowingly. "I know you."

"Just get ready, while I put this in the garbage," and then she reached into the waste can and grabbed the length of rope that had no doubt been around the neck of Henry Wilmarth just nights ago.

"Eew!" Sonia shrieked.

Hazel loped out of the cabin. *She really is loaded up with pregnancy hormones or something.* Outside, she flipflopped across the front yard toward the end of the drive, but slowed to take a grimacing glance at the outhouse. In her mind, the tentacular newborn squalled, its sucker-mouth pulsing. *Jesus* . . . A large plastic garbage can sat across from the mailbox. She pried off the lid, then held her breath at the stink. But before she dropped the noose in, she caught herself peering down.

Several objects she couldn't identify lay atop a garbage-filled bag. An arrangement of leather straps were attached to metal platforms, while from each of the two platforms, sharp steel spikes sprouted. A long leather strap had also been dropped in the can, with a buckle, yet it was much too lengthy to be a belt.

She picked up one of the platforms.

When she noted wood-splinters embedded in the saw-teeth she could guess that they were the things workmen used to climb telephone poles; a brand name was etched on the spikes, SPORT CLIMBERS, INC. Next, she picked a receipt out of the trash, which read, HAMMOND'S OUTDOOR GEAR, BOSSET'S WAY, N.H. *Lineman Spikes, one pair, $199.99.* The next item: *Tree Scaling Belt, one, $69.99.*

"Did Frank buy these?" Hazel wondered aloud, but then the date told her that could not be. These items were purchased not only before Frank had arrived, but two days before Henry Wilmarth committed suicide.

Hazel barely knew Wilmarth, though he definitely did *not* strike her as a sport climber or an athlete of any kind.

The last item on the receipt made the discovery all the more dark.

Rope, sisal, 3/4-inch, 20 ft., $10.00

Hazel stared out at nothing. *Why would Henry buy tree-climbing spikes? Unless . . .*

Unless he originally planned to hang himself from a tree? Then thought the better of it?

It made the most sense, she supposed.

She dropped the rope in the can, then noticed one more thing: a metal can, which at first she thought must be a can of paint until she picked it up for closer inspection. TREE PATCH, it read. It was empty yet the can's side contained traces of some tarry substance. *Oh, like when you cut a branch off a tree, this is the stuff you smear on the stub.* She shrugged, then put the can back in the garbage, replaced the lid, and went back to the cabin.

3

Astonished, Sonia said, "This squirrel burger is *wonderful!*" after just one bite. "And to think I had my doubts."

"The muskrat's excellent, too," Hazel complimented the stringy yet aromatic chunks on her sampler platter. "Tastes like smoked duck, and the possum reminds me of turkey drumstick meat." Then she took a crispy bite of the next selection: deep-fried hognose snake.

"Don't tell me," Sonia suspected. "Tastes like chicken?"

"Nope. More like trout, and very good."

Hazel let her gaze glide over the tavern: wooden tables, wooden walls, and wooden floors. The aromas from the kitchen were delectable. A long bar stretched across the rearmost wall, tenanted by working-class . . . *Rednecks,* she could find no other word. Most of the tables were occupied by groups of rough-handed and coarse-voiced men. It impressed her, though, that when she and Sonia had entered, the clientele had scarcely taken note of them. *Looks like we're the only women here other than the wait staff.* She would've at least expected to be ogled a bit, especially considering her scant shorts and top and Sonia's overspilling bust, but there was really none of that. *I guess I feel out of place if there're no perverts lusting after me.*

"Waitress?" she asked. "I'd like to order another entree, please."

Sonia looked surprised. "You just ate an entire Roadkill Platter and now you want more?"

The chuckling waitress was the ultimate cliche: stocky, pear-shaped body; bunned hair; eye makeup that looked applied with a butter knife; and a name tag reading ASENATH. "It must mean she likes our food. Bet they en't got restaurants like this in the city."

"It's such a unique surprise," Hazel said. "Everything's even better than I imagined."

"I'm glad, and by the looks'a yew, ya could *use* a little meat on yew're bones." The waitress huffed like Aunt Bee on *Andy Griffith.* "And if ya want *my* recommendation, order the perch. It's a nine-ounce fillet on a bed of fresh-water mussels and crawfish tails sauteed in garlic butter."

Hazel nodded resolutely. "I'll have it."

"Anything else for you, hon?" Asenath inquired of Sonia. "Seein' you'se got a young 'un on the way, don't'cha forget you gotta eat for two."

"No, thanks." Sonia cradled the bulbous belly. "The squirrel burger's enough for both of us. I'll be content just watching my 105-pound friend eat more than a football player."

Hazel shrugged. "I've always eaten like a pig, but I never gain an ounce."

"I was the same way, sweetie," Asenath assured, then her body fat giggled as she laughed, "so just you remember what they say about gift horses!" and then she left to put in the order, laughing all the way.

"I'll bet the fish is really frozen," Sonia whispered. "Places always say it's fresh, then you find out it's been in the deep freeze for a year and came from Viet Nam."

"Ain't *nuthin'* here not fresh, missy," a crackly voice surprised them both. "I'se'll stake my repper-tay-shun on it."

Hazel and Sonia both suppressed a shock when they turned to see an elderly man in a wheelchair passing between tables. Shrivel-faced and feisty-eyed, he wore a hat that read LUNTVILLE V.F.W. But the feature which stalled both Sonia and Hazel's tongues was the unfortunate fact that the old man had no hands.

Finally Hazel managed to reply, "That sounds like quite an endorsement, sir."

"Calls me, Clonner, hon, not sir. Clonner Martin," he said in an out-of-place southern accent. "When I'se first moved here ten years ago, this dump was just a bar full'a S.S.I. rednecks, so's I tell the owner, I say, 'When God were passin' out brains you must'a been in the butt line. With alls the critters in these woods and alls the fish in Lake Sladder, you could make a killin' if'n ya turnt this hole in the woods into a restaurant.'"

"Well, I'm glad he took your advice," Sonia said.

The old man—Clonner—cocked an eye. "Take my advice? Hail, the cocky rube told me to kiss him where the sun don't shine'n threw me out. So's I just said the hail with him and up'n bought the place fer, like, next to nuthin'."

"Oh, so *you're* the owner," Hazel remarked. "I must say, I've been to some good restaurants in my life, but this is definitely the most unique."

"Thank ya, thank ya, sweetie. It's all's about takin' advantage of ak-sess-er-bul resources and ident-er-fy-in' the market. We'se got skiers in the winter and campers in the summer. Why not give 'em somethin' they cain't get nowhere's else?"

"You're a true marketeer, Clonner," Sonia said. "I would never have thought squirrel could be so good."

"I trap squirrel, possum, muskrat, snake, you name it, since I were a kid, and fished too. Cain't do it now, a'course," and he honked a laugh, holding up his stumps. "So's I got my half-wit nephew and his ex-con buddy doin' it." He wheeled the chair around and pointed to an oblong opening in the wall through which the kitchen could be seen. Right up in the opening two rustic-looking men in their thirties busied themselves fileting fish. One was chunky-faced and bearded, with shaggy brown hair; he chewed his lip as he worked. The other—taller and slim—seemed more at ease with the work, whistling as his knife finnicked through slabs of clean white meat.

"See them two losers there? That's them. 'Bout all they'se good fer is trappin' and fishin', but I guess that's better than nothin'."

Hazel looked at them. *Rednecks tried and true.*

The old man, next, pointed his stump right at Sonia. "Anyways, missy, if yer friend here say her perch ain't the freshest fish she ever et, I'll pay yer whole check."

"Oh, I'm sure it will be, Clonner," Sonia replied, embarrassed now that her remark had been overheard. "You've convinced us. But . . . where exactly *are* you from? Your accent is southern but everyone else here has a *New England* accent."

Clonner nodded confidently, nubbed arms crossed. "I'se from Luntville, West Virginia, missy. Moved up here ten years ago, bought a couple pieces a land cheap. Got sick'a bein' around rednecks, ya know?"

He paused for effect, then the three of them burst out laughing.

"And lemme guess. You gals? I'll'se bet yer from Proverdence."

"How did you know?" Hazel asked, amazed.

"I saw the Brown U. Sticker on yer car," and then he honked another laugh.

"You really are something, Clonner," Hazel said.

"And don't be put off none on account I ain't got no hands," he went on. "Some folks are, but, hail, it's no big deal. First sixty years'a my life, I had hands"—he shrugged—"now I ain't. I got me a pair'a hooks but don't like 'em much."

Before Hazel could think better of it, she asked, "Clonner, how . . . how did you lose them?"

"Blammed dye-ur-beet-iss," he said nonchalantly. "Runs in the fambly's what the doc tolt me. A Hindu feller, or swami. Older brother Jake had it too, so's they cut off the poor bastard's feet. But me? I gots it in the hands, and I guess I must'a pissed God off a time or two 'cos right after the swami doc cut off my hands, I got a whopper of a case'a arthritis so's I gotta roll my old butt around in this chair." He raised a nub as if there were still a hand on it and he wished to raise a finger. "But you know, way I see it is my life's *still* a blessing. Heart's still beatin', sun's still shinin', and I'se still drinkin' beer, so I got a lot ta be thankful fer."

"That's a wonderful viewpoint, Clonner," Hazel said, then felt a twinge of guilt. *Sounds like something my father would say* . . . It made Hazel more mindful of all she took for granted.

Now Clonner peered curiously at them. "Guess that one slipped by ya, huh?"

"What's that, Clonner?" Sonia asked.

"I mean, I thought shore you'd be thinkin' 'How in tarnations does a fella with no hands even *drink* a beer?'"

Hazel and Sonia looked at each other, duped.

The waitress set a can of Bud on the table next to him. "Here ya go, Clonner."

"Best thing 'bout owning yer own bar is ya drink fer free!" he exclaimed, and then he leaned very carefully over, got the rim of the can between his top and bottom front dentures, then tipped his head back and drank.

Hazel and Sonia stared.

"See? Ain't no big deal," he said. "I best take a peek in the back'n make sure I ain't gettin' ripped off blind. But you girls take care'a yourselfs, and thanks fer stoppin' by."

"It's been a pleasure talking to you, Clonner," Hazel said. "And we'll be back for the all-you-can-eat fish-fed pork."

"Best pork ya ever had, so's you do that. And if'n ya need anything er got any questions 'bout the area," he added, wheeling away, "just you come'n ask me."

"Thank you, Clonner," Sonia bid.

When he was gone, Hazel observed, "What a wonderful, high-spirited old man."

"Yeah. Poor guy's got no hands but he's still got a big smile on his face. Me? I pitch a fit like there's no tomorrow if I break a nail or if Frank's five minutes late."

I need to have more of his outlook, Hazel thought, but she knew it was all mental talk. Even now, she was surveying the tavern, sliding her gaze over various men to fantasize about which ones she'd like to have sex with. Several men played darts in one corner, jabbering in restrained revel. Two more played billiards with serious looks on their work-worn faces.

When she blinked, she caught on a breath, and suddenly saw herself stripped, gagged, and blindfolded, with her hands tied behind her back. She'd been bent over the pool table while one sturdy man stood behind to methodically sodomize her. The other deftly plunged the fat end of a cue stick in and out of her vagina like someone churning butter . . .

Hazel shivered out of the vision.

Sonia was smiling coyly. "What are you so intent on?"

"What?"

"You know what I mean. Since we walked in here you've been eyeballing everyone in the place."

"No, I haven't," Hazel blurted.

"Oh, I know. You're looking for that guy we saw when we first drove by. The woodsman-looking guy."

Hazel frowned, said, "I am not," but thought, *She's right.* "But now that you mention it, I don't see him anywhere."

"Gee, I guess that means he left, Hazel," came some sarcasm from Sonia.

"But his truck's still outside."

"Ah, I see, you're *not* looking for the guy but you memorized what kind of truck he has."

Her cell phone jangled, then she moaned when she looked at the caller ID. "Damn. I should have never gave my cell number to my father."

"That's terrible, Hazel"—now Sonia looked genuinely annoyed. "How can you just disregard your father like that? He's a very nice man, and you duck his calls like he's a telemarketer." A sharp frown. "You *are* going to answer it, right?"

Hazel shrugged.

"Answer it!" Sonia snapped. "Don't be such a shit."

"Hi, dad," Hazel finally picked up. "Sorry I haven't been in touch."

The tinny voice on the other end seemed to vibrate. "Oh, thank God, Hazel. I was so worried. I've been calling your home line for weeks–"

Hazel took the phone outside, for some privacy. "I've been real busy grading papers for the summer session. I *meant* to call you, but . . . you know how it is."

The tinny voice tempered. "I didn't even know you had a cell phone until that fine young man Ashton gave it to me . . ."

Yeah, dad? You should've seen that 'fine young man' pissing on your daughter last night. She held back a laugh. "I just got the cell, dad," she lied. "I didn't have time to call you because right when the session ended, Sonia and I went up to New Hampshire to meet with her fiancé. We're there now."

"New Hampshire? How long will you be there?"

"Just a week or two."

Disappointment seeped into her father's tone. "I was so hoping you could come to the grand opening of the new parish, but that was two weeks ago. It's a beautiful church, honey . . ."

"Oh, I'm sorry," she kept making excuses. "I forgot. But when I'm back, I promise, I'll come and see it."

"Hazel. You know I want you to do more than just come and see it." The voice sounded forlorn now. "You need to come *back* to church, come *back* to God. It would make me so happy for you to be my choir director. You sing so beautifully . . ."

Oh, Jesus, this is a drag. "I'm really busy with school, dad. Between teaching and working on my doctorate, I really don't have time."

A pause, then, "There's always time for God, honey."

"I'll call you in a few days, okay? And I will come and see you when I'm back, I promise," she struggled to end the uncomfortable call.

Was her father choking up? "I love you, Hazel—"

"I love you too, dad," she nearly whined.

"And more important than that, *God* loves you. But sometimes I don't think you believe that."

I DON'T believe that, came the instant thought. *Why would God love a reckless, indulgent pervert like me? Every thought in my head OFFENDS God . . .*

"Hazel? Are you there?"

"Yes, dad. I have to go now but I will keep in touch–"

He chuckled. "At least try to not duck *all* my calls."

Hazel sighed.

"Goodbye, honey," her father bid. "Go with God . . ."

"'Bye," she said quickly and ended the call.

SHIT! that's so uncomfortable! She knew the reason she didn't like talking to her father was because even the mere sound of his voice made her feel guilty. *My head's a cesspool, and he wants me to go to CHURCH!* She turned despondently, leaning against a front post. How could anyone be so at odds with themself? A pickup truck parked only feet away, and out strode two more working-classers, either loggers or construction workers. All brawn and wide shoulders, muscled legs, tufts of hair spilling from their collars. "Howdy," one said with a half-smile. Hazel eyed his crotch, said, "Hi," and watched them enter the tavern. *Go with God,* she repeated her father's words but at the same time fantasized: she'd been hauled atop the pickup's hood. The first redneck lay right on her head and fucked her face; an elephantine penis seemed to bend down into her throat and bug her eyes out with each thrust. The other pumped her pussy with a small toilet plunger . . .

Sick, sick, sick, she thought.

Fwump! came a sudden sound.

Behind the tavern a large man effortlessly tossed a huge garbage bag into a dumpster. *It's him!* It was the "woodsman." This close Hazel felt tiny. *He could roll me up in a little ball and just fuck me, squash me into the dirt . . .*

"Excuse me," she rushed. "Do you have the time—"

He disappeared through a backdoor, never having heard her.

Hazel shuffled back in, hoping her perch was ready, or anything to get her mind off the carnal muck that seemed to cover her like slime.

"Are you sure?" Sonia said from the driver's window. "That's a long walk in this heat."

"The cabin's only a couple miles. I just feel like a walk"—she patted her stomach, which was protruding now—"I need to work off some of this food."

"Well, all right. But if you get tired, just call me on your cell and I'll pick you up."

"Okay."

Hazel watched Sonia back the Prius out from amid the phalanx of pickup trucks, then drive away. She felt stuffed now, yet antsy. The call from her father, she knew, had thrown her off kilter. Yes, she knew she was a crummy daughter. She knew her father was a good man who loved her very much and would do anything for her, yet still she avoided him. He made her think of *herself* too much, and this frustrated her. She felt frustrated, too, in not being able to meet the woodsman, though why she couldn't imagine. *He's just a backwoods manual laborer.* She could only presume her fascination denoted some subconscious—and perverse—fantasy.

Shit . . .

Over the treeline, the horizon began to flame as the sun inched lower. *Maybe a couple miles of walking'll clear my head . . .*

The winding road back toward the cabin was paved but soon Hazel found herself veering off on a wide dirt road. If she had her bearings right, it should navigate her toward Lake Sladder, which she'd love to see. Intermittently, she passed clusters of trailers set back in the woods. They seemed hidden. Flaps of laundry fluttered on clotheslines. The forest thickened the farther she proceeded, the tall pines and oaks seemed closer and closer together. Suddenly she felt uneasy, bare-legged and flipflopped when snakes and briars could be all around. *Go with God, go with God,* her father's voice kept harassing her. She'd devoutly attended church up until the end of high school, long after her sexual obsessions had made themselves plain in her psyche. *Did I ever really believe in God?* she asked herself now but then was certain that she did. *So when did I stop?*

No answer.

Her father had always been a Methodist minister, and owned a small truck dealership on the side. The new parish was his dream. Hazel knew how much her father wanted her to come back to church—he blamed "liberal, atheistic university life" for steering her away—but now, in this vibrant heat and fresh outdoor air, she suddenly realized that it had not been waning faith but instead a sense of overriding self-disgust. She felt she didn't belong in church, that for someone who so eagerly pursued sexual debauchery as herself, her presence in the pews would be hypocritical. *I've got enough to feel bad about . . .* Her mother had abandoned her marriage only months after Hazel had been born, and though her father had never offered details—"It was simply God's will, and that's good enough for me"—Hazel had overheard some relatives verifying that her mother was actually quite a tramp. *Now I know where I got my sex-pot genes,* she thought. Sometimes she wondered the most ludicrous things: *Is my mother an Asthenolagniac? Is she a Asphyxiphile or a Maieusiophiliac?* Hazel had to laugh.

Suddenly she stopped; it seemed her mind had been meandering along with her feet, for now she realized the dirt road had forked and she'd unconsciously veered with it. The trees stood surreally still around her. Up ahead—ten yards? Twenty?—a man stood with his back to her. Just . . . *standing* there.

Hazel's eyes thinned. *There's no reason to be afraid . . . so DON'T act afraid.* She took confident strides forward. "Excuse me, sir. I think I took a wrong turn back there. Could you tell me how to get back to the—"

Her throat sealed off the remaining words when the man quickly turned. Her purse fell to the dirt. The man wore a shabby, stained T-shirt, smudged jeans, and—

Holy shit, what IS this?

—a mask. A Peter Pan mask.

Hazel didn't actually shriek until she turned around and found a second, taller man blocking the road behind her. This one, dressed just a shabbily, wore a Snow White mask.

The several-second pause was her biggest mistake; by the time she attempted to flee perpendicularly into the woods, Peter Pan had already had his hand gripping the back of her top. One swoop of his arm flung her into the dirt.

Stereophonic chuckling descended. A knife to her throat chaperoned words in what seemed a southern accent. "Don't'cha make no noise or'se I'll cut'cher throat'n bleed ya to death while we'se fuckin' ya."

Hazel's heart hammered as a dirty hand hauled her top over her head. Two dirtier hands mauled her breasts while Peter Pan grabbed her hair. "What a big-ass pile'a steel wool this is," he chortled. He rubbed her face in his crotch. The denim of his jeans smelled unmistakably of fish.

Snow White said, in a syrup-think New England accent, "Yew heerd what she said, said she eats like a pig. Well, haow 'baout we see if she fucks like one tew?"

Someone from the restaurant, came Hazel's frantic deduction. *But, shit! The restaurant was packed!*

Now a hand pawed her crotch. "Bet'cha she got a shaved pie."

"Neeeew . . ."

"Shore. Young gals these days, 'specially the collerge gals, all shave it. Bet'cha it is."

"Aw'right, then, yew're on. Winner gets his nut'n her fust."

Hazel's flipflops were flung away and her shorts were peeled inside-out and off.

"Well dew tell!" said Snow White. "I en't never *seed* a chunk'a red pussy har like thet!"

Mortified, Hazel tensed when one of them grabbed a fistful of her abundant pubis plot and *pulled.* Pain prickled; the skin of her sexual mound pulled out.

"*Big* ass pussy fer such a little thing."

"Ee-yuh. Nice big lips on it." The eyes behind Snow White's eye-holes leveled. "Best jew keep them eyes shut, reddy-head. Less yew see'a us, better the chance we durn't kill ya."

Hazel's eyes sealed shut.

"Flip her over naow. I wanna see whar her shit come out."

"Dag straight."

The rough hands flipped Hazel over like a sack of flour. Her buttocks was parted.

"Shee-it!" affirmed the southern voice. "That ass is fresh cornbread right out the oven!" and a fingertip shimmied in the anal opening.

"Well-used, tew. Yew kin tell by lookin'. More like'a slit instead of a hole. Means she's no stranger to gettin' it in the ass." Belt buckles clinked. "Well go on. Yew got fust dibs."

Hazel sensed her attackers changing positions. She grunted; her cheek dragged in the dirt as her hips were hauled up. With her eyes closed, she seemed to *sense* more. She heard the sound of a throat being cleared, then—

Hhhhock!

A mucoid lump landed in the crack of her buttocks after which a penis of more than modest girth pushed through.

"Shee-it," came the immediate complaint. "This stringbean's asshole tain't tight at all. And fer such a li'l thing?"

"Heh, heh, heh. Told ya it looked well-used. Probably had more cocks goin' in it than shit comin' aout."

In spite of the reeling horror, Hazel was able to register the grievance, and—

"Ho boy!" Peter Pan delighted.

—Hazel deftly tightened her anus. *So I've got a big asshole, huh,* she managed to think. *How's this for big, you redneck garbage-pile?* Her dexterity enabled her to tighten the sphincter and hold it for a considerable length.

"Aw-aw-aw, *man!* All's a sudden, she's tighter than a li'l boy's ass!"

Snow White's New England drawl cackled. "Haow would jew know abaout li'l *boys'* asses?" and then a guttural peal of laughter fluttered up.

"Just a figgure'a speech, ya know?"

Now, with a mechanical promptitude, Hazel began to oscillate the intricate muscle without any relent at all, opening and closing at a pace that matched her heartbeat.

Her sodomizer was panting, grunting almost in distress as the penis plunged in and out. "I'se swear on my mama's grave this is the *best* dang cornholin' I ever had!" and then he began to shiver, his strokes picking up, and:

"Ah, fuck—ahhhhhhh!"

Hazel easily felt the hot spurts eddy into her bowel. She felt sickened, yet thrilled. Eventually the invading penis slid out of her.

"Cain't believe my dick spit that fast."

"Your dick *always* spits fast," Snow White laughed. "En't had the 'sperience I had. Naow yew get aout my way," Snow White said, "'curz it's my turn. And while I'm jiggin' up her shit, yew best thank the lady for bein' setch a good sport, eh? Mebbe like a Nor'east Mustache?"

"Wish I'd thunk'a that!"

As the taller man popped a considerably larger erection through her sphincter, Peter Pan pulled her face off the ground and wiped his deflated penis across her upper lip. *Oh, you MOTHERFUCKER!* she thought. Now she had to smell remnants of her own excrement.

All the while, though, the question beat like a drum in her head: *What will they do to me when they're done?*

"Well I'll be gard-durn't if yew en't right," Snow White railed, pumping her. "She larnt proper, I'se tellin' yew. Just as I'se sarten my daddy fucked sheep, I'm *durn* sarten this is the tightest backside I ever buggered."

"Tolt ya!"

"Make it tighter, reddy-head, make it tight as yew can, less yu'd ruther me'n my pal here cut yew're li'l cupcake tits off'n choke ya tew death on 'em."

Hazel summoned every iota of strength in her body, focused it on her sphincter, and *squeezed*...

"Ee-YUH!"

More sperm slopped into her bowel; Hazel could feel that this deposit was considerably more voluminous than the first man's. The cock spasmed in curious *quivers* as the assailant's balls drew up against her vagina.

The man exhaled. "If'n this 'un could make her asshole any tighter she could likely cut PVC pipe."

"Or bust an empty Bud bottle, fer shore."

"Ee-yuh. Tew bad we en't got one." His hips nudged closer to Hazel's buttocks. "Loosen up naow, reddy—theer, good."

Hazel was cruxed. *He just came so . . . what's he doing now?* He seemed to be adjusting his hips like a golfer just before making a shot.

"En't done just yet," and then—

Oh my God...

—he began to urinate.

"See, what I always larn't was that if yew're gonna *cum* up a bitch's ass, yew might as well piss up it tew, eh?"

"Dag straight."

Hazel winced with her face in the dirt. *And I thought I was sick in the head.* Heat *blossomed* in her lower abdomen; she could feel her bowel swell and swell–indeed, she could even feel pressurized urine tracing up the convolutions of her large intestine. After what had to have been two full minutes, the flow had not abated. *For shit's sake, buddy! Are you gonna piss all fucking day?*

"Like pullin' the truck up to the fillin' station!" cawed Peter Pan.

"Ding-ding-ding-ding-ding . . ."

When no more urine remained, Snow White slowly withdrew. Hazel thought of a fat, shaved rat being dragged out of her ass.

"En't much I'd ruther dew'n piss up a gal's backside. Just supthin' that tickles me pink abaout the ideer of a gal filled with piss."

Peter Pan clapped in degenerate glee, and when he did so, his limp cock jiggled. "I'se hear that!"

Hazel collapsed to her belly. All that piss bloating her bowel made her feel buoyant. Her brain seemed like something diced into dozens of nuggets, and each nugget struggled but failed to fully reconnect with the others. She couldn't quite contemplate the potential that she would be dead soon.

"Come tew think of it . . ."

Suddenly she was being dragged across the dirt by her hair, until she was arranged in a sitting position against a tree.

"Time this bitch got filled up both ways. I done filled up her ass, so's why'n't jew fill up her belly?"

"Yeah! It's been a spell since I done that!"

Hazel's skewed faculties didn't register their intent until Peter Pan was standing with his revolting-smelling penis right in her face.

"Open up."

Hazel glanced upward through half-closed eyes. "What?"

"Come on, red! Crank that cock-sucker open." The smiling Peter Pan mask looked ludicrous as such words were emitted from it. "I'se gonna pee in yer mouth'n yer gonna drink it."

Hazel blinked. Hadn't she had enough yet? When she gazed down at herself, her lower abdomen bloated such that she looked half-pregnant herself. *I'm sitting in the woods, raped and naked, with my belly sticking out 'cos some redneck just used my ass for a urinal,* she thought very concretely.

"No," she said.

Peter Pan's eyes looked incredulous. Snow White's gaze slowly roved over. "Say *what?*"

"I'm *not* going to drink your piss," Hazel said. She shrugged. "I don't care any more—my life's a piece of shit because *I'm* a piece of shit. My father's the most wonderful man in the world and I treat him like a bum—I *avoid* him because I'm too lazy and indulgent to bother. The only person I truly love—a woman, by the way—

thinks we're only 'buds,' and I've got more mental problems than an abnormal psyche text." She held up dirt-smudged hands. "Go ahead and kill me. I'm done."

Peter Pan flicked his knife. "If'n that's the way ya want it—"

Hazel smiled as the blade lowered. *I guess it is . . . and I'm fine with that.*

"New, new, new"—Snow White's hand intervened to pull the knife away. "En't no sport in killin' a woman who en't afeared, and anyway, she's just playin' with us naow."

"Playin'?" questioned Peter Pan.

"Ee-yuh. She don't keer if she live're dies, but ya knaow what?"

"What?"

"We'll tie her up'n take her back to the shack." Snow White got down on one knee and looked right at her through his eye-holes. "Then tonight weer gonna snatch ourselfs thet pregnant one." He pronounced "pregnant" as *preg-ernt.* "Ee-yuh, li'l reddy-head heer thinks she can fuck with us. Afore we kill *yew,* we'll kill yew're knocked up friend fust."

Hazel gulped. For the first time she opened her eyes fully and looked at him.

"I'm gonna pitchfork that snippy bitch right in her big belly. Then I'll'se fuck her while the tot's blood's sloppin' out her cooze. All while yew're watchin'. Heh, heh, heh . . ." His real eye winked in the eye-hole. "Think I'm lyin'?"

"All right, I'll do it," Hazel shrilled and opened her mouth.

Chuckles fluttered more about her head. Peter Pan stood before her; her sitting position allowed a near-perfect alignment between the rogue's crotch and Hazel's mouth. Every muscle in her neck tensed from the sudden gust of crotch-stink. "Tain't pissed all day . . ."

"Shuh hope yew're thusty, hon."

Peter Pan pinched her cheek till it hurt. "Listen up. I'se got my own system, see? You open yer mouth, I piss in it till it's full. Then I stop and you swaller. Then ya open up agin'n I fill 'er up agin, and we'se go like that, ya hear?"

Hazel rolled her eyes. "How methodical. So I'm to assume this isn't the first time you've forced a woman to drink your piss—"

Whap!

A hard palm impacted the side of her head.

"Fust time?" cackled Snow White. "We been fillin' tramps with piss for a coon's age."

"Oh, a coon's age, huh? I've always been curious," Hazel tempted fate. "Just how long is a coon's age?"

Whap!

Hazel's head bobbed on her neck.

"You sassin' us?" inquired Peter Pan, the end of his limp penis poised between index finger and thumb.

"And, reddy? Heer's somethin' else yew need to know," and Snow White knelt down and spread Hazel's legs wide. "If'n yew don't swalluh every maouthful, then—"

Smack!

—his fist pounded her sex.

"—I'se gonna punch yew in yew're cunt."

Hazel moaned from the impact, her groin throbbing. "All right," she wheezed. "I got it."

"Then git ready, reddy!" Peter Pan celebrated.

Hazel braced herself: eyes sealed, neck craned and back arched, mouth locked open. An instant later, her oral cavity was being filled with hot urine, then the stream stopped and Hazel tensed, then gulped it down.

She teetered where she sat.

"Open!"

Through a throbbing mental disgust, Hazel forced herself to adhere to the "system." She opened her mouth and let it be filled again.

And again.

And again.

And again and again and again . . .

She could find no simile to apply to the taste. She could only think of it as mineralish and anti-sapid: something revolting yet in defiance of description. She seemed to be able to *smell* it going down her throat. But the worst sensation of all was simply all that liquid heat being deposited from mouth to stomach.

Snow White's New England drawl piped up as if amazed: "She shuh is chuggin' it daown like a champ, eh?"

Peter Pan *eee-hawed.* "And I'se got *plenty* more store up fer the bitch!"

Hazel shut the words out and opened her mouth again . . .

And again and again.

Oh my God is he ever going to finish?

On the thirteenth swallow, she hiccupped, thought, *Shit!* and out gushed an entire mouthful.

Smack!

Her face ballooned; she nearly threw up. The impact of Snow White's knuckly fist to her majora felt more like a swift and very pin-point blow with a mallet. It made her kidneys and even her ovaries hurt. *If he does that one more time he might rupture my uterus,* she thought through the sickest daze.

"Gawd *dog,* I trooly dew *love* punchin' gals in thur pussies."

"Yeah, man!"

Three more mouthfuls and three more swallows ensued before Peter Pan's bladder was at last depleted of all its contents.

Hazel felt her belly and bowel *slosh* when she sidled over, whining and in tears.

"Naow thet's what I call fillin' a bitch *up.*"

"Look-it that gut!"

Indeed, all that urine made her look inflated.

"Huh belly? Shee-it! Haow 'baout them *nips* on her?"

Only now did Hazel become consciously aware of this incident's most obscene element of all: she was vibrating in a state of accelerated sexual arousal.

"I'se don't believe it!" Peter Pan exclaimed. "Her dang nipples're stickin' out like the spark plugs on the boat motor!"

"Aye, they are, heh, heh, heh! T'is a very especial kind'a gal who gets horny whilse havin' the holy ever-livin' *hail* raped aout'a her, huh?"

That, Hazel thought, *would be me.*

The dichotomy raged. She was horrified, disgusted, and sickened unto *death,* yet her libido betrayed all such undisputable facts. Sodomized, beaten, and filled with urine, yes, by two men who might very well kill her, but . . .

She had never felt so turned on in her life.

"Hands'n knees agin," Snow White ordered. "We en't finished yet, girlie."

They're going to ass-fuck me AGAIN? she wondered. Automatonically she assumed the position ordered, then—

Pumph!

—Snow White's workboot pressed down across her shoulder blades, the force of which rammed her face back into the dirt. "Keep thet gorgeous li'l butt stickin' up, reddy-head, so's ya can show us a piss gusher."

"A piss . . . *what?*"

"Blow alls my piss aout yew're ass, reel hard, see? We wanna *see* how far it shoots."

You've GOT to be shitting me! but what choice did she have but to accommodate the perverse command? She jutted her rump up, took several deep breaths, then tightened her abdomen and *HEAVED* . . .

"Ho boy!"

"Yew see thet?"

Hazel's anus dilated, and she blew a veritable *plume* of sullied urine out of her bowel. It *vaulted* from her in a way that made her think of a water cannon.

Petr Pan giggled. "Baby, looks like you'se just shot a fuckin' quart'a piss out'cher ass TEN FEET!"

Great . . .

Snow White clapped. "I'se seed a lot'a gals blow piss aout thur butts in my time, but nevuh *thet* far! Naow's time tew empty huh belly as well, eh?"

"Only fittin'," and then Peter Pan knelt beside her in the fashion of a wrestler. He put her in a headlock, forearm about her forehead, as she remained straining on her knees. "Now if'n ya *bite?* I'll crack yer purdy neck, ya hear?"

"Bite . . . what?" she mumbled.

"And dun't yew ferget," added Snow White, "whut we'll dew to yew're pregnant friend. I'll stick a boat-hook up her pussy and drag the baby aout by his nose, ya heer?"

He and Peter Pan guffawed.

Hazel knew the score when Peter Pan isolated two dirty fingers and pressed them to her lips. She opened her mouth, then said fingers slid in and pressed hard against the back of her tongue.

The vicious pressure took her by surprise; her gag-reflex responded like a thrown switch. Her belly prolapsed, then—

Uuurp!

She vomited up a great, caustic well of urine. It sounded like a bucket of water being upended. Her assailants cackled. Then the fingers jammed back deeper and pressed—

Hazel's stomach spasmed and splattered another gust of hot, food-flecked urine into the dirt. Her eyes spun in her head, and her abdominal muscles cramped. "No more, please!" she sobbed—

Uuuurp!

Back the fingers went, past her tonsils this time, to trigger another release.

"That's a good girl," cooed Peter Pan.

"This shuh beats hail aout'a watchin' TV."

It had to have been some very obscure recess of her psyche that allowed Hazel to contemplate: Of all the times she'd been violated—and had *invited* that violation . . .

THIS was the most grievous.

"I curn't BELIEVE what I'm seein'–no suh! This sick bitch is playin' with huh-self whilse yew're makin' huh *puke!*" Snow White railed.

After another gust, bile dangled from Hazel's lips and spots swam before her eyes. Had she heard him correctly?

Oh, yes . . .

When Peter Pan's fingers jammed back yet again, Hazel realized her right hand had come up between her legs to coddle her clitoris.

"Might as well just empty the bitch . . ."

Hazel convulsed through several more go-rounds. In a grand finale, then, the fingers pressed down harder than ever and, this time, didn't let up. A frighteningly large wet spot of urine and bits of food carpeted the dirt before her. Her belly pumped and pumped and pumped and Hazel gagged and gagged and gagged. She'd long since given over to dry-heaving, yet still the invading fingers persisted. She hacked, wretched, bucked, and flopped. Nothing was coming up now, yet the fingers wanted more. When they finally withdrew several minutes later, Hazel believed she'd been just one spasm short of throwing up her stomach.

Wracked, cramping up, and dizzy to incognizance, she rolled over, wheezing, after Peter Pan at last released her. This sociopathic abuse of her body left every nerve in her body buzzing in raw lust. She lay in the great stain of her own piss and vomit, and masturbated openly.

Peter Pan chuckled. "Any other gal'd be scared shitless but this 'un's horny as a mare!"

"One of a kind," Snow White remarked but pronounced "kind" as *conned.* Hazel played with her clitoris, slipping it between her fingers like a watermelon seed as Peter Pan seemed to marvel at her distended nipples.

"Pinch them harder!" she panted.

She half-shrieked when he obliged, twisting the areolae as if they were wood screws. Hazel's ass clenched, she bucked, then came convulsively. In the "afterglow" she lay in a near-paralysis, as if run over.

Snow White was rummaging through her little purse. "She shuh en't much for money. En't got but twenty piddlin' dollars on huh." He stuffed the bill in his pocket, shaking his masked head.

"Do I look like a fuckin' ATM?" she snapped at him.

"She's got huh-self a lotta spunk, I'll give huh thet."

"Yeah, man."

"What's this heer?" Snow White asked and removed a small bottle of Pond's.

"It's hand lotion, Einstein!" Hazel yelled.

"Don't get smart," but, of course, Snow White pronounced "smart" as *smot.*

"Reddy-head taken everything we give huh, and she still en't beggin' for huh life."

"So's I guess that can only mean . . . ,"

Peter Pan sealed Hazel's mouth closed with an open palm, then pinched her nostrils shut with two fingers.

Her eyes bugged; she mewled into her closed mouth. Peter Pan's chuckles grew darker and darker as her vision dimmed. She flopped in the dirt like a pinned frog. Her lungs expanded . . .

They're killing me. For real this time.

The chuckles grew echoic as Hazel's consciousness faded to black.

Had she died? She felt sinking very quickly, falling down an endless hole in the ground . . .

A faceless voice very far away whispered: *Hazel, my child, I adjure you . . .*

Her breath whistled when the hands came off her face. She hacked and sucked in air simultaneously, shuddering. But—

But—

A monstrous pressure–an *obscene* trespass–begat her first

scream in earnest. *What IS that?* She heard more chuckles like some sound-effects trick that turned each utterance into a hundred, along with . . .

Along with a sickening wet *schlucking* sound. Something huge was pumping in and out of her vagina to the extent that she thought she was having a baby in reverse.

"Take a looky, reddy!" Peter Pan guffawed.

A hand jerked her head up, forcing her to look down between her spread legs. At the same time she smelled the absolute worst stench of her life. *He's not—He's not really—*

Snow White sat between her legs. He'd removed one of his boots; hence the stench: the appalling odor of a big unwashed-for-days redneck foot. He'd smeared the hand lotion over it, she could only guess, and now had most of his entire foot stuck up into her vaginal barrel.

"Theer ya go, ee-yuh!" he celebrated. "Theer ya go . . ."

schluck, schluck, schluck, went the sound.

The atrocious thing pumped in and out of her, at times broadening her vaginal lips to a stretched pink rim.

"Nothin' like a good ole foot-fuckin' ta break a sassy gal's starch!" Peter Pan hooted.

schluck, schluck, schluck

"Ee-yuh, ee-yuh," Snow White grunted. "En't foot-fucked me a bitch in . . ."

"What?" Hazel yelled. "A fuckin' coon's age!"

The rapists burst out laughing.

"Come on," Peter Pan egged on. "See if'n ya can get it all the way up her."

The horrendous foot flexed inside, then Snow White raised his ass off the ground and—

"Eeeeeeeeeeee-YUH! Thar she goes!"

When the foot slunked into her all the way to the ankle, Hazel, very understandably, shrieked.

And then down came Peter Pan's hands to seal her mouth closed and pinch her nostrils shut again.

schluck, schluck, schluck

Her convulsions redoubled. She heard a distant buzzing in her head, then once more her lungs began to expand. The chuckles flitted about like bats far away. *This is it,* came the calm thought through the appalling subventions. The cross on Hazel's sullied bosom felt like a red-hot ingot over her heart, and as her life began to descend into unutterable darkness she pleaded, *I'm know I'm not worth saving, God, but could You at least know that I'm sorry for my sins?*

Her brain de-oxygenated, the effect of which hit her like a potent opiate, and even as her mind went totally black, she knew she was masturbating, knew even that she'd climaxed at the immediate point of de—

Turmoil. Pandemonic commotion. The hands flew off Hazel's face. She yelped in a breath when the foot was yanked out of her plundered vagina like a lollipop pulled from a greedy toddler's mouth. Hazel shivered in near-death as her lungs siphoned in air. What was happening? When she managed to lean up, an intense white light burned in her eyes. *The light at the end of the tunnel of Death,* she thought for sure, but then why were her attackers still present? Snow White and Peter Pan seemed charged into panic, swearing under their breath. "Haow yew fuckin' like thet?" "Come on, we gotta git!" Frantic footfalls pounded the dirt, then their manic silhouettes fled into the trees.

I must still be alive, Hazel presumed.

Very slowly, her vision began to clear. Evidently the foot-game had been going on a while, for the sun had sunk lower. That's when she realized that the intense white light in her eyes was actually a pair of headlights on a vehicle.

A huge, wide-shouldered shape approached, then lifted her up.

"Holy Moses, yew all right, miss?" came a genial yet heavy voice.

Hazel simply lay limp in arms that felt secure as metal rails. "I, I—," was all she could say.

"Don't'cha worry. Them men're gone," the thick northern drawl told her and then she felt herself being carried a short distance and placed in the passenger seat of what she thought must be a pickup truck. Her rescuer disappeared a moment, then returned with her purse and scant clothes. He placed a blanket over her. When he got behind the wheel, Hazel was finally able to say, "Thank you. You saved my life."

His form looked fuzzy. "Aw, naow, I doubt they'd'a kilt ya but they was rough customers, all right. I'll tell ya, though, if that one fella was doin' what it *looked* like he was doin' . . . well, I almost wish I could'a kilt them myself." A pause. "Lotta evil folks in this world, it seems."

Hazel hugged herself beneath the wrap as the pickup pulled away. Had God answered her prayers, or had it merely been luck? Finally her vision came back sufficiently to make out details of her rescuer . . .

I don't believe it . . .

It was the brawny man she'd seen taking out the garbage. The "woodsman."

"You must be one'a the gals stayin' up the Wilmarth place."

"Yes," she blurted. "My name's Hazel Greene."

"I'm Horace Knowles. Growed up 'raound heer." He shook his head, which was topped by think, straight-black hair down to his collar. "Some'a the best campin' and hikin' you'll evuh find in our area." The peaceful drawl sounded checked by anger. "Then ungodly stuff like this happens. It could drive tourists away. Curn't ever understand why some folks are just so . . . *bad*."

So evil, Hazel thought spontaneously. "Oh, but my friend and I aren't really tourists—her name's Sonia, by the way. We just came up to meet her fiancé. He inherited Henry Wilmarth's cabin."

"I only met Professor Wilmarth once. Very nice man, and it's a dag shame what happened . . ."

"Yes . . ."

"Well, best not think'a that. 'Specially after what'choo been through. Won't take but twenty minutes to git yew to the county sheriff's."

Hazel rubbed her stomach beneath the wrap; it still ached from the forced-vomit contractions. *County sheriff's . . ."*Don't bother, Horace. But if you could drive me back to the cabin, that'd be great."

Only now did she note the rest of his face: chisel-jawed, dark-eyed, whiskers. *He's a redneck Adonis,* Hazel thought. But Horace looked alarmed by her comment. "But, miss, you *was* raped, weren't ya?"

Buddy, the shit those animals did to me make your typical rape look like babies blowing bubbles. "Yes, but I'm not really comfortable reporting it to the police. It's impossible for me to give a description; they were wearing masks."

Horace nodded grimly. "I think I git what'cher sayin'. Lotta women don't report bein' raped 'cos half the time they en't believed."

She could've laughed. *All women are sluts who ask for it.* "Yeah. They didn't cut me or anything. I'm actually very lucky."

"The grace'a God it weren't wuss," Horace said.

Hazel stalled on his words. Without conscious direction, her fingers slid up between her breasts and touched her cross.

"If'n yew're shuh," he said, "then I'll have ya back at the cabin in no time."

Hazel felt cosseted in relief now. But then—"Oh, wait a minute. I'm *filthy!* I don't want Sonia to see me like this; she's pregnant and it would definitely distress her. Is there a motel around? I need a shower *really* bad."

"Keziah Mason's lodge is full up, I'm pretty shuh, but yew're more'n welcome to get washed up at my trailer."

"Thank you, Horace. You're a godsend."

Only minutes later she was walking awkwardly into a modest mobile home wrung with wind-chimes; her hand kept the blanket wrapped about herself.

Horace carried her things in behind her. "En't much but it's home."

"It's very well-appointed," Hazel said of the interior. It didn't look trailerish at all but cozy. Plush couch and carpet, dark walls, framed pictures.

"Right in heer," he said and opened a narrow door. He handed her a towel. When she took it, she lost her grasp on the wrap and it fell partway open, revealing her furred pubis, her belly and one breast.

Horace immediately turned away.

"Ooops," Hazel said.

"I'll be in heer if'n ya need anything."

"Thanks."

The bathroom was a tiny compartment but to Hazel, just then, it couldn't have been more luxurious. She felt enslimed by filth—indeed, by *evil*—and she needed desperately to wash off all the unmentionable grime. She imagined that she'd been dragged bare-assed by devils through a shit-trench in Hell. The scalding water in the telephone-booth-sized stall made her bristle; she moaned in delight as the layers of sweat, dirt, and urine were sloughed away. Now that she'd been removed from the danger, she grew more aware of the toll her body had taken, most especially her vagina. It ached from the horrendous insult paid to it, and when Hazel thought most objectively about exactly *what* had happened, she cringed. *A foot. A big dirty redneck FOOT!* She lathered her pubis up in a great poof of suds, rinsed it off, then relathered but *still* felt filthy. She wished for a douche bottle full of Listerine; she wished she could hook a hose to the shower nozzle and flush herself out like a radiator. She had to settle for inserting the bar of soap into her vaginal inlet, popping it out, then working her fingers in.

Once dried off and re-dressed, she limped back to the front room. Now her sex throbbed in a steady ache. She heard a strange swooshing sound that wavered in and out, then found Horace sitting at a potter's wheel in a smaller room off to the side. His foot pumped a pedal which spun the wheel as his hands expertly molded a curvaceous vase out of wet clay. A kiln sat in the corner. From pegs on the wall hung an array of knives, styluses, and other clay-working tools, while shelves opposite housed multitudes of finished products: bowls, flower pots, tubular wind chimes, paperweights shaped like swans, butterflies, etc.

"You're quite a craftsman," Hazel complimented of the wares.

"I'm a potter," Horace said without looking up. He pumped the pedal. "I make mainly wind-chimes, and regional knickknacks fer tourists. Lotta my stuff's for sale at the Pickman's Curiosity Shoppe on Main Street. Yew'n yer friend might wanna stop by'n take a look."

"We will," Hazel promised, gazing around at the all the displayed objects. "So this is your main occupation, and you work at the tavern on the side?"

Horace laughed under his breath. "More like the other way 'raound. But t'ween this'n my job at the tavern I'se can pay the bills a right easy."

Hazel didn't hear the last of his words, for something on the top shelf snagged her eye. She reached up, took it down.

It was an intricate and very finely crafted clay box, about five inches long, four wide, and four high. Slightly lop-sided, its angles slightly off, its sides slightly unparallel. *Just like the box at the cabin, only clay instead of metal* . . . The same bizarre glyphics adorned its sides and lid: series of v's,<'s,^'s, and >'s, interspersed irregularly by ~'s. She felt sure that its dimensions were identical to the box at the cabin. The only difference other than its composition was an absence of the curious bas-reliefs on the sides and center of the lid: the unsettling figures. After a lengthened surveillance, too, the glyphs seemed varied in some way, or perhaps more plentiful than on the body of the cabin box.

"There's a box very similar to this at the cabin."

"Metal, goldish color, right?" Horace asked.

"Why, yes."

"That was the model I used to make the template for this." Horace pointed to the box in her hand. "See, a while back, Professor Wilmarth brought that gold box over. He said it was very old, from Egypt're some sech place. And he wanted me to duplicate it, said the angles hadda be exact, and said he'd pay me five hunnert dollars for a prototype. Said if I did a good job he'd pay a tidy sum more for a whole bunch of 'em—thirty-two more, he said."

Hazel stared at the recital. "So Henry Wilmarth paid you to make this box?"

"Ee-yuh, he did. Cash money, too. Felt bad takin' that much but he said skills like mine was wuth a respectable wage."

"When was this, Horace?"

"Oh, last spring, I s'pose."

"Before the Mother's Day Storm in St. Petersburg?"

"Oh, ee-yuh. Was like in March, I think."

She tried to get the story straight. "And he said he wanted to buy *more* of these from you?"

"If'n I did the job right. Said the angles hadda be exact, and, well, I'll stake my repper-tayshun that the angles *is* exact"—he pointed to an array of protractors, compasses, and polycarbonate angle-stencils hanging on the wall. "They'se exact, all right. Said it didn't need to be metal, though, clay was fine, and he said it didn't need the same drawings on it. The metal box had these creepy drawings that looked sort'a like monsters."

Hazel felt a modest chill when she recalled the bas-relief figures. Had the figures seemed hostile and tentacled? She shivered.

Horace pointed to a sheet of graph paper tacked to the wall. "Just the dimensions'a the box hadda be the same. But the engravings—the little and V's and sech–hadda be *different*."

Hazel examined the graph paper, and on it noticed an off-angled exploded diagram depicting the box's four sides and the lid. "Different," she muttered.

"Ee-yuh. See, I even made these templates for each side and the lid"—next, he held up plastic sheets into which the glyphs had been copied and cut out.

"But he never contracted you to make the rest of the boxes?"

"New. Never heard from him directly again." Horace set the vase aside and washed his hands in a small sink. "Kind'a weird. He was always in and aout'a taown's what I heerd. So's when I finished the first box I left a letter under his door, tolt him it was ready for him ta take a look at. A while later I get a letter back thankin' me for my trouble but sayin' he didn't need any more of the boxes. Plus a check fer another five hunnert."

"And when was *that?*" Hazel felt driven to ask. "Was it before or after the—"

"It were after that big storm he survived in Florida, ee-yuh. Like end'a May or early June."

Hazel gazed perplexed at the box. When she opened it she found a similar interior: seven struts supporting an egg-shaped metal band. "Did Professor Wilmarth ever say what the box was for?"

Horace dried his big, beefy hands with paper towels. Hazel stared at them, imagining one clamped to her throat and the other rockering her sex . . .

"I seem ta recall him saying it was a *crystal* box. S'posed to hold some sort'a crystal. Said he hadda bunch'a friends who wanted 'em. What's the word he used?" Horace squinted. "Gemologists, I'se think."

Hazel blinked. *A crystal. A gemstone? Didn't Henry's letter mention a STONE, that he also referred to as the "ST"?*

"It's full dark naow. I best get yew back."

Hazel limped after him out to the truck. Storm clouds roved overhead, consuming a beautiful moon. *Looks like rain tonight.* She idled her thoughts as Horace drove the bulky truck out of the boondock cranny and pulled back onto the main road.

What a day . . . She felt strangely at ease and very definitely *un*traumatized in spite of the horrific scene earlier. Worse was she felt an inkling of arousal, no doubt ignited by her proximity to this handsome, strong-as-an-ox bumpkin who'd saved her.

"You're very modest, Horace, but you know, I think those men really were going to kill me."

"Mebbe but, new, I don't think so. I hadda hankerin' it was the Fish Boys, just a gut feelin' but, shoot, I curn't prove it."

"The Fish Boys?"

"Couple local fellas, en't good fer much. Rumor is they both done time fer small stuff, but even *them* fellas en't got the belly fer killin'. Were probably just a couple poachers passin' through. Lots'a poachers out, all the time hot for whitetail deer, moose'n beaver. 'S'illegal to hunt moose'n beaver, ya know."

Hazel sighed. "Horace, that's not what I meant." Her hand drifted to the marble-firm thigh filling the denim. "I meant that whether you saved my life or you didn't, I'm still indebted to you. The only way I can think to thank you is . . ."

Her hand slid over a crotch that felt *packed. Feels like this hayseed's got a pound of ground beef stuffed in there.* Her finger slid greedily up and down the zipper . . .

"Horace, pull over," she whispered in his ear.

"Aw, well, I dun't know, Hazel . . ."

"Pull over, pull over . . ."

Horace groaned, then pulled the clattering truck onto the shoulder.

At once she felt feverish. She unfastened his belt, opened his pants, and pulled down his fly all in a series of movements that seemed synchronized. He wore no briefs. The musky scent of a day's work wafted up when her hand ladled out all that warm, soft meat. *My God,* she thought, dizzy, gently squeezing the mass of scrotum and coiled cock.

"Aw," he muttered.

The mass came alive, an erection quickly lengthening. Hazel ringed her thumb and forefinger about the shaft to help it along and in doing so felt it swell to a column so hard it barely yielded to her pressure. A swatch of foreskin bunched at the top; she delighted in gently pulling it down and feeling all that delicate skin slide silkily up and down over the hot pillar. In the dashlight she noted veins fat and long as earthworms. Horace fidgeted in his seat as she continued to slowly stroke. Once fully hard, it began to beat; Hazel was almost flabbergasted by its size: the girth of a Red Bull can but inches longer. She wanted to suck it all down. She wanted to sit on it and let it all burrow into her. *I just got raped to within an inch of my life by two guys sicker than Richard Speck, and NOW look what I'm doing . . .* Why should she even *try* to understand herself?

This cock is gorgeous, she thought, stupefied. *It's a fucking work of art . . .* Next, she scooped up the scrotum which filled her entire hand, was almost giddy as her fingers explored each testicle, each almost the size and weight of a hen's egg. The excitement she induced made the balls start to draw upward on their intricate tethers, then she grabbed the shaft again and slid the foreskin all the way down, baring a plump, fat-slitted corona. Drool filled the considerable piss-slit. Even this minutia of sexual anatomy fascinated her, and due to the organ's atypical size, she wondered if it were possible to . . .

Hazel held the column close with one hand, while the thumb and forefinger of the other opened the delicate slit. Horace flinched, while Hazel delighted in being able to admit the end of her pinky finger fully into the egress of Horace's urethra, something she'd never been able to do before.

But what now?

I've got to suck it, I've just GOT to . . .

She leaned over to fellate him but just as her lips would meet the glans . . .

"Aw, ya know," Horace pushed her away, "this en't settin' right with me, Hazel. En't nothin' 'baout yew, it's just . . ."

Hazel stared at him.

"I just curn't let'cha dew this, much as I'd wanna." It was with difficulty that he managed to stuff those marvelous balls and beating cock back into his trousers. "See, I got me a honey–Lillian's her name–and, see, she's over in the Iraq right naow. She's in the signal corp. I'd be a low-daown dag dirty *dog* to fool 'raound with another gal while my baby's over there fightin' fer my freedom. New sir, a fella couldn't get no lower."

Oh, for God's sake! An ethical redneck!

"So I just hope yew understand and durn't take it personal," he said and got back on the road.

Hazel put her face in her hands and laughed. "You're a good man, Horace, and you have no idea how lucky your girlfriend is. They sure don't make many men like you these days." She sighed.

"And now I guess you think I'm a super slut for pulling a move like that . . ."

"New, durn't worry none. We all gots our thing."

"I just didn't know how else to thank you . . ."

He raised a finger. "Come by the Curiosity Shoppe. It'd make me look good to the owner if'n ya bought something, and I'll bet there's plenty theer you'd fancy."

"I'll look forward to it, Horace."

"And like I said a'fore." He smiled contentedly behind the wheel. "Durn't thank me, thank the Lord . . ."

The rain had just started when Hazel entered the cabin. Lights burned softly in the front room, but Sonia wasn't there. "Sonia? I'm back."

"Oh—In here."

Hazel followed her friend's voice into the small den. Sonia sat at Henry Wilmarth's desk, studying an array of papers.

"Wow, that was some walk," Sonia said without looking up.

"Took longer than I thought, and—"

Finally Sonia's eyes looked up in exclamation. "What's wrong! Are you hurt?"

Hazel limped in. *Well, I just got foot-fucked, if that's what you mean.* "I guess I'm not in the good shape I thought. Sore all over. I was so tired halfway back, I hitched a ride with a local."

Did Sonia offer a suspicious frown? Suddenly thunder rumbled, then rain began to patter the roof.

"And I got back just in time," Hazel added. She leaned over the desk. "Looks like some serious Nosy Parkering going on here."

"I took the liberty of looking over Henry's papers," Sonia defended herself.

"Feminist doctrine. Sounds good to me." Hazel noticed lots of papers written by hand, many of which appeared to be in foreign languages. "And?"

Sonia sat back, sighing. She adjusted her position in the seat to accommodate her swollen belly. "A whole lot of really bizarre rigamarole."

"This is definitely Latin," Hazel said, picking a sheet up. "And it also looks like—"

"I know. Not a photocopy but an old style mimeograph," Sonia augmented. The sheet was purple-tinted and frayed. "I haven't seen something like that in decades."

Hazel skimmed a few lines. "I took some Latin, but most of this is illegible. Terrum Per Me Ambula? Something about 'walking the earth . . . '" She squinted. "'Per qua spheres opportunus' means 'by where the spheres meet.' And . . . 'Non in notus tractus tamen inter illud tractus?' Damn, I don't know. Maybe "Not in known spaces but between them?""

Sonia showed her another paper. Hazel recited, "'They frendo civis . . . '" She blinked. "'They crush the cites,' or something like that."

"Weird."

On the back, a Post-It was stuck. It read in cursive script: *Mimeo of hand-copied intercession page of A.A. I believe someone scrivened the page from the Wormius translation of A.D. 1228. Either the Bibliotheque Nationale in Paris, or the copy in Lima.*

"Beats me," Hazel said. "What about the others?"

Sonia handed her a frayed 8 x 10 photograph that looked almost as worn as the mimeograph. The back read, in the same script:

Probably illegally photographed p. of rumored copy of Greek trans. of N. (Theodorus Philatus, A.D. 950) that escaped condemnation and burning ordered by Patriarch Michael, A.D. 1050 . (Is this the copy thought to be hidden in Vatican?)

"Greek, huh?" Hazel noted. "Good luck translating *that*."

"Yeah. And the notations look like Henry's handwriting."

"It makes sense. It's his stuff, and something he was obviously studying with some interest."

"Transcriptions of Latin and Greek, from the Middle Ages and older? Printing presses didn't even exist then," Sonia seemed stifled. "So somebody accessed original copies of the texts, which *had* to have been handwritten, and then copied certain parts in their own hand?"

Hazel shrugged in resignation. "I guess. But so what?"

"Henry Wilmarth was a *mathematician*, Hazel, and a scholar of *geometry*. But this stuff looks like old folklore or something. And there's not a single number or equation on any of these pages."

"Sonia!" Hazel blurted. "How do you say 'I don't give a shit' in Greek?"

"Don't be a smart-ass," Sonia smirked back. "But now, look at this."

Another dog-eared 8 x 10. At the bottom, clearly scribed in fountain pen and *not* in Henry Wilmarth's hand, were the words: *one of only two extant sheets of Al Azif, pilfered by Deacon M. Bari days before the fall of Const.* The photo itself, however, was immediately recognizable: a hand-drawn exploded-diagram of a box whose planes were not quite even. On each plane were drawings of the same geometric shapes (v's,>'s,^'s, >'s) that Hazel recognized from the metal box.

She took the box down off the shelf and compared it.

"It's the same," she deduced. "The dimensions and the symbols."

"Yes, and isn't that interesting?"

Hazel's brow rose. "Actually, yes." At once she felt animated. She was about to tell Sonia about the similar clay box that Henry had contracted Horace to craft, but thought better of it. *Find out about this first.* "And the 'fall of Const.' *has* to be the fall of Constantinople, right?"

"Uh-huh. The mid-1400s. This is some really old stuff, Hazel. Now . . . look on the back."

Hazel flipped the photo over and saw a brief scribing in Wilmarth's hand: *See File 293.* "Looks like our work's cut out for us now." She strode to the file cabinet.

"It's not there. There are no numbered files," Sonia informed. "No folders, even."

Hazel hauled open each drawer and found some to be empty while others appeared full of school papers. "You're right." Her eyes narrowed at the desk. "What about the desk?"

"It's locked."

"Have some initiative!" Hazel complained. She stalked to the kitchen, then returned with a broom.

"What are you—"

Hazel jammed the broom handle into the handle of the first desk drawer, and yanked hard. The lock-piece in the old wooden desk cracked easily.

"Hazel!"

"Henry Wilmarth is dead, right? And he left Frank the cabin and all of its contents, right?"

"Well, yes, but—"

"So, now, this is really *Frank's* desk, right?"

"Sort of, I guess, but—"

"So, by feminist doctrine, the desk is yours too."

Sonia laughed. "Feminist doctrine, huh?"

Hazel knelt. "Honestly, what's the big deal? The guy's dead." She searched the drawers, yet found nothing in the way of numbered file folders. Mostly just trade journals and old school curriculums and syllabi. Also a magnifying glass and a stapler. She went *Yuck!* when she lifted a bottle of Kessler's whiskey out of the bottom drawer, then, "Oh, double-yuck!" and she lifted out a revolver.

"Is it loaded?" Sonia asked in a hushed tone.

"Don't know, don't know how to find out, and don't *want* to find out." She returned it along with the bottle, then reached all the way back. "Hmm." She pulled out a digital camera.

"Check it!" Sonia said excitedly.

Hazel turned it on, then giggled, "Wouldn't it be a riot if there were pictures of Frank and Henry Wilmarth, like, making out and doing each other?"

Sonia made an appalled face. "Hazel, you're sick!"

"Just a thought." She checked the menu on the tiny screen, then slumped. "Damn. The memory card's empty."

"So much for that."

"And so much for the mystery of File 293." She was about to close the last drawer but then stalled when she noticed an oddity. She leaned closer.

Scrawled in ballpoint, against the wooden side of the drawer, was this word: *Yog-Sothoth.*

Whatever the hell that is, Hazel declared to herself, *why would Henry Wilmarth scribble it on the inside of his desk?*

"Maybe the file's up at this cottage Frank's at."

Sonia nodded. "Maybe, but if I asked him, then he'd know we were going through Henry's effects."

"He probably wouldn't be too happy about that."

"No."

Then an idea occurred to Hazel, quick as a beacon going off. "Wait a minute! Maybe it's not a paper file but a *computer* file!" and she hit the power button on the laptop sitting at a small table flanking the desk.

After booting up, Hazel and Sonia both said "Shit," in near-unison. A password box flashed on the screen.

"Any idea what Henry's birthday is?" Hazel asked.

"He was too smart—and too eccentric—for that." Sonia mulled the thought. "What was Frank saying on the phone earlier? The father of geometry?"

Thrilled, Hazel typed in EUCLID, then received a PASSWORD INCORRECT tag. "Damn."

"Oh, well," Sonia gave up. "It's none of our business anyway."

"Of course it isn't, but I'm dying to know what that box is all about. Aren't you?"

"Yes, but we'll never get into the computer. Just shut it off."

Hazel's hand hovered over the mouse. *Hmm. I wonder . . .* She looked back into the bottom drawer.

"What are you *doing?*"

"Type as I read," Hazel instructed, squinting at the arcane scrawl. "Y-O-G-hyphen-S-O-T-H-O-T-H."

Sonia did so, frowning. "What's that?"

"It's written down here. Sometimes people write their passwords in an out-of-view place in case they forget it. I do the same thing with my bank account number for when I'm checking online."

Sonia clicked the tab. "You were right!" she squealed.

Hazel looked up at the glowing screen background. She smiled. "Now, let's see what we can dig up . . ."

A simple search for the number "293" pulled up a directory *full* of numbered files, almost a thousand of them.

When Hazel opened File 293, she found it to be five jpegs, one of each side of the metal box, plus the lid.

"He scanned the box?" Sonia asked.

"Looks like it," and she pointed to the scanner sitting above the computer. The next page showed the same five jpegs only each glyph was circled in red ink and assigned a number which corresponded to the list of chronological numbers below, and to each number was assigned another number but in degrees.

"Henry measured the degrees of every angle on the box and indexed them," Hazel presumed.

"Scroll down, maybe there's more."

Hazel did so but only found the typed words: *Quotients for Power Schematic of original ST carrier.*

"There's that damn S-T again," Hazel muttered.

"I guess the degrees of each angle constitute an equation."

Hazel peered queerly at the screen. "But for what? And what the *hell* is the S-T?"

"Some kind of a stone, right? Isn't that what Henry's instructions implied?"

Hazel nodded, then decided to tell her . . ."Remember the guy we saw earlier who you called the 'woodsman?'"

"Yeah, the hunk of beefcake you have the hots for," Sonia said with a smirk.

"Whatever. He's the guy who gave me a ride home today, but he took me to his place first, a trailer out in the woods."

Sonia glared. "Oh my God, Hazel! You didn't!"

"No . . ."

Sonia wagged a finger. "I know you, Hazel. You're kinky and spontaneous. In this day and age you can't just pick up men and *do* them. The sexual revolution is dead, and STD's are what killed it."

Hazel sighed. "I didn't *fuck* him, Sonia. Jesus." *All I tried to do was suck him off, THEN I would've fucked him . . .* "I'm trying to tell you something, okay? The guy's name is Horace—"

"*Horace?*"

"Horace Knowles. He's a potter, sells his stuff at a shop in town. But he had a box identical in size to this metal one, only it's made of clay."

Sonia's previous perturbation faded. "You're kidding."

"No, and it was Henry Wilmarth who paid him to make it, last spring, before the storm."

"Why on earth would he—"

"I don't know, but he also indicated he might want Horace to make a whole bunch more of these boxes, but later—when he got back from Florida—he cancelled the order."

Sonia turned the metal box in her hand. "Boxes just like this . . ."

"Yes, the same dimensions, the same asymmetry." Hazel took the box from her friend and studied it, puzzled. "It's the same size, all right, but I'm positive that the engravings are different. They're the same types of configurations but on Horace's clay box there are more of them, and in different sequence."

"Now you're losing me."

"The only thing Horace could tell me about the box is that Henry said it was supposed to hold a *crystal.*"

"How . . . strange." Sonia seemed flustered now, interested to an extent but addled by something. "Hazel, I've been sitting too long and now my back's killing me. Help me to the bed, will you?"

Suddenly Hazel's attentions were diverted. She helped Sonia up from the desk and carefully piloted her into the main room. Only a few lights burned out here, and the rain could be heard teeming from the open windows. "At least the rain cooled things down . . ." The queen-sized bed sat in one corner, while the couch, TV, coffee table, and entertainment center sat in the other. *I wonder if I'll get to sleep in the bed with her,* Hazel quietly hoped. She sat Sonia on the edge of the bed.

"God, I'm so tired all of a sudden," Sonia murmured.

Hazel's eyes fell on her friend's bosom, and the beautiful bolus of flesh that contained a new life. She gazed at Sonia's drowsy face. *My God I love you.* "Go to sleep then. It's been a long day."

"I can't, Frank's calling at nine." She yawned. "Wake me up at eight-thirty, will you?"

"Sure," Hazel said, cringing on the inside. In her mind she saw herself rolling Sonia's maternity dress up, parting her legs, and pressing her face into all that warm fur. "I'll be in the den, prying some more into a dead man's privacy."

Sonia chuckled, eyes closed.

Back at the computer, Hazel took to clicking on random files—anything to get her mind off of Sonia. Many of the files were brief, typed notes, like:

File 67: invariant intervals seem to be rectilinear, which suggests a designation for dimensionality reliant on a non-existent power source. S to the 2nd power cannot possibly equal Y2 + Z2

Or: *File 745: The carrier for the ST can only be a manner of uplinkage, which harnesses energy from available space, even a perfect vacuum! Yes! (See File 691)*

File 691: It seems to me that Alhazred possessed only a partial understanding of quotient potential. Euclid MUST have been in possession of original box and perhaps even the ST itself, circa 270 B.C., and made notes that Alhazred copied and input along with the schematic in Al Azif . . . In Euclid we know that there are only 10 axioms and postulates but the schematic (File 13) PROVES the existence of an 11th. Of course Alhazred wouldn't have understood this! He was an occultist, not a mathematician!

"All right," Hazel groaned, and clicked on File 13 . . .

File 13:
v = S
^ = T
< + E
> = (D)imensionality
Fluctuations of power rely on the sum total of each degree of every v, ^, <, and >

Hazel blinked. "S equals space, T equals time, E equals energy?" she asked the air.

The file's last line read:

~ = the square root of the former times .33.

Now her head was beginning to hurt. *All right, I'm bored now. I should stick to what I know: Hemingway, Fitzgerald, and Faulkner.* She was about to turn the computer off when she thought, *Oh, what the hell?*

She clicked on the very last file . . .

File 944:
v><<^~<v~^^>v^~v<^>>v^<v>>^v~v~v^<v><^~<> = D + S + E + T to the 33rd power!
Thurnston! Frank! My God, this is it!

Hazel scrolled down in the body of the same file and found another exploded diagram, like a box opened up and unfolded. Unlike the first, which was a digital scan of the metal box, this was hand-drawn with the meticulousness of an architect, a veritable blueprint of another box. Each section was filled with more of the glyphs, abundantly more than the sections of the metallic box. Hazel felt certain: *This is the schematic for the clay box that Horace made . . .*

It occurred to her then that since she'd opened the very last file, why not look at the very *first?*

click

File #1 was another jpeg, radiant in its brightness and clarity. The picture showed an egg-shaped gemstone which at first looked black as obsidian but then, after a blink, appeared to possess the hue of dark red wine. Within the crystal's body she thought she detected darker and lighter scarlet striations. The entire stone glimmered from hundreds of minute facets.

She held her gaze, then realized that the crystal had been photographed on this self same desk.

Below the picture was a legend that read: THE SHINING TRAPEZOHEDRON.

Hazel stared as if the screen were a chasm. *Shining . . . Trapezohedron . . .*

The S-T . . .

It had to be.

I've GOT to find out what this thing is . . . Resurged now, Hazel zipped the cursor back to the index and determined to peruse every file in the directory if need be, until she discovered the purpose of this puzzling red-black crystal.

That's when a great clap of thunder shook the house, then all the lights went out.

Hazel flew out of the seat when the shrill shriek sounded in the other room. She plunged into nearly full darkness until lightning flashed and showed her that the bed was empty. "Sonia! Where are—"

"I'm in here—oh, damn it!"

Hazel used her cellphone to light her way toward the voice. *I thought she was in bed!* but then she found Sonia standing awkward and naked in the metal washtub beneath the primitive shower.

"Are you all right?"

"Yes, but I almost fell when the lights went out," Sonia fretted.

"You scared the crap out of me; it sounded like a horror movie in here. You told me you wanted to take a nap."

Dripping wet and clotted in soap bubbles, Sonia grumbled. "I know, but even as tired as I was I couldn't sleep. Every time I'd start to drift off, I'd start thinking about Frank up on top of some dumbass mountain in the middle of a dumbass thunderstorm and probably getting hit by lightning."

"You really are a worrywart," Hazel laughed.

Sonia paused, looking off as if something unpleasant entered her mind. "And then, when I finally *did* fall asleep"—she shivered—"I had the most *awful* dream . . ."

"What happened in the dream?"

"I was covered in some kind of slime, and then-and then, this thing that I guess was an octopus tentacle started to go into–" Sonia squeezed her eyes shut hard and vigorously shook her head.

"What?" Hazel egged on. "A tentacle started to go *where?*"

"Oh, Hazel, it's too gross to talk about. Don't make me think about it . . ."

Tentacle, Hazel reflected, of course recalling her own daymare in the outhouse: the atrocious, tentacled baby with a sucker for a mouth.

"So I decided to take a shower in this dumbass metal tub," Sonia continued, "and that dumbass water pump!"

"Just stand there and don't move; you're liable to slip. I'll be right back." *Honestly,* Hazel thought. *She's like a little kid all of a sudden.* She quickly found some candles in the kitchen, lit one, and returned. Sonia shrieked again when more thunder boomed. "Relax," Hazel said.

"Help me finish, will you?" Sonia pointed to the crude pump-handle.

"Sure . . ." Hazel worked the pump as Sonia finished lathering herself.

"This is a first: a shower in spring water. But that water-heater thing works; otherwise it'd be ice-cold."

"I feel sorry for the settlers in Colonial days."

"They probably didn't even *bother* washing. You know, the first bath tub wasn't even invented until the 1800s."

"Gross." Hazel kept pumping, only allowing herself to look indirectly at Sonia's body. *Good Lord . . .* The simple sight of her made Hazel's groin jitter. The swollen breasts and even more swollen belly, all gleaming. Pregnancy had stretched Sonia's nipples out to lovely dark-pink circles, inches wide; Hazel imagined herself slowly licking each circumference in an inward spiral, then stopping on the distended papillae, to suck. Her eyes followed the trails of suds as they coursed down Sonia's shapely legs.

I can't stand this . . .

"I'll just be another minute."

"Take . . . your time."

Did Sonia grin over her bare shoulder? And did her hands linger as they soaped the milk-gorged breasts? Next, she sudsed the nest of dark hair between her legs . . .

Now Hazel's sex began to moisten, in spite of all that had been done to it today. She knew she could never tell Sonia about the rape; likewise, she was surprised by how unaffected she felt now, only hours after the brutal fact. Instead, her attention remained fixed entirely on Sonia, on her shining body, all those voluptuous curves, all that perfect warm white skin. One of Hazel's therapists had once declared her *erotoscopic.* "You're much more like a man in the spontaneous way you react to sexual imagery," the woman had said. "Not only are you erotomanic, you're *erotoscopic*. A merely arousing *image* triggers your libidinal system . . . *instantaneously.* Very rare among women. In fact *all* of your paraphilic disorders are exceptionally rare among females. Consider yourself unique, Hazel." *Fuck you,* Hazel had thought in response. In little more than a year she'd gone through half a dozen therapists and had wound up abandoning them all.

Still, the image of Sonia in the shower seemed to percolate in Hazel's psyche . . .

"You can stop pumping now."

"Careful stepping out." Hazel opened a towel and wrapped it around Sonia's shoulders.

"Thanks." Sonia tucked the towel above her bosom, then winced when more lightning flashed in the tiny window. The candle light flickered, throwing their shadows on the wall. The shadows jerked.

"Let's get out of here. This room's creepy."

This whole cabin is creepy, Hazel decided. She grabbed the candle and followed Sonia back into the main room.

Hazel let her heart slow down. Even in the frumpy towel, Sonia's beauty raged in her eyes. She felt like masturbating, but where? *Impossible.* "At least it sounds like the rain's falling off," she remarked to distract her.

"Is it?" Sonia went to the front window. Now there was just a trickle. "Yeah, but with our luck the power'll be out for a week."

THUNK

All the lights snapped back on. "See what you get for being cynical?" Hazel said and snuffed the candle.

"Oh, damn it, I keep forgetting—" Sonia fished through her travel bag and withdrew a plastic bottle.

"Forgetting what?"

"This stuff." She held up the bottle. "It's this special lotion I saw on TV. All the stars use it. It helps prevent stretch-marks." She took off the towel, and tossed it to the bed, again standing utterly nude before Hazel.

"Oh, let me!" Hazel couldn't resist. She reached for the bottle but Sonia wouldn't let her take it.

"No, Hazel, it's not a good idea. You'd get carried away, and you know it."

"Bullshit. The only reason you won't let me is 'cos you're afraid it'll turn you on."

"Oh, so *that's* what you think?" Sonia cast a sharp gaze, paused, then handed the bottle to Hazel.

My lucky day. She squeezed the creamy beige liquid into her palm, then gently smoothed the cream over the center of Sonia's stomach. Hazel was marveled; she couldn't believe how *tight* the fetus-filled abdomen felt, how *firm* it was. She rubbed in repetitious circles very slowly, then paused to trace a fingertip about the nub of her popped-out navel. When she flicked back and forth—

"Stop!" Sonia giggled. "It's tickles!"

"Oh. Sorry." Hazel squirted more into her hand and repeated the process, all the while growing more and more dizzy from the warmth, image, and presence of her friend. *I love you so much I can't stand it,* she could've wept. Now she glided her hand to Sonia's breasts and began to gently rub. When Sonia tensed to object, Hazel cut her off, "Women get stretch-marks on their boobs, too, you know."

"Yeah, I guess they do . . ."

Hazel's hand slid into the shape of each breast, very daintily caressing. She giggled, unable to help it, "These really are big, Sonia—"

"Tell me about it. They're heavy, too. Between my boobs and junior here, I'm surprised I don't need a backbrace."

Hazel liberally applied more lotion—

"Come on, you're using half the damn bottle," Sonia objected.

"Noooo," and then Hazel's fingers began to tease one of Sonia's spread, pink nipples.

Sonia snatched the bottle away. "That's enough, thank you. I can't get stretch-marks on my nipples—"

"How do you know?"

A coy smirk came to Sonia's lips but before she slipped her robe on, Hazel was certain her friend's nipple-tips were twice the size they'd been in the shower. *She's all turned on now but she'll never admit it.* At least there was *some* satisfaction.

"Oh, I found a picture of the S-T," Hazel revealed. "It was the very first file in Henry's index."

"The S . . . Oh, you mean the stone?"

"Um-hmm. It's a big crystal; Henry took a digital picture of it right on his desk."

Sonia grabbed her arm. "Show me!"

In the study, however, the laptop sat dead. Hazel pushed the power button but only an error screen came up. "I don't believe it! The storm crashed the computer."

"But it's a laptop. The battery should've kicked on the instant the power went out."

Hazel lifted up one end of the laptop. "There's the reason it didn't—no battery." The battery slot was empty.

"Oh, no. Frank'll be furious."

"Not if we don't tell him," Hazel reminded. "Oh, gee, I don't know why the computer doesn't work. Must've been a power spike."

"I don't really like lying, Hazel."

"It's not lying. It's merely circumventing the truth."

Sonia laughed. "I guess it'll do. What else was in those files?"

"An exploded diagram for *another* box. The symbols on it were different, and I swear they're the same symbols on the clay box that Horace made."

"You and your Horace . . . Anyway, what did the stone look like?"

Hazel had to think about it. "It was beautiful but also kind of . . . I don't know. Disturbing? Don't know why. Sometimes it looked black, other times maroon, and there were threads of red inside. Henry called it the Shining Trapezohedron."

"That's a mouthful."

"I think a trapezohedron is a crystal whose surface is composed entirely of polygons, if I remember my geometry right."

Sonia picked up the metal box on the shelf. "And it's supposed to go inside this?"

"Yeah, or—I guess Henry had the clay box built for the same purpose. I got the idea that the clay box—with the new symbols—is supposed to be an upgraded version of the metal box, at least that's what some of the text files seemed to imply."

"Damn." Sonia frowned at the dead laptop. "I'd love to see that picture, if only for curiosity's sake."

"Later I'll go on my own laptop and read some help files about rebooting and recovery techniques—"

From the main room, Sonia's cellphone went off. "That's Frank!"

Sonia rushed to the room, snapped up the phone. "Hi, honey! How are you?"

Hazel followed, then stood right next to her, her ear inclined toward the phone. Distantly she heard Frank say: "'—s're fine up here." Some crackling. "—damn lucky I found the cottage before the storm started."

"Is there electricity in the cottage?" Sonia asked.

Frank seemed to laugh over more static. "No way, just candles. But you wouldn't believe how much of Henry's stuff is stowed away. It'll take a long time to go through it all, I'm afraid."

"Bullshit, Frank!" Sonia snapped. "You're coming back tomorrow, like you promised, right?"

Hesitation, then more static. "—ght not be able to make it by tomorrow afternoon, honey. Tomorrow night, maybe."

"Frank, that's unacceptable!"

The crackling and static seemed to double. "—you hear me? I'm sorry, honey, but Henry left a lot of papers, and—"

"Yes, and all you have to do is destroy them like he ordered! So *do it* and get back here!"

"Just try to bear with me—"

"The only thing I'm *bearing* is your child in three or four weeks! You could at least be considerate enough to spend some time with me!"

Wow, she's really pissed, Hazel thought.

After another wave of static, Frank said, "I want to at least read some of this work before I destroy it, honey. Can't you understand that?"

"No!"

"It's my field of study. Just give me till tomorrow evening, okay?"

Sonia's teeth ground. "*Early* evening!"

"Okay—"

"Promise!"

"Baby, I promise. In the meantime there's plenty to do around there. I'm sure you and Hazel'll have a great time. Walk the nature trails, check out Lake Sladder, go for a country drive. You could even—" but then the crackling increased tenfold.

"Frank, I can barely hear you!"

"—breaking up from the storm . . . bad cell reception . . . call you in the morning—"

"You better!"

"—love you, honey . . ."

Sonia was vibrating in place she was so irritated. "I love you too, but if you're not back tomorrow night, I'm gonna kick you in the balls so hard—"

"—breaking up worse now . . . better go. Goodnight . . ."

The connection fizzed off.

Sonia snapped her phone closed and put it on the nightstand. Her face was *pink* in anger. "That son of a bitch just burns me up. 'Oh, come up to the cabin, honey. We'll have a lot of fun.' Fun, my ass. I'm about to have a *kid* and he's up in some cottage on a mountain dicking around with a bunch of geometry papers."

Hazel rolled her eyes. "Sonia, give the man a break. All he's really doing is carrying out a colleagues last wishes."

"Yeah?" Sonia huffed, then sat down on the bed. "Or maybe he has a girl with him up there."

Hazel couldn't resist some coyness: "Oh, but I thought yours was an *open* relationship."

"Only with my *preapproval,*" Sonia replied, stone-voiced.

"A *conditional* open-relationship, I see." Hazel had to laugh. "I wouldn't worry anyway. Frank's too self-absorbed to have a lover on the side. Why would he orchestrate this whole cabin-thing just for that? You really think he's fooling around when his mentor only died a few days ago and happened to leave him the entire estate?"

Sonia settled down. "You're right. And he *is* too self-absorbed."

"So just don't worry about it. Take some advice from a friend. You're kind of cranky right now, so why don't you just go to bed? You'll feel a lot better tomorrow."

Sonia smiled meekly, nodding. "You're right, as always. I'm sorry my skewed hormones keep finding their way to you." She kissed Hazel on the cheek. "Goodnight."

"I'm going to try to fix Henry's computer, but I won't make a peep." *Kiss me again, kiss me again,* beat the thought.

"That's okay."

"Oh, and . . . where am I sleeping?"

"In the bed, silly!" Sonia laughed. "You're so paranoid. What, did you think I'd make you sleep on the couch?" She chuckled into the main room and started turning off the lights.

Hazel watched her raptly, then snapped out of it several moments later. *My head is such a mess I can't believe it.* She typed in some recovery commands into Henry's laptop, had no success, then retrieved her own laptop and set it up on the desk. *At least it's not the Blue Screen of Death,* she thought. She left the study door cracked only an inch, and as she read through some trouble-shooting files, one eye kept glancing every so often to the bed, where Sonia lay on her side atop the sheets. *How can I love someone so much and yet it's so wrong?* Nothing seemed fair. Her own sexual anomalies were unfair as well. *Sick, sick, sick,* she thought, remembering the orgasm she was sure she'd had even as Peter Pan had been strangling her whilst a foot had been sunk into her sex. *Why can't I just be normal?* But in the back of her mind came a reply, in her father's voice: *Come back to God.*

She covered her mouth to stifle a delighted squeal when she saw that Henry's laptop was at last reloading; in a moment she was able to access the directory full of Henry's files. When she reclicked File #1, the screen filled with the startling image of the Shining Trapezohedron.

Its undefinable color captivated her. Each facet of the complex polygonal surface glimmered. She found herself staring as her mind lost focus, but then a vertigo jolted her like two fingers snapping before her face. It had been ten p.m. when the computer got back to rights but now it was eleven. *I must've dozed off and not realized it . . .*

She clicked on the zoom feature and moved the cursor to a random facet. Each click thereafter brought the sparkling jpeg closer and closer, until the entire screen was a vitreous black-maroon.

The image that now filled the frame looked like nothing at first, just that odd color, but as she looked more intently . . .

Did she hear the piping of *flutes?* The music—if it could even be called that—resounded very faintly yet seemed structured and discordant at the same time. Hazel jerked her head around, then even put her fingers in her ears, but the minuscule cacophony prevailed. *Aural mirage,* she thought. *Probably fatigue-born, probably some traumatic-stress reaction.* When a breath caught in her chest, the maniacal sounds had vanished.

"What was *that* all about?" The more she looked at the zoomed image, the more taken by it she felt. She thought of cavemen staring in awe and wonder at a fire, or gazing at stars while having no idea what they were.

She felt droopy now, yet somehow motivated, and next thing she knew she'd opened the bottom desk drawer. Her hand glided past the revolver and without forethought from her, landed on the magnifying glass.

What am I—

She put the glass to the computer screen, began to stare . . .

Her mind bent, it *stretched* as if her skull had dissolved, leaving only her raw brain which was siphoned through her eye-holes and somehow sucked into the image on the screen. She thought of out-of-body-experiences, something she'd never believed in, had dismissed as hopeful hallucinosis, but now—

Her eyeless vision was forced to gaze; it plummeted like a stone dropped from a plane, soaring. The closer she got to whatever it was she was falling toward, Hazel saw cities, or things like cites: a geometric demesne of impossible architecture which extended in a long vanishing line of horrid black—a raging *terra dementata.* Concaved horizons crammed with stars, or things like stars, sparkled close against cubist chasms. She saw buildings and streets, tunnels and tower blocks, strange flattened factories whose chimneys gushed oily smoke. It was a necropolis, systematized and endless, bereft of error in its moving angles and lines. It was pandemonium. Gutters ran black with noxious ichor. Squat, stygian churches sang praise to mindless gods. Insanity was the monarch here, ataxia the only order, darkness the only light. Ingenious, unspeakable, the monarch stared back . . . and smiled.

Hazel saw it all. She saw time tick backward, death rot to life, whole futures swallowed deep into the belly of history. And she saw people too. Or things *like* people.

One of the things was waving at her, with a tentacle.

"E uh shub nleb nbb lrrg glud blemmeb," came the words.

Hazel's disembodied consciousness stared and drooled.

"Nub krebb nebb e uh yurgg flurp ey ftagn—"

Several of the things were now waving at her with their suckered tentacles. Their faces stared intently back, *upside-down* faces covered with carbuncles.

"Gub nbb grlm naabl e uh nuuurrlathotep."

When Hazel finally shook off the terror's glimpse, she found herself face-down on the floor. The magnifying glass lay cracked. *What the hell?*

A nightmare, of course. She'd fallen asleep at the screen. A tiny clock in the other room was gently chiming midnight.

Oh, shit, I feel hungover.

She dragged herself up, looked at the computer screen, and groaned. YOUR COMPUTER IS BEING SHUT DOWN DUE TO A GENERAL PRODUCTION ERROR. Then the screen turned black.

Great.

She sat back down and rubbed her eyes. The vision she'd had seemed lodged in the back of her mind like a blood clot. *What WAS that?* She'd been fatigued to begin with, and was likely also suffering some delayed stress from her rape. And then? *I fell asleep at the screen and had a nightmare. Big deal.*

But what a nightmare it was. *Tentacles. People with tentacles, and upside-down faces like overcooked pies.* They'd been talking to her.

"Bedtime," she determined. She pulled off her top and stepped out of her shorts, then tiptoed into the main room where Sonia could be seen sound asleep on the bed. The fans were on, blowing air all around. She was about to get into bed herself but faltered. *Oh, no . . .* She had to go to the bathroom, and since there *was* no bathroom in the cabin . . . *No way. I'm NOT going to the outhouse,* she knew immediately. *Not at midnight.* Her only other option?

Bears pee I the woods, so I guess I can too. She found a flashlight in a kitchen drawer, then a door at the rear of the house let her out. At once she was taken aback by the dense, half-deafening chorus of crickets and peepers underscored by the dripping forest now that the storm had passed. Clouds thinned overhead, letting moonlight fall down behind the house. Oddly, she sensed she could feel the light on her nude body. Her skin prickled at a scant, tepid breeze which rustled through the woods.

She came off the short steps, wandered a moment, then squatted abruptly next to an old charcoal grill and began to urinate. *Oh, that's better . . .* The most morbid thought struck her just then: *How much of Peter Pan's piss is coming out in mine?* He couldn't have made her throw up every drop, could he? Wouldn't a little of it, if only a trace, have metabolized in her own body? She pursed her lips as if tasting something disgusting.

It was still coming out. *Come on . . .* In a scenario such as this, how could she *not* imagine herself being spied on by some night-prowling pervert? Then she closed her eyes, and all at once, the image was drilled unwillingly into her head: the Tentacle People from inside the crystal had converged on her. Two held her aloft on their ropy arms while a third positioned its corrupted face between her thighs, then opened the puffily lipped mouth that was located on its runneled forehead. It drank up her piss as fast as the stream could arc out of her, and when it began to ebb, the lips closed around her sex and sucked, until every last drop had been coaxed from her bladder and pilfered through her urethra. Hazel squirmed in the unyielding, tentacular embrace. But now that the thing had quenched its thirst on her liquid waste, waste of the solid variety was its next desire. The hideous mouth slurped lower and began to suck hard on her anus. Finally her intestines gave into the pressure and began to release their wares, and when they'd been sucked flat, the lumpen-faced monstrosity began to sloppily eat. Was the thing squealing in exuberance? Its own tentacles writhed in delight. Hazel was dropped to the wet ground then, and saw aghast that it was not only the arms of her visitors that were tentacles, but their legs too, for they wore blushing scarlet robes embroidered in gold, within whose borders were gold-stitched glyphs similar to those on the box. When the robes parted, she could see that their legs were stouter, more venous tentacles with widened, circular suction cups for feet, and, worse, their genitals seemed rolled up like gray, meaty hoses at their groins. Two of the things moved between her legs now, while the third remained at her shoulders with one of its rubbery arms girded about her throat. When it began to constrict, boa-like, Hazel's body tensed, stretching out, then the fleshy noose tightened till her tongue stuck out and she couldn't breathe. That's when the other two unreeled their cocks and began to gibber in some insane excitement. Balloon-cheeked now, yet erect-nippled, Hazel peered up in the moonlight and saw the exact nature of their penises: two feet long each, and reminiscent of the ends of elephant trunks. The trunks wasted no time in burrowing into her vagina simultaneously. The eyes like pustules planted on their cheeks gazed down on her terror-rigid body; the swollen-lipped mouths panted and drooled. Hazel began to orgasm in salvoes; it was like a *seizure* of pleasure colliding with the terror of asphyxia. Her ass wriggled in the dirt as she came time and again, even as the netherworldly genitals pumped gouts of hot, chunky slop deep into her sex . . .

Hazel's eyes snapped open at a mental lurch. She remained squatting, though she'd finished relieving herself. *Just like me. A head full of perverted SHIT* . . . What could compel her mind to manufacture such a detestable vision? She took several deep breaths, began to stand up—

"Shub nbb grlp naabl nith."

Hazel gasped and fell backward on the verge of shrieking. *It can't be!* She shot her flashlight beam in the heinous droning's direction but there was nothing there.

I am really out of it tonight, she thought once she'd calmed down. *There are NO TENTACLE PEOPLE in the woods!* She went back in the cabin, locked the door, then went to bed and fell immediately into convulsive sleep laden with putrid-smelling dreams and black, mindless gibbering.

4

Next morning, a little local driving around led them to the none-too-surprisingly named Main Street which comprised a small downtown area. Knickknack shops, some antique, used-book, and hand-dipped candle stores, and several eateries took up most of it, plus a tiny post office and a bait shop. After rising, they'd decided to come here upon Hazel's affirmation, "I'm so hungry I could out-eat a couple of truck drivers"; additionally, she wanted to stop by the Pickman Curiosity Shoppe and fulfill her promise to Horace. The little shop sat right on the corner.

"Interesting little downtown area," Sonia said after breakfast at a diner called simply The Diner. They walked idly down the barely occupied street, passing shop windows. "I would've thought it'd be more redneckish, like the tavern."

"I think a lot of rich people come here during skiing season," Hazel said innocuously, but then she noticed Sonia smiling at her. In fact, she'd caught her doing that several times already this morning, even immediately upon rising from bed. *Why's she keep smiling at me?* She felt skewed to begin with: a lousy night's sleep, the dreams, the things her tired mind had imagined seeing in the jpeg of the crystal, not to mention being raped. Sonia's periodic smile seemed scolding, the way an adult might smile at a child who'd done some minor thing wrong. Furthermore, Sonia seemed much more perky today, bright-eyed, skin glowing. She wore a colorful maternity-cut sundress bursting with floral patterns. Even her body seemed to glow obscurely through the dress.

Hazel had dressed in khaki shorts and a T-shirt tied at the midriff. The shirt displayed the face of Mark Twain and read along the bottom ENGLISH MAJORS MAKE GREAT LOVERS, and then showed the Brown University crest. "You want to look in any of these shops?"

"No. Maybe later. I'm happy just walking around with you."

The remark made Hazel feel off-guard; it had sounded almost intimate. But then Hazel was doubly surprised when Sonia was suddenly holding her hand.

"I'm so lucky to have a wonderful friend like you," Sonia said.

Hazel looked at her and didn't know what to say. But she knew what to think. *I love you. I love you so much it hurts . . .*

"Oh, there's the place you want to go," Sonia said, and pointed to Pickman's on the corner. "I'd be very interested in meeting this *Horace* fellow," and then Sonia slipped Hazel another of her arcane smiles.

What is WITH her today? "Yeah, he's a potter but he also works on the side at the tavern." She passed a barber shop, a nail salon, then Hazel's gait slowed at the next store: HAMMOND'S OUTDOOR GEAR. *Same store where Henry Wilmarth bought the rope he used to hang himself with,* but then she recalled what else he'd bought: pole-climbing boots, of all things.

"Let's cross here," Hazel said after a car passed.

Sonia was smiling at her.

Goofy, Hazel thought. *Hormones or something. Mental note: don't EVER get pregnant. It makes you weird.*

A cowbell clanged when they entered the curiosity shop. The store smelled stuffy, and the gaunt, dim-eyed man behind the counter *looked* stuffy. He sat poised behind the register, his thumb through a palette as he eyed a large half-painted canvas on an easel. Oddly, he wore pressed slacks, a nice button shirt, and a tie. *Ever hear of smocks?* Hazel felt like telling him. "Hello, ladies," his voice creaked like an old door hinge. He dabbed at the canvas with a thin brush.

"Hi," Hazel said. "We're here to see Horace Knowles. He said he'd be in today."

The man—who surely wore a toupee—didn't look at her. Instead, he spoke as he dabbed more paint. "Ah, Horace. He was indeed supposed to restock today but called at the last minute. Another job came up, he claims."

Shit. "Oh, well, we'd like to look at his pottery."

He frowned, then fidgeted with his ear. That's when Hazel noticed he had a hearing aid. "Blasted thing. Ah, but—yes—Horace's work can be found on the west wall. And should you be interested in original oils, my personal gallery can be found in the east room."

Sonia stifled a laugh at the odd man; Hazel merely smirked. *East, west? Gee, I forgot my compass.* She took a quick peek at the proprietor's current canvas: a skeleton with long, flowing blond hair held an infant skeleton at her bosom.

"Madonna and child," the man informed her. "Do you like it?"

"Uh, oh, yes. It's very interesting," Hazel blundered. *Do you think you could come up with something* less *original?* She grabbed Sonia's arm and directed her toward the display shelves full of pottery.

Finely fired vases, ashtrays, and ring boxes sat arrayed on the shelves. Sonia picked up a porcelain bullfrog with abnormally large eyes. "This stuff's pretty cool. It's different without being cliched."

"The stuff he had at his house was even better," Hazel said, examining a star-fish-shaped trivet.

"I guess I'm a little . . . jealous . . ."

Hazel sighed and looked at her. Sonia was smiling that wide-browed smile of hers again. "I told you," she whispered, "I didn't do anything with him, and even if I did, why would you be jealous anyway?"

"Come on . . ." Sonia took a few steps, then stopped to look at an assortment of porcelain-tubed wind chimes. "Oh, I *love* these."

"Don't change the subject," Hazel insisted. "What is with you today?"

Sonia only kept smiling, cocked a brow, then kept looking at the chimes.

Men are right. Women are nuts. Hazel collected a half-dozen pieces of Horace's pottery and took them to the counter.

"I say, you must genuinely admire Horace's work," noted the man. "He's a fine potter."

What I admire more than his work is his COCK, but that's another story. "He's not just a potter," Hazel insisted, "he's an artisan. A guy with this kind of talent? He could make a fortune at the crafts shows in Providence."

"Hmm. Ah, well . . ."

Hazel was deliberately talking Horace up, if only as a gesture of gratitude for his saving her yesterday. The man set his pallette aside and wrapped up Hazel's purchases. It was during this process that Hazel's notice was flagged by a quick, dark-red sparkle. This Mr. Pickman wore a ring quite atypical for men: a clunky polished stone the size of a small gumball. It's color reminded Hazel of the Shining Trapezohedron.

"What an interesting ring . . ."

"It's corundum, from Nova Scotia. Very rare. Said by the Druids to bring profit to the wise."

"Oh."

He raised his hand, eyed the ring, then Hazel. "Quite like the color of your hair, I'd say. You have lovely hair, if you don't mind my saying so." Then the thinnest smile came to his very narrow and very dry lips.

The words and the creaking voice made Hazel's skin crawl. Did she feel her nipples actually shrink? "Thank you, sir. Have a good day."

"Not interested in the gallery, I see."

"Oh, we'll be back later!" Hazel assured and hauled Sonia out of the store. "'Bye!"

Sonia looked reprovingly at the large bag of items Hazel had bought. "Didn't know you were so fond of porcelain work."

"I just wanted to get some souvenirs," Hazel commented.

Sonia took Hazel's arm. "Where to now?"

"Let's stop by Horace's trailer."

"Do we *have* to?" Sonia almost pouted. "I don't really feel like sharing you today."

Sharing me? Hazel didn't get it. They wandered down the sedate, shop-lined road, back toward the car. "The real reason I want you to go is 'cos you need to see the ceramic version of the metal box."

"Oh. Right."

Hazel let Sonia in the passenger side, then drove. It was hot for this early in the day; Hazel was perspiring at once. Last night's torrential rain made everything steamy now. The paved road wound through trees in a wide swath; even the woods were misty with humidity whenever Hazel took a glance. Several dirt and gravel turnoffs passed them. FISH - HALF MILE, read a rickety wooden sign at one of the turns. *Horace said... Fish Brothers?* Hazel's mind ticked. His hunch as to the identity of her rapists. Could the sign mark where they did business? *Don't be ridiculous,* she scolded herself. *There're probably dozens of fishermen working Lake Sladder.*

She forced her mind off the topic, to concentrate on her bearings. *Here it is,* she believed, then turned right onto an unpaved road.

"These woods are spooky all of a sudden," Sonia remarked. "And look at the mist."

Within the woods, tendrils of gaseous moisture seemed suspended. "From the rain, plus the heat," Hazel replied, then she took an casual glance at Sonia. Sonia was smiling.

"All right. What is it?" Hazel demanded.

Sonia fingers diddled with some of Hazel's curls. "What is what?"

"The smiling. The *look*. All morning long you've been giving me that *look*," and then Hazel tried but likely failed in mimicking it.

Sonia's voice descended to something like a sultry octave. "You were terrific last night."

Hazel winced. "What, fixing Henry's computer? I wouldn't call that a *terrific* job; it crashed again later."

"Come on . . ."

Hazel snapped her gaze. "Sonia, you're really goofy today."

"Oh, I know I'm moody but you definitely caught me in the *right* mood last night." Suddenly Sonia leaned over and put her lips right on Hazel's ear. "You were just . . . so . . . *good*."

That's it. Hazel pulled over on the shoulder, then leveled her eyes. "Sonia. What are you talking about?"

Sonia looked swoony. "It was lovely. I've never come like that in my life. Not even with Frank."

Last night? Hazel's eyes blankened. "What, uh, what—"

Sonia gave a shrill laugh. "Oh, so you're pretending you don't remember? That's fine."

Hazel continued to stare, more into vacant space than at Sonia. "Seriously. I . . . don't remember . . . Did we . . ."

If one could nod lasciviously, Sonia did just that. She put her arm about Hazel's shoulder, leaned closer, then traced the tip of her tongue up the side of Hazel's neck. "You're irresistible today. But then, if you want to know the truth . . . you're *always* irresistible to me."

Hazel began to shake very subtly. She wasn't ready for this. Words she longed to hear but never had were being spoken to her now. *We must've had sex last night . . . but I . . . don't . . . remember . . .*

"And if you don't remember *that*," Sonia said, now stroking Hazel's thigh, "you have the worst memory in the world." Her hand slipped up Hazel's Mark Twain shirt; Hazel's nipples erected like tiny hard-ons when fingertips played over them. Then the fingers spidered down to her crotch and began to gently strum.

Hazel was stewing in a repressed frenzy of bliss, lust, and love. Now her crotch was being rubbed more directly. She felt her fluids rush.

"And you're so unselfish, sweetheart," Sonia whispered. "You didn't even let me do anything for you."

"I—I didn't?"

The lewd smile broadened. "Oh, I know! Did you get into that bottle of whiskey in Henry's desk? *That's* why you don't remember."

Hazel felt torn by opposites. She was being felt up and sexually stoked by the only true love-interest of her life, yet the aggravation of no recollection maddened her.

Sonia's lips came back to her ear. "Take these shorts off. I need to go down on you—"

"In the car?" Hazel exclaimed.

"I know how you feel about me," the whisper continued to beat. "Don't you want me to?"

"Yes!" Hazel shot. "But . . ." *What is going on?* "But not *here.* It's broad daylight." Her nipples felt like tingling, hot stones; her sex was *thumping* in her shorts. *This is crazy. I've got to get my head together.* "Let's-let's wait . . . till we're done here," she stammered.

Sonia, ever smiling, slid back into the passenger seat. "I get it. Hard to get–"

"No, no, it's just—"

"I know how you like games, Hazel. I don't mind playing them . . ."

My God, my God . . . Hazel pulled back onto the road. What could account for her memory failing to recollect a love-making session? *And I KNOW I didn't drink Henry's whiskey. I HATE whiskey.* What then?

The situation was impossible; Hazel could scarcely reckon it. She pulled into the winding lane leading to Horace's solitary trailer. Sonia's hand continued to play in Hazel's lap, titillating, then withdrawing, coaxing more tingles and moisture.

She's driving me nuts . . .

Grass grew closer to the trailer; Hazel pulled up and cut the engine. "I just want you to see the clay box," she made the excuse but for the life of her she didn't know *why* it was suddenly so important. Perhaps it really wasn't. She needed to sort her thoughts; either that or Sonia was playing some games herself, some *cruel* ones.

"Fancy place," Sonia said, grinning. "Like the Trump Tower."

"Be nice. Not everyone who lives in a trailer is white trash."

"And I can imagine what went on in *this* trailer last night—"

"Would you stop with that!" Hazel tried to sound serious while at the same time giggling when Sonia's finger began to tickle her belly button. "Nothing went on."

"That's fine. Okay, let's go meet *Horace,*" but then Sonia quickly grabbed Hazel's shoulders, pulled her face to her, and began to kiss. The kiss delved, first ravenous, then outright lewd. Sonia's tongue invaded Hazel's mouth, tussled with her tongue, then actually began to suck it. All the while, Hazel began to melt in her lover's arms. She could feel Sonia's heat radiating from her flesh through the sheer sundress while the nipples hardened beneath the fabric to shapes like cleats. She broke off the sloppy kiss long enough to say, "Here," and then Hazel almost shrieked when she noticed Sonia had dropped her dress straps to reveal her raging bare breasts. Hazel could've disintegrated at the abrupt sight of them. "To hell with Horace. Let's go back to the cabin and *fuck.*"

Hazel reeled. "Cover those up! He might see—" She cast a nervous glance at the trailer's tiny windows, fumbling to pull Sonia's straps back up. The frustration nearly brought tears to her eyes. Confusion and arousal seemed to pack together in her psyche like someone kneading dough. *All this time I've wanted her more than anything and now all of a sudden—*

Sonia's hand found its way back to Hazel's crotch. "You can see Harold later—"

"Horace!"

"So start the car, turn it around, and drive us back to the cabin. Frank's coming back tonight, remember? Let's spend the whole day in bed." Sonia's eyes glittered, but suddenly her expression lost all of its whimsey and turned dead serious. "You have no idea how much I need to be with you now."

The words winded Hazel. "Okay—" and her hand touched the key but then the trailer door *clacked,* and out walked a looming, smiling, and very brawny Horace.

"Too late . . ."

"Guess we have to go in now," Sonia said in sing-song voice.

Hazel wanted to bang the wheel with her fists. *Why is she fucking with me like this?* She tried to calm down, got out, and put on a smile. "Hi, Horace. I hope we're not intruding."

"New, not et all," boomed the voice of the big man. "Quite nice ta see yew agin."

"Horace, this is my friend, Professor Sonia Heald."

Sonia extended her hand. "Hello, Horace. A pleasure to meet you."

"Ee-yuh. Likewise. Gettin' ready fer a new addition, I see."

Sonia put a hand to her belly. "I'm looking forward to being a mother but I'm getting sick of being an *expectant* mother, if you know what I mean."

"I heer ya, Miss Heald. My own ma tolt me I weighed twelve pounds when I come into the light'a day."

Sonia focused on the very large man. "I believe it."

"She got huh-self dag tired'a carryin' *me* 'raound. God dun't make much easy, she said. He en't supposed tew, I guess. But every new life is shuhly a gift from God."

The introduction grew awkward; then a steady breeze set dozens of porcelain wind chimes into a radiant clamor. "Best we get inside," Horace offered and showed them in.

"We stopped by Mr. Pickman's shop earlier but you weren't there," Hazel said. "He said you were busy."

"Shuh am," Horace replied. "Durntedest thing, tew. But fust . . ." He slid a chair over for Sonia to sit in.

"I just wanted Sonia to see the your clay replica of the box."

"Oh, ee-yuh. Be right back," Horace said and disappeared into his work room.

"That man is *huge,*" Sonia whispered. "You wouldn't think a guy that big would be into *pottery.*" She leaned closer. "And I can see why you're so attracted to him. The big ones aren't my type at all, but *you?*" Then came another cunning smile.

"Stop it!" Hazel whispered back.

"And just remember. The more time we waste here, the less we'll have to make love before Frank comes back."

The fusion of anticipation and confoundment only dizzied Hazel more. She almost screamed when Sonia lifted out one of her breasts and said behind her grin, "Suck this for me, will you, please?"

Hazel's hands blurred to re-cover her friend. "Why are you *doing* this to me?" came her propulsive whisper. "You've never been like this!"

"It took last night to make me realize how much I've taken you for granted." Again, that dead-serious gaze. "I feel bad about that."

"Stop! Not here . . ."

The trailer floor actually bobbed a little when Horace rejoined them. "Heer it 'tis." He passed the clay box to Sonia.

"That's amazing," Sonia commented, examining its asymmetrical shape. "It *is* just like the metal one at the cabin."

"But all those little hieroglyph thingies are different, aren't they?" Hazel bid.

"Yes. It looks like they're more of them." She looked to Horace, who stood huge, arms crossed. "This is fascinating work, Horace. And do I understand correctly that Henry Wilmarth asked you to make it?"

"Ee-yuh, 'tis true." He glanced to Hazel as well. "And I just took five more out the kiln. 'Tis why I wurn't at Mr. Pickman's shop today. I 'spect he's ruther displeased."

"Five more?" Hazel inquired. "But yesterday you said Henry changed his mind and didn't order any more."

Horace nodded. "It were someone else. Strangest thing, tew. Found a letter in my mailbox this mornin' ordering thirty-two more boxes, which was what Henry asked for at fust but then decided aginst."

"Who . . . was it?"

Horace shrugged. "Durn't know, letter weren't signed, just said he represented Henry's gemolergy friends and they wanted more boxes. Thought it were a mite foolish, a joke mebbe, until I opened another envelope inside that had five thousand bucks in it. Cash. Curn't say no to five thousand bucks. Lord, I en't never had that much money in my hand at once . . . ever."

Hazel and Sonia looked at each other. "How peculiar," Sonia said. And Hazel, "But they just left the letter? No one knocked on the door to talk to you?"

"New. Just left the letter'n cash in my box and left. No name on the letter or nuthin'."

"And this person said that 'Henry's friends' want the boxes?" Sonia asked for clarification.

"Um-hmm."

"A gemology club," Hazel recalled from their conversation last night. "Isn't that what you said?"

"Ee-yuh."

"How curious." Sonia pinched her chin. "Frank never said anything about Henry having an interest in gems."

"Yeah, but he and Frank are *geometry* professors, Sonia," Hazel pointed out. "Cut gemstones are covered with facets comprised of *geometric* configurations, just like the *gemstone* Henry referred to as the 'Shining Trapezohedron.'" Hazel' eyes again beseeched Horace. "And Henry said the box is to store a *gemstone,* right?"

"A crystal, he said." Horace took the box back from Sonia. "I curn't make much sense out'a any of it. Figure it's just the man's hobby, wants special display boxes for crystals. I durn't ask questions 'baout stuff I durn't know. I just dew the work."

"This is quite a mystery," Sonia said.

Yeah, Hazel thought. *It couldn't have been FRANK who left the letter. Right now he's up on the mountain in some ridiculous cottage.* Hazel's thoughts stalled. *Or is he?*

Sonia rose, a bit awkwardly, and handed her purse to Hazel. "Horace, do you mind if I use your bathroom?"

"Please dew." Horace led her to the cramped hall. "Sorry it's so small in theer."

"I'll be fine, thanks."

The narrow door clicked. *At least it beats the outhouse,* Hazel mused. *Or going in the backyard.* "At the very least, congratulations on your new work order."

"Thanks much. 'Tis shuhly a lot of money someone left in my mailbox. Would ya like to see the others?"

Hazel followed him into his small workroom. The air was warmer here, from the kiln. Sitting on a tray were five more freshly fired boxes. Horace showed her his technique, holding up a plastic version of the box—an "inside-out mold," he called it and explained how he would first oil the plastic box, then apply clay around it, after which he pressed pre-made plastic template cards on each side and the lid; this pressed in the sequences of glyphs directly into the clay's surface. The inside-out mold was then slipped out, and the clay shell fired in the kiln. "Pretty labor intensive," Hazel remarked.

"New, new, just the mold and templates. Once I got them right, the rest is a snap. Kind'a fun, actually."

Hazel looked more closely at the five new boxes and was astounded by how precise they each were. Several times, though, her eyes flicked to Horace's crotch—his *packed* crotch—and she found that, now, she couldn't have been any *less* interested in his sexual endowment. Knowing that she'd soon be making love to Sonia seemed to sweep her mind clean of all its dirt, of all those fetishes and paraphilias and kinks and perversions. *Sonia is my cure* . . . The idea of a sexual romp with this mountain of muscle named Horace, or with any man for that matter, seemed as boring as playing solitaire.

Just then she heard a muffled cell phone ringing, not hers but Sonia's. She pulled it out of her friend's purse, saw that it was Frank calling, then said, "Excuse me a minute, Horace."

"Shuhly."

"Hi, Frank, it's Hazel," she answered, stepping back into the living room. "Sonia's in the bathroom—"

"Thank God," came Frank's odd reply.

Hazel frowned. "What time tonight will you be back?"

"Mmm. That's the catch. I've found more of Henry's work up here—it's spellbinding, so—"

"Frank," she deliberated. "Answer the question. What time *tonight* will you be back?"

A static pause. "It won't be tonight, Hazel. Maybe tomorrow afternoon but I can't even guarantee that. There's just so much sheer *data* up here."

"That's shitty, Frank!" she almost yelled. "Sonia's pissed off enough as it is. You don't get your ass back to the cabin tonight, you might not have a fiancé anymore."

"Listen, listen," he sounded desperate yet enthralled. "Make her understand. This is important to me—"

"It sounds like a crock of shit! She thinks you've got another woman up there with you!"

"For God's sake, that's ridiculous." Did he sound out of breath as well? "Sonia can fly off-the-handle sometimes, so I need you to do me a big favor—"

Hazel's teeth ground. "Don't make me be the messenger, Frank!"

"Just tell her, please. If I get on the phone with her, she'll go off the deep end. So, please, Hazel just tell her that—"

"Frank! Be a man and talk to her yourself. She's in the bathroom, just wait a second and I'll give her the phone."

"No, no, it's very important. I've been reading all of Henry's notes he stashed up here at the cottage. I think-I think he's wrong. I think the theory can actually work."

"I don't give a *fuck* about the theory, Frank," Hazel snapped, then noticed Horace raise a brow in the other room. She scurried toward the small bathroom. "I'm passing the phone to Sonia in the bathroom right now. *You* tell her—"

"No. Tell her for me. Tell her my cell phone died while we were talking."

"No! And don't you *dare* hang up, you selfish, inconsiderate prick."

"You're a peach, Hazel. I'll make it up to you. If you could see this work up here, you'd understand—"

"Don't you *dare*—"

Frank hung up before Hazel could get to the bathroom. She slumped in the hall, then returned to the living room. *She's gonna shit a brick when she hears about this . . .*

Sonia came out a minute later. Hazel dreaded what must come next. "Thanks for showing us the boxes, Horace. We've got to go now."

"Pleasure havin' yew. Stop by any time."

Hazel scribbled her cell number and passed it to him. "Give me a call in a few days. We'd love to take you out to dinner or something."

"Why, thanks much, I will."

Back outside, Hazel opened the car door for Sonia, who looked shivery in repressed excitement. "All right, I've seen the box, so let's *go,*" and then Sonia couldn't have looked more wanton over to Hazel.

Hazel stalled at the driver's door. *This is NOT going to be easy.* "Listen, Sonia . . ."

"What?"

"Um . . ."

All those lascivious edges to Sonia's expression dulled instantly. She *knew* something was askew. "What is it, Hazel? I'm not liking the vibes right now."

Hazel gulped. "When you were in the bathroom . . . Frank called. And I answered."

"Oh, good. What time did he say he'd be at Henry's cabin?"

Hazel's flipflops shuffled in the grass. All the way down the driveway, though, there was only mud from last night's rain. "He's still at the cottage. He's . . . not coming back tonight. Tomorrow afternoon maybe."

Sonia's eyes suddenly possessed a glare that could cut stone. She took out her cellphone, dialed Frank's number, then waited. Obviously Frank's voice mail came on, not Frank himself.

"Frank, it's Sonia. What are you pulling? I will *not* be treated like this. What? You're *avoiding* me? I'm too much of a pain in the ass to *talk* to? Well hear this: if you don't call me back right away, I might just stick this engagement ring right up your ass." Tears began to dot her cheeks. "You're the one who wanted to be a father and right now my stomach's sticking out like a pickle barrel from *your kid.* Call me back, or you'll be sorry." Then she hung up.

The incident squelched Sonia's previous horniness like a bucket of water on a campfire. Her glare cut into Hazel across the roof of the car.

"I told him to wait for you but he wouldn't," Hazel said. "He was afraid you'd blow a gasket. He wanted me to tell you that his cell phone was dying."

Sonia wiped her eyes. Her silence was the most unpleasant aspect of the event.

"I was rushing to the bathroom to give you the phone, but he hung up."

More tense moments ticked by. Wind chimes sang innocuously. Sonia remained silent, staring her ire out into the woods.

"He said he found more of Henry's work, important stuff," Hazel added. "It got him all jazzed up, you know, that theory, the non-Euclidian stuff. I mean, the guy *is* an academician. He gets as excited about geometric principles as we get over the themes and variations of *Moby Dick.*"

Sonia's disjointed glare grew even sharper. *"Don't you stick up for him!"*

"I'm not!" Hazel all but wailed. "I don't even really like him; if I had my way, you wouldn't even *be* with the jerk! I called him a selfish, inconsiderate prick!"

If only traceably, Sonia smiled. "You're sweet, Hazel. And I'm sorry you're in the middle of this. But you know me—better than anyone probably: I need to be by myself for several hours—"

No! Hazel's thoughts screamed.

"I'm too frazzled and, believe me, I won't be very good company for awhile. I'm going to drive back to the cabin and just try to decompress from this, okay?"

Hazel stared. "Sonia, please—"

"I'm sorry I led you on, but that was before Frank pulled this move." Sonia wiped her eyes, appeared to be straining not to fall apart. "Just let me be by myself for a little while."

"You're going back to the cabin without me," Hazel droned, her own tears threatening now.

"I have to. Please understand; don't be mad. But you know how I get. Whatshisname can drive you back later, okay? Or just call me in a few hours . . ."

Hazel was teetering in place, staring over the car's roof. "I'll make you forget all about Frank." She gulped. "I love you. Please– give me a ch–"

"It's best this way," Sonia said through a choke. "Just . . . forgive me."

Sonia got into the car and drove away.

Hazel felt like a circuit breaker that had just been thrown off. She stared through nothing as the Prius disappeared around the bend of trees. She wanted to scream, cry, and laugh all at the same time, but instead she remained mute in place, vibrating from the crushing disappointment. *One inch away from my dream coming true . . . and Frank had to fuck it all up . . .*

She felt warped now, twisted; she felt as though pieces of her psyche had been cut off and absconded with. *Always me, always me . . .*

The trailer door clacked again when Horace came out; he seemed hesitant. "Wurn't listenin' deliberate naow but couldn't help but heer. Yew're friend seems quite bent aout'a shape 'baout somethin'."

"Yeah," Hazel sighed, dabbed her tears.

"And yew tew. Anythin' I can dew?"

Hazel flinched, gave a mauled smile. *Shape up.* "Just girl-talk, Horace. Young and dumb, that's me. It'll all be okay."

"Ee-yuh, I shuh hope so."

But would it really be okay?

Horace came down the steps and surprised her by offering a glass of ice-water. "Heer. It's turrible hot; yew'll likely feel better after takin' some'a this."

"You're very thoughtful, Horace." The cold water down her throat roused her; it focused her previous idea to something, all of a sudden, thrilling. *Sonia's in no condition to climb the summit . . . but I am . . .* She looked up hopefully at the towering Horace. "Are you familiar with an old cottage built way up on top of the summit?"

Horace mulled the thought. With his arms crossed, his biceps bulged to the size of baking potatoes. "If'n yew mean Whipple's Peak, well, ee-yuh. I 'member when I was a little shaver, my gram used to talk abaout it, tryin' ta sceer me, I 'spose. Said it were sittin' right at the edge'a the cliff, and didn't have no front door." He pronounced "door" as *doe-uh.* "Said it were haunted and'd been there since before white men ever came heer."

"Built by Indians, in other words."

"New, 'cos that's what I asked'n she said Indians *couldn't'a* built it 'cos they didn't know haow ta cut stone. See, my gram said the cottage was made'a gray blocks—granite."

Gray blocks, Hazel's mind wandered. *The Gray Cottage, that's what Frank called it.* "I'd like to go and see it, Horace. But . . . how do I get there?"

Horace chuckled subtly. "Ah, well naow, see, I dun't think it really exists, Hazel. Just a wive's tale—"

"Yeah, yeah, but let's just say that it *does* exist," she pressed him. "How would I go about looking for it?"

The large man shrugged, then pointed high to the west. "En't no other way but to just walk all's the way up the summit, and I'd imagine it'd be half a day at least gettin' up there. See all that mist?"

Hazel's eye followed the direction of his finger. It was just a tree-covered pinnacle, at least a half mile up. *Mist?* she thought. She strained her vision.

"Foller the line up where there en't no trees."

Now she saw it. There must've been a mudslide or avalanche of some kind, eons ago, for now she detected a swath against the summit's most extreme rise covered only with brush, no trees. At the very top, as far as she could see, lay a blanket of pale mist.

"But I wouldn't go up there if'n I was yew," Horace went on. "It's like Sleepy Holler, and the Goat Man, yew know? Cum't possibly be a stone cottage up there when ya think abaout it."

"Why not?"

"Impossible to carry all them granite blocks up there." Horace rubbed his chin. "A'course, my gram *did* say she saw it huh-self when she was young, though. So . . . who knows?"

Interesting. Hazel kept her eyes on the distant smear of mist.

"She said there was 'sposed to be *treasure* in the cottage but she couldn't get it on account she couldn't get *inside*. Like I said, weren't no door."

A stone cottage . . . with no door? Could Frank really be lying that intricately? Hazel didn't think so. *The cottage MUST exist; Henry even mentioned it in his suicide note. And Frank really IS there, right now.*

And if he isn't back by tomorrow afternoon . . . I'm going to try to find it . . .

"Strange tales 'baout that cottage, I'll say. But every place got a few sech tales."

"Urban legends, backwoods legends, they're all the same," Hazel remarked. "It's part of human nature to tell stories but then I guess every story that's ever existed is based in some way on fact."

"Ee-yuh. And heer's somethin' else, if'n yew wanna talk abaout strange." His big hand touched her back and urged her toward the driveway. "Tell me what'cha think, but just walk up along the edge."

She saw what he meant; the entire driveway was a trough of mud from the rain. She'd walked gingerly along the forest's rim.

"Them prints there are mine," he said, pointing to a track of large footprints going to the mailbox and then back to the trailer. "But naow . . . see thet?"

They stood at the bulky mailbox. Footprints impressed in the mud came to, then from the box.

"Tracks from whoever left you the envelope and money," Hazel observed. She saw nothing odd about it.

Horace held up a finger. "Stay along the edge'n yew'll see."

She followed him farther past the driveway's end, into the mud-splotched road itself; all the while, Horace's finger pointed down at the tracks. With each print left by the mysterious deliverer, Horace counted out, "One, two, three . . ."

What's he driving at? Hazel wondered.

" . . . thirty-one, thirty-two, thirty-three."

Horace and Hazel stopped. But so did the tracks, nearly in the middle of the road. The tire-tracks from Sonia's car coursed well away from them and, hence, couldn't have covered up any additional footprints.

"Strange?" Horace asked.

"Very strange," she admitted, gazing at the termination of prints. *Thirty-three steps in, and thirty-three steps back. Then . . .* It was as though the person who'd delivered the envelope had appeared and then vanished into thin air.

Between the footprints and the prospect of finding the Gray Cottage, Hazel hoped for enough mental diversion to forget about her almost-sex session with Sonia. It worked . . . for a while anyway. She passed on Horace's offer for a ride, electing instead to walk back to town on the paved road. Dense pine and oak lined both sides of the way, breaking up only periodically to show small crackerbox houses stuck back at the ends of short driveways. As she walked, the day's heat and humidity glazed her. *Not even sure where I'm going.* Several persons either sitting on front porches or fussing with shrubs waved casually at her. *What did Sonia call this place? Hooterville?* Ma and pa in rocking chairs, bumpkin women hanging clothes on the line. But she had to stop at the next house she came to: a county sheriff's car sat parked there while the officer himself had his hands full keeping a quarreling couple apart.

"Just you calm daown now, the both of ya's," he warned. Meanwhile a fortyish man in a sleeveless T-shirt and beer belly raged red-faced at a mop-haired woman who sported an even *bigger* beer belly. "Been married to huh durn neer twenty years, payin' the bills, workin' my tail off!" He pronounced "workin'" as *wuckin'*. "Naow I sees she's gettin on with another man!"

Hazel walked by, only ten feet from the conflict, trying to act like she was not listening. *Here we go. Backwoods love gone sour. The good old Domestic Dispute . . .*

"I en't never cheated on yew, Cal, and it's dag *shitty* to say so," the jowly woman wailed back, fists waving. "And after all I done for yew?"

"Shee-it, woman!"

Hazel smirked. By the looks of the dowdy, overweight woman and her red nose, it would take a secret suitor with very *low* standards to be a party in infidelity. *Take what you can get, honey . . .*

"Now, come on, Emma!" barked the sheriff. He held the woman off as though she were a pit bull. "Cal reely ketch you with another man? Admit it if'n he did—"

"He did nothin' of the sort 'cos there *en't* no other man!" the woman cracked.

"If there en't no other man!" the husband bellowed back, "then who done gave yew that ring!"

Hazel glanced at the woman's piggish hand at the same time the sheriff did. Glittering on her finger was a roughly cut deep-scarlet ring.

Hazel wasn't sure but she wondered, *Wasn't Mr. Pickman wearing a ring just like that?*

Not that it mattered. Hazel stepped up her pace; she'd had enough listening to angry rednecks. As she headed away, she heard the woman yell, "I done told yew! I faound it! Warn't no man give it to me!"

Hazel was glad the confrontation was behind her.

Another half-mile and she was on Main Street. Intermittent passersby nodded to her, yet one woman frowned when her husband gave Hazel's legs a good look. *I guess I'm just killing time,* she supposed, looking into some windows. Every time she thought she was feeling better, though, stray images began to hector her. *I could be with Sonia right now. Right NOW . . .* She winced. *Goddamn Frank. Talk about getting torpedoed.* Soon the images turned lewd, but didn't involve Sonia at all. When just an hour ago she'd felt cured of her kinks and demented fetishes, now they all poured back into her head like cement from a mixer. She recalled the feeling of being pissed in by Snow White yesterday, only to likewise be forced to drink more piss straight from Peter Pan's rancid cock. Then she could feel the ghosts of his dirty fingers jammed down her throat, to make her vomit it all back up. She shuddered as she walked, appalled by the violation; nevertheless, all the disgusting memory did was throw her pervert switch, and next thing she knew her sexual nerves were buzzing. *Oh, no, not again . . .* Even as nauseousness grew, her sex moistened.

Sick, sick, sick, came the dismal thought. She wouldn't even admit to herself why she'd come here in the first place, but now she had to face it . . .

The Fish Boys . . . That's what Horace said.

Her angst was twisting her up. She needed to find these Fish Boys . . .

She wandered a bit, glancing in random shop windows. A Rite-Aid store appeared round the corner. She went in to get a Sierra Mist but had to do a double take when she passed a line of ten people at the photo counter. They all stood chatting amiably, beneath a sign that read PASSPORT PHOTOS.

THESE rubes? she wondered, passing them to the checkout. *That's an awful lot of rednecks getting passports, of all things . . .*

Oh, well. She walked around some more, mainly taking in the distant scenery. The green, wooded hills closer, and mountains miles off. Everything seemed pure here; even the sky looked *pure.*

Eventually she meandered into Bosset's Way Woodland Tavern. *Someone in here must know where I can find the Fish Boys.* It was the only way to discover for herself if they, indeed, had been the ones who mauled her.

The place stood two-thirds empty, yet cigarette smoke hazed the bar area. Quiet, work-weathered rednecks either chewed the fat over beers at the tables, or—*clack!*—played pool. One elderly couple, obviously tourists, marveled over plates of possum-sausage hoagies. Hazel drearily took a seat at the long empty bar.

"Waal, hey thar, sweet pea," greeted a corpulent barmaid with bunned hair and an apron. "What'll it be?"

"How about a beer?" *Alcohol just makes me more fucked up than I normally am,* she admitted. *So why did I just order a beer?*

"Comin' right up! Ooo, and I just love yew're hair! What a lovely color!"

"Thank you," Hazel said. *My hair looks like steel wool dipped in barbeque sauce. What are you–correction: YEW–talking about?*

Her brain seemed to tick as she sat there. She felt so sick right now, yet so anxiously demented. *Motherfuckin' Frank. Fucked me over six ways till Sunday. If he really does have a girl with him, I'm gonna cut his cock off and put it on a stick.*

Clunk. The barmaid set down her beer. "Thar yew go, cutie pie." The broad face seemed enthralled by Hazel. "Hope yew durn't mind my sayin' so"—chubby fingers reached out and actually pinched her cheek—"and yew might not believe this but thar was a time when I was just as pretty and slim as yew—"

"Yeah, Ida!" someone yelled from the pool table. "Back when Eisenhower was president."

The barmaid's face bugled, pig-eyed. "Just you hush thar, Nahum Gardner! Lest I tell Nabby what it *looked like* yew was doin' in the men's room other night!"

Guffaws cracked in the air.

Hazel glumly sipped her beer. *Redneck paradise.* She thought of ordering lunch but realized she had no appetite. All that filled her mind were images of sex with Sonia—sex she'd likely never have. But when she tried to think of something else, she winced at what her mind produced: being pissed on, being cracked in her face, being choked and held up off her feet as some faceless thug fucked her . . . *God* . . . She thought of calling Ashton, whom she knew loved her, but she shrugged the idea off. *I only want to be loved by Sonia and that's NEVER going to happen.* She glanced errantly at the pool table, noticed one stocky man with bulging muscles and hair pouring over his T-shirt collar. In the vision she saw him fornicating with her on one of the bar tables, duct tape slapped over her eyes and mouth. He gulped from a beer bottle while he stroked, but then he suddenly withdrew, creamed her labia with his sperm, and slunked the beer bottle in her, fat-end first . . .

Hazel rubbed her forehead and groaned, her sex squirming, swampy with need.

"Oh, new, that's right, I never got chance tew tell ya 'baout it, Hannah but, ee-yuh, all's I need is my passport, then I durn't think it'll be long afore I go." It was Ida, the barmaid, now yammering excitedly on the phone. "Ee-yuh, Sao Paulo it's called. Not shuh whar it 'tis but I think it's one'a them beachy places . . ."

Hazel's eyes narrowed. *This woman is going to SAO PAULO?* Nothing more unlikely could've occurred to her.

"Oh, goodness, yes! I en't had me a vacation in *yeers!*"

When Ida hung up, Hazel *had* to ask, "Did you say you were going on a vacation to *Sao Paulo?*"

"Why, yes! I'se so excited!" the woman beamed. "Do you know whar 'zactly it 'tis, hon?"

"Yeah, it's in Brazil."

Ida's eyes blanked. "And, uh, whar's that?"

She getting a passport to go to Sao Paulo and she doesn't

even know where it is? Hazel was flummoxed. *She must've won a sweepstakes or something.* "South America, the south western coast. But it's not on the beach like Rio, it's more like thirty miles from the ocean. Read about the place before you go there because, well, it's not exactly a tourist hot-spot any more."

"No . . . beaches?"

"Not unless you've got a Land Rover. I'm sure there're buses that go to the coast but in South America even the buses are suspect. Highwaymen, insurgents. And Sao Paulo has one of the highest population-densities of any city on earth, almost twenty million people and most of them live in extreme poverty. There's death-squads, gangs, drugs, pick-pockets, you name it. And there are Marxist terrorist cells that love to kidnap Americans." Hazel sipped her beer. "You might want to try Rio, instead, or some of the beach resorts south of there."

"Why, I say . . . ," Ida blurted. "I never would'a thought they'd be sendin' me tew a place like *that.*"

Yeah, a sweepstakes she must've won, Hazel knew. "Oh, and by the way. Do you know where I can find the Fish—" but before she could finish, the phone rang.

"Be right back, sweetie . . ."

Just as Ida parted, a stool scuffed the floor several spots down. In it a wide-shouldered, grizzle-faced man sat. He wore a sweat-stained T-shirt that read ACME TREE TRIMMING AND HAULAGE. He sat almost dejected, rubbing his eyes as though fatigued or mentally frayed. "Dang," he muttered.

"You look like you're feeling about as good as I am now," Hazel offered.

The man glanced over, bleary-eyed. "Howdy'n, waal, ee-yuh, not feelin' up ta snuff. Had the wust night's sleep ever." He sputtered. "Nightmares, yew know?"

"Well, I had a doozy myself," Hazel replied. "Must be in the air."

A big hand glided over. "Name's Nathaniel—call me Nate. Nate Peaslee."

"Hi, Nate, I'm Hazel." When she shook the large, steel-firm hand, she imagined it clamped to her throat while he rubbed the wet end of a huge penis back and forth over the nub of her clitoris. *Stop it! Stop it!*

"I once dated a psych major who said the best way to disarm the memory of an unpleasant dream is to talk about the dream itself," she said.

He shook his head, gruffed a sound. "Curn't 'member ever havin' a nightmare so *reel.* Dreamt I woke up in my bed and somehaow *knowed* that someone were in the house. Then I thought shuh the place was on fire"—he pronounced "fire" as *far*—"'cos thar were this black mist all abaout, like seepin' up through the seams in the floor but when I sniff, it durn't smell like smoke no ways. Smelled kind'a like fresh meat're fish. Next thing I knowed I'm lyin' in bed but curn't move a muscle ta save my life but I ken *see* some fella walkin' araound my place, mutterin' all this jibber-jabber. Looked like he was weerin' sunglasses, of all the durnt things."

"And that's it?" Hazel asked. "That's the dream?"

"Ee-yuh, all's I ken 'member. Didn't sleep me a *wink* after thet."

Shit, buddy, she thought. *My nightmare's got that beat by a mile.* "Say, Nate, have you ever heard about a really old cottage up on top of Whipple's Peak?" she thought she'd ask.

His eyes narrowed in contemplation, then he perked up and said, "Ee-yuh, naow's yew mention it. En't thought 'baout it in yeers. Some place no one knows who built. Never seed the place myself but my brothers did, hiked all the way up thar back when we was little kids—"

Ida, clearly eavesdropping, lumbered from the back. "Oh, naow, Nate, durn't ya be fillin' my friend's head with all that tripe!" She looked earnestly to Hazel. "Honey, thet en't nothin' but tall tales. Thar en't no haunted cottage up on Whipple—"

"But my brothers done seed it when we was little," Nate insisted.

A reproving glance. "Nate, yew're brothers may be fine, hard-workin' fellas but they both lie like a couple'a rugs."

Nate stalled. "Waal, curn't argue with yew thar, Ida."

"Okay," Hazel said, "but there's something else I need to know. Can either of you tell me where to find some people known as the F—"

The phone rang again, summoning Ida, while simultaneously, Nate's cell phone rang.

Jesus! Hazel could've screamed at her luck.

"Aw, god-durnt it," Nate said. "Rush job at the Curwen place, huh? I was just abaout to grab a samb-witch, but—Aw, all right." He hung up, jangling his keys. "Gotta run, Hazel. Boss is payin' double-time so's I guess lunch ken wait. Nice talkin' tew ya, though."

"You, too . . ."

A moment later he was out the door.

The Fish Boys, the Fish Boys, Hazel turned the words over. Was Fate preventing her from finding out their location? *Fate or God,* came a second, unpleasant thought.

The pool table men left, high-fiving after their game, and when Hazel turned to look she now found the bar empty. She could still ask Ida about the Fish Boys . . . *If she ever quits yacking on the phone!* Several yuppie-looking young men came in next, in hiking gear. They wore Boston College shirts—the enemy. *Dead end. They wouldn't know either.* Ida put another beer down for her, with the phone tucked between cheek and chin. *I guess you're gonna run your mouth all day,* but then Hazel blinked after having noticed a crimson sparkle.

How do you like that? Ida was wearing what seemed a scarlet ring identical to Mr. Pickman's and the woman who'd been arguing with her husband . . .

A sound like a squeaky bearing snapped her attention, then a crackly voice, "Aw, now, there she is! Hazel, ain't it?"

Hazel turned to see Clonner Martin wheeling up in his chair. "Hi, Clonner. Nice to see you again." She hopped off her stool and sat across from him at the nearest table. "How are things going?"

He huffed, raising his stumps. "Still got no hands, but the sun's still shinin', the world's still turnin', and I'm still drinkin' beer, so's I'm just fine."

Hazel smiled, shaking her head. She remembered his similar optimism yesterday. "You're quite an inspiration, Clonner."

"Aw, hail . . ." He ordered a beer for himself. "I do all right. A dang sight better than Luntville, West Virginia."

"Oh, that's right. You grew up there. Didn't you say you had a brother there too?"

"Yeah, sure did. Jake."

Then Hazel grimly recalled that Clonner had lost his hands to diabetes, while his brother lost his feet. Suddenly she felt charged up in a small way; the old man's mere presence helped put away her own angst and doldrums. It refreshed her to hear the snappy, crackling southern accent as opposed to the low-throat drawl of the true locals. "What urged you to move here of all places?"

Clonner took a good swig of beer by biting the can's lip. "Pot luck, I guess. Saw an ad for the land in the back'a *Field'n Stream.* Price was right and I'd just come inta some money so's I said hail'n come up to check it out. Never went back. Were all ready sick'a the heat'n skeeters." Another swig and he rambled on, "Bought me a piece'a lakeside property with a shack on it, and a decent double-wide on a couple acres just down the road. I'se live in the trailer, and my loser nephew'n his deadbeat buddy live in the shack. And like I told ya yesterday, darlin', I'se also bought me this bar once I seed how bad it were suckin' wind. But I'll be danged if'n I ain't doubled the profits."

"But you still have land in West Virginia?" Hazel inquired, somehow fascinated by the whiskery old man.

"Naw, naw, hon, solt it all, I did. Hadda a hunnert acres'a crap land in Russell County. Weren't worth squat, it wasn't, but then some business fella up'n offered me some *long* coin fer it. He were from a mining company and the land was worth fair scratch 'cos of the gypsies on it."

Hazel stalled. "Gypsies?"

"Yeah. So he and his mining company bought it all and here's I am." He shook his head. "My whole blammed life, though, I never once knew of a mine in the area and shore as hail never saw no gypsies or hurdy-gurdy folks on it." He scratched his chin with a stump. "Reckon he wanted to get the gypsies to work in his mine under the table."

Hazel squinted. "Clonner, I think you mean *gypsum,* not gypsies. It's a mineral used in construction materials."

Clonner gaped. "Ya don't say! Shee-it, all this time I thought it was gypsies. I'll tell ya, a fella learns somethin' new every day!"

Hazel had to control herself not to laugh. "Yes, I'm sure your land had *gypsum* on it, and that's why you were paid well." *What a character . . .* "Oh, and I'm glad I ran into you, Clonner. Are you familiar with some people—brothers, perhaps—known as the Fish Boys?"

Clonner almost dropped his beer out of his dentures. "Oh, yeah, missy, I'se sorry to say I am. 'S the two losers I just tolt ya I let 'em live in my lake shack, my fat'n useless nephew Clayton and his goin'-nowhere pal Walter Brown. They sell their catch to the local restaurants. They'se also trap'n filet woodchuck, possum, muskrat. In fact, I pointed 'em out to ya yesterday." He pronounced *pointed* as "purnted," and then gestured the waist-high opening in the wall in which Hazel remembered seeing two men fileting fish.

"Oh, so *those* guys are the Fish Boys," she acknowledged, and now she felt a twinge of suspense. The bearded fileter had been overweight while his partner next to him had been tall and wiry-slim. *Peter Pan was fat,* she remembered, *and Snow White skinny and tall* . . . Maybe Horace had been correct with his hunch.

"Where can I find them, Clonner? Where's this lake shack of theirs?"

The question almost caused the old man to audibly moan. "Aw, missy, now, you don't wanna go *there.* What'cha wanna find them two white trash loafers fer?"

Hazel laughed. "You certainly don't speak very highly of your own nephew, Clonner."

"He's a lazy, fat putz and his buddy Shot Glass ain't nothin' but a skunk and a weasel."

"*Shot Glass*?"

"Aw, yeah, that's Walter's nickname." Clonner made a *pppppht* sound with his lips. "*Great* nickname fer a al-ker-holik. Shot Glass come here from Brattleboro, Vermont, more'n likely 'cos of the husbands of too many redneck tramps he were messin' with. Only friend my nephew's got–peas in a pod. Oh, shore, I guess they'se decent fishermen'n trappers but they ain't good for nothin' else. Deal I made with 'em was they pay me some two-bit rent ever month with the fish'n game they catch, but then they blow all their scratch on booze and don't hardly pay me squat." It was clearly a sore subject to Clonner. "Cain't kick 'em out, though. Clayton's blood, after all." At last, his gaunt face seemed to grow *more* gaunt. "Say, Hazel, what'choo askin' 'bout them two no-accounts fer anyway? Did ya say ya wanted to know how ta *find* 'em?"

"Well, yes," and she was disturbed by how effortlessly the lie arrived. "My friend Sonia and I want to cook out on the grill tonight, so I need to get some fresh fish. Then someone mentioned the *Fish* Boys so I thought they'd be a good bet."

Clonner shrugged. "Aw, well, they do bring in a good fresh catch, I'll give the pair'a morons that." His stump waved toward the front door. "Just go on down the road a half-mile, then turn toward the lake on Zadok Spur it's called. Go on a spell, there be the shack."

Bingo! Hazel thought. "Thanks very much, Clonner." She tried to pay her tab but the old man wouldn't hear of it. "Yer cash is no good in *my* bar, sweetie. But just you do me a favor if'n ya catch up to Clayton'n Shot Glass."

"Sure, Clonner."

"You tell those two beer-soaked, do-nothin' *bums* that it might be nice, just once, fer them ta actually pay their blammed rent like ever-one else in the world!"

"I'll do that, Clonner. See you soon." Hazel smiled at him then left the bar.

The shift from morning to early afternoon brought more heat and humidity; it came in waves. *Shouldn't have had those beers,* she thought at once. She was already buzzed, a feeling she didn't typically like. Nevertheless, each step she took down the road brought a refreshing excitement to her. *Clayton Martin and Shot Glass Brown . . .* Would they really prove to be Peter Pan and Snow White? And if they were . . .

Why wasn't she *afraid* of the prospect?

She found the turn-off, the oddly named Zadok Spur, in less than ten minutes. Here, though, the asphalt ended, leaving a narrow road even muddier than Horace's. When she thought of walking within the forest's fringe, one step told her it was useless. Evidently the land here lay very low; last night's showers had turned the forest's carpet of leaves and detritus into swamp. *To hell with it,* she consigned. *Mud washes off,* and she took off her flipflops and marched unfazed through the slop. She didn't care how dirty her feet got, anyway. *The rest of me just might be a whole lot dirtier in a little while . . .*

More excitement welled, however unspecified. Sweat drenched the Mark Twain T-shirt now, to the extent that it stuck to her chest like a wet veil. Nerves squirmed in her nipples which had distended a half-inch, and between the heat and the considerable walking, her shorts worked up tight into the cleft of her buttocks. When the mud-trench of a road broke, she felt woozy . . .

There sat the aforementioned shack, just off the shore with the flat glass of Lake Sladder shimmering nearly as far as she could see. From the shack, a ramshackle pier extended, while a decrepit boat sat still in the water, heaped with nets and fishing rods; animal pelts hung up on a two-by-four frame. *Well here they are,* Hazel thought, ankle deep in mud. *The Fish Boys.* In only minutes she'd have the answer to her question . . .

Her feet schlucked as she approached. She glanced at the shack's small windows and—

What's that noise?

She heard a sound like a vacuum cleaner, though by the looks of the place, and her impression of its tenants, she couldn't imagine much housekeeping going on here. A awful stench blew into her face from a garbage can just beyond the porch; *Ugh,* she thought, looking it, for it contained piles of fish heads along with the heads of possums, squirrels, and other mammals. A wooden door stood open, from which the machine-sound emerged. *Great design,* she thought in sarcasm, for the shack had been erected below a slight rise before the shoreline; the excess rainwater from the woods had clearly entered the teetering building at one end.

BUY YOR FISH HEER, read an incredulous painted sign. MUSKRAT, POSSEM, WOODCHUK - CHEAP.

Hazel felt no hesitation when she stepped onto the facsimile for a front porch and entered the shack without knocking.

The vacuum sound deafened her. It was a disaster of a domicile: busted recliner chairs sitting askew, a warped table full of empty beer cans, a television with a coat hanger for an antenna. Various wires looped from the ceiling; a dented refrigerator, a microwave with a crack in the window, and a hot plate comprised the kitchen, while pots and pans dangling from the ceiling. The only true lamp in the place sat on the counter, but it was shadeless. A fat, brown-haired man was opening the fridge for a beer. He had a beard. *Clayton,* Hazel realized. *Clonner's nephew.* He went to the counter and began the grisly task of fileting some skinned animal the size of a dachshund. A second man busied himself at the opposite end of the shack: tall, wiry, stubbled-faced and sunken eyed. His long hair was the color of a dirty sheep. *Walter "Shot Glass" Brown . . .* Indeed, Hazel had seen both men fileting fish at the tavern yesterday. Shot Glass paused to chug a can of beer, then returned to his noisy duties, for he was the one behind the deafening sound. The shack's far end dipped enough to form a low spot which had accumulated an inch of water on the floor. Unmindful of the possibility of electrical shock, Shot Glass tramped boot-footed through the water, wielding a two-foot-long clear plastic tube an inch in diameter; this tube was connected to a long, black hose stuck to a machine that looked like an engine analyzer at a gas-station, only very old. The man was vacuuming up the water that lay in the dip, the shack's crude sleeping area, she could see, for two ratty, steel-framed beds occupied the nook. Mattresses lay sheetless and stained.

Hazel merely stood there, looking around.

"Yo! Yo!" Clayton, the fat one, yelled to his partner. He set down his bloody fileting knife. "Shot Glass!" He banged a pot on the makeshift kitchen counter. "Turn that dang thing off!"

Shot Glass looked up amid the siphoning cacophony; water slurped loudly into the tube. He noticed Hazel standing there, then flicked the machine off.

"We'se got company," Clayton said.

Shot Glass set the nozzle aside, then tramped out of the water. He peered, weasel-faced. "Who're yew?"

Hazel crossed her arms below her bosom. "Clayton, Walter, a.k.a. Shot Glass–the Fish Boys, huh? Nice to see you again. And just so you know, I didn't file rape charges yesterday, but I did tell some people I was coming here now. So if I, say, disappear, the police will know where to come. Keep in mind, there is still a death penalty in New Hampshire."

Both men looked at each other, narrow-eyed.

"But that was some job you guys did on me yesterday. The foot-fuck especially."

"Clayton, what's she talkin' 'baout?" Shot Glass asked.

Hazel snapped, "You stupid redneck dimwits!" then she pointed to a cluttered shelf on which sat two plastic faces: Peter Pan and Snow White. "If you're gonna rape a woman half to death, at least have enough brains to hide the evidence!"

The shack stood silent several moments, Clayton and Shot Glass at a loss for words. Clayton gulped, and . . . was Shot Glass nervous when he went to the refrigerator for another beer?

"So . . .," Hazel began. "Here we are, and since I've just told you that I never filed a police report, what does that tell you two think-tankers?"

"Eh?" asked Shot Glass.

Clayton scratched his head.

Hazel sighed. "You guys know what *carte blanche* means?"

"Eh?"

"Cart . . . *what?*" Clayton inquired.

"Free pass?" Hazel continued. "Consensuality?"

Shot Glass swigged more beer, frowning. "We durn't know what yew're *talkin'* 'baout."

"For shit's sake," she muttered. "Listen, I have some problems—some *psychological* problems. They have names, for all the good they do. One's *erotomania.* Another is chronic transitive *paraphilia.* One doctor even said I was *sexually pathological.* It means I have destructive sexual fantasies that are severe enough to cause detriment to my life. I don't expect you guys to know what any of this means since you both probably dropped out of school in the fourth grade—"

"Try seventh, there, missy!" Shot Glass cracked as if offended.

"'Bout the same here," Clayton twanged.

"Wonderful," Hazel groaned. "But here's something you *can* understand. I'm *sick in the head.* Sick as in *sexually* sick. I have fetishes and fantasies that exist on an *obsessive* level."

Shot Glass's face seemed to lengthen in contemplation. "Yew mean yew're, like, nympho?"

"Yes!" Hazel celebrated. "You finally got it!" She peeled off the moist T-shirt, bearing sweat-misted breasts erect with the most obvious anticipation. Then she stepped out of her shorts. "Any time now. It should be pretty clear to you two dopes that I'm ready, willing, and able."

Chuckling, it was Clayton who lifted her up by a hand to her crotch and the other to her armpit.

"On the bed," Shot Glass directed. "Guess we didn't tune the bitch up good enough yesterday."

Clayton slammed her down on a dirty mattress. Springs squeaked. "Think of me as an all-you-can-fuck buffet," Hazel panted. "Do anything you want."

"Anythang?" Clayton asked, taking off his smudged jeans.

She flinched when Shot Glass pinched her labia. "Just don't kill me or cut me. Oh, and—*please*—no foot stuff."

The men roared laughter. Clayton, pantsless now, sat on her stomach, his groin reeking. He cleared his throat, then let a wad of phlegm splat between her breasts.

"Thar's some ripe chest-peaches, heh, heh, heh!" Shot Glass remarked.

"Yeah, and I'se gonna fuck 'em fierce," Clayton promised. He lay his erection in her modest cleavage, then pressed both breasts together. He began to hump. Hazel felt the mucous-slick organ slide back and forth. Meanwhile, Shot Glass was working two, three, then four fingers into her drenched vagina. When the thumb nudged in and all the fingers closed to form a fist, Hazel bucked in a crest of agonizing pleasure. Shot Glass pistoned the fist back and forth while traversing clockwise and counter-clockwise, and when he pinched her clitoris—quite hard—Hazel came in a series of clenching, eruptive spasms. She shrieked when the fist pushed in deeper. The bed rocked. Then the great weight of Clayton lifted as he raised his penis up, stroking the slick skin. He quickly leaned forward, put his gorged corona right against her nostril and—

"Here's some nose drops for ya . . ."

—ejaculated with force. Most of each jet of semen shot right down the nostril till she gagged, hacked, and then could feel it sliding down the back of her throat. Clayton tapped the rest off against her lips.

"Kind'a like blowin' yer nose backwards, huh?" the fat man reveled.

"Ee-yuh," Shot Glass agreed. "And I done got the dirty whore off already." He shimmied his hand out of her, wiped it off on her face, then said, "And haow's this fer an ideer?"

Shot Glass moved away as Clayton dismounted her. Hazel lay squashed on the atrocious bed, stomach sucking in and out. *More, more,* her thoughts pleaded. Her fingers stroked her aching, thumping sex. "Set 'er up, Clayton," Shot Glass ordered next, but what was he doing? Clayton man-handled her to a sitting position, while he himself sat right behind her, and vised her neck in the crook of his elbow. "Aw, yeah!" he hooted. "That'll really fuck the bitch up!"

Hazel flicked her eyes to the right—*What's he doing?*—but all she saw, very briefly, was Shot Glass take another swig of beer and smack his lips. Then he disappeared from the edges of her vision.

"Ee-yuh, this'll likely put some zing in her day . . ."

Hazel clenched at the loud, abrupt sound: the scream of the vacuum pump being turned back on. Clayton's hand slapped across her mouth, then her eyes shot wide when Shot Glass reappeared holding the long clear nozzle at the end of the vacuum's hose.

"Let's see what this does ta her nipples, eh?"

Hazel's back arched when the nozzle was applied to her right areola. The instant contact was made, the nozzle's rim sealed against her flesh and the motor's whine doubled from the resistance. She watched half in terror and half in fascination as the clear tube sucked her areola out an inch, then an inch and a half. When it seemed that the motor would burn up from resistance, Shot Glass took to turning it on and off, on and off, over and over, the pressure sucking the nipple out, then releasing. Hazel squirmed in the bed from the delicious pain.

"Hot damn! Would ya look-it that?" Clayton yelled.

"Ee-yuh siree," Shot Glass commented after turning the machine off. "En't thet dandy ta look et?" He removed the nozzle to reveal Hazel's molested nipple, which had now been sucked out to something the size of an unshelled walnut, only raging pink. "Yew could hang yew're hat'n coat on it," and then the machine's deafening whine resounded and the process was repeated on her left nipple, on and off, on and off, over and over.

Now both nipples stuck out similarly, gorged with blood.

"Do her pussy now," Clayton suggested.

"Wait a minute, time out," Hazel roused enough from her sick daze to object. "That's a bit much, I'm afraid."

Crack!

The impact of Shot Glass's hand across her face slapped half of her consciousness out of her.

"Yew said *anything,*" he reminded, and then once again the vacuum was turned back on. Now Clayton pulled her knees back to her shoulders, to protrude her vulva. All that filled Hazel's head was that mad, deafening sound . . .

The nozzle's rim sucked right up tight against the opening of her sex. At once the pink labia was pulled taffy-like into the tube. Both men stared in glee at her crotch. All that nerve-charged, hypersensitive flesh seemed to fill the first inch of the nozzle as though the suction were drawing her vagina inside-out up into the tube. On and off, the switch went amid Clayton and Shot Glass's dark laughter. On and off, on and off . . .

After several minutes of this Hazel was nearly convulsing—two inches of her vaginal flesh—the vaginal *metus,* might be the proper term—had been sucked up into the tube. The machine's insane whine rose and rose as more and more resistance was met, and again Hazel began to climax, this time via the most perverse means of her life. When three inches of metus had been drawn out, Shot Glass shut the machine off.

"Dang!" Clayton exclaimed of the visual effect. "That plumped her pussy up fierce, it did!"

"Ee-yuh, shuh did."

Gog-eyed, Hazel looked between her legs; her labia appeared swollen, like the lips of a boxer who'd just lost the fight. The demented activity had trebled the blood supply to this tender area, leaving it to throb in a viscous tingle.

Shot Glass chugged more beer. "Heh, heh, heh. 'S'one tough cooze *this* tramp's got."

Clayton twisted the still-protruding nipples till Hazel yelped. Then he ran fat fingers through her deep-red pubic hair till they found the marauded labia and began to diddle with it.

"Shore is fun fuckin' with gals."

"'Specially sick pups like this 'un heer," Shot Glass added, unbuckling his trousers. He manipulated several pillows beneath her rump, while Clayton remained sitting behind her. Her cross lay stuck between her breasts by semen and mucous.

Shot Glass knelt between her legs. "Ee-yuh, only one thing a fella can dew with a pussy plumped up like this'n that's *fuck* it."

The erection looked a good eight inches, uncircumcised. He peeled the abundant foreskin back, then ran the dome up and down the folium of her sex. "Shit, the bilge pump got this sick bitch so horny she's leakin' like a sieve," he said.

You can say that again, came the panting thought. *Now stop toying with me and FUCK me . . .*

He banged his cock in hard to the balls, then began to hump her with vigor. Hazel's vagina felt effervescent from the previous suction, as though the pump had generated new webs of nerves. Shot

Glass pulled his cock all the way out, then banged it all the way back in, over and over and over, until the bed was rocking so violently it must've been close to collapsing. Incredulously, though, the man maintained his fornication with one hand on his hip, and he swigged beer from the can in his other hand.

Joggling, Hazel winced up. She had to ask, "If all you drink is beer, why is your nickname *Shot Glass?* Seems to me you'd drink shots . . ."

His face was twisting up as orgasm impended. "Eh?" Balls slapped the bottom of her elevated ass. "Waal, yew'll see." He winked at Clayton. "Choke the hose-bag up some—git some spark in her. Just be keerful ya durn't kill her—"

Hazel gagged when both of Clayton's meaty hands clamped her throat and squeezed. *This again,* she thought in the most despairing delight. At once she grew dizzy and dim-visioned. The cock continued to bang in and out. Each time Hazel's consciousness began to blacken, Clayton's grip released enough to bring her back a moment. Her head lolled and her tongue stuck out through a droopy smile. Her sex was being plundered now; it was squirming around the piston-rod of resilient flesh. All the while, the higher and higher she got, the combination of rising sexual sensations merged with the effect of decreased oxygen to the brain producing a heroin-like euphoria. For the third time, she began to climax hard . . .

Her consciousness fell into dead space; the black-out seized her, lingering. Through cracks in the lightless curtain of her soul, she saw her father peering at her, in tears . . .

She revived as if rising from a tar pit. When her eyes reopened she saw nothing at first. Her heart was missing beats but eventually corrected itself. When her vision finally focused . . .

What's he . . . doing . . . now?

The scene formed in front of her. She remained on the bed, her ass propped and legs spread wide. Shot Glass remained kneeling between them, though he'd withdrawn his erection and was now frenetically masturbating . . .

"Aw, fuck, theer! Theer she goes!"

Clayton giggled manically behind her.

Shot Glass did not spend himself on her belly as she thought he would. Instead—

Oh my God . . .

—he was carefully masturbating into the object of his namesake: a shot glass. Hazel watched with incredulity at each white spurt that fired into the tiny glass.

"Uuuuuuuuuh . . . Ee-yuh . . ."

When he'd finished, his cock fell away limp. He held the shot glass up for her to examine.

Clayton giggled slobberingly into her ear. "See? That there's why they call him 'Shot Glass . . . '"

"I'm like thet coffee, yew know? Chock Full'a *Nut.*"

The shot glass was almost full to the top with sperm.

"Heer ya go, reddy-head. Open up."

Hazel's eyes crossed at the prospect. "No way. That's ridiculous. You can't possibly expect me to swallow that much cum."

Whap!

All of the air in Hazel's lungs vaulted out. Shot Glass had pile-driven his fist straight down into her solar plexus. At the same time, Clayton had reapplied his asphyxiating grip to her throat.

She flopped fishlike on the bed, face bluing. It had been fun before but now it was excruciating. She couldn't breathe.

Shot Glass's voice sounded as though it was coming from the end of a long echoic tunnel. "Curn't believe the sass'a this 'un, eh?"

"Dag straight. Ya do a bitch a favor, then she talks shitty to ya."

"Curn't have that, new-sir."

Clayton released the grip; Hazel turned limp as wet rags on the bed, wheezing.

"Naow," Shot Glass addressed her. He held the shot glass forward. "Yew were sayin'?"

Aw, jeeeeeze . . . Hazel craned her head back and opened her mouth. Both men chuckled as the shot glass was tipped, and nearly an entire ounce of semen was poured into her mouth. Nauseated, she let it sit there, dreading the inevitable, then she counted to three in her mind and swallowed.

"Yew're welcome," Shot Glass sniggered.

"Look at it this way, red. Ya just got free lunch."

Both men climbed off the bed.

Exhausted and still out of breath, Hazel could only remain sitting up in the filthy bed, staring at them. Shot Glass, limp dick dangling, went to the refrigerator for still more beer. Clayton looked all the more ludicrous: fat, dirty, and without pants. He thunked toward the back door. "Be's right back. I gots ta pee."

"Me tew," Shot Glass said and for a moment moved toward the door as well. But then he stopped on a dime.

"Wait a sec', Clayton. What're we thinkin'? Why we goin' aoutside when the toilet's right *heer?*"

He pronounced *toilet* as "tur-let."

Hazel's face seemed to wither, and by now, she didn't even have the energy to object. Shot Glass knelt up to her on the mangy bed. He slipped the flaccid cock right into her mouth. Hazel squeezed her eyes shut, waiting for his void, but instead, he held off, and called out, "What jew doin', Clayton? Come on."

"Huh?"

Shot Glass waved him toward the bed. "Get right up heer next ta me'n get yew're willy in her yap. Let's *double-fill* the bitch. Both the same time."

Fat, stupid, and pantsless, Clayton hesitated. "Aw, shee-it, Shot Glass. I don't know. My dick stuck in there right next ta yers? Sounds kind'a queer, don't it?"

Shot Glass frowned. "En't queer if'n it's a *gal's* maouth we're pissin' in!"

Clayton shrugged, gut roll hanging. "Guess yer right," and then he knelt right up next to his partner and slid his penis into Hazel's already burdened mouth. Both men began to giggle as the whizzing commenced.

Dual hot jets fired into the back of her throat. Hazel put the whys and wherefores out of mind, to solely concentrate on her task. Her throat worked desperately, machinelike, to swallow the urine in enough time to make room for more. She strained forward, not daring to think what might happen if she regurgitated, or simply hacked on them.

"Theer, ya go, theer ya go," Shot Glass kept saying, fist to hip, pissing away. "Seems a waste ta piss in the lake when we'se got a perfectly good gal's breadbasket ta pee in."

"I hear that!" railed Clayton.

They pissed for several minutes more, Hazel managing to swallow almost all of it. Yesterday had been *nothing* compared to this. Just how much in liquid volume could they possibly *put* in her?

And worse, exactly how much *piss* could a 105-pound woman drink before her stomach burst?

When she thought she would die, the dual jets abated. The men withdrew, chortling, leaving Hazel to sit spread-legged, pot-bellied, and filled to rupturing with atrocious, sloshing heat.

"Tune ya up enough, did we?" Shot Glass asked, grinning as he reached for yet another can of beer.

Fuck, Hazel thought.

"Now do our laundry'n git this placed cleaned up," Clayton yapped, then both of them roared laughter.

Why on earth did I ever come here? she asked herself, then plodded off the bed. Her stomach did indeed audibly slosh as she trudged back to the "kitchen" and dazedly put her shirt and shorts back on. *I'm out of here and I'm never coming back . . .*

"Have a nice day, sweetie!" Clayton bid, yuckling. "'Member ta put on a happy face!"

"Shuh ya durn't wanna stick araound?" Shot Glass blared. "Yew know. We could cuddle some, hold hands'n read poetry."

The shack nearly rocked from their laughter. Hazel staggered toward the door, stupefied. It was some inner-sense, however, that halted her at the entry. She coughed, blinked, took a deep breath. *I need to get all this piss out of me,* her mind wandered but at the same time her eyes had roamed to the can-littered table. Next to an opened bag of potato chips rested a travel book, *New York City for Dummies.* Also, in the dip of a corroded couch cushion was another book, *Fodor's Guide to Mexico City.*

This didn't sound right. She pointed to the books. "So you guys travel, huh? *You* guys?"

Both of the men looked at each other as if concealing some secret satisfaction. "Aw, ee-yuh," Shot Glass affirmed. "I'se goin' to Mexico City'n Clayton heer's goin' to New Jork."

Hazel peered at them in spite of her exhaustion. "Travel *much,* do you?"

"Waal, new, en't never traveled to speak'a. But we figgure why not? Hard-workin' dudes like us? Weer entitled to a vacation."

Hard-workin' dudes . . . "Mmm. How peculiar," Hazel murmured.

"What thet, missy? Sumpin' *wrong* with us goin' on vacation?" Shot Glass snapped.

"You guys just don't strike me as traveling types. And you're best friends, presumably."

"So?" Clayton demanded, holding a beer. He *still* had not put his pants back on.

"Since you're friends," Hazel conjectured, "I would think you'd travel together—"

"What, you sayin' weer *homos?*" Shot Glass tested her.

"For God's sake!" Hazel exclaimed. "Neither of you have traveled before but one's going to *New York* and the other to *Mexico City?* Why those places, and why not together? It just seems . . . odd to me." The only thing more unlikely was the lowbrow barmaid, Ida, getting ready to go to *Sao Paulo,* of all places. This wasn't adding up.

Shot Glass's patience was ruffling. "Odd, huh? Waal I'll tell ya, only thing seems *odd* to me is *yew* still standing theer. We just bilge-pumped yer tits'n pussy and then put enough piss in yew ta fill a kiddie pool."

"Yeah," Clayton moronically concurred. "Best you git-cher ass out'a here, 'less'n we decide to do a *real* job on ya."

Hazel's volition told her to move toward the door at once—to *leave* . . . She even saw Clayton errantly rubbing his cock, which suddenly looked half-hard again. *If these two scumbags get their dicks up again . . . I know exactly where they're gonna put them . . .*

Nevertheless, her feet remained where she stood.

She put a hand to her nauseous belly, then looked back at them. "I need to know how to get to a place called the Gray Cottage."

Silence.

Shot Glass froze mid-sip. Clayton slowed playing with himself as he peered at her.

"En't never heerd'a no Gray Cottage," Shot Glass told her with a sharp smirk.

"Me neither," Clayton gruffed, oddly defensive.

"Bullshit," she retorted. "You know what I'm talking about. What is it with people around here? The barmaid at the tavern says the place doesn't exist, while two other people I talked to say they've heard of it but don't know how to get there, and now you two jokers say you've never even *heard* of it. But it *does* exist; I know that for fact."

"Oh, dew ya naow?"

"Yeah. It's supposed to be up on Whipple's Peak someplace, where all that mist is. You guys live here, you *must* know of a trail that leads to it."

Shot Glass flapped his hand. "Aw, it en't up on Whipple, it's way over at Mount Washington—"

"Oh, so you *have* heard of it," Hazel challenged, and when he'd told her *that*, she received the immediate impression that he was deliberately giving her false information.

Why?

The dilapidated room grew tense. Shot Glass rubbed a fist in his palm. "Yew sassin' us again, girlie?"

"Yeah!" Clayton demanded. "Sounds like youre' gittin' too big fer them whory britches. Want us ta loosen 'em up a tad fer ya?"

"Yew ask tew many questions, reddy-head, and it's gettin' my dander up. So why'n'chew get aout'a heer afore I kick you in the cunt so hard yew're fuckin' ovaries slide aout'cher nose?"

"What is the *big deal?*" Hazel insisted. "All I'm asking for is a little help finding this place. Shit, it's the least you could do."

Shot Glass's neck stiffened as his eyes leveled. "What'chew mean by *thet?*"

Hazel sputtered. "For fuck's sake! I just let you two animals use my body for Pervert Party Central! All I'm asking for is a favor! Tell me how to find the Gray Cottage!"

"Oh, so we owe *yew* a favor, huh?" Shot Glass mocked. "Waal, then . . . Clayton!" he snapped. "Hold her up!"

The fat one had already slipped behind, and in a second he'd chicken-winged her. She shrieked when he pulled her elbows so close they touched.

"All right!" she screamed. "I'll leave! Let me go!"

"Heer's yer favor, missy—"

Fwump!

Hazel's body jerked up when Shot Glass kicked her right in the crotch, punter-style. Clayton didn't let go when the impact drove her feet off the floor. Then the pain set in . . .

Had he broken her pubic bone? She could only pray that the violence didn't burst any organs or cause internal bleeding.

"Heh, heh, heh. Think yew larnt yew're lesson 'baout askin' questions thet en't yew're business?"

Half-doubled over, Hazel drew her gaze up to see Shot Glass standing tall and snide, arms crossed. She took note of his hand . . .

Another one . . .

He wore a scarlet-stoned ring.

Her voice ground like gravel. "What's that ring you're wearing?"

Shot Glass's face drew seams when he stared closer. "I'se durn't believe this! We just warnt the bitch not to ask questions, so what she dew?" Shot Glass bellowed: "Ask another question!" He reached up and grabbed the light fixture hanging from the kitchen ceiling, then—

He shattered the unshaded bulb against the counter-top, then . . . put on a black rubber glove.

Hazel began to squeal and kick, but the effort was useless; Clayton only tightened his grip on her elbows. Shot Glass pulled her top up, then, with the gloved hand, squeezed her right breast. The nipple remained distended from the suction machine.

"Don't you dare!" she screamed. "Don't you—"

Zap!

Shot Glass meticulously touched both of the broken bulb's lead-stems to Hazel's swollen nipple. After the zap there was a crackle.

She flopped upward from the shock, which felt more like the impact of a two-by-four than an actual shock. Though the contact lasted only a second, her legs agitated involuntarily. The entire right side of her chest throbbed in a strange sensation of tingling, burning, and numbness.

"One more time fer posterior sake," Clayton urged. "Like my daddy used to say."

Even in her horror and unrelieved agony, Hazel couldn't help it: "That's *posterity,* you dogshit-for-brains, useless fat vagabond—"

Zap!

crackle . . .

The second jolt zapped her left nipple. Hazel howled.

"What'chew think, Clayton? She larn't huh lesson?"

"Yes, yes, I have!" Hazel wheezed.

"Naaaaw . . ."

The third jolt kicked her feet a yard off the floor and bent her spine forward like a pretzel. Shot Glass had reapplied the bulb's 110-volt lead-stems this time to Hazel's crotch . . .

She fell limp in Clayton's arm's, vibrating in the aftermath.

"Had enough, reddy-head?"

Hazel, barely cognizant, nodded.

"Durn't come 'raound heer no more. Weer sick'a yer red-hairt pussy'n sass. Clayton?"

Hazel's heels dragged against the floor as she was moved out to the porch, stood up limply at the step, and *pushed.*

She bowled forward, staggered, then fell—*splat!*—into the sea of mud that made up the driveway. She landed face-first.

"Heh, heh, heh—Yew think little missy'll be back tomorrow?"

"Shore hope so! We'se can have tea'n crumpets!"

Nothing particularly sentient occupied Hazel's mind at that moment, only her awareness of her outrage and her pain and her stupidity. Just one coherent thought sparked: *I'm SO LUCKY to be alive* . . . Mud-spattered, she eventually teetered to her feet, then cupped her aching crotch with her hands. Her nipples sizzled in a low, steady pain. Then she groaned when she remembered that she was still full of beer-piss. She staggered away down the drive, Shot Glass and Clayton hew-hawing laughter behind her. When she took a final dismal glance back, she saw that Clayton, too, wore one of the crude, crimson rings.

Oh my God, oh my God, oh my God, her thoughts droned with each imprecise step. Flipflops long gone, her bare feet eventually *schlupped* their way off the driveway to the paved, secondary road. She paused when her heart skipped a few beats, then managed to pull herself back from a probable fainting spell. When more awareness sparked, she bent over right on the road's shoulder, jammed two fingers down her throat, and forced herself to vomit. Gushes of urine flew out—more than a few. *I must be the only woman in history to vomit up redneck piss TWO days in a row . . .*

When it was all out, she staggered on, then turned onto a wooded nook which led down to the lake shore. Next thing she knew she was trudging into the cold, raw water to let all the horrendous filth of the day wash off of her body.

I asked for it, and I got it, she thought. *No one to blame but myself.* She took her shorts and top off in the water, rung them out and rinsed them over and over. When she came back to shore, she examined herself for physical damage. Fortunately no bleeding was in evidence between her legs, and no marks from the shock through her shorts. Her breasts were another story, though. The suction machine had been bad enough, but the electric jolts left them twice as swollen, with a minute burn-mark on either sides of the areolae. *Thank God,* she spared the final thought, then rung her clothes out as best she could, re-dressed, and went back to the road.

She knew what had compelled her to go there: her sickness, her *paraphilia*—triggered by the disappointment of missing her chance with Sonia. *I don't even remember getting it on with her. I must've done it in my sleep . . .*

But what had urged her to ask questions, questions that only irked her detestable assailants further, to the point of molesting her, of beating her, electrifying her?

Too many things were brewing now. These odd rings, commonplace rural folk anticipating trips to *Sao Paulo, Mexico City, New York?* And Frank's uncharacteristic absence and bizarre behavior. Then the problem still remained: was there really an ancient stone cottage up on the mountain? Hazel felt certain there was. *So why can't I get a straight answer from anyone?*

A half hour of walking revived her. The pain receded somewhat, but by now her senses sharpened. She could've been maimed, critically injured, or killed, she knew, yet somehow she'd escaped those fates and was now walking home as though nothing happened. *And that's what I have to act like when I'm back at Henry's cabin,* she knew. *Like nothing happened . . .*

The day bloomed beautifully before her: flawless sunlight beaming through a cloud-free sky. The dizzyingly tall trees on either side shimmered in luscious, shifting greens. Birds sang *en masse.* Before long she was actually smiling as she limped along the road, but the smile faded when her cellphone rang and she saw that it was not Sonia but Ashton.

Just what I need . . . Why didn't she want to answer it? She liked Ashton but . . . She let the voice mail get it, waited a moment, then listened: "Hazel, it's me again—big surprise. I don't know why it's so hard for you to answer the phone but . . . Anyway, call me back, will you please? I've probably left a half a dozen messages since you left; I just want to know that you're okay. I suppose I'd be worried to death but I just spoke to your father and he says he talked to you yesterday." A long pause on the line. "I just . . . miss you. Oh, and I wanted to tell you about your father's new church; I had a look at it this morning. It's beautiful, and, well, you know, your father's a little bit hurt that you haven't been there yet—"

Oh my God! Hazel thought. *If it's not my dad making me feel guilty, it's Ashton!*

"So why don't we plan to do that when you're back from this trip, okay? It would make your father very happy . . . Anyway, uh, I hope to hear from you soon, and I love you—"

That was enough for Hazel; she put the phone away. *Now is not the time for some guy to be telling me he loves me,* and then she immediately thought of Sonia . . . and continued to curse herself for not even being able to remember what had happened between them last night.

When she'd made it back to the cabin, she felt frantic to wash. *Quiet,* she thought, for Sonia was napping. The ceiling fans were blowing, and the shades had been pulled down over the open windows, leaving the place grainy in half-dark. She stripped off her clothes, then snuck to the shower cubby. She pumped the cumbersome shower, the cold water raising gooseflesh. Perhaps it was a subconscious endeavor to punish herself by not heating the water first. Teeth chattering she lathered herself, scrubbed hard, then rinsed off but it was necessary to repeat the procedure two more times before she felt clean. *Obsessive-compulsive,* she half-joked to herself; she even scrubbed her tiny cross and then actually splashed Listerine on it. *Forgive me, forgive me,* came the aimless thought, and then she wilted when she looked down at her wet, naked body: the abused nipples still protruding from the suction machine, and her aching sex swollen and over-tender from the vicious kick, compliments of Shot Glass. *Bastards . . . Pieces of shit . . .* But of course she'd only wound up getting what she'd asked for.

She tip-toed back to the front room and put on clean shorts and a halter, then paused to look dreamily at Sonia who remained asleep atop the sheets. *I should get into bed with her,* she considered but then realized that would backfire. Sonia's mood would remain ruined by her upset over Frank. Instead, Hazel grabbed her camera, then quietly went up the metal ladder next to the shower room, pushed open the trapdoor, and climbed onto the roof.

The sun *blazed. Now THAT'S what I call scenery,* she thought. If she positioned herself right, she could look straight down the direction of the driveway through a wide break in the trees and see just how expansive Lake Sladder was. The parts of town that were visible looked tiny but meticulously detailed. She took several photos.

Without realizing it, she was craning her neck. Another lucky vantage point showed her the ominous rise of Whipple's Peak which now, for some reason, looked so immense it appeared unreal. After squinting—*There it is!*—she made out the clot of mist that Horace had indicated. The mist hung just before the bluff, which looked so steep now it made her dizzy to imagine being up there. But—

What's the cause of that mist? It just seemed to sit there at the peak, a pale smear.

Was there really a cottage concealed within it?

And is Frank really there?

She dawdled around some more on the roof, then caught herself eyeing a very tall tree—a white pine, she believed—that spired right next to the cabin, so close that she could stand on the eave and touch the bark. She heard birds rustling amid the density of branches, noticed several bowls sticking out of the trunk like holed warts. She smiled when she noticed sparrows nesting in one. Next, though, she was leaning over slightly, hands on knees . . .

A track of splintery gouges were evident in the bark—she thought oddly of teethmarks—spaced by several feet and appearing fairly regular. The tracks led at least fifty feet up the fat, towering tree.

What the hell are those? she wondered but then the answer snapped. The gouges could only have been made by something metal, and that's when she remembered those pole-climbing boots that Henry Wilmarth had mysteriously left in the garbage can.

He must've used them to climb THIS tree, she realized for when she looked around at the other trees in proximity to the dwelling, they were all free of the gouges.

Why on earth would he want to do that?

Hazel was back down the ladder and sneaking out the front door a minute later. *I'll bet the garbage men already came,* she suspected but when she opened the can at the end of the drive, the implements were still there. *Henry was almost sixty, and if he could do it, I can do it,* she reasoned. She collected the spiked boots and buckled strap of leather that the receipt called a "tree-scaling belt."

"Can't hurt to check it out," she talked to herself, and besides, from a position high in the tree she'd be able to get some spectacular pictures. She tip-toed back through the cabin, grabbed a pair of work gloves from the kitchen, then went back up to the roof. *I'm a twenty-two year old with a Masters degree,* she reminded herself. *I should be able to figure this out . . .* She sat awkwardly on the roof and strapped on the spiked boots. Standing, then, was even more awkward, but she managed to clip-clop to the eave, flail the scaling belt around the great pine's trunk, then thread it behind her back and secure the clasp. *And now . . .* She put one spiked foot against the tree, took a breath, then hopped off the eave, sinking the second boot into the bark as well. *Simple!* All that remained was the incremental process of hitching the belt up several feet, leaning back, then stepping higher with each boot. She used the previous track-marks as a guide.

Ten minutes later she was nearly sixty feet aloft, within the middle of the tree.

Oh, wow! She leaned back, feeling utterly secure by the belt and spikes. She aimed her digital camera, forwarded the zoom, and snapped several stunning pictures of Lake Sladder and the town. She also noticed several tree bowls protruding, a few sporting nests crowded with tiny peeping birds. She took several more pictures.

But the original track-marks that Henry had made . . . proceeded higher.

Hazel proceeded higher. *I'm a natural!* she celebrated. Soon, she was nearly a hundred feet up the ancient tree, surrounded by heavy branches. The next series of snapshots would be even better.

She contemplated going higher but noticed that Henry's track-marks had stopped. *Don't get carried away,* she considered. Better to retreat and get back into the cabin; then she could download the pictures into her laptop and see them in better clarity. She was about to do just that, when . . .

A tree bowl, dinner-plate-sized, stared her right in the face just as she prepared to lower the scaling belt. Yet no bird nest was evident. Instead, the hole within had been filled with something black and—when she touched a gloved finger to it—tacky, like tar . . .

That tree-patch stuff, she recalled. The empty can had been tossed in the garbage.

The rest was simple deductive reasoning. When Henry had scaled this tree less than a week it ago, he'd done so for the purpose of filling this bowl with patch. However . . .

None of the other bowls have been patched, she knew. *So . . .*

Why had a man nearly sixty, bent on suicide, climbed a hundred feet up this tree, just to patch a single bowl, then go back down and put the climbing gear in the garbage?

At once Hazel pressed a gloved hand into the black semi-shiny surface of the patch material. It hadn't hardened much; the sun kept it pliable as modeling clay.

There's something in here, she knew for a fact, and then began to pull out sloughs of the tar-like patch. After digging half of it out and flapping it down to the ground, she felt a bump within the bowl. The bump moved. She twisted her fingers around, then—

Come out, you fucker!

—extracted the tar-covered lump. A thrill pumped through her when she noted its basic egg shape, and its length of four inches and perhaps three in depth.

This HAS to be it! Henry hid it HERE!

The Shining Trapezohedron.

Less than ten minutes later, she was back in the cabin, the scaling gear abandoned. She stood bent over the kitchen counter and commenced with the effort of cleaning the odd stone, first wiping off as much of the tar as possible with paper towels, then scrubbing more meticulously.

A half-hour later, she thought, *Fuck!* Her wrists and fingers ached. The thin layer of tar that remained would require much more effort to remove completely. *I need some kind of cleaner,* she resolved. Doing it this way would take forever.

"Oh, there you are," came Sonia's groggy voice from behind.

"Shit, sorry, I must've woken you—"

"No, no." Sonia, hair tousled, got a soda from the fridge. "I've been sleeping for hours—jeez."

Hazel looked at her. "Did—" she began, then bit her lip.

"No, I haven't heard from Frank, that asshole." Sonia rubbed her eyes. For a woman who'd just had a several-hour nap, she looked, if anything, like she needed *more* sleep. "It really bothers me."

Hazel struggled for something to say in consolation but knew there was nothing.

"Anyway, I'm really sorry I abandoned you at Harold's trailer."

"Horace," Hazel corrected. "And it's okay. You needed your own space. I had—" Circumstance forced her to pause. "I had a nice walk around," but then thought, *Actually, I got raped, beat up, and electrocuted AND I had a ton of orgasms. See how fucked up I am?*

"I'm glad," Sonia said, then squinted at the black lump on the counter. "What is *that?*"

"The Shining Trapezohedron, believe it or not."

"The stone Henry said he got rid of?"

"Um-hmm. Long story short, I found it stuck in a tree bowel and covered with that black tree-tar stuff."

Sonia chuckled. "So much for Henry's 'irretrievable' disposal."

"Actually, it was pretty clever. Something he didn't want found so he hides it close to the house—"

"The last place anyone would think to look. Like Poe's 'Purloined Letter.' But how did you—"

Hazel shrugged. "I lucked onto it," she said. "But it's covered with this black stuff and I can't get it off. I'm dying to see it cleaned up. The jpeg on Henry's computer was astonishing—the colors, especially—so the real thing will be even better."

"Tree tar, huh? If you used a Brillo, it might scratch the surface."

Hazel scrubbed her hands now. "I'll have to get cleaning solvent—"

"Any hydrocarbon would probably work fine, rubbing alcohol, gasoline—hell, maybe even Henry's bottle of whiskey."

"I'll do it later—my fingers are cramping from all this scrubbing." Hazel followed her friend into the front room, where they both sat on the edge of the bed. Sonia was staring off into space.

"Stop worrying," Hazel whispered. "It's not good for you."

"I don't know if I'm worrying or *seething.*" Sonia anxiously clutched her knee. "I'm thinking . . . that maybe I should just call off the wedding."

Hazel knew she had to be careful in any attendant remark. "Listen. Sonia. I'm *not* sticking up for him, but I think that would be a serious overreaction."

Sonia rubbed her temples. "You're right, and I *do* overreact to things but—Jesus!—this really hurts."

Hazel put her arm around her. "Men are tubesteaks—that's just the way it is. We put up with their shit and they put up with ours."

"How fair of you!" Sonia managed a chuckle.

"Just let him get all this Henry stuff out of the way, then he'll be fine. And if he's not?" Hazel spread out her hands. "Then we'll pull his balls off and hang them on the rearview mirror like sponge dice."

Sonia laughed sluggishly. "I wish I could be as matter-of-fact and sensible as you. I'm going to try, at least." She stilled herself a moment. "But . . . isn't it human nature to be jealous sometimes, or suspicious or insecure or paranoid?"

"Sometimes, sure."

"And what should I do if he's not back tomorrow afternoon? What if he calls up again and makes more excuses for not being here?"

"Well . . ."

Sonia wrung her hands. "If he's not back tomorrow . . . I'm going to climb up that fucking summit or mountain or whatever it is and confront him."

Hazel hugged her. "*That's* reasonable, *if* he's not back tomorrow afternoon. But you're not going to go, *I'm* going to go."

"Hazel, it's my headache, not yours."

"You're eight months pregnant and have doctor's orders not to exert yourself," Hazel reminded. "I actually talked to some people today, about how to get to the cottage."

"Really?" Sonia asked, surprised.

"Horace says his grandmother told him the place was right at the top where that fog bank is. He also estimated it'd take a half a day just to get up there, so that's why I'm going, not you." Hazel felt confident about the task, should it become necessary. "But let's just give Frank another day and see."

Sonia nodded. "You're wonderful, Hazel. I don't know what I'd do without you . . ."

The words made Hazel's head go light. Then she could've melted when Sonia kissed her on the cheek.

Please, please, Hazel pleaded.

"I'm just so tired, I don't get it." Sonia yawned with a frustrated expression. "I shouldn't be this tired, especially after the nap."

"Stress," Hazel offered. "Worrying about Frank's got you worn out." She hugged her, resisted making an advance, then just smiled and said, "Get some more sleep. I'll wake you up for dinner. I noticed a grill out back—we'll have a cookout later. I'll cook you something."

"Mmm," Sonia murmured, "you're sweet . . ." Then she was asleep again.

Hazel spent the next few hours trying to get Henry's computer back to rights–to no avail–and another hour after that trying to get all the tar off the Shining Trapezohedron: impossible without some sort of cleaning liquid. She put it out in the car, knowing that in the morning the sun would heat it up and make the tar less adhesive. She truly did want to see the crystal in all its shining spectacle. Later, she drove into town and bought some fresh walleye from a market, plus some asparagus and potatoes. After waking Sonia at six, they'd had a fabulous backyard feast.

But her friend's distress over Frank's behavior never let go. Sonia remained distracted and on edge, in spite of an obvious effort not to seem that way. They sat outside till past dark, watched fireflies and listened to peepers, then went to bed.

Hazel essentially *winced* herself to sleep, first, from trying to banish the obscene dichotomy: the abhorrent things the "Fish Boys" had done to her along with the fact she'd received an extraordinary satisfaction from the foray. Also, being in the bed with Sonia but not being able to make love to her only compounded her frustration. Worse was knowing that last night they'd shared some potent intimacy but, of course . . . *I don't remember any of it* . . . Several lovers in her past had complained that she talked in her sleep but was also periodically subject to sleep-walking. *Last night I guess I was sleep-FUCKING.* Consciously missing out on what she wanted so dearly only made her feel more dismal. Eventually, though, she did drift off to the soft hum of the ceiling fans—

—the night cocoons you as you lay naked and sweating in the bed, but all you see is darkness at first. Has the backdrop of your sleeping mind turned into a black chasm? Suddenly your spirit spins propeller-like as huge, wet words croak and echo in the chasm and begin to spin, spin, spin, spin around with your mauled spirit: *algolagniac one who receives sexual satisfaction from pain dritiphily sexual stimulation derived from being covered with or in proximity to filth asphyxophile one who longs to be strangled during sex biastiphilia sexual obsession with being brutalized and raped hybristolaglia the desire to engage in sexual congress with degenerates and criminals asthenopagniac one attracted to being humiliated and overpowered and beaten cyesolagnia sexual excitement from pregnant women urophily the compulsion to be urinated on.* Then:

sick sick sick sick sick

Then:

you you you you you

And round and round you spin as more huge, wet, sloppy words cram into the spiral: *Hazel my child I adjure you my dear friend Frank if you're reading this then I am already dead eat the cum out of the toilet is the key by where the spheres meet this ungodly harlot needs to die full of the cur's jism anyway uh I hope to hear from you soon and I love you the tenets of Non-Euclideanism have the potential to produce unlimited energy they could transpose objects of unequal weight and mass between two points of vast distance en't much I'd ruther dew'n piss up a gal's backside you don't understand I've found still more of Henry's work up here—it's spellbinding when a gal gets a pussy full'a Shoggoth cum it don't take but a minute or two letter weren't signed just said he represented Henry's gemolergy friends and they wanted more boxes thought it were a mite foolish a joke mebbe until I opened another envelope inside that had five thousand bucks in it my dreams have turned ghastly indeed tinged by a grotesque carnality unlike anything in my experience sometimes even—I swear—people (or things* like *people) make utterances in my dreams that reveal information which I verify later en't never heerd'a no gray cottage yogsothoth and his retinue were are and shall ever be not in spaces known but between those spaces waiting the ghosts of all those dead from the storm follow me everywhere please come back to church come back to God it's where you belong honey please don't insult my memory Frank—*

—forget that goddamned stone ever existed . . .

The black blood of the chasm clears and then . . . you can see. You can see *yourself.*

"Just got me a hankerin', yew know? 'N I carn't think of a reason not tew."

"Shit-yeah, Shot Glass!"

"I gotta *see* what's in this heer big belly, heh, heh, heh . . ."

Your spirit plummets when you realize you are back in the nefarious shack of the Fish Boys. You sit nude on the rot-wood floor, your sex aching, lines of gelatinous sperm up and down your chest like slug trails, like white snot. You can smell it wafting up–all that sperm spattered on you in sport. Shackles gird your ankles; a chain between them is bolted to the floor. You look up . . .

"You fuckers! Stay away from her!" you scream bloody murder. "I swear to God I'll kill both you loser redneck motherfuckers if you lay one hand on her!"

Sonia has been stretched across one of the foul-stained beds, nude, gagged, and shivering in horror. She lay in an X-configuration, ankles and wrists tied to each bedpost. Her great gravid stomach sticks out, gleaming in sweat, the navel popped out like an acorn of flesh.

Shot Glass smooths callused hands over the slick belly. "Heh, heh, heh. Heh, heh, heh," then his gaze shoots to you. "Weer gonna make this big-belly-bitch give it *up,* reddy-head." He stands grinning with his limp cock dangling from his zipper. "And *yew* get to watch."

"Yeah!" Clayton rails, giggling and jumping up and down. He stands fat and malodorous as ever, his pants off, fecal smears at his hairy buttocks. He reaches into a can of lard, scoops out a handful, and spreads the pale glop over the end—

"What are you evil cocksuckers doing!" you scream.

—of the clear plastic nozzle that you're all-too-familiar with. Then he kneels at the edge of the bed and, after some finessing, manages to insert the tube several inches into Sonia's vaginal canal.

"Take that out of there! Don't you dare, you sick pieces of shit! Leave her alone!"

Shot Glass winks, then turns on the bilge pump.

The motor screams. Sonia's body goes rigid as she arches her back on the bed, trying to scream through her gag. Shot Glass and Clayton's wicked laughter can barely be heard over the pump motor's rising, insane whine. Shot Glass pushes down on her belly while Clayton pushes the nozzle in deeper.

"Git aout'a theer! Git aout!" Shot Glass hoots, then turns the machine on HIGH.

The motor's scream is now deafening. It is a sound truly forged in Hell. Sonia squirms on the bed, balloon-cheeked as the industrial suction works harder against what can only be her cervical cap.

"Stop it! Stop!" you scream over and over till your eyeballs are fit to eject, but even from the bottom of your lungs, your pleas cannot be heard over the motor's scream.

Whole minutes go by like this . . .

Finally, Shot Glass and Clayton cast incredulous expressions when the bilge pump cuts off and the insane whine grinds down to nothing.

Clayton scratches his beard. "What happened?"

"Bilge pump's motor burnt up!"

"Dang! Bitch's pussy done wore it out!"

Shot Glass shakes his head, drags the nozzle out, and looks perplexed at it. "Didn't even bust her water. En't that somethin'?"

"Shore is, Shot Glass!"

Sonia's eyes are insanely wide now as she shudders on the monstrous bed.

Thank God! you think. But—But what now? "There, you've had your fun! Now let us go! I'll give you money, I'll give you the car–anything, just let us go!"

"Heer thet, Clayton?"

"Shee-it!"

Shot Glass goes to the counter, then reappears with not one but two lamps, each with shattered bulbs.

Oh my God NO . . .

"En't never seed a baby come aout afore," Shot Glass said. "So's weer gonna make yew're friend have aout with it." He holds up the lamp-ends. "One way're another, that kid's comin *aout.*"

Then the madness resumes. Sonia begins to flipflop on the mattress as Shot Glass and Clayton each wield a lamp, bearing the live lead-stems to her nipples. You hear the familiar *Zap!* followed by a crackle. Sonia's teeth can be seen grinding her gag. After a while, tendrils of smoke trail up from the tortured areolae. "Naow thet we got'er primed," Shot Glass remarks, "let's do daown heer."

You scream and scream and scream as they begin to alternately zap Sonia's navel and clitoris.

Zap!

crackle . . .
Zap!
crackle . . .
Zap!
crackle . . .

Repeatedly, they hold the lead-stems down for several seconds, which causes Sonia to convulse and actually sizzle. Her hair stands on end, and even the tuft of her pubic hair swells out from static. Then they begin to zap all around the circumference of her swollen stomach.

By the time they stop, you've screamed your throat raw. Sonia lay still alive, shuddering with her eyes peeled open. Her eyes' whites have long-since turned red from hemorrhage.

Shot Glass now appears annoyed by their repeated failure to effect miscarriage. "This bitch's womb is tougher to crack than a fuckin' floor safe, Clayton. I durn't understand it."

"Shore is one tough cunt."

Burn marks pock Sonia's belly. There's an awful redolence in the room which can only be seared skin and burnt labial flesh.

"Lemme just go get the twenty-pound sledge," Clayton offers. "Shee-it, we'll *beat* the kid out of her."

"Please please please, just STOP!" you rasp. "Why are you doing this?"

Shot Glass frowns over at your query. "Why we doin' it? What'cha think, missy? Weer doin' it 'cos it's *fun!*"

Then they both begin to cackle again, Clayton actually flapping his penis up and down in amusement.

"New, the sledge en't special enough, Clayton—"

"Special?"

"Ee-yuh. Got no style, yew know?"

"Style?"

Shot Glass rolls his eyes. "Clayton, any ole moe-ron cud think'a thet! We need sumpin' en't been done afore. Hmm . . ." He swigs some beer in rumination. "Aw, I got a ideer!"

"Please my God I'm begging you would you PLEASE not do this! Do it to me, not her! Just PLEASE let her go—"

"Clayton, I'm sick'a heerin' that 'un. En't nothin' wuss than a sassy bitch with a laoud moauth. Haow 'boaut shuttin' her up?"

With surprising agility, Clayton thumps over and—

Smack!

—sweeps a rank bare foot right across the side of your head. You topple over, your chains straining and your senses shatter like a window.

It's mostly a grainy veil of semi-consciousness that cloaks your mind now. "Heh, heh, heh. Heh, heh, heh," you keep hearing. You hear your chains clink as you attempt to drag yourself forward. When you try to keep your eyes open, they keep dragging shut.

"Heh, heh, heh. Heh, heh, heh . . ."

Your hand slides across your chest, through tacky sperm, to desperately touch your cross. *Help me, God,* comes your hypocritical supplication. But the cross has changed.

It's now a pentagram.

You try to focus, to shove back the crushing urge to faint. More chains clink as you knee your way toward Sonia. On hands and knees, then, you look at the mangy bed—

And your heart slams in your chest.

For however long you've been dazed or unconscious, now you see what they've been up to.

You leap forward off your knees in an offensive reflex. Tiny warbling squeals can be heard leaking from Sonia's gag as Shot Glass prepares a fair length of rope about the middle of Sonia's stretched stomach.

He ties a knot—"Heh, heh, heh!"—then slips a wooden rod beneath it. Amid the madness, you think one word: *Tourniquet* . . .

Clayton giggles as Shot Glass begins to turn the rod . . .

Your screams fly like glass shattering. Your ankles bleed from the metal fetter and you strain across the floor, useless. Half a turn of the rod sinks the rope into Sonia's belly, like someone tightening a string around a beach ball.

"Crank it, Shot Glass! Crank it!"

"Give it *up!*" and then he casts the most evil grin at you when he slowly turns the rod further. You actually hear the rope creak.

You scream yourself senseless. "I'll do anything! ANYTHING! *Just stop!*"

Shot Glass peers at her. "Anything?"

"YES!" you bellow.

"Hmm." Shot Glass chews his lip, holding the rod to maintain the tourniquet's tension around Sonia's belly. "Would'jew, say, eat Clayton's shit?"

Your mind wobbles. "YES! Just take that rope off her!"

He hesitates, reverses the rod till the rope hangs slack. "Okay, reddy-head, Yew got yew're self a deal. But just so yew know. Clayton eats big so ya gotta figure he *shits* big."

Clayton giggles uncontrollably now. Pantless, dirty, and fat, he thunks toward you, fingering his penis in exuberance. "Down on yer back'n open wide, reddy! I'se gonna shit right in yer purdy mouth!"

At least they'd cancelled their torture of Sonia. You lay back as instructed, open your mouth, but almost scream as Clayton crudely squats right over your face. The canyon of his shit-flecked buttocks lowers, then the vision trebles in horror when he widens that buttocks with his hands to lend a more concise view of puckered, pimpled anus.

"Clayton, try'n feed the turds direct inta her maouth. I'd be pleesed as punch ta see thet."

"Shore thing!"

Open-mouthed, you wait. The abominable cleft now hovers only inches from your lips. When the even more abominable sphincter begins to dilate, you slam your eyes shut.

"Here she comes!"

Clayton's anus squeezes out a stout, firm stool that—

"Eeeeeeeeeeee-YUH!"

—that miraculously slides right between your lips. When it lowers to the back of your throat, you have no choice but to sever it with your teeth, go tense, and swallow. The odor of the process can be imagined, but the taste?

You cannot think about that . . .

With each desperate swallow of each stool-segment, you only have time to re-open your mouth to admit *another* segment.

"Aw, noaw, yew're cheatin'!" you hear Shot Glass complain. "The deal's off if'n ya cheat! Curn't just shalluh, yew gotta *chew . . .*"

The entirety of your soul moans now, but you must do it. It's the only way to save Sonia. You actually chew the next segment, your belly quivering in revolt to what's being forced into it. It's as though your whole face is trying to seal shut against the outrage, but you keep eating none the less; even your mouth shudders as it attempts to manipulate the warm, tight stools. One after another they descend from the hellish clough. Your tongue cannot help but detect corn, arcane grit, bean casings, and other mysterious fecal debris. All you can do is mush it up and gulp it down, your spirit screaming all the way.

"Ee-yuh, naow *thet's* entertainment!" you hear Shot Glass roar.

After another grunting minute or two, Clayton's bowels are relieved. He is kind enough to wipe his ass with the back of your limp hand but you're essentially too mortified to really notice. You're practically convulsant as you lay gog-eyed on the floor with a belly full of hot shit; you're all too aware of its heat and the sense of grotesque *fullness* within you.

Your teeth are creamed with feces, your mouth lined with it. You're helpless to stop the rich, horrendous stench that eddies from your mouth with every breath . . .

But I did it, by God, you think. *I did it!*

"Unlock these shackles and let us go now," you demand.

Shot Glass stands up, parting his hands. "I always keep my promises. A man who durn't keep his word en't wuth nuthin.' Clayton. Let her go."

"Shore, Shot Glass."

You look up expectantly, but then—

"Oh my God, you fuck!"

Clayton turns around and starts pissing hard in your face.

And Shot Glass begins to crank the tourniquet rod once more.

"You lying scumbag evil pieces of redneck FUCK!"

"Heh, heh, heh! Heh, heh, heh!" Shot Glass keeps cranking the rod. The rope constricts tighter and tighter against Sonia's belly. Her body actually bows upward now, with only her heels and her shoulder blades touching the mattress. "Heer she goes, ee-yuh! Ee-yuh!"

Clayton can only maintain his giggling as he shakes the last of his piss off in your face. Then he goes to the bed and removes Sonia's gag—

The scream that bursts from her throat cracks every window in the shack.

"Heh, heh, heh! Heh, heh, heh!"

The rope creaks, digging deeper.

"Pop the kid out!" Clayton cheers.

"YOU CRAZY PSYCHO WHITE TRASH SCUM!" you bellow.

Shot Glass now stands up to crank harder. He pulls against the rod like a lever that won't quite give. Sonia's shrieks sound like brakes with no pads but in between, Shot Glass looks at you and says, "Durn't know what'cher all bent aout'a shape over no ways, reddy. This en't nuthin' but a dream."

"Yeah," Clayton agrees. "*Your* dream. Which means it's just a bunch'a shit from *your* head."

The rope keeps creaking. "But what ya gotta understand is that, here? In this place? The shit from your own head mixes with the shit out theer . . ."

You stare at the madman's words. The revolting mirage from the outhouse—the man with the upside-down face—had said the same thing, hadn't he, and as that idea occurs to you your eyes rove back to, first, Clayton, then Shot Glass. They've changed . . . as if their revelation to you has triggered an allegorical metamorphosis . . .

Their faces are upside-down, the effect of which only makes their sneering, shuck-and-jive, backwater grins all the more hideous. And their genitals—normal only moments ago—now sport maroon spheres for glans and scrotums like sacks of grapes.

"Clayton, heer it comes!"

"Git it! Git it!"

One other thing: their arms have transformed to stout, heavily suckered tentacles.

Sonia's final shriek whistles through the air. There's a long, loud *Crrrrunch* and then a gush of splashing water. You look away just as Sonia's belly begins to collapse.

"Heh, heh, heh . . ."

Shot Glass and Clayton jump up and down in monstrous jubilation, tentacles writhing. A baby begins to hack, and the last thing you see is Shot Glass's inverted face moving closer and closer to yours, the upside-down grin widening, and he explains, "Waal, missy, theer en't but one more thing I have ta say ta yew. Wanna know what it 'tis?"

Your eyes feel lidless as you stare.

"Gub nbb shub naabl e uh bleb nuuurrlathotep . . ."

You scream so hard that blood sprays from your mouth and you—

—woke up in bed next to Sonia, glazed in sweat and shivering beneath the caul of granular darkness stretched across the room. Hazel could hear her heart thunking down. *Oh my God, another nightmare . . . What the FUCK is wrong with me?*

She lay still, recovering from the mudslide of detestable images still in her head. *Calm down, calm down, it's all over . . .*

She turned her head to the left and found Sonia sleeping contentedly. Then she turned her head to the right—

She could see the narrow door to the den; it stood open a few inches, and the desk lamp threw a widening wedge of pale-yellow light on the floor. Had she left the light on earlier, or had Sonia? The prospect made little sense, since Hazel would've noticed it before going to bed.

Something smelled *meaty* in the room, even with the overhead fans going. But her attention was snared not by the odd smell but by rapid, irregular *clicking* sounds which she recognized immediately.

A computer keyboard.

Her eyes widened where she lay, staring at the crack in the den door.

Someone's . . . typing. On one of the computers . . .

There could be no doubt unless, of course, this was another dream . . ."Who's in there?" she called out, but her voice sounded scratchy and feeble in the grainy dark. "I can hear you typing."

"You don't hear anything, Hazel," a man's voice replied quite nonchalantly. "So just shut up."

The voice—she was positive—belonged to Frank.

"Frank, what are you doing in there? How come you didn't wake us up when you got back?"

An annoyed sigh in between pauses of the keyboard. "Because I'm not back." Then a chuckle. "I'm still up at the Gray Cottage. This is a dream, Hazel. Haven't figured that out yet?"

Dream, my ass, she determined then climbed off the bed . . .

She could do little more than *try* to get off the bed, however. She propped up on her hands, tried to swing her legs out but suddenly a horrendous pressure was pushing down on her. Was she having a stroke, a heart attack? *No,* she realized. *No symptoms, no pain. So why*—It was as though the gravity of the space she occupied had increased tenfold. "Frank! This is fucked up!" she yelled, yet the brassy exclamation did not stir Sonia from her sleep.

Another chuckle from the den. "Hazel, the only thing fucked up in this house is *you.*"

"Asshole! Help me up!"

Her plea was answered only by more key-clicking.

What was he doing in there, even if this *was* a dream? And if truly a dream, then that would have to make it—what? *A dream within a dream within a dream?* came the absurd consideration. Meanwhile, every muscle in her back and arms strained quite failingly against the increasing weight, pressure, or gravity; something invisible was essentially squashing her back down to the mattress. A moment later she lay flat on her back again, and she couldn't move. The paralysis permitted her to move only her head, back and forth. When she snapped her gaze back to the right, her eyes flicked lower, to the floor before the den . . .

Wisps of black smoke seemed to be sifting upward from the floor. *Fire! The cabin's on fire . . . ,* but then in her scrutiny she realized it couldn't be smoke.

Smoke didn't smell like *meat.*

"It's not really smoke," Frank elucidated from the den. "You can think of it as a gas-phase effluent . . ." The wedge of light swelled as the den door creaked open. A shadow stood huge in the wedge, then shrank quickly as Frank ambled out. He looked down at Hazel from the foot of the bed.

"It's a conduction-flux, Hazel"—he grinned—"from the spells."

The spells, Hazel repeated the word in her mind. Even in her trepidation, she frowned at him. "Who do you think you are? Van Halen?"

Frank wore sunglasses in spite of the room's meager light. "Hagar," he said and laughed.

"And what's this about spells?"

"Spells, Hazel—occult theorems that manipulate the angular invariants of the surface of the Shining Trapezohedron." He leaned over and rubbed her bare leg. "You know what that is, don't you? The Shining Trapezohedron?"

Hazel was about to say yes, was about to tell him that she'd found it and locked it in the car, but then retracted the affirmation without knowing why. Instead, she credulized the lie with an incomplete truth. "Oh, that red gemstone on Henry's computer. File Number 1. I saw the picture of it. What the hell is it?"

"What the hell is it?" he murmured. He wore khaki pants, loafers, and a short sleeve shirt with the tails out. His hair look disheveled, and overall he appeared tired and dirty. "You don't need to know because you would never understand. You're a lit-head and a sex-maniac."

"Thanks . . ."

"Henry chickened out, just like my father. So he threw it away, the asshole. The system works in sequences of 33, but without that crystal we only have 32. It reduces the power-quotient by ten to the 32nd power."

Hazel smirked her confusion. *What's he talking about?*

"Don't you see? Henry *knew* he was screwing us over. That's why he got rid of it."

Hazel sighed nervously. "Frank, this doesn't feel like a dream. It feels real."

"Three cheers to God, then, hmm? For creating the human mind and all its ten trillion synaptic connections. Quite a piece of work, to be able to do all those things and *still* produce dreams with such clarity, such accuracy, and such sheer authenticity that we don't even believe they *are* dreams." His hand slid up the inside of her thigh, played through her abundant pubic hair, then gave her crotch a squeeze. "Did that feel real?"

"Yes!" she yelled.

"But how can that be? If this were real, Sonia would've woken up. You have a very loud voice sometimes, you know that?" He sputtered. "It reminds me of my mother, which I guess is one of many reasons I've never liked you."

"Oh, that's just great, Frank!"

"This one, on the other hand . . ." He wandered over to Sonia who remained asleep on her side. He pushed her over on her back, then kneed onto the bed. His fingers slipped the straps of her nightgown down, then he lifted out the large, bulbous breasts. "God, those are great tits, aren't they? Shit." He played with them, infatuated. "I *love* these tits, Hazel, but the problem is . . . I fucking *hate* everything else that's attached to them."

"You really are a shitty person, Frank."

"Yeah," he chuckled. "I am. But I'm a sucker for big tits, I guess. Drop a couple loads, then next thing I know she's got me believing I'm in love with her and we should have a kid." He pushed the nightgown up over Sonia's swollen belly, then grimaced in disgust. "I should've made big-bellied whine-machine get an abortion."

"Frank! That's awful!"

His brows raised over the sunglass rims. "Think about what you just said. It's *awful* for me to say that?"

"Yes!"

"But it's *your* dream, Hazel, just like the fat guy told you in the other dream. It's *your mind* that put those words in my mouth, so what does that really mean? Does it mean that *I'm* awful?" He thumbed open Sonia's labia, then smirked. "No. It means that *you're* awful."

Hazel exhaled a long breath in frustration. "This dream sucks, Frank. I just want it to end."

"Of course you do." He walked back over to Hazel. "But between looking at your body and my fat, knocked-up manatee of a fiance's tits, I've all of a sudden got some lead in the pencil, if ya know what I mean." He stood at Hazel's side of the bed now, closer. It was then that Hazel noticed the oddity: his *breath.*

Whenever Frank spoke, his mouth seemed to expel breath-fog, like when one talks in cold weather.

Only *this* breath-fog was black, like sooty smoke.

"Why is your breath—" she began.

"Just more conduction flux." He smiled more sharply behind the black oral mist. "The spells reverse the valance of proximal molecule chains—it's all geometry, Hazel—and one of many results is a *directional* yield. Fictility. It involves an inversive model of a quadric surface within angular hyperbolean variants. For instance, right now you probably feel like an invisible water bed is lying on top of you, right?"

"Yes!"

"Ah, well, consider, this"—he leaned over—"if I put my finger, just *one finger,* behind your head, and lift—"

He did this, and Hazel's head raised off the bed as though it was instantly weightless.

"See? My brain waves—my *thoughts*—manipulated the desired valance."

His finger continued to lift her head up, then her back, until she was fully sitting up, and then—

He continued to direct his finger, forward now, and down. Moments later, she was bending forward as her back bowed . . .

"What are you doing?"

"Sonia said you're double-jointed or some shit, used to be a gymnast."

"So?"

"I want to see you go down on yourself." A smoky chuckle. "Don't know why, really. It's just the idea of you sucking yourself off really rings my bells . . ."

The bizarre task, impossible to most, was easily achievable for one as nimble as Hazel, though it had been awhile since she'd bothered. She gave into the perverse request, however, relaxing her hip joints and spreading her legs to an extreme. *Concentrate,* she thought, Frank's finger still pushing. She imagined her spine going rubbery, then it bowed further until her pubic hair tickled her lips. She extended her tongue, ran the tip between the folds, and felt the forbidden thrill.

"No, no, not just the tongue," he ordered. "Get your *whole mouth* down there on your pussy and suck."

She relaxed more, folded over now in a human convolution. She smelled her own musk as each tiny increment of effort brought her closer and closer until—

"There," Frank said, satisfied. "You did it. Now suck it."

Her labia still ached from the various tortures the day had brought, but once the outer vulva was drawn into her mouth, she enjoyed the intense yet soothing sensation. She sucked her own folds, played with them between her lips. She heard Frank's zipper come down.

"Suck your whole clit into your mouth," he panted, leaning over close to watch. The meaty smell of his black breath gusted into her crotch. "Suck it like it's a little cock and get yourself off . . ."

Hazel did so, coaxing the clitoris, hood, and immediate flesh upward via suction. Her saliva clicked as the suction grew systematic.

"Good, good, yeah," Frank gusted, and with his approval came the sound of his own masturbation. "Suck it off. Make yourself come . . ."

Hazel filled her head with many of the day's debauches; nauseating to typical women, these images had her whining in only another minute, summoning waves of imminence that made her groin throb. She let it all replay in her mind: being mauled, man-handled, tit-fucked, and fisted; being slapped, choked, and bilge-pumped; being forced to swallow a shot glass full of sperm and then letting not one but two male bladders be emptied into her stomach. All these repugnant images left her enfrenzied as her mouth desperately plied her own sex.

"Think about Sonia," was what Frank's black voice whispered next. "Pretend that's *her* pussy you're sucking . . ."

The mere words set her off; her pelvis bucked up against her mouth as the potent spasms broke.

"Good, good . . . Suck, suck . . ."

She came till she thought she'd collapse into herself. She was actually crying it had been so good . . .

When she wanted to teeter over, Frank jerked her face up. Thumb and index finger of his left hand dimpled her cheeks to give her fish-lips, while his right hand pressed his glans right to the hole and–

"There . . ."

Globs of sperm flowed between her lips onto her tongue, eddies of it. When he'd finished he kept her cheeks pinched together and pushed her head all the way back.

"Swallow now."

Hazel nearly vomited when she did so. *Oh, gross . . .* The sperm tasted unlike any she'd experienced—it tasted *wretched.* It tasted the way old sperm smelled on a dried up wet spot three days old.

The room's occult gravity slammed her shoulder blades back down on the bed.

"You're something, you know that?" Frank's words misted. He pulled his zipper back up. "You're every perverted male fantasy in the flesh, Hazel. You are the personification of Woman As Object, a sexual spittoon, a *thing,* Hazel, that exists solely as a receptacle for every twisted desire to ever comprise a man's most carnal obsessions." He smiled below the foolish sunglasses. "You're *meat,* and what's worse is that you're content with that role. You walk the earth with only one true purpose: to be fucked. You're a human condom, Hazel—a *fuck*- dump—and that's all you'll ever be."

"Fuck you," she drooled.

Frank's black voice puffed as he spoke. "Find the Shining Trapezohedron and you'll be rewarded," and then he turned and walked out of the cabin, counting each step.

"One, two, three . . ."

When he was gone, Hazel's awareness was hauled down into utter, ghastly *black.*

"It's almost noon!" the voice pried into her sleep. "Don't you want to get up?"

Hazel's eyes clicked open. When she tried to speak, her tongue seemed glued to the roof of her mouth. *What?* she thought, then, *Oh, God . . .* Blocks of sunlight came one by one into the room as Sonia opened the shades.

"Here's some coffee." Sonia smiled down at her, setting a cup on the nightstand. She wore another bright, flowery sundress.

"Is it really noon?" Hazel groaned. A headache twinged at the back of her skull.

"Almost." Sonia seemed perky, energized, as she busied about the room.

At least she's not still down in the dumps, Hazel considered. She sat up naked in bed, rubbing her eyes. *Damn.* "Sorry I slept so late. That's not like me."

"No problem."

Hazel was going to mention her nightmares but then thought better of it when she recalled the slowly reforming details.

"I was doing work anyway."

"What work? Summer session's over. You're on vacation."

Sonia sighed. "This morning I checked my email and found a note from Administration. They lost all my student evaluations—the entire student roster—for all my classes in the session. So now I have to re-collate the *whole friggin' thing,* and send it back to them. They have to have it for the quarterly stats."

"Bummer," Hazel said. "I'll be happy to help."

"Thanks, but it's really something I have to do. It'll probably take a couple more hours." Her smile beamed. "At least it'll give me something to do while Frank's on his way."

Frank. . . Hazel tried to blink away the remnants of the nightmare: Frank's black sunglasses, his black breath, ugly comments, and rotten sperm . . .

Sonia sat next to her. "And I'm sorry about yesterday."

Hazel could've groaned. "You don't have to ap—"

"You're right, I did overreact." Sonia laughed and rubbed her baby-bump. "Knocked up, you know? Crazy hormones. I don't know how Frank's been putting up with me the last eight months."

Well, that's a change, Hazel thought. *He's not the Big Bad Wolf anymore.* "He said he'll be back this afternoon," she tried to sound confident, "and I'm sure he will be."

"I know. I keep forgetting. Frank's not just a self-absorbed *guy,* he's a self-absorbed *college professor.* And by now his phone battery *is* dead, it's got to be. Like you said, once he gets all this Henry stuff out of his system, he'll be fine."

Hazel nodded through a distraction. Of course she *knew* that last night was indeed a dream . . . her mouth was lined with the most awful taste. She hopped off the bed. "Well, you get back to work. I've got to take a shower and decide what I'm going to do today," but as she moved away, Sonia's hand caught her wrist.

"Wait!"

"What?"

Sonia kissed her lightly on the lips. "Thanks for being such a good friend. I don't know what I'd do without you."

Hazel looked at her, hoping the moment would turn serious, but then Sonia's expression turned to one of concern. Her finger daintily touched Hazel's left nipple.

"Your nipples look swollen . . ."

They ought to, Hazel thought. "They get that way sometimes, that's all. Period's coming," and then she strode naked for the shower.

In the cubby, she brushed her teeth, brushed her tongue, gargled with vehemence, then let the cool water blank her mind. But there was still the Shining Trapezohedron to clean, and she did want to take another stab at uncrashing Henry's computer. *Frank might know what to do,* she considered. She sudsed her pubis thoroughly, then blushed in the spray when she recalled dreaming of performing cunnilingus on herself. *I didn't really do that in my sleep, did I?* She couldn't imagine. What bothered her most, however, was the prospect she'd only now let come to the surface of her consciousness. Sonia seemed confident that Frank would indeed return this afternoon, but . . .

What if he doesn't?

Hazel knew that she would have to find the Gray Cottage herself.

Today she dressed in fluorescent-green flipflops, a shortish stone-washed jean skirt, and a sleeveless tee that read: APRIL IS THE CRUELLEST MONTH, BREEDING LILACS OUT OF THE DEAD LAND – T.S. ELIOT. She rolled her eyes when she saw her reflection in the little mirror: both nipples stuck out like pegs between the lines.

Hazel couldn't identify what brought the idea to mind when she came back out. "Didn't you say that Frank's father lived in Concord?"

Sonia sat at her laptop in the den. She never looked up from her typing as she answered, "Yeah. I went up there with him once—pretty depressing place. It's practically a nursing home."

"So Frank's father is an invalid?"

"He walks fine, the problem is he's totally blind. Frank always felt bad about not having enough money to get him in a nicer facility. At least now, with Henry's inheritance, he'll be able to." Sonia looked up. "Why do you ask?"

Hazel fiddled with the metal-version of the crystal box. "You're busy for a while and I'm bored. Can I borrow your car and drive to Concord? I want to ask Frank's father about the Shining Trapezohedron."

"The wh—Oh, the crystal."

"Yeah, and I want to ask him about this gemstone club Horace mentioned. That sounded pretty weird."

"That along with an anonymous letter and five thousand in cash."

"I mean, come on. A gem club? Did Frank ever mention anything about Henry Wilmarth being in a geology club of any kind?"

"Nope. But he obviously knew about this Shining Whatever, 'cos Henry's last instruction asked him not to bother looking for it," Sonia reminded. "I'm kind of curious myself now. You really want to drive to Concord?"

"Why not? It can't be that far."

"From here, probably less than an hour." Sonia checked her address book on the laptop, then quickly printed out the address of Thurnston P. Barlow. "Just use the map in the car, you shouldn't have any trouble. It's not far from the New Hampshire Technical Institute."

"Cool. See ya later."

"Oh, wait, and while you're there, bring back some carry-out, okay, for the three of us. I'm dying for Chinese!"

"Sure."

"Beef with chow fun noodles!"

"You got it," Hazel smiled. "See you in a few hours."

She skipped out of the house, into breezy heat. The car's interior was scorching; she left the door open to air it out, then picked up the paper bag containing the Shining Trapezohedron. The tree patch had indeed softened in the heat but still left a tacky mess. *I'll work on this later,* she resolved, then was in the car and on her way.

Southward on Interstate 93 had in forty-minutes' time brought her to Concord. Revolution-era architecture was seen in every direction; the town seemed neat as a pin yet too small for a state capital. A few minutes later she'd parked and was entering the The Ammi Pierce House - Assisted Living Apartments. Frank had referred to the place as a "shit-hole," but Hazel found the exterior clean, stately, and impressive. The shit-hole came *after* she'd entered when at once she was accosted by nursing-home odors and distant babbling. *Jesus . . .* These weren't really apartments but just single rooms, like a boarding house. Hazel signed in at the shabby front desk; then the clerk—a gaunt, balding man with a giant adam's apple—came around the desk to take her to Mr. Barlow's room. The clerk's gaze seemed to brush over her nipples through the T-shirt. He took her up to the second floor. The tannish carpet smelled rotten; she forced herself not to look to closely at variously shaped stains. A man in white-garb pushed a cart at the end of the hall. *A male maid,* she guessed. The man looked at Hazel blank-faced, then pushed onward.

Creepy joint.

When she knocked on Mr. Barlow's door, a hushed voice said, "Please, do come in."

The room was dark—*Of course it is! The man's blind.* "Hi, Professor Barlow. My name's Hazel Greene. I'm a—"

The dark form in the corner's voice possessed a surprising vitality. "Ah, yes. Frank's mentioned you. You're his fiance's friend."

"And her teaching assistant at Brown, yes, and I know Frank pretty well too."

"Feel free to turn on a light and have a seat," and when Hazel did so she was shocked to note the haggard state of Thurnston Barlow. He was a scarecrow in oversized clothes, but appeared clean, recently shaven, stark white hair neatly combed. Hazel knew the man to be in his sixties but the figure facing her from the armchair opposite looked in his eighties. Sunken cheeks, sunken eyes, face pallid like wax; overall he appeared *drained* of life. She could only see the very bottoms of his irises. The rest of the apartment looked as infirm as he did. *Poor bastard,* she thought.

Thin, bloodless lips barely moved when he continued, "And now you, Sonia, and Frank are taking a respite of sorts, at the late Henry Wilmarth's cabin, correct?"

"Yes, sir."

"Henry was a brilliant man." The voice was uncannily zealous to be spoken from someone so emaciated. "It's quite a shame what happened. In hindsight, though, I wasn't all that surprised."

"Really?"

"He was quite a different person when he returned from St. Petersburg."

The Mother's Day Storm . . . Hazel tried to focus on her task yet she kept feeling an annoying distraction. She felt antsy . . .

"I suspect Frank or Sonia apprized you of the fact that I am completely blind," the old man went on, "and I'm sure you've heard from time to time that the blind are known to compensate for their visual detriment by developing an excess acuity in other senses."

"Yes, I have heard that."

"So I hope you're not offended by my saying"—he paused and sighed—"that you smell intense and absolutely lovely . . ."

Hazel chuckled. "I'm not offended at all, Professor Barlow."

"Around a place like this, a sharpened olfactory sense is more a curse than a blessing." He smiled, dead-eyed. "You've livened up an old man's day more than you can know."

"Well, I'm glad of that," and only then did Hazel realize that she'd unknowingly spread her legs in the jean skirt. Had the man been able to see, right now he'd have a bird's-eye view of her pantiless crotch. The idea instantly moistened her. "I think what you're smelling is my shampoo. It smells like blueberry muffins. The guy I'm dating likes it."

"Blueberry muffins and, well . . ." A thought faded. "In that case I envy your beau," he said and laughed.

Oh my God, she thought. She noticed the old man's baggy crotch: a lump was forming it. *He can SMELL my pussy . . . and it's making him hard . . .* The awareness fascinated her. "Anyway," she tried to keep on track, "I guess I should've called first, so I hope this isn't an inconvenience—"

"Not at all, Hazel. Any friend of my son's is always welcome here, unconditionally." Another laugh. "Not that *here* is any great prize."

The distraction was cutting into her now. Her sex was seeping, from the simple knowledge that her scent and her presence was giving the infirm man an erection—that, and the knowledge that he couldn't *see . . .*

Very, very slowly, she hiked her skirt up to her pelvis, then rolled her top up, while saying, "I came here to ask you some questions."

"The questions of the young bring only delight to retired academicians, believe me."

Now Hazel sat spread-legged on the chair, her skirt peeled all the way back, her bare tits plump as peaches from arousal. *I'm exposing myself to a blind man,* came the bald and thoroughly unfeeling thought, and with it her own nipples inflamed further and the groove of her sex began to flood. Meanwhile, the "lump" in Thurnston Barlow's baggy convalescent slacks lengthened. Hazel's vision grew hazy but she managed to ask, "I'd like to know about the Shining Trapezohedron."

Barlow's eyes, however dead, seemed to darken. The strangely energetic voice seemed to corrode when he replied, "How do you know about– Frank didn't tell you, did he?"

"No, sir, but there were some references to it on some letters Henry left on the desk. Sonia and I weren't exactly prying but we couldn't help but see them. Henry referred to it as a 'graven image,' and a 'golden calf.' What on earth did he mean? It's just a rock, right?"

The man seemed crestfallen now . . . and his erection was ebbing. "It would be pointless for me to explain, Hazel. You'd have to be a very deft mathematician with a sound knowledge of physics to even come close to understanding." The old man seemed to falter through a thought. "You don't have it, do you? The stone?"

"No, sir," she lied. "Henry's letter said he disposed of it."

Barlow's bony hands rubbed his face. He went silent.

"Professor Barlow? Are you all right?" Hazel gulped. "If I've upset you in some way, I apologize."

"No, no, it's just . . . My God. You wouldn't believe what we almost got ourselves into." He cleared his throat with difficulty; if anything, he looked even more skeletal now that Hazel had raised the topic. "What you have to understand is that Henry Wilmarth was a genius–a genius with the potential of an Edward Teller."

"Edward *Who?*"

"Oh, of course, you wouldn't know that. He's the man who invented the hydrogen bomb."

Hazel struggled with her curiosity and her raging arousal. She couldn't keep her thoughts straight. *What's he talking about?*

The old man leaned toward an augmented telephone sitting beside him. "Pardon me a moment, but I need to call Frank—"

Hazel draped her knees over the arms of the chair, baring her furred pubis even more extremely. "You probably won't be able to get him. Right now, it's just Hazel and me at Henry's cabin."

Barlow's face webbed with concern. "So where's Frank? He's supposed to be there destroying . . ."

"Yes, sir, destroying Henry's documents and files. He felt it would be deemed quackery and only bring ridicule to his name."

"Quackery," Barlow muttered.

"This theory the three of you were working on. Non-Euclideanism."

Pale white brows popped up. "You're very resourceful. But do you know what that *means?*"

"Haven't a clue. Frank tried to explain but it went right over our heads."

The old man's voice sounded guttural. "I'm glad it did. There are some things people don't need to know, Hazel. It's better that they never even *consider* them in the most farfetched fancy. Fortunately Henry Wilmarth realized this before it was too late. I pray God Frank does the same. So . . . *where* is he? He's *not* at the cabin now, you say?"

"No, sir, he left right after Henry's funeral several days ago," she said while at the same time running the pad of her middle finger up and down the slickened groove of her sex. *Pervert, pervert, pervert,* she condemned herself but kept doing it nonetheless. The sensation made her want to hiss through her teeth, but she knew she dare not. Not only were the blind known to develop an accelerated sense of smell but an accelerated sense of hearing, too.

Barlow was about to further his questions but Hazel interrupted. "Would you excuse me a minute, sir? I need to use your bathroom if you don't mind."

"Oh, of course." The crabby hand pointed behind him. "To the right. It may not be the cleanest bathroom—I've no way of knowing, of course." He smiled. "I'm at the mercy of the housekeeping staff."

"I'll be right back," she said and strode off.

In the bathroom, she glared at herself in the mirror. *What are you DOING? You came here to TALK to the old man, not PLAY WITH YOURSELF in front of him!* Fuming, she urinated, flushed, then washed her hands, all of a sudden crawling in prickly heat. It was her sickness, she knew, sinking in like it always did. Whatever perverted brain cells in her head made her like this . . . they were sparking now with vigor. *No, no, no,* she groaned to herself and pulled her top over her head. She took off her skirt and now stood naked.

No, no, no . . .

She took care to make no noise when stepping out of the bathroom. She peeked around the hall entrance and, sure enough, Frank's father was tremble-handedly caressing his crotch. She stepped back to the bathroom, closed the door loud enough for him to hear, then walked back out.

"I'm back," she said and gingerly lay her clothes over the chair. She sat back down, prickling all over now by the fact that she was sitting completely nude in front of a blind man. "Where were we? Oh, yes, were we talking about–"

The old man faltered. "Hazel, I—I'm delighted to talk to you but I'm afraid I'm terribly side-tracked right now. I've been blind for almost five years, but—but . . ."

Hazel pressed her hand flat against her sex and made slow circular motions. "But what, sir?"

He seemed hesitant. "Would you mind terribly if I touched your face? I'd really like to see you and, of course, touch is the only way the blind can really see."

Careful. Be VERY careful. "Sure," she said and hopped up. She stood immediately before him, bent over, and took his hands. Then she placed them on her face.

The fingertips trembled all about, from forehead to throat and back again. "Oh . . . my. You're so beautiful, so lovely."

"Thank you," she whispered.

The dead eyes looked up. Now his fingers were trembling at her collar bones, and Hazel's vision just got hazier and hazier and the sickness sunk deeper, drenching her brain like a sponge.

Two tears glittered in the old man's eyes. "Please . . . ," came the driest peep.

Hazel grabbed his wrists and pushed his hands down to her breasts.

"I *knew* it," he whispered. Now his entire form trembled in the chair.

Her own voice parched. "I have some problems, Professor Barlow, and . . . as I'm sure you're all too aware of now. I try to think of them as frivolous little fetishes, little kinks, but I guess they're a lot more than that. I rationalize what I'm driven to do by telling myself that if no one gets hurt, it's okay. But that's pretty naive, I suppose . . ."

The old man's hands smoothed over Hazel's young breasts, then down her waist, over her abdomen. "Blind men dream of this, Hazel. There is no other fantasy for us, really . . ."

As the hands tended her breasts, Hazel looked down between his arms, down the flat of her stomach and the formidable puff of dark-red pubic hair; she spied the old man's tented crotch and noticed the dime-sized wet spot there. How long had it been since he'd touched a woman? How long had it been since he'd experienced this proximity and actually gotten an erection? Had climaxed?

Barlow's hollow breaths quickened. "What a beautiful moperist you are, Hazel."

Her breasts jiggled when she laughed. "*Moperist?*"

"That's the name of this particular fetish," his voice rose and fell. "One who commits 'mopery' is one who becomes sexually aroused by exposing oneself to the blind."

Mopery, huh? "That's a new one on me," she said, moving her pubis closer. "I'll have to put it on my list."

Now the old hands were molding her hips, circling her belly, probing her navel. “But certainly you’re not *aroused,*” Barlow whispered. “A young, beautiful woman such as you couldn’t possibly be aroused by a blind old man . . .”

Hazel took his hand and put it to her sex. She manipulated one of his fingers right into the sopping-wet slit. “So you think I’m not aroused, huh?”

She drew the trembling finger in and out, tightening herself.

“Please,” he pleaded. “Let me . . . taste you . . . It’s been so long.”

Hazel needed no time to contemplate, nor weigh the subjectivities of the situation. Most of her conscious thought felt filmed over. She pressed Barlow back in the chair, then effortlessly hopped up, placing each bare foot on a chair-arm. Professor Barlow quivered and moaned, blindly looking up in wait. Only once did Hazel’s conscience ask, *What am I doing?* Only once.

She raised her right leg straight up like a punter at the peak of the kick, then pressed the sole of her foot against the wall. From here she merely inclined her pubis, leading it straight to the thin-lipped mouth of Frank’s invalid father. The alignment was perfect.

Hazel’s pose tensed her back and leg muscles to tight cords when the sexagenarian tongue delved into her folds.

The old man mewled in something like pleading delight. Hazel urged her clit closer. Soon, though, he got the hang of it, perhaps old memories rekindled, as his tongue movements grew rhythmic.

Beneath his mewls, she could hear him desperately pawing his crotch with one crabbed hand. *Don’t over-excite him . . .* ”Just relax,” she whispered, abdominal muscles tightening. “Take your time.”

Hazel’s sphincter and vulva began to pulse. The inside of her mind felt like a dam, holding back a seamy gulf of deviant images she longed to bathe in. When the damn burst—

Hazel hissed, her pussy spasming.

—the images gushed through—*men coming in her face, pissing in her face, locking her down bent over in a pillory to be sodomized en masse*—and came right in the old man’s face, her sex like a steaming sponge being squashed. She felt her own juices squirt out of her like an overripe fruit being bitten into. She kept her sex pressed to Barlow’s mouth as she continued to come with every flinch of her pelvis.

Careful, careful, she kept telling herself. *He could have a heart attack,* but she couldn't discipline herself one bit. She slithered down to a squat, unbuckled his pants, and took his penis out.

"Oh, dear," he wheezed, dead eyes gazing up. "You're such a lovely, lovely . . ."

This is one hard-as-a-rock cock for an old man, she thought. She finessed it in her hand. *Bigger than Frank's too, I think.* The pole of aged flesh quivered in her hand. Barlow cringed when her fingertips teased over the slippery glans. The piss-slit looked agape, a tiny, famished mouth hanging open. "Relax," she whispered, then adroitly fed the tip into her vulva and slowly declined her squat until her sex swallowed the entire thing. The awkward position caused the cock to touch her in areas not typically explored. She slowly began to ride her pelvis up and down. "Don't move," came her next whisper. "Just relax and let me do all the work . . ." She stepped up her rhythm, running her open hands over his sunken chest, thinking, *Don't die, don't have a coronary,* but then the man gasped and went into a series of feeble bucks. Hazel sighed, feeling the hot, gluey threads leap up into her vaginal canal. "There, there, that's good. Just relax and come . . ."

Moments later, the old man lay limp in the chair, a stick-figure in too-big clothes, when Hazel tightened her vaginal muscles to squeeze out the last semen and sensations, then daintily climbed off him.

I should NOT have done that, she feared, standing now to look at him. "Professor? You're all right, aren't you?"

The gaping-mouthed face nodded. "Yes, yes, I—"

"Don't talk just yet. Just rest and get your breath back. We'll talk in a few minutes. Let me get you a glass of water."

He nodded again, mouthed *Thank you.* Hazel put her clothes back on and went into the kitchen.

Give yourself a pat on the back, Hazel. You just came close to fucking a poor old blind man to death. You are the pervert's pervert. Each day you manage to find yet another new low. She poured a glass of water, was about to return to him, but noticed an opened door. *Bedroom,* she realized. There was almost nothing in it, just a bed and a dresser. Barren walls whose corners were rounded by cobwebs. On the dresser, though, stood a singular oddity: a framed picture. *Why would a blind man have a—,* but then she figured the picture must have sentimental value, whether he could see it or not.

It hadn't been touched in years, though, as quarter-inch-thick dust proved. Hazel picked it up, wiped it off.

Three men in hiking gear stood in front of Henry Wilmarth's cabin, all bearing timid smiles. Frank to the left, looking young, vibrant, eyes burning with a thirst for knowledge. He had to have been in his late-twenties when this was taken. To the right stood Thurnston Barlow, in no way resembling the withered shell in the outer room. *Early fifties,* Hazel estimated. He stood sturdy, confident, strong, yet radiating the aura of an academician.

In the middle stood Henry Wilmarth, whose smile seemed less timid and more *knowing.* Intense-eyed, lips pursed within the scholarly beard. Cupped in his hand at waist-level was the Shining Trapezohedron.

Interesting . . .

Perhaps Professor Barlow put the picture here because it reminded him of better times. Dead eyes notwithstanding, maybe he pictured it here in his mind every day and mused upon what it meant: a part of his life that had purpose.

The picture seemed sad. Hazel flipped it over, hoping for a date, but found instead a small photo slipped under the frame's lip. She took it and out stared.

No human subject stood within the snapshot's border. Photographed amid brambles, vines, and closely converged trees was a small building made of uneven stones. Unshuttered windows stood in deep embrasures of finely hewn rock; even the meager, slanted roof appeared to be made of *sheets* of stone, slate, perhaps. Mist clung around the dwelling's only visible corner. No door of any kind was in evidence.

The Gray Cottage, Hazel's thoughts croaked.

So . . . it really did exist. For whatever reason, seeing the picture made Hazel's heart quicken.

She set all back to rights and returned to Professor Barlow, who'd been able to catch his breath. "Here I am," she said to alert him, then took his hand and placed the water glass in it.

He smiled, exhausted. "What an angel you are, Hazel. What a blessing . . ."

Hazel wilted. *I'm a sex-freak, I'm a deviant, erotomanic paraphiliac. When men rape me and force me to drink their piss, I*

LIKE it. When they choke me unconscious as they're fucking me . . . I come. She could've laughed. *An angel? A blessing? I don't think so . . .*

"I had a pretty good time, too, you know," she dismissed. But now that her perversions had been slaked, she felt steadfast. "Among other things, we were talking about Frank, Professor."

His slack face stilled, then showed recognition. "Oh, yes. And you'd mentioned that he *wasn't* at Henry's cabin yet. So . . . where is he?"

Hazel elected not to confess to having seen the snapshot. "He went up to the top of Whipple's Peak, to a place called the Gray Cottage," and then she studied Barlow's face very closely.

The old man suddenly went rigid with distilled anger. "For God's *sake.* He was expressly instructed *not* to do that."

"Is this cottage . . . still there?"

"Yes," the old man croaked. "Henry and I went there several times many years ago." He made a bony fist. "Damn it!"

"Sonia's none too happy about him being up there. She's due in a few weeks and wanted to spend as much time with Frank as possible."

Barlow's agitation made him visibly shake. "Really, I must call him—"

"He's been up there several days, last we heard from him was yesterday." Hazel sat back in her chair, thinking. "His phone battery's got to be dead by now."

Barlow feebly felt for a button on the phone, pressed it, and said, "Frank," into a pickup that was undoubtedly connected to a voice-recognition program. The speaker phone began to ring. Frank's voice-mail came on immediately, and after the beep, Professor Barlow snapped, "Frank, this is your father! You're not supposed to be at the goddamn cottage; it's fit to collapse so leave at once! I'm serious, son. I've never asked *anything* of you in my entire life, but I'm asking now. Leave the Gray Cottage and go back to Henry's cabin. Leave at once! It's a disgrace for you to be up there when you've got a pregnant fiancé waiting for you—you should be ashamed of yourself. And hear this, son: when you're back, you call me. You and I are going to have a long talk," then he jabbed his finger into the off button.

"Wow, looks like I just got Frank in big trouble with his dad."

Barlow wrung his old hands. "Frank has an obstinate side, but one thing he's never been is greedy. That's why this surprises me."

"Greedy? I don't understand."

"Earlier you asked why Henry called the Shining Trapezohedron a golden calf. It's very much a *false* icon, Hazel."

More perplexity. "So there's a correlation between the crystal and the Gray Cottage?"

"Indeed there is."

"Frank said he's been detained there because Henry left a great deal more paperwork in the place, said it'll take him a while to destroy it all."

"Listen—" He sat upright, arthritic hands on knees, and stared directly at Hazel with his useless eyes. "Forget about it all, Hazel. Frank'll likely see the light once he thinks about things, puts two and two together. All I'll tell you"—he pointed a bony finger—"That stone, that horrid crystal, has . . . a power."

"Come on, Professor."

He seemed to calculate his next words. "It's a good thing indeed that Henry disposed of it, but let me just speak my mind. If for some reason you, Frank, or Sonia find where Henry hid the stone, throw it into the lake, bury it, put it in the garbage–anything. And whatever you do . . . *don't* look at it."

This was getting strange. What bothered Hazel most was the conviction with which Barlow made his comments. "Why, sir? It's just a stone."

"It's far more than that. It's a *seducer.*"

Maybe I should just leave, she considered. *I'm probably agitating him at this point.* But still—

She *had* looked at the crystal, hadn't she? Not the stone itself, but the jpeg on Henry's computer. And she'd *seen* things.

No, I THOUGHT I saw things . . .

"The metal box, too," the old man continued. "Destroy it. Let's just say you'd be doing me a favor."

"You're really confusing me, sir. Don't *look* at the stone?"

He seemed animated now, tense in some unexplained resolve. "Precisely. If you look at it long enough . . . it will make you want to do things, Hazel. It came very close to making Henry Wilmarth do something abominable—"

"What?" she almost yelled.

"—and it did the same to me." He laxed back in the chair, somehow looking even older now, more infirm. "Henry was stronger than me, I suppose. He was able to say no to it in time, before it got its hooks in him. I, on the other hand, wasn't so lucky."

All right, this is useless. The man's getting carried away. He's probably part-senile by now. Semi-precious gems don't have POWER. You can't say NO to a hunk of rock. "What do you mean by *that,* sir?"

He pointed to his eyes. "I looked too long, my dear. And when I realized what the Shining Trapezohedron was trying to do to me, I resisted . . . For that resistance, I was punished."

Hazel's eyes shifted as she looked at him.

"The crystal is what made me blind." He took a breath. "And remember what I said earlier? That the blind are able to hone other senses to a higher clarity via the loss of the vision?"

"Yes."

He rubbed his face as if weary. "It's not just smell, taste, and hearing, you know. It's also certain intuitions. For instance when I asked you before if you had found the Shining Trapezohedron, you said you hadn't." A very silent pause. "You were lying, weren't you?"

Hazel froze. "Yes, sir, I was."

"And you found it *where?*"

"Henry put it in a tree bowl, then covered the bowl with tree-patch. I happened upon it by pure coincidence."

The old man seemed lost now, yet he also seemed desperate *not* to appear that way. "I suppose I may have sounded a bit over-dramatic, Hazel. But can't you do this for me?" He made a parched chuckle. "Can't you appease this nutty old man? Please. Put the stone *back* in the tree bowl, cover it up, and, for God's sake—*don't* tell Frank you know anything about it. Will you do that for me? Please?"

"Yes, sir, I will," she said. *Big deal. It's just a rock.*

"Thank you. And, please, tell Frank to call me when he gets back to Henry's cabin, all right?"

"Sure."

The man was winding down. *I guess I fucked out any energy he might have,* she thought. "I have to go now, Professor."

"Yes–I'm getting very tired and I'm afraid the nurse will be by shortly with my medications."

Hazel's eyes narrowed. Blind, yes, and old, but he didn't seem to be sick. "I hope you're not ailing from anything serious, sir."

"No, no. Blood pressure, arthritis—the inevitable afflictions of old men." He seemed even to struggle smiling. "But, please, stop by again anytime. It's been a pleasure . . . being in your company. You're a wonderful, generous person."

I guess that's the urbane way of thanking a nymphomanic woman for fucking you. She got up. "I'll come by again soon, I promise. Goodbye, sir."

He raised a palsied hand to wave.

Hazel left, thinking, *Does he really believe all that? Don't look at the stone because it has POWER, it'll get its HOOKS in you?* She closed the door and turned only to see whom she'd previously dismissed as a janitor pushing his cart right up to Professor Barlow's.

"How nice," he said. He was looking right at her breasts, where her nipples still stuck out noticeably against the fabric of her tight shirt.

"Pardon me?"

"How nice to see Professor Barlow with a visitor," the man went on. He was fortyish, bulky, drab. He opened a drawer on the cart and withdrew a small paper cup. "His son comes around once in a blue moon but that's about it."

Hazel noticed now that what he pushed was not a cleaning cart but a med cart. Multiple drawers were loaded with pill bottles.

"So you're the nurse for the residents?" she asked.

"Just the pharmacist."

"I wasn't aware that Professor Barlow had a blood pressure problem–"

The man was in the process of stealing another glance at Hazel's distended nipples, but her question snagged him. "He doesn't have high blood pressure. What gave you that idea?"

"He just told me."

"Oh," he said stretching the word. "I can understand that, I guess. He doesn't want you to know. His blood pressure's picture perfect. Wish mine was."

Hazel was getting aggravated. "So what *is* wrong with him?"

He shook the little cup of pills. "Let me put it this way. These pills? They're anti-psychotics."

"Anti—"

"Professor Barlow is completely, utterly, one-hundred-percent insane."

I wonder if Frank's back yet? she asked herself when she got back to the cabin. Something felt weird when she got out of the car and looked at the wooden building. The entire drive back had sapped her brain; between Thurnston Barlow's bizarre remarks and Frank's suddenly erratic behavior–not to mention Sonia's mood swings, and the various other tidbits of either mystery or claptrap, Hazel had trouble thinking straight.

And now this . . .

The cabin *looked* empty, but why would she receive that impression? *I've had the car all day, so there's nowhere Sonia could go.* She tried to shirk off the disquieting impressions as she headed up the front walk with a take-out Chinese order and the bag containing the Shining Trapezohedron (she'd also bought a can of gem polish at a drug store near the restaurant) but then peered at something white just off the driveway. *A paper ball?* she wondered.

It was even more disquieting picking it up, for it lay only feet from the notorious out-house. Every time she saw the archaic structure, she shivered at the recollection of the "daymare" she'd had. *Find the stone . . . and you'll be rewarded,* the slush-voiced, upside-down-faced rapist had told her. *Frank said the same thing in the dream I had last night . . .* Hazel's stomach tensed as the dream-bits hovered over her.

The object was indeed a sheet of paper rolled up into a ball, as if someone had dropped it there. The ball crinkled as she unrolled it.

"Now what the hell is *this?*" she muttered.

Tight handwriting filled both sides. Hazel's gaze seemed to warp as she examined it: a list of names, addresses, phone numbers, and Social Security numbers. Each entry was numbered, and the first on the list were—

1) Hannah Bowen, 610 LaFanu Wood Rd., Bosset's Way, NH 03266 - 161-14-6557 - Ph: 646-262-0051

2) Emma Freeborn, 368 Bierce Spur, Bosset's Way, NH, 03246 - 464-18-9571 - Ph: 646-202-4978

3) Nabby Gardner, 4285 Machen Creek Dr., Bosset's Way, NH, 03246 - 410-42-2649 - Ph: 646-301-2476

The list went all the way to 33. Hazel noticed several familiar names, such as Ida Saltonstall, more than likely the barmaid at the tavern; and Nathaniel Peaslee, whom she met there as well. Richard Pickman, the dour artist and shop-owner, was on the list, too, and so were Walter Brown and Clayton Martin, the men whom she'd solicited for rape . . .

More weirdness. Why would there be a handwritten list of thirty-three local residents on a piece of paper in the yard? *Something Henry had written?* but, no, she'd seen enough of his characteristic penmanship to know he hadn't been the scribe.

Frank, the name dropped in her head like a bell-toll.

"Sonia, I'm back!" she called out when she barged into the cabin, "and I didn't forget the Chinese . . ." She stood still, waiting for a reply. A quick glance showed her the den was unoccupied. "Sonia?" Hazel stowed the take-out in the refrigerator, already knowing full well Sonia wasn't in the cabin. *Frank must've finally come back, and they're out for a walk,* she hoped, yet her gut told her something altogether different. She hurried to the den, searched for a sample of Frank's handwriting, but could only find Henry's. For the hell of it, she turned on Henry Wilmarth's computer—even knowing it had crashed for good—then sat down with a rag and began to clean the tar-patched crystal with the pungent cleaner she'd just bought. *Works like a charm* . . . She was surprised by how efficiently the solvent dissolved the tacky black muck. Within minutes, the scarlet crystal glimmered.

Wow . . . She held it up. The black striations woven within the stone's ruby-red seemed to move. Next, she took down the metal box and compared it side by side to the Trapezohedron. The glyph-like engravings on the box corresponded identically to many of the angles of the stone's shimmering facets. *Whatever you do . . . DON'T look at it,* Professor Barlow's warning resounded in her head. He wanted her to dispose of the crystal and destroy the box.

Hazel stared into the stone . . . and saw nothing.

Foolishness.

She felt tempted to gaze more deeply into it now, but to her surprise, Henry's computer suddenly booted up. She put the box and the Shining Trapezohedron back into the bag, then turned her attention to the computer, immediately accessing the massive index of Henry's notes. She clicked a random file toward the bottom—

Strange . . .

She was looking at a list of cities. *BIG cities,* she realized as her eyes scanned the list.

PRIMARY
1) Tokyo/Yokohama - 32.1 mil
2) New York Metro - 17.8 mil
3) Sao Paulo - 17.7 mil

And the list continued down–a long list. Hazel knew at once that the list comprised the most heavily populated cities on earth. The last three were—

31) Bangkok - 6.5 mil
32) Johannesburg - 6 mil
33) Chennai - 5.9 mil

—and then it ended. Hazel peered, confused. *Thirty-three local residents on one list, and thirty-three major metropolises on another list.* Why was the number thirty-three suddenly popping up everywhere? *More of the nightmare,* she reckoned, and then her stare lengthened. *Didn't Frank say in the nightmare something about sequences of thirty-three?*

All this mess was making her head spin. The very next file was a list of the same names on the list she'd found outside, though not alphabetical this time—

1) Nahum Gardner - Tokyo
2) Clayton Martin - New York
3) Ida Saltonstall - Sao Paulo

—and right on down, listing every name on the handwritten list.

Thirty-three names, thirty-three cities . . .

But what on earth could any of this *mean?* Hazel clicked on another random file and found a queue of jpegs. But the file-name was ST. PETERSBURG

Oh my God, she thought when she opened the first one.

What was it? A great mass of shapes filled the sky, fronted by a city-scape just before dawn. The shapes were a merge of colors: brown, black, gray. Hazel wanted to believe they were storm clouds but if they were they were unlike any clouds she'd ever beheld. They seemed part-solid, part gaseous, and though she knew it was her imagination, she could swear she detected immense malformed *appendages* sprouting from the mass. *Henry took this just before the storm hit last May,* she realized.

The next jpeg caused her to jolt. The ill-colored mass now seemed to be lowering on a city block, consuming high-rise condos and spiring office buildings . . .

And the next: All the stone blocks of a skyscraper had been caught in a freeze-frame, blowing out as if bombed and leaving only a steel skeleton.

The next one: Buildings concussing along a boulevard, while cars, mailboxes, debris, and *people* were blown down the street.

A final file showed a pile of human bodies massed against a wall: limbs contorted, faces frozen in an appalling death. Many of their arms and legs looked like the flesh had been corroded off, leaving curled bones that were somehow yellowed and rubbery . . .

Hazel closed the file down at once, her stomach clenching. *Holy shit, that's horrible . . .* The news had blamed the tragedy on multiple-vortex tornados—a rare fluke of nature—but, but—

Hazel knew what a tornado looked like. None had been visible in the jpegs.

She grew sicker and sicker as her mind played over every question. To clear her head, she went to the kitchen for a soda, then returned and found herself staring at a smaller desk along the back wall, where Sonia had set up her own laptop.

How could I have missed that!

Sonia's laptop sat opened, its flowery screensaver roving, and taped to the keyboard was a quickly scrawled note.

HAZEL: FRANK CALLED JUST AFTER YOU LEFT, SAID HE WASN'T COMING BACK TILL TOMORROW. CALL ME THE MINUTE YOU GET IN. LOVE, SONIA

*Oh, no, no, no—please. Tell me she didn't—*She snapped open her cellphone and dialed.

"Hazel! Thank God," Sonia answered, sounding winded.

"What happened?"

"The asshole made up more excuses about not coming back to the cabin," Sonia seemed to temper her words. "So I just *have* to know. I don't think he's ever been to this goddamn Gray Cottage, if it even exists at all."

"It does, at least according to Frank's father. I saw a picture of it."

"All right, fine, but that's why I did this. If Frank's not there, then I *know* he's been lying to me all along—"

Hazel's lips tightened. "Sonia, please tell me you're *not* climbing up to the top of Whipple's Peak."

"I had no choice!" her friend squealed. "He's been lying to me for days and I have to know why!"

"Sonia! You're eight months pregnant! The exertion could make you have a miscarriage!"

"I'm being careful, I'm taking it slow—"

"Bullshit! Come down right now!"

A pause, heavy breathing. "I can't, Hazel. I think I'm almost there. It's cooler all of a sudden, and there's a lot of mist . . . I'm going to sit down a minute and catch my breath . . ."

Hazel couldn't have been more infuriated. "You're overreacting again! I can't believe you'd do something this crazy!"

A winded laugh. "Crazy, huh? You want to hear something *crazy?* Frank was in Henry's cabin last night while we were both asleep."

Hazel's stalled. She remembered her dream: *I dreamt of Frank . . . in the cabin. Last night.*

Impossible.

"Look at my laptop," Sonia instructed. "I left it on deliberately so you could see."

Hazel jiggled the mouse to find Sonia's computer already logged online. But the screen name at the top wasn't Sonia's, it was Frank's, and right now she was looking at the website for the U.S. State Department. "Sonia, what's this all about? The State Department?"

"I was going stir-crazy with paranoia, Hazel. So I went onto Frank's account–he doesn't know I have his password."

"Why would you do that?"

"Why do you think? I wanted to see if he was getting emails from another woman."

"And?"

"He wasn't but . . . look. Look at the URL trail."

Hazel frowned, fulfilling the request. Several dozen URL's shot down the screen, all from the State Department's website. Hazel looked closer, then, and saw the page that had been repeatedly accessed was:

"Online applications for United States passports?"

Sonia was catching her breath now. "Yep. That's what Frank was doing when he snuck in last night. I have *no idea* why he'd be requesting passport applications for dozens of local residents. Look at them."

Hazel scrolled down to the first URL, found the application and saw whose name and info had been typed in.

"Hanna Bowen," she said aloud. Then she clicked the second access: "Emma Freeborn." And the third: "Nabby Gardner."

"They're all locals, Hazel. It's crazy. I counted the total number and it was thirty-three. For God's sake, why would Frank *do* that?"

Hazel's stomach was already twisting. Those first three names were the first three on the handwritten list *and* the corresponding city-list. "Give me a second." She checked the rest and inexplicably found, in alphabetical order, thirty-three Bosset's Way residents. The names on the paper and the names on the online applications were identical.

"Are you there?" Sonia asked.

"Yeah. Listen, Sonia, there's a whole bunch of weird things happening all at once. I found out more about the crystal, and I found out more from Frank's father . . ."

"Thurnston? What did he say?"

She continued to stare at the handwritten list as she talked. "It's too complicated to explain on the phone. But I've got some ideas." She could hear Sonia walking again—her break over. "Just stay where you're at. You're jeopardizing yourself and the baby by hiking all the way up Whipple's Peak. Just sit down, take a nap, and I'll be right up. I'm slim and in good shape, I'll bet I could be up there in a few hours."

"I wish you would come up, Hazel," Sonia said, her tone growing thin.

"I will. Right now. But don't exert yourself anymore."

"Just keep in cell contact. I've come all this way, I can't stop now."

"Yes you can, damn it!"

"And—" A long pause stretched over the line. "Jesus . . ."

Hazel squeezed the phone to her ear till it hurt. "What?"

"This fog or mist or whatever . . . It's really thick right now." Her footsteps could be heard crunching. Then:

They stopped.

"Oh my God . . ."

"Sonia, what is it!"

Sonia's voice lowered to a hush. "I found it, Hazel. I found the Gray Cottage . . ."

"Don't go in! Frank's father said it's about to collapse!"

"Doesn't look like it, it looks solid." Another pause. "I have to go in now, Hazel. If Frank really is in there, I have to confront him. And if he's not . . . then I guess that means he's been shacking up with some girl at a motel somewhere." "Don't go in the cottage!" Hazel kept yelling. "Wait till I get there!"

"No, no, Hazel. I have to go in. This has been making me sick. I'll call you back in a few minutes—"

"Don't hang up! Don't hang—"

The line severed.

Crazy! she thought. *This whole thing's crazy!* She was out the door in seconds, back in the car, and then speeding off onto the road which would take her to the bottom of Whipple's Peak . . .

5

What happened? Sonia thought. She lay in a muggy daze when she awoke. But . . .

Awoke?

What was she awakening *from?*

She lay on a cold stone floor. Above her stretched a small ceiling that, like the walls, was composed of stone. She could remember nothing until . . .

The cottage. The Gray Cottage. She couldn't move. Memories filtered back in the tiniest trickles. *I was pissed at Frank so I hiked up Whipple's Peak and—and . . . I found the cottage, didn't I? I'd been talking to Hazel on the cell, and . . .*

Nothing. Darkness.

Think! she ordered herself.

She was too disoriented. Nothing came back to her in sequence. A door . . . that opened into thin air. Scarlet heat. Strange words. Two eyeballs on the stone floor. Chuckling that was somehow like black slop. A mind-boggling orgasm. A sucking sound.

Her heart thudded in her chest.

After a few more groggy minutes, Sonia was able to incline herself up on her elbows. Immediately, she burst into a round of screams.

She saw that she lay there naked, but that's not why she was screaming.

Naked, yes, but she also saw quite easily that she was no longer pregnant.

And then—*then*—she remembered everything:

Sonia hangs up with Hazel just as she sees the Gray Cottage emerge from rising smears of pale mist. It's a strange building, indeed. Stone block walls, their seams tinged dark with fungus and mildew; an uneven slate roof over which pour festoons of ivy; narrow, iron framed windows whose glass is so dingy with age that its nearly black. But—

No front door.

She walks a circuit around the cottage, first the south wall, then the east, then the north, then—

Sonia shouts aloud when she sees that the building's westerly wall has been built flush against a sheer cliff. Had she taken one more step—

Her hand comes up to her chest.

—she would've fallen a half-mile straight down.

But who would build such an odd structure? And why on earth would Henry have chosen it as a place to work?

These things don't matter, though, for Sonia is intent only on one thing: finding Frank.

The prick. He's probably got a woman in there with him right now, a YOUNG woman, a freshman probably. Making a monkey of me while I carry around his kid . . .

She begins to check the windows. *A house with no door. It's madness.* All the windows are maddeningly locked—

Yes!

—save for one.

It creaks open, and a bewildering fresh-meat smell sifts out. *For shit's sake,* she thinks, frustrated. *Can I even do this?* She gets one leg up and over, the window's embrasure pressing her crotch. A grunt, then a deep breath, and she manages to shimmy herself through, the narrow frame barely clearing her gravid belly. *Christ!* But now . . . she's inside.

Several candles light the stone-walled room. There's no reason to call out for Frank for she instantly sees that the room—the entire cottage—is unoccupied. Her fury rises. It's not just unoccupied, it's *empty.* No furniture, no pictures, no lamps, no adornments of any kind. And furthermore—

No evidence of the additional papers, documents, and books regarding Henry's "research." In fact, there's not a single book in the place, not a file cabinet nor folder. Nothing. Except . . .

She walks cautiously to the corner. She stares, leaning over. At first she thinks it's a prank, some made-in-China rubber Halloween geegaw, but only a moment of observation shows her that it's very real: two bloody eyeballs on the floor.

Sonia steps back, her skin crawling. *Whose . . . eyes are they?* the question whispers at the back of her mind. She knows that some mode of action must be taken—escape, most likely—but she's unable to focus on that notion. Instead, she just keeps stepping backwards—

Thump

The wall stops her, then the faintest humming sound begins to waver about the room. She keeps still, keeps silent, as she sees tendrils of mist start to rise from the seams in the floor's stone blocks, but unlike the pale mist outside, this mist is *black.*

Very slowly, Sonia turns around.

It's not a wall she's facing, it's a door, and she quickly calculates that the door exists on the *western* wall, the wall built flush with the precipice outside . . .

It's a Colonial-style door: heavy, nine panels, an oval brass doorknob, ornately flared hinges. A sheet of yellowed paper that she thinks must actually be vellum has been tacked to the center panel.

Sonia reads the vellum aloud . . .

"'The Old Ones were, the Old Ones are, the Old Ones shall be. Not in the spaces we know, but *between* them. Yog-Sothoth is the gate whereby the spheres do meet . . .'"

Numbed by her own confusion, Sonia lifts the paper and reads more archaic scrawl on the other side.

"'The earth gibbers with their Voices; the earth mutters with their Consciousness; where reverence to their Word lingers, and upon where their Totems are blessed, they come. They come and they roil the seas. They smash the forests. They crush the cities . . .'"

Sonia takes a breath, then reads a final line:

"'That is not dead which can eternal lie, and with strange aeons even death may die.'"

Sonia gulps. The words bring pressure to her head; there's an awful taste on her tongue. She looks closer at the door and sees that its panels are covered with glyphs that hadn't been there before, glyphs like:

v><<^~<*v*~^^>*v*^~*v*<

The markings on the metal box, she knows, but as she stares, the rows of glyphs multiply until they're swarming all over the wood, and they're *moving,* they're opening and closing, and that's when the door knob begins to turn.

Sonia has every intention of turning tail and running but when she tries to—

She can barely move.

She shrieks when she looks down, sees those tendrils of black mist now crawling up her legs with a feeling like warm earthworms, then up and over her belly, then over her shoulders. They're holding her there. Eventually some of the tendrils adhere to her sundress. They roll the dress down her body, and then they roll down her panties, and a second later she's totally nude, shivering, and rooted in place. And then?

crrrrrreak

The door swings open, and Sonia sees only the sky and the vast landscape stretching for miles.

Her vocal cords are paralyzed now. Her lungs try to heave out screams but to no effect. She's trying to scream because several robed and hooded figures seem to ooze out of the thin air just beyond the door, and with great slushing sounds they step forward and enter the room.

Ropy arms reach out for her: tentacles of shiny, gray-pink flesh. The faces in the hoods seem inverted; they're hardly faces at all but lumpen and brown like plops of excrement. Lips like boiled bratwursts turn up to monstrous smiles, to be licked by tongues like slabs of liver. Gold embroideries line the fringes of the maroon robes, and when the robes part, Sonia throws up at the sight. Stouter, vein-lined tentacles comprise their legs, and betwixt them hang curled-up snouts of meat for genitals. The feet they walk on are inverted funnels of unearthly flesh.

Sonia begins to lose consciousness, but the noxious mist holds her up like a harness. She thinks she can hear a mad sound—flutes?—something that sounds crazy like a record playing backwards. All the while, the tentacular things come forward; they are exuberant by the sight of her naked body; they squeal and titter and flail their boneless arms.

One's great rotten mouth exists on what would be the forehead; it sucks down against Sonia's mouth, the slimy liver for a tongue pushing through her lips and roving down her throat till she begins to gag. The others embrace her with their tentacles, molest her breasts, dabble at her pubis, churn over the bloated belly in delight. From behind, one of them inserts its morbid penis up into her rectum, chittering, and in only moments begins to ejaculate some form of sperm that feels hot and chunky, like bean and millet soup, while the others openly masturbate in place, the ends of their tentacles rolled around the ends of the horrid cocks, and then they titter in unison, ejaculating on her in gouts, spattering her belly, spattering her breasts. The netherworldly semen looks and smells like vomit.

When their revel is finished, one of them leans its abomination for a face toward her and says, "E uh shub nleb nbb lrrg glud blemmeb," and then they all pick Sonia up and carry her through the door . . .

She doesn't fall as she would expect or even *hope* at this point. Are they walking on clouds? But, no, they seem to dissolve into the air and prolapse—

—someplace else.

Uneven angular walls of shiny red rock striated with black compose the room she hovers in now. Yes, hovers. She seems to be levitating, her back parallel to the scarlet floor. The air here feels somehow like warm oil. When Sonia looks around she finds no sign of her appalling escorts: she's alone.

And hovering.

An unseen force spreads her legs wide. She feels a pressure-drop. She tries to scream again but still no sound is permitted to escape her throat when a great bruise-colored hose of flesh six inches wide and dozens of feet long unravels from above. Snakelike, it roves around her, as if examining her, then rears its "head" which is actually no head at all but a rimmed, pulsating cone. Encircling the inside of the cone's lips are scores of pink fleshy things like tongues from which clear drool dribbles. The cone rises, backs up, then lowers very slowly, homing in, and attaches itself to Sonia's splayed crotch.

It begins to suck her sex.

In mid-air she goes rigid. The suction intensifies, and then the entirety of the hose begins to *pulse.* All those dozens of tiny tongues are slavering about the inside of her vulva, summoning the lewdest sensations. Several tend her clitoris simultaneously while others rove and slurp and lick deeper into her vaginal barrel. All the while, the suction increases, and even as an orgasm of incomprehensible tenor begins to impend, Sonia knows what this maleficent hose or tentacle or snake or *whatever* it is is trying to do:

It's trying to suck out her baby.

Struggling is futile. All she can do is hover in the air and *feel.* Feel those tongues squirming over every inch of her sex inside and out, madly ministering to her clitoris, and stoking the most ecstatic sensations she'd ever known.

Her orgasms *erupt.* Her sex *beats* as it begins to give up one delirious climax after the next. Her eyes cross. Her entire body quakes with each potent spasm . . .

Then something *snaps.* She hears a tiny, muffled *gush,* and feels something escape her insides. She can't imagine what is it, though, for she is still too lost in the throes of her climax. Nevertheless, that gush is the sensation of her water breaking.

Soon the climactic spasms transform to something else: contractions of labor.

Sonia knows now, yet all she can do is stare in ultimate horror as the hose pulsates harder and the suction escalates, and her body quivers and then—

She feels something huge . . . *leaving* her. Her swollen belly begins to shrink and her vagina gapes as her fetus and placental mass is sucked right out of her womb into the hose. Her jaw feels unhinged as her mouth hangs open at this most iniquitous theft.

She sees the lump of her baby slowly sliding up the hose like a snake swallowing an egg several times its own girth–

—and then she's sucked out of the impossible scarlet room and–

Slam!

—jettisoned back into the Gray Cottage.

The door slams shut, and Sonia passes out.

Sonia lay nearly as paralyzed as she'd been in the recollection. Her hands ran desperately over her newly deflated stomach. *My baby's gone my baby's gone my baby's gone,* the words siphoned round her head.

Yes, those monsters on the other side of that door had taken her baby. She rolled over, shrieking her outrage and no longer caring if she lived or died, and she began to crawl naked back toward the door. She would go back—yes! She'd open the door and go back and confront them and fight them, by God . . .

But before she could reach the door knob, the door began to open on its own. This time, however, it was not the robed abominations who crossed the threshold. It was Frank.

Well. THAT'S fucked up, Hazel thought of the oddity. The front door to the Gray Cottage was on the cliff-side wall. Just what kind of a house *was* this? Before pulling her head back, she chanced a momentary glance down the steep, stump-pocked precipice. She wobbled a moment in vertigo, then hauled herself back.

Jesus!

It had taken over four hours to mount Whipple's Peak, an arduous uphill climb through dense forest, weblike vines, and fallen branches.

She could see, though, where someone had half-blazed a trail with a machete–Frank, no doubt. The cottage sat in a cocoon of pallid mist.

Entirely made of stone. Hundreds of years ago? Isn't that what Horace said? Each finely cut stone that comprised each wall was larger than a cinderblock; Hazel couldn't imagine what they weighed apiece. Nor could she imagine how people so long ago had gotten the blocks all the way up here.

"Sonia!" she bellowed at the top of her lungs, banging on one of the narrow windows. She'd called repeatedly on her cell, but Sonia hadn't picked up. She'd called Frank, too, for all the good that had done. *Motherfucker. Whatever he's up to, we'll get to the bottom of it now.* She circumscribed the huddled cottage and at last found a window that was open. Her lithe frame made it easy to slip inside, and once she did that . . .

All she could do was stand and stare.

It was not the vacant cottage interior that drew her shocked gaze, nor was it the antique door hung with a sheet of yellowed paper. It wasn't even the two sloppy objects in the corner that appeared to be gouged-out eyes.

It was Sonia.

She lay naked, smudged, and very still. It occurred to Hazel that she might well be dead but instead of immediately rushing to her, she paused . . .

Is her . . . No, it couldn't be . . .

It was either imagination or the angle, but momentarily Hazel thought that Sonia's pregnant belly was slightly larger than it should be.

But that was impossible.

At once, Hazel knelt before her friend. She patted Sonia's face, praying, *Please, don't be dead!* and felt a crushing relief when Sonia's eyes fluttered. Her gaze looked skewed, half-insane; her mouth was a tiny "O" as she gazed upward.

"Hazel," she murmured.

"Don't worry, I'm here—"

Sonia began to shudder where she lay. "They—they took my baby!"

She's in shock, Hazel determined. "Sonia, calm down. I don't know what happened here but no one took your baby."

"Can't you see! I'm not pregnant anymore! I—" but then Sonia leaned up enough to see that she was indeed still very pregnant.

She screamed for a full minute. "That's impossible! Hazel, I went through the door, they *took* me through that door—"

Hazel tried to control the hysterics. "You had a nightmare or something, Sonia. You couldn't have gone through that door; it opens to the cliff. If you'd gone through that door you would've fallen all the way down to the bottom of Whipple's Peak—"

"No! No! You don't understand! We went through but it turned into another place. These things, these monsters! They had tentacles for arms and legs and rotten, upside-down faces and they wore robes, and they—they took me to this room that was black and red like the crystal, and then a *giant* tentacle with a sucker at the end came down and sucked out my baby!"

What am I going to do? Hazel fretted. *She's delirious.* The only question was *why?* And why was she naked?

Sonia cradled the bloated abdomen, her eyes lidless in turmoil. "But then-then . . . Shit, I can't remember!"

"Try to, Sonia. Take your time."

Sonia stared into space, then, instantly, her face turned white.

"Frank," she croaked.

"What about him?" Hazel rushed. "Where is he?"

"I—I . . . Hazel, I know it sounds crazy but after those things took my baby, they threw me back in here and I wasn't pregnant anymore!"

"Fine, fine," Hazel tried to humor her. "But you were saying something about Frank? Where is *Frank?*"

"Then the door opened again and Frank came out! And he dragged me back through the door but this time I went to *another* place, and—and—"

"And, what, Sonia?"

Sonia's screams made Hazel clack her teeth.

"They put another baby in me, a *different* baby," Sonia was suddenly whispering. "One minute I wasn't pregnant anymore, then the next . . . I was."

She's had a psychotic episode, that's got to be it. "Sonia, listen to what you're saying. You believe that you're carrying a *different* baby in your womb now?"

The whisper drifted. "A *monster* baby . . ."

All right. Shock. A mental breakdown, plus whatever Frank's done to her. I've got to get her to a doctor, Hazel knew. But that wouldn't be easy. Getting a half-crazy pregnant woman all the way back down the trail would take . . .

All night, if she doesn't miscarry in the process.

But she had no choice.

"Come on, we're going home." Hazel got Sonia on her feet, got her shoes and sundress back on. But she had to ask, "Sonia. Whose eyes are those?" pointing to lumps in the bloody puddle. "Are they—"

"They're Frank's," Sonia said and gulped. "He said he pulled them out himself and then those things replaced them with red crystals, smaller versions of the Shining Trapezohedron. Frank showed them to me—"

"Sonia, you're delirious—"

"—when he took off his sunglasses."

The comment froze Hazel's stare. *Sunglasses. Just like . . . my nightmare . . .* But then Sonia had insisted that it was no nightmare at all, that Frank had really been in Henry's cabin last night. Yes, the reference to the sunglasses bothered Hazel very much, and also her mentioning robed "things" with "tentacles" for arms and legs. All too similar to what she'd seen—or *thought* she'd seen—in the jpeg of the Shining Trapezohedron . . .

Somehow, now, she knew that the focal point of all this weirdness, and all this insanity, was the Shining Trapezohedron.

Hazel had it with her in the plastic bag she'd brought, along with the metal box—

And along with the pistol she'd found in Henry's desk drawer.

It took a great deal of effort to assist Sonia in squeezing her girth through the narrow window. But after she got Sonia all the way back outside . . .

She paused, still in the cottage.

"Hazel!" Sonia shot a whisper. "Come *on!*"

"No, wait." Hazel turned. She was looking back at the door. "I have to *see,*" and then she strode for the door.

"No! Don't! It's some other place, Hazel! Some other dimension! If you go in there, they'll put a monster-baby in you too!"

We'll see about that, Hazel thought. She didn't hesitate to turn the knob and swing the door wide.

Hazel shouted. A gust of wind nearly took her off her feet. The lowering sun filled the room with an orangish tinge, something to be fully expected, and beyond stretched the heavily wooded valley, the lake, and the town.

"Do you see this, Sonia?" she shouted over the wind. "It's just the town down there! There's no monsters! There's no other dimension."

"That's what you think . . ."

The wind whistled. Hazel began to push the door back against the fading gust, but she stopped when she thought she heard:

"Don't go, Hazel. You don't understand. There are *wonders* that await."

Though the words wavered with the wind, she knew they were Frank's.

"It's Nyarlathotep," the voice eddied back. "The messenger."

"I'm not hearing this!" Hazel screeched to herself. "It's hallucination!"

"Help us deliver the message, Hazel—yes, you and Sonia. Wait till the conduction flux refreshes, then *you* can come in here too . . ."

Hazel slammed the door shut, then slipped out the window.

"I know you heard him, Hazel . . ."

"I heard nothing," she denied, taking Sonia's arm and leading her through the pale mist. "I only *think* I heard something—"

"Frank."

"—because of the power of suggestion."

"I'll bet you saw black mist, too," Sonia insisted.

Hazel stiffened.

"That's what Frank's breath was like whenever he talked. It was black, not like this mist out here, but like the mist that crawled up from the floor. It held me there . . ."

Hazel shook it off, urging Sonia along. *Don't think. Just walk.*

And a long walk it was, with Sonia stumbling and talking nonsense all the way. It was past midnight when they'd finally reached the bottom of Whipple's Peak, and were back in the car and on their way out.

"Where are we going?" Sonia murmured from the passenger seat. She lolled groggily, cradling the great belly with distaste.

"I'm not sure," Hazel said. Her hands gripped the wheel as her mind raced for answers.

"Oh, I'm so tired . . . But I don't want to go back to the cabin."

"Sonia, we're *never* going back to the cabin, or that fuckin' cottage either, unless it's with dynamite."

The tires hummed over asphalt; in front of them, the headlights bored into the darkness. "I'm thinking we should just drive back to Providence, get you to a doctor—"

"Yes! For an abortion!" Sonia moaned at the sight of her belly. "I have to get this monster out of me, and there's no point worrying about Frank. He's one of *them* now, in the other dimension."

She's hopeless, Hazel realized. But too much of what she'd said still simmered in her. She didn't believe in portents, nor did she believe in shared dreams. But what other explanation could there be? *Something I either don't understand or haven't thought of yet, so forget it.* But one thing she could *not* forget was the plastic bag in the back seat.

That fucking crystal, and that box. Her mind ticked as the car whizzed through the road's long curves. *And right now Horace is making more of them, because someone unidentified had paid him to . . .*

It had to be Frank.

The tire-sound had lulled Sonia to sleep. *The Shining Trapezohedron, and the box,* Hazel thought. *Somehow they're connected to everything that's wrong . . .*

Maybe Horace could remember something more that Henry Wilmarth said. There was nothing else to go on . . .

Instead of heading straight out of town, Hazel pulled off on the tree-lined dirt road to Horace's.

Thank God he's home. She saw lights on in the trailer and his pickup parked out front. Sonia remained asleep so Hazel grabbed the bag, jumped out, and trotted to the trailer.

On the rickety porch, she paused as a breeze set off a dozen tubular wind chimes. It was a lovely, melodic sound, even in its disorder. But then, between the notes, tiny words seemed to wander to her ears . . .

"Hazel, my child. I adjure you . . ."

She winced, shook her head, and strode on.

"Horace!" she yelled, banging on the thin metal door. "It's me, Hazel! Please! I need to talk to you!"

She banged but there was no answer. *Could he be asleep? Through all that racket?*

She tried the knob, found it unlocked, and went in. Silence and dim lights greeted her. The TV was on with the sound off: a Japanese chef on some flamboyant cooking show. He brought a cleaver straight down the middle of a coconut, splitting it in half. "Horace?" she called. Each footstep caused the trailer floor to creak. Her brow furrowed; she entered his workroom . . .

What she noticed first was that Horace wasn't present. What she noticed second was that the shelf on which he'd been storing the clay boxes was vacant.

What she noticed third was the suitcase.

It lay open on Horace's worktable, a standard-sized Samsonite. It was filled with dozens of the clay boxes. Hazel didn't bother counting them but if she had, she'd have counted exactly thirty-three of them.

The mystery order is finished, she realized. *But WHERE is Horace?*

Careful footfalls took her through the trailer's depths. The cubby-sized bathroom? Empty. A storeroom and a small bedroom? No sign of Horace either. Only one more door remained, at the hall's end.

As she approached, she heard a sound–a wet sound–that instantly reminded her of fellatio. Slick, steady, rhythmic. She froze. *Shit! Maybe his girlfriend's home on leave! Maybe she's in there right now . . .*

The slick, wet sound drew on.

The door stood minutely ajar. Hazel put her eye to the gap and looked down.

You've got to be shitting me . . .

In the slice-like gap, she was able to detect what could only be Horace's bare hips. He lay on the bed, and at his groin, a suitor was indeed performing fellatio. But Horace's fat penis, which she'd seen in all its turgid glory only nights before, was flaccid, yet his suitor was sucking with gusto nonetheless. Certainly all men experienced erectile dysfunction on occasion, even sexual works of art such as Horace. This, however, was not the oddity that roused Hazel's concern.

The "suitor" was not Horace's girlfriend. It was no girl at all, in fact.

It was Mr. Pickman, from the curiosity shop.

There's no way Horace is gay, she resolved. *No way.*

None of her business, true, but Hazel pushed the door all the way open. Mr. Pickman continued to tend to Horace's groin, sucking voraciously at the very flaccid organ. Horace lay still on the bed, jeans down to mid-thigh. The angle of the door blocked his head from Hazel's view.

"What are you doing?" Hazel demanded.

Mr. Pickman paid the query no mind at all. He just kept going at it, head bobbing steadily, bad toupee askew. He'd perched himself at the edge of the bed.

"Mr. Pickman!" she bellowed. "Horace! What the fuck is this?"

Pickman's head slowed, then stopped. He looked up quizzically, and when he recognized Hazel standing there, he smirked.

"You're shitting me, right? You two are *lovers?*"

The smirk deepened. Then Pickman, first, straightened his toupee, then fiddled with his hearing aid.

"Blasted thing. Cost six thousand dollars," he muttered.

Hazel could not repress being taken aback.

"Step farther into the room, miss, and all your questions shall likely be answered." He chuckled. "Well, one of them, at any rate."

Hazel did so, turned toward Horace . . . What she saw slammed her back against the wall.

The reason Horace lay so still during the oral ministration was now clear: he was dead. His face was split, his head having been halved very precisely from the center of the crown of his skull to his adam's apple. Blood drenched the pillow on which his head lay.

It was perhaps Hazel's rather demented subconscious that framed the exact words to her demand: "Why are you sucking a dead man's dick?"

Aggravated, Pickman stood up. "Well, if you *must* know, it's something I've always longed to do," came the high, creaky voice. "You see, I've always loved the man but, as is generally the case, Horace was not bent to the same proclivities as I. What's the old saying? You can have what you don't want, but what you want you'll never have?"

Hazel was mortified. "So, what? You told him you wanted to suck his dick? And then he turns you down so you kill him?"

"Oh, no, no, no," he fussed. "I knew Horace would never consent, but I always imagined his cock was magnificent. It was providential that I'd never get to see it while he was alive, but what's the harm, really, now that he's dead?"

"Somebody cut his *head* in half!" Hazel shouted. "If it wasn't you, then who was it?"

"Oh, I confess to the deed"—he bent over—"but I did not end Horace's life for the reason you seem to be harboring." He rose again, hoisting a double-bladed ax. "I did it with this, and not too bad of a job, if I may say so. But you must understand that I didn't *want* to kill Horace. I was instructed to."

"Instructed by who?"

"Our emissary."

Emissary? "Is his name Frank? Frank Barlow?"

Pickman paused. "I never did get his name, but nevertheless he's our indoctrinator. An amiable enough chap, I suppose, if a bit testy at times." Pickman pointed toward Hazel's cross. "Like your Jesus, he can walk on water."

Hazel's tone lowered. "Was he wearing sunglasses?"

Pickman seemed surprised. "Why, yes! So you know of him."

She had to keep her eyes averted from Horace so she could think. *Frank ordered this fruitloop to kill Horace, AFTER Horace finished the clay boxes.* "And you're the one who put all the boxes in the suitcase, right?"

"Right, again." He huffed. "But they're hardly mere *boxes,* miss. I'd explain but I'm *certain* you'd never understand. Understanding only comes after indoctrination."

"The box is some kind of a carrier or activator for the Shining Trapezohedron, isn't it?"

"Indeed it is," Pickman said. "I'm impressed."

"Horace told me the box is supposed to hold the crystal, like some sort of a storage box, but Wilmarth's notes referred to it as a 'power carrier.' The only thing I can guess is that you put the crystal in the box, then . . . something happens."

"Something incredible," Pickman intoned, but now his eyes had drifted down to the sagging plastic bag. "Miss, if I may? Is *that* the Shining Trapezohedron you have there?"

"Yeah," she said at once. "And the gold box from Henry's cabin."

Pickman contemplated something. "Give it to me, please, then you may go. I've no instructions to kill *you.*"

"I'm not giving you shit," she blurted.

Pickman's eyes rolled; he hefted the ax. "Need I remind you of the implement in my hands? If you *don't* give me the crystal, I'll simply take it, after I do to you what I did to Horace."

Hazel pulled out the revolver and pointed it.

"My, oh, my . . ."

"Yeah." Hazel eyed him with complete disdain. "Why did you call Frank an 'indoctrinator?'"

Pickman sat down at the bed, took a last forlorn glance at Horace's dead genitals, and slumped. "Because he indoctrinated us all–the chosen. He helped us see the truth, he brought us into the fold, when he came to us."

"In dreams?" Hazel reasoned. "He came to you in a *dream,* and there was black mist coming out of the floor?"

Pickman looked quizzical. "Surely *you* haven't been indoctrinated." He looked closely at her hands. "If so, you'd have a ring."

"Like that one on your finger?" she challenged, noticing the uneven scarlet stone, just smaller than a marble.

"Yes. I'm afraid I was being disingenuous when I told you it was a Nova Scotian corundum."

Hazel was getting a headache trying to make sense of this. But there was still the objective problem of what to do with Mr. Pickman. Questions, however, continued to peck at her.

She noticed no such ring on Horace's corpse.

"Horace *wasn't* 'indoctrinated,' as you say. But he still must be part of what's going on. He made all those boxes."

"He's no more a *part* of it than you are, miss. He was merely an unknowing pawn. Our only interest in him had to do with his skill as a craftsman."

"So he didn't really even know what he was making."

"No, the poor fool. And when he'd completed the task . . ." Pickman raised the ax.

"You killed him 'cos you didn't need him anymore."

"I'm afraid so."

Frank, she kept thinking. *It's all centered around Frank.*

"So Frank indoctrinated certain people into this cult of yours—"

"Not a cult. A congregation."

"Fine. But what's this got to do with thirty-three passport applications for a bunch of local rubes?"

"My, you do know a lot," he said. "But I'm afraid on that note, I'll elect to keep silent."

Hazel leveled the gun.

"I'm not afraid to die, miss, because, in a sense, I *won't* die, just as the emissary promised." He smiled, pointing again to her tiny cross. "Our god is much more generous in the dispensation of immortality that *yours.*"

What was the name I heard? Hazel strained her memory. "Narl-something? Narlo . . ."

"Nyarlathotep . . ." His thin-lipped grin beamed. "Give me the Shining Trapezohedron and you can enjoy the fruits of the Messenger as well."

"Nyarlathotep. The Messenger." Hazel stared. "But . . . who is he a messenger for?"

"And even greater god," Pickman whispered dreamily. "Yog-Sothoth."

The word was familiar, wasn't it? *Yes! Henry's computer password!* "All right. Then what's the message?"

"I'm afraid it's not for me to say—"

Bam!

Hazel's hand jerked up when she squeezed off one round into Mr. Pickman's belly. The ax clunked, and Pickman was shoved to the wall where he slumped to the floor, blood pouring.

Agony contorted his face. "Whuh—why did you do *that?*"

Hazel shrugged. "Let's see. One, you murdered Horace and I *liked* Horace. Two, your pursy face pisses me off. Three, I *hate* that arrogant, pedantic tone of voice of yours. And four?" She glowered at him. "Your paintings *suck.*"

Pickman gurgled, looking up at her appalled. Hazel put the gun down and picked up the ax. She lined the blade up with the middle of Pickman's head, steadied herself, then took a deep breath and raised the ax high, arching her back, lifting up on tiptoes, and then—

Swoosh!

She drove the blade back down in a perfect arc. The impact split Pickman's head in half, in fact, splitting the entire neck and stopping only at the sternum.

Somebody needs a hug . . . and I guess it's me. She looked at Pickman's halved head, then rationalized that he deserved it for killing Horace. An eye for an eye, a cut-in-half head for a cut-in-half head.

Hazel grabbed the bag and walked back to Horace's work room. She had every intention of retrieving the suitcase full of clay boxes but when she looked down, that intention became moot.

The suitcase was gone.

"Fuck."

She left the trailer in haste, fairly sure that her nostrils had detected the smell of raw meat . . .

Hazel drove just short of lead-footing it, soaring down the road's long curves, heavy-boughed trees passing on either side. *The only guy in this whole fucked up town I trust is dead. So, what now?*

The tires shimmied through another winding turn. *Wait a minute. There IS one other person I trust . . .*

Several minutes later, her headlights roved across the front of Bosset's Way Woodland Tavern. The parking lot looked full. "Sonia, I'm going inside to talk to Clonner, then I'll be right back out, okay?" She nudged the groggy Sonia. "Okay?" Sonia nodded sleepily, mumbled something, then drifted back to sleep.

Finally. Some decent luck. When Hazel got out, she immediately saw the feisty, old Clonner Martin sitting by himself in his wheelchair just outside the front door.

"Clonner!"

"Well, hey there, Hazel!" the old man cracked a greeting. "Stoppin' by fer a late one, I'se see. Well, we're always glad to have ya."

She rushed right up. "Clonner, I came here to talk to you–"

"Somethin' wrong? You look a tad troubled. Well, whatever it is, I'se sure I can help out."

She leaned closer, eyes wide in the dim lights. "There's a whole bunch of things happening that aren't right. Some of the people around here have . . . changed. I know this sounds nuts, but there's some kind of weird cult activity going on, and it all has to do with Henry Wilmarth and some things we found in his cabin."

Clonner's wizened face seemed suddenly contemplative. "If'n ya wanna know the truth, Hazel, that don't sound nuts at all. And you'se right 'bout some folks changin'. There's some other really queer stuff I been hearin' too, like folks waitin' fer *passports,* of all things, and—"

"And some very unlikely locals anticipating trips to other cities, some of them *international* cites."

A look of dread came to Clonner's eyes. "I heard the same type'a stuff, just over the past two days. And I heard somethin' else, just tonight . . ." Clonner looked to either side as if checking for eavesdroppers. "Come on in, we'se'll go talk in my office . . ."

So it's not just me, Hazel thought in a wash of relief. Strange, though, that the tavern was so quiet in spite of the full parking lot. She opened the door for the old man, waited for him to roll in, then entered behind him.

There must've been thirty people inside, all sitting at tables or at the bar, chatting quietly as they sipped beers. "Low-key night," Hazel said.

"Aw, yeah, we'se not all rowdy rednecks here." Clonner moved his wheelchair to a table, where Ida the barmaid immediately brought him a beer. "Actually, we'se just havin' our nightly meeting, hon."

Hazel's eyes scanned the interior. She saw several women amongst the patrons, but mostly men. Several she'd seen before, like Nate Peaslee, whom she'd met earlier. *Hadn't his name been on that list?* she asked herself. Also, the man and woman—Cal and Emma, she thought—who'd been arguing the other day, with the sheriff playing referee. Plus some others she'd seen around town.

Very slowly, every single person in the bar turned their heads to look at Hazel . . . and grin.

Hazel shrieked when the door banged open behind her, and in walked Clayton and Shot Glass, carrying Sonia inside.

Several men rushed her in a blur; one got her in a neck-lock, the other picked her up by her ankles.

Both had scarlet-crystal rings on their fingers.

"Not you too, Clonner!" Hazel wailed as they carried her to a table and slammed her down on her back. "I thought you were a good person!"

Clonner guffawed from the chair, cracked, "Then ya thunk wrong," and took a swig of beer by denturing the can's lip. "We'se amazed that a gal with yer college smarts could be so blammed stupid. How come ya didn't leave town?"

"Because I trusted *you!*" and Hazel squirmed uselessly against her marauders as they flipped up her denim skirt and pulled her T.S. Eliot T-shirt up over her breasts. A woman stepped forward and handed them some rope. Hazel instantly thought of the pistol—then wilted when she realized she'd left it in the car.

"The Fish Boys tell me you'se're one *hail* of a dirty girl," Clonner remarked.

"Ee-yuh she is," Shot Glass agreed. "En't never met one dutty-ur. Drinks piss like a champ, eats the nut, begs fer it in the ass, and comes when yew choke her aout."

"Dirtiest dang whore you ever seed," Clayton contributed, and then they both carried an unconscious Sonia back into the kitchen.

Clonner showed gleaming but misaligned dentures when he grinned. "So you think yer dirty?" He winked. "*We'll* show ya dirty."

The harder Hazel struggled the more violently she was man-handled. "Haow's *thet* for a pile'a hair?" one commented and *cracked* her exposed pubis hard with his palm. Then Ida, the fat barmaid, wriggled her fingers through it. "Aw, naow, Wilbur Whateley, durn't yew be disrespectin' my li'l friend heer," and then—*Kuuuuur-HOCK!*—she spat into the rust-colored tuft. Next, a man with a bent spine hobbled up, and said, "Shee-it, Ida, if I curn't dew better'n thet, my name en't Charlie Ward"; the twisted codger stuck both thumbs into Hazel's labia, pulled the thumbs apart, then leaned over and—*Kuuuuur-HOCK!*—expectorated right into her vagina. "Thar yew go, honey. Mebbe yew'll git'cherself a hock baby naow." One of the other men who'd tied her up addressed them next: "Yew light-weights durn't know nuthin'." *Smack!* He rammed his fist into Hazel's jaw, knocking her senseless, but as her mouth gaped—*Snnnnnn-ORT!*—he blew a wad of mucus into it after thumbing a nostril closed. Then he pushed her jaw closed and forced her to swallow. "Haow's *thet,* eh?"

The room all applauded.

Hazel reeled on the table. She'd been trussed up with some expertise: her right wrist lashed at the crook of her left knee, and vice-versa; she was a human ball. Two other overweight women played gigglingly with her breasts. "Sech a cute little thing, en't she?" one of them complimented.

"I could et her up!" shrilled the other.

Hazel snapped her gaze to Clonner, gnashing her teeth. "What did you mean when you said it was your nightly meeting?"

Now it was Clonner who played with her breasts—with his stumps. "Don't'choo know yet?"

"It's Frank, isn't it? The *emissary!*"

Clonner's bushy brows elevated. "That it is. See, the whole list's in-dockter-nated now. Takes a day for most, but a few, like, Nate Peaslee there, it takes two, three days."

She remembered Peaslee telling her his dream. *The black mist. The man with sunglasses* . . . Nate grinned at her, then pinched a nipple till she gave off a shrill shriek. He, too, wore one of the marble-sized scarlet rings.

"It's something about sending people to other cites—*big* cities," she grated.

"Aw, now, just you don't worry 'bout that," Clonner said. "What you *need* to be worryin' 'bout instead is what shape you'll be in when we'se done with ya." The old head on the skinny neck craned up, and he shouted to the back, "Clayton! Fetch the Crisco!"

Clayton's fat face appeared in the opening in the kitchen wall. "What fer?"

"Don't question me, boy! Just do it, ya useless, no-rent-payin' fat waste'a space!"

"Awwwww . . . ."

"What are they doing back there with Sonia?" Hazel demanded. "Do anything you want to me, but—*please!*—don't hurt her."

"Oh, we'll do anything we want, hon," the old man said.

"For God's sake, I'm begging you!"

"God's sake? The Devil's? Naw, it ain't 'bout none of that," and then he wheeled around to the other side of the table.

Now that she was trussed up in a ball, they'd arranged it so her ass was just past the table's edge. When she looked around again, she saw everyone in the room circled about her. Several women—all decidedly unattractive and middle-aged—but mostly men, and she saw now that they *all* wore the scarlet rings. *Those rings HAVE to be made from the same mineral as the Shining Trapezohedron,* she felt sure. But the original crystal remained in the car with the pistol. Maybe she could barter with it, because if her loathsome dream about Frank had really been *true,* then the crystal was something they wanted very much. *And they DON'T know that I have it . . .*

From the back, Clayton waddled out, beer belly swinging. He carried a can of Crisco . . .

Hazel didn't wonder what it would be used for.

"Make yerself useful, Clayton," Clonner ordered, holding up his stumps. "Slick me up."

"Shore, grandpap." Clayton scooped out some of the Crisco and began to spread it over Clonner's stump-ends.

"I've seen the list, Clonner," Hazel barked a distraction. "Everybody in this room is on it, aren't they?"

"Just about. A'course, I ain't on it 'cos I ain't got no hands. Cain't work the box." He glanced over. "You *do* know what the boxes're fer, don't'cha?"

"To hold the Shining Trapezohedron."

"Yep. These all folk's'll be doin' the work; my job's just to watch over 'em'n keep 'em out'a trouble 'fore it's time for 'em to go." Now he was rubbing his stumps together, like a chef stropping two knives. "I'm gonna prime ya up now, girl."

She felt the nub of one stump rubbing against her vulva. Before he could insert it, though, she blurted, "But aren't you one man short?"

Clonner hesitated. "Ya don't know what'cher talkin' 'bout. Not countin' me, we gots thirty-three here. Twenty-eight men, five gals." He looked to Peaslee. "Ain't that right, Nate?"

"Uh, well, I think so, Clonner."

"Yeah?" Hazel challenged. "What about Pickman, that fruitcake from the knickknack shop?"

The room stilled. Clonner traversed his chair. "Pickman's here, ain't he?"

Everyone looked around, then someone said, "Shee-it, she's right. He en't heer."

Someone else interjected, "Aw, forget it, Clonner. The bitch just tryin' tew bide for time."

"Time shuhly durn't matter for this 'un," voiced another redneck.

Clonner eyeballed her between her thighs. "Where's Pickman?"

"Let me and Sonia go and I'll tell you . . ."

"Hmm, lemme think . . . Aw, ya know what?" Clonner raised his greased stumps. "I don't give a shee-*it!* He'll turn up." He wheeled up closer between Hazel's legs. "And now I'm gonna stump-fuck ya till ycr eyeballs switch sockets."

"Eeeee-doggie!"

"Give huh a fuckin' she'll never forget!"

"Git 'em *all* the way in, *all* the way in, Clonner!"

It's a psycho-redneck hootenanny, Hazel thought in the grimmest awareness. She tried to relax her groin—knowing what was surely coming–but couldn't help but flinch when Clonner pushed the first stump into her vagina. In and out very slowly at first, but then faster and deeper, each slick, perverted penetration stiffening every muscle in her body. Then—

Not there too . . .

The other stump was punched into her anus and shoved deep.

Hazel's scream concussed throughout the room.

She was being churned; when one forearm went in, the other pulled back, and soon the grotesque trespass took on a regular rhythm. With each penetration, the crowd clapped, like following organ notes at a baseball game. "Come on, gals!" someone hooted. "Get in line and get ready to squat!" *Squat?* Hazel managed to wonder through the consternation. The forearms pistoning in and out made her feel as though her internal organs were being rearranged.

"Oh, me fust!" Ida giggled, floppy tits bobbing as she approached the table. She pulled up her dress and peeled off her panties—

Two men helped her up onto the table.

"What this heer floozy needs is a good face-warshin'."

"Ee-yuh!"

The other four women stood in line, removing their panties as well, while Ida squatted over Hazel's face. The woman's spread pubis looked horrendous, a great sprawl of hair which even trailed down the insides of her thighs. Two fingers pressed into the top of the rooster-wattle vulva, baring the urethra. "Heer yew go, hon," Ida said and began to piss.

The rank stream bored into Hazel's face. Ida swivelled her hips to sway the urine back and forth, up and down; it *gushed* down the sides of Hazel's face. Once the stream sprayed across her eyes and leaked in, stinging. When the urine-flow retarded, Ida flinched her inner muscles, flexing out the last few jets right against Hazel's lips.

"Yew like thet, baby?" she inquired, then tensed, cracked a gassy fart, and got off the table. The crowd roared.

One after another, the remaining four women followed suit, each middle-aged vagina more ghastly than the previous. One's looked like a tumbleweed with a pile of chewed beef jerky in the middle, and another's piss smelled like asparagus. Hazel could barely breathe throughout the entire process; occasionally one of Clonner's forearm penetrations derricked so deeply that her mouth shot open, permitting a flood of urine.

When the women were finished, the applause raised to a din, and in a final gesture they all leaned over and spit in Hazel's face.

Dripping piss, Hazel croaked, "Why are you doing this to me!"

The entire room answered in perfect unison: "Why *not?*"

At last, old Clonner's arms began to tire. Just a few strokes before Hazel thought sure she'd be ruptured internally, the greasy stumps were dragged out, then Clonner wheeled around to rub the stinky sticks across her face. Hazel wished her head could somehow withdraw fully into her body, like a turtle's.

"Yes, sir, that shore was a dandy time," Clonner exclaimed amid more applause. "Back where's I come from, they call that a *ruckin'*." Hazel whirled a dazed glance around and saw now that all the men had their pants open and were idly masturbating. She relaxed against her bonds, then glared at Clonner.

"I killed Pickman, back at Horace's trailer."

"Oh, did ya now?"

"Yeah, and then I called the police and told them I was coming here," she lied.

"Jew heer thet, gang?" someone exclaimed. "She calt the cops!" and then everyone laughed when the man stepped out of the crowd.

A man in a county sheriff's uniform.

"Lyin's a sin, girlie," Clonner chided. "And by the way, this here's Sheriff Tom Malone."

Fuck, Hazel thought.

"You didn't call no one, and if'n ya had, it wouldn't matter. 'Cos we'se protected."

"Yeah?" Hazel spat. "By Frank? Then where is he?"

"Naw, not Frank—"

"By Nyarlathotep?"

Clonner's beady eyes widened. "You know more'n we thought. What'chew know 'bout Nyarlathotep?"

"He's the Messenger, and—what?—he comes here through the Shining Trapezohedron? Is that how it works?"

"What'd'ya think, folks?" Clonner addressed the crowd. "Think we oughta tell her . . . or ya think we oughta fuck the shit out her?"

The crowd roared, men frantically wagging their dicks.

"Nyarlathotep's the messenger for the greatest god of all, honey."

"Yog-Sothoth!" the room cheered.

"And the rest'a the Great Old Ones." He rolled himself back to the table and looked deeply at her. "Yog-Sothoth's the gate, and he'll come though that gate once Nyarlathotep's message has been delivered. A'course, that's the *least*'a yer worries right now, sweet cakes." He shot his gaze to the clamoring crowd. "Line up, fellas, one at a time! We ain't done fuckin' this 'un up—not by a long shot!"

It was then that twenty-eight men—all having fondled themselves to hardness—lined up at the table's edge.

"Tramps like this needs ta be reminded what they'se here for!" Clonner incited like a team coach. "They'se also need ta be reminded that their butt-holes ain't just fer shittin'! So give it to her hard, men! I want each'a now to give her a good throttlin' right up her backside first, then finish up in that big red-hairt pussy'a hers. With any luck we'se'll get her pregnant *and* give her a great big shit-infection up her cooze!"

The men rallied, cat-calling, whistling, stirring into a psychotic hormonal frenzy. *Get ready,* Hazel droned to herself. What point was there in being terrified? *This'll probably take a while . . .*

And take a while it did.

Each man in turn stepped up and deftly sodomized her. They all seemed to stay their orgasms for an inexorable amount of time, and one of them, Nate Peaslee, she thought, pounded his erection in and out of her anus for ten solid minutes. But several stokes before they'd come, each and every one pulled out, slid their penises right into her vagina, then ejaculated. The entire ordeal lasted at least two hours, and was accented by the incessant sound of their hips slapping her buttocks. She was relieved upon each release of sperm into her sex, if only because that meant another one was finished. She felt the separate ejaculations—some quite hefty—slowly ooze out, whereupon each drooled down between her ass-crack and splatted on the floor. Men who'd finished sat back with a beer to watch the rest, and a number of them—to her misery—took a second turn. One man, however, did *not* spend his seminal wares in her . . .

Oh, no, she moaned when she saw him and his bobbing erection come around the side.

Walter "Shot Glass" Brown.

"Cum't be greedy naow," he said, standing spread-legged and jerking off in a manual blur. "I know haow much'ya like it—" and then he clenched up, slowed his strokes, and positioned the shot glass. "Ee-yuh, theer it 'tis, ee-yuh . . ." One thick, milk-white spurt after the next fired into the glass until it was—

"Filled ta the blammed top every dang time!" Clonner celebrated, and then the rest resumed their applause.

Hazel didn't bother resisting now, for she knew that if she did it would only bring a worse death for her and Sonia. She didn't even need to be told to open her mouth.

"Heer ya go, reddy-head, jess the way yew like it—straight up'n neat!" Shot Glass emptied the shot glass into her mouth; its contents slid out in a single, viscid lump.

Hazel's throat clicked when she swallowed.

"Naow is thet a down'n dirty hoo-er or is it not?" someone shouted.

"Good job, missy," Clonner rolled up. "Ya done took all these horny fellas without battin' an eye. We'se proud'a ya."

Hazel barely heard the snide babble. The pain at her sex and rectum throbbed right along with her heart.

Clonner announced to the room, "All right, folks, fun's over fer now. You best all git home. It don't look like the emissary's comin' tonight, so we'se'll just all meet here tomorrow same time."

The crowd murmured goodbyes, high-fiving, back-slapping, and began to depart. Was it her imagination, or was her attention focusing deliberately on the tiny sparkle of blood-red light that glimmered from the tiny stone on all of their fingers?

The ordeal, at least, seemed to be over, but . . .

Is it really?

Hazel's limbs unfolded and flopped to the table when someone cut her bonds. She could sense the warm glob of Shot Glass's sperm in her belly; it seemed to curdle there.

"'Course, it could'a been worse, huh?" Clonner addressed her.

Hazel gaped at him. "You're shitting me, right?"

Clonner shrugged bony shoulders. "It's only Shot Glass's cum we made ya eat. I mean, we could'a been real assholes and made you eat *everybody's* cum, right?"

Hazel coddled her aching vagina with her hands. "Well, yeah, I guess that's true."

Clonner held up his stumps. "So, dang, girl, the least ya could do is thank me. Jiminy Christmas, gal's're so ungrateful these days, ain't they, boys?"

Shot Glass and Clayton were the only ones who remained. They drank beers up at the bar. "Ee-yuh, they'se shuh are, Clonner," Shot Glass agreed, then Clayton, "Ungrateful, ungrateful, ungrateful!" Both men hopped off their stools, Clayton bringing Clonner another beer.

Hazel sat up on the table's edge and winced at the old man. "Let me get this right. You want me to *thank you* for not making me drink *everybody's* cum?"

"Dang tootin', and I'se a bit offended ya ain't already."

Hazel's face lengthened in despair. *For God's sake . . .* She knew she had no choice. "All right," she sighed. "Thank you, Clonner, for not making me eat everybody's cum."

Clonner clapped his stumps together and guffawed. "Who's ta say we didn't?"

Clayton appeared, with his big fat shuck-and-jive uneducated redneck grin. He was holding an aluminum cake pan. When he declined it slightly Hazel saw a *slew* of semen in it.

"You didn't!" she shouted.

"We ain't a bunch'a dopes 'round here, hon," Clonner said.

"Afore we started fuckin' yew," Shot Glass informed, "we put this heer pan on the floor, so's when all that nut fall aout yer pussy, it landed in the pan."

"And guess who's gonna drink it?" Clayton added.

Am I really going to let them do this to me? Hazel wondered. She took the pan. *If I don't, they kill me, and they kill Sonia. If I do . . .*

She looked narrowly at the aggregate sperm of twenty-eight men. The pan lay covered with the pearlescent slime, and it all drooled down to the corner when she tipped it some more. *And some of those guys came twice,* she dismally recalled. *That a LOT of sperm . . .*

"Well?" Clonner urged.

Hazel's head droned. She looked at the pan one more time, then sighed.

"Un-fuckin'-believable!" Clayton railed.

"This heer gal should win some kind'a award!" Shot Glass exclaimed.

"Hardest-core tramp I ever seed in my life!" Clonner added.

Hazel brought the pan's corner to her lips, tipped it up, and let all that sperm slide into her mouth and down her throat.

"There." She smacked her lips. "Happy now?"

"Yer one of a kind!" Clonner cracked. "Would'a bet everything I got you wouldn't'a done it." He winked. "The test's almost over now, hon, and so far, you'se got straight-A's."

Hazel sneered, ignoring the snotty aftertaste. "Test?"

"Ain't but one more thing you gotta do, and if'n ya do it . . . you can go."

Hazel laughed. "What kind of an idiot do you think I am? You're never gonna let me go."

"Shuh we are," Shot Glass said. "Durn't need ya for nuthin' reely." He walked back to the bar with Clayton.

"Serious?" Hazel said to Clonner.

"Shore."

"And Sonia, too, right?"

"Well"—Clonner shook his head—"ain't gonna lie to ya, but yer knocked up friend ain't here no more. I had a couple'a the boys drive her out the minute she got here."

"Drive her out *where?*"

"Don't matter none. See, she's important. But you're . . . *not.* So, if'n ya wanna walk out'a here, all's ya gotta do is one more thing."

Hazel was about to ask what but then heard muted chuckling behind her—plus a whizzing sound. She looked toward the bar and saw Shot Glass and Clayton simultaneously urinating into a beer pitcher.

Fuck, she thought. *What else could I expect?* She said a brief, feeble prayer as she heard the pitcher filling. *God, please let it be so that if I do this, I'll walk out of here alive. Okay? Please?*

"Help an old fella out, Clayton," Clonner said next. Shot Glass brought over the pitcher, which looked about two-thirds full not including the foam. Clayton pulled down Clonner's zipper, fished inside with his fingers, and withdrew—

Holy shit . . .

—a little corroded, fleshy nub.

"What happened to your *dick?*" Hazel had to ask.

"Aw, no big deal. That swami doc gave me what they call a *penectomy.* Cut my willy right off, he did, on account it was goin' ta rot, juss like my hands. Gangrene, he said, from the blammed dye-ur-beet-iss. All's he left were that little nub. But I cain't complain, had plenty'a nuts in my time," and then Clayton hoisted him up from behind, while Shot Glass positioned the pitcher. "Ahhhhhhh," the old man sighed as he let it all come out. The stream frothed, whipping up more foam. But Hazel was wincing . . .

"What's wrong with your piss? It looks—looks . . . *pink.*"

"Aw, some glommerus shit're some such—you'd have to ask the swami. Somethin' out'a whack with my kidneys, so's my piss always got a little blood in it."

It looked like pink lemonade whizzing from the nub of flesh. Hazel's stomach was already roiling. When the old man's bladder was drained, the pitcher was almost full, and tinged with the faintest pink. Being coerced to drink piss was bad enough—as the past several days could attest—but, somehow, the idea of *blood* being in it made the prospect infinitely worse.

Hazel sat sullen on the table edge. Her eyes dimmed when Shot Glass, uttering, "Heh, heh, heh," placed the pitcher into her hands.

"Come on, reddy!" Clayton hooted.

"Shows us what yer made of," Clonner added.

"Durn't disappoint us," Shot Glass finished. "Heh, heh, heh . . ."

Hazel raised the pitcher and began to drink. She tried to pace each swallow, to get as much into her as quickly as possible: *Chug . . . Chug . . . Chug . . .*, like that. The taste, of course, was unmentionable, and worse was the foam and the heat. The process seemed to *pump* the heat into her belly in fast, even measures. *Chug . . . Chug . . . Chug . . .* With each swallow, her toes involuntarily flexed, and her pectorals clenched, causing her breasts to jerk. Her mind reeled by the time she'd drained the level only by half.

Chug . . . Chug . . . Chug . . .

"She's shuh gonna dew it!" Shot Glass yelled.

"Shore is!" came Clayton.

Clonner: "I ain't had me this much fun since my first Hock Party!"

Chug. . . *Chug*. . . *Chug*. . . , and then the remnant foam spilled into her mouth and she was done.

The men clapped heartily, well, at least Shot Glass and Clayton did, but Clonner clapped his stumps as well. The plastic pitcher clattered to the floor, and Hazel fell back on the table. She held her belly through the most dispiriting moan.

"You wasn't kiddin', Shot Glass! She shore chugs piss like a champ."

"Tolt yew."

"And all that nut ta boot!" Clayton chimed in.

Hazel grunted when she sat back up. "Now. Let me guess," she said. "I ask if I can leave, then you rednecks all cluck laughter and say no, right?"

The three men all looked at each other. "What'choo talkin' 'bout?" Clonner piped. "We done said if ya drunk up all that piss, ya could scoot. So . . . scoot."

Hazel did not, could not believe it. Belly pushed out, she slowly slid herself off the table. *No,* she felt sure. *They're bullshitting. I KNOW they are* . . . She took several careful steps toward the door, then glanced over her shoulder.

"Thinks weer jivin' her," Shot Glass laughed.

Clonner laughed harder. "Go on, git! Ain't no reason fer us to keep ya here!"

Clayton grinned, "So ya best leave . . . 'fore we change our mind . . ."

"And we'se know blammed well ya ain't stupid enough to go to the cops."

Hazel eyed them.

"'Cos we got thirty-some witnesses—includin' the *sheriff*—who'll *swear* you come in here all drunk'n disorderly, tryin' to hustle guys for tricks, and actin' all crazy," Clonner added. "You don't count fer shit, so git'cher dirty ass out'a here'n go back where ya come from."

Shot Glass nodded, squinty-eyed. "Forget abaout that preggered friend'a yours, forget abaout this taown'n forget yew evuh came heer."

The old man traversed his chair and rolled toward the bar. "Clayton, git that TV on and see's if ya can find a sports ticker."

"Ee-yuh," Shot Glass said, grabbing more beers. "Dyin' ta see haow the Sox done against the Yankees."

Hazel's mouth fell open. *Could it . . . really be true?* She still didn't believe it. She tiptoed toward the door, took one last glance behind to see them all looking up at the television. Then she ran out of the bar.

No one stood in wait outside. Crickets throbbed, and the parking lot lights blared. Piss sloshed in her belly when she jumped in the car, started it, and slammed it into gear. She'd need to turn left to take the road out of town, but this idea made no conscious presence in her mind. She cut the wheel hard-right.

Then floored the gas.

The Prius plowed right through the front door into the bar, begetting a sound like a wrecking ball. The deafening crash made her grin. The vehicle's penetration crossed the tavern's front section, exploding windows, flinging tables and chairs aside, and then it collided with the long bar itself, where Shot Glass and Clayton sat. Shot Glass was jettisoned ten feet to the right, while Clayton and his bulk was thrown left, right into a very surprised Clonner, whose chair toppled onto its side. Clonner's stumps flailed when he tumbled across the floor.

Planks fell on the car's roof, while more clattered here and there. The television squawked something about someone named Wang throwing a "perfect game" and the Red Sox losing twenty-six to nothing, but Hazel didn't know anything about hockey. She got out with a great grin, walked about the wreckage, then poured herself a draft beer.

NOW it's Miller Time . . .

She traipsed around, looking at her handiwork. *Oh, goodie!* she thought. *I think they're still alive.* Each of the men lay in some state of serious disarray, but it was Clayton she approached first: face bloodied, nose smashed, one foot twisted all the way around. He blubbered, shuddering on the floor.

Hazel prodded his big belly with her foot. "Hey! Clayton! Don't die! Don't pass out!"

Puffy eyes and a ballooned face looked up at her. "Ya crazy tramp! Look what'choo done ta me!"

"Well, what did you expect, after the twenty-eight-man gangbang?"

"Shee-it! You tolt us yerself ya was a nympho! Alls we done was give ya what'cha asked fer!"

"Clayton. I did not ask to drink a cake pan full of sperm or a beer pitcher full of redneck piss." She stepped on his smashed ankle, and he screamed. "Tell me where Sonia is."

His crushed voice sputtered. "I don't know, I don't know–"

"Really?" The lemon-squeezer on the bar was practically calling her name. It took Hazel no time at all to snatch it up and haul Clayton's pants down, revealing his terror-shriveled genitals. She placed his right testicle into the lemon-squeezer's cup, and with no preamble pressed the handles together . . .

The sound–actually a wet *crunch!*—thrilled her, but much more gratifying was the deep, walrus-like caterwaul that exploded from Clayton's fat throat.

"Clayton. Where's Sonia?"

"I don't know, I'se swear!" he bellowed. His face looked twisted, eyes flipping back and forth.

She placed the left testicle in the squeezer.

"Wait, wait!" he begged. "I 'member now! They'se took her to the bus station!"

Hazel looked at him, said, "You're lying," and then–

cruuuuunch

–the left testicle was pulped. *He doesn't know,* she determined, *and neither does Shot Glass.* The only one who might know was Clonner.

Clayton now lay as a mass of convulsant, whimpering fat. From the bar she plucked a glass swizzle stick, lubed its end with spit, then slipped it all the way down his urethra.

"Naw, naw, I'm begging ya's . . ."

Snap, Snap, Snap!

That done, she approached Shot Glass, who lay bulge-eyed, both legs broken at the shins. Should she use the lemon-squeezer? *Hmmm,* she thought. Evidently, Hazel was on a urethra kick today, for after another sip of beer, she grabbed the lamp next to the cash register, pulled it around, then turned it off. She shattered the bulb, baring the two lead-stems. Then . . .

Down came Shot Glass's pants.

He boo-hoo'd like a baby when she arranged the flaccid meat of his penis. Once or twice, he tried to jerk away, but for this he was rewarded by Hazel's hand squeezing the fractured area of a shin. "In ya go," she said, daintily working the bulb's first lead-stem into the despairing piss-slit. Then she merely inclined the lamp a few inches until the second stem touched one hairy ball.

And she turned on the light.

It was a rock 'em, sock 'em good time watching Shot Glass stiffen up and convulse on the floor. Several times she clicked the lamp on and off, to cause his yowls to alternate. After a minute or two, the whites of his eyes turned tomato-juice red, his balls began to smoke, and his cock began to turn gray and shrink, for in a sense, it was cooking.

When it looked like he was about to croak, Hazel removed the lamp. "Haow yew like *thet?*" she asked.

He blubbered something, barely conscious now, his tongue protruding.

"Could've been worse, though, right?"

He must've heard her, for his reddened eyes widened at the words.

"I mean, I could've been a real asshole and crushed both your balls like I did Clayton. The way I see it, you should thank me, and frankly I'm offended that you haven't already."

He made coarse, hacking noises, trying to speak.

"Say 'thank you, Hazel, for not crushing my balls like Clayton.'" She wagged a finger at him. "If you don't, I *will* crush 'em *and* electrocute your dick some more."

Shot Glass's cheeks gusted breath, his tongue still sticking out; however, in spite of this impediment, he made feeble noises that crudely repeated what she'd ordered.

"You're welcome," she said and—

cruuuunch

cruuuunch

—crushed both balls with the lemon-squeezer anyway.

That was about it for Walter "Shot Glass" Brown. *Okay,* she thought. The television still jabbered on, now about someone with the name "A-Rod" getting two grand slams. Hazel presumed that this person must've won the hockey game so he'd been rewarded with two free breakfasts at Denny's. She glanced over and saw Clonner trying to move away from her on all fours. "Oh, don't leave, Clonner. We need to have a chit-chat."

She poured herself another beer behind the bar, then hunted around. *This'll have to be good . . . Ah!* On a shelf she found a roll of duct tape, and in the corner, a plastic bucket. She brought them around, grabbed the plastic bag out of the car, and slammed her foot down on Clonner's back which threw his legs and stumped arms out.

"Crazy bitch!" he cracked. "I'm calling the sheriff!"

"Really? *How?*"

"Fuckin' women are all nuts, they is! I'm handicapped, fer shit's sake!"

Hazel waved the pistol in his face. "Listen, Clonner, I could shoot out your knee caps and elbows with this gun, electrocute what's left of your dick with the lamp, and crush your balls with my lemon-squeezer, and you'd probably tell me where Sonia is, right?"

His waxen face glared, stumps struggling on the floor. "I don't know where she is'n even if I'se did, I wouldn't tell ya' cos what those things'd do to me fer spillin' my guts is a million times worse'n anything you can think of!"

"What *things,* Clonner?" Her eyes thinned. "The Tentacle People?"

"The minions'a Yog-Sothoth!"

Hazel still refused to believe it. Those had been hallucinations, or tricks of light when she'd stared into the jpeg of the Shining Trapezohedron.

"You're going to tell me where Sonia is," she said and pulled the plastic bucket over. Then she stuck her fingers down her throat . . .

It was a Niagra Falls of vomit that gushed out of her mouth: sperm, beer, but mostly sudsy urine. *Lots* of it. With every depression of her fingers, her stomach sucked in, and out gushed more, one dizzying heave at a time. It took several minutes to get it all out, and upon doing so, her abdomen ached fiercely. Yet in spite of the discomfort, she smiled in deep satisfaction, for the bucket now stood about half-full. *But it has to clear his nose,* she knew, so, to add to the level, she squatted over the bucket and urinated. It had been awhile, and she was delighted to see that her own contribution had increased the level by another inch at least.

"Get it yet, Clonner?" she asked.

"*You'se* the one who don't get it, ya crazy psy-kerpath! I don't know where yer friend is!"

"But you told me you ordered your men to take her away."

"Yes!" he spat, and then the poor man's dentures fell out. He gummed the next words, "It were the emissary who tolt 'em 'zactly where to take her!"

The emissary, she thought. *Frank.* Instantly she got the hunch that Clonner was telling the truth. By now, of course, and quite understandably, Hazel was in the middle of a solid bout of temporary insanity, yet some aspect of her reason remained very much intact, proof of her mettle. From the bag, she removed the Shining Trapezohedron.

"Where in tarnations did'ja find *that?*" Clonner yelled, amazed.

"Doesn't matter. But you know what it is and you're going to tell me." She held the egg-shaped crystal between them, then turned it in the barlight; it glittered like stardust. Thurnston Barlow had told her *not* to look at it, but the stone's arcane beauty made it impossible. Her head tilted as her eyes grew wider . . .

Were the facets actually moving, the angle of each polygonic plane changing? It simply couldn't be, she *knew* this, yet the more deeply she looked into the crystal's scarlet-black depths, the more she felt it pull on her own mind.

"Jesus!" she shrieked, and dropped the stone.

She could've sworn she'd seen a face—*Frank's* face—grinning back at her.

It was as though her brain was pudding that someone had their hands in, and those hands pulled out when she'd dropped the crystal.

That horrid crystal, has . . . a power, Professor Barlow's words creaked back.

Hazel jiggled her head to shake out the images, then looked at Clonner. He remained lying like a pile of clothed sticks, yet he was shivering with his eyes squeezed shut.

She poked him. "What exactly does this do?"

Clonner desperately shook his head.

"Open your eyes!" she shouted. "I won't make you look at it."

The old man begrudgingly obeyed, lower lip trembling.

"How does it work?" She picked it up again, removing the metal box from the bag. "What—like *exactly*—is it supposed to do?"

"Just forget it!" he cracked.

"It goes in here, right?" and she opened the box and eyed the metal band within. She turned the crystal in her hand . . .

"Fer Jesus' sake, don't *do* that, girl!"

She lay the crystal on the band . . .

"It's a rock in a box, Clonner! It's not *magic!* How can you *believe* that?" but even as she'd asked the question, she had to wonder what *she* believed.

She held the opened box before his withered face. "So what now? I'm supposed to say some *magic words?* I'm supposed to utter an occult spell, or babble out some geometric equation? What? Tell me!" Her eyes narrowed on the box. "Am I supposed to close the box?"

"Don't close the box, ya psycho bitch!" Clonner yelled, and just as Hazel's fingers did indeed close the intricate lid on the box–

She shrieked at a loud *Bang!* from outside, loud as a howitzer going off, and more planks clanked to the floor from the abrupt concussion. The lights blinked on and off. It seemed as if the ground beneath the tavern had hiccupped, tossing the building up an inch and letting it slam back down.

The concussion caused Hazel to drop the box, where it clattered open on the floor. The Shining Trapezohedron rolled out.

"Don't do that again!" the old man wheezed. "It ain't time! Things ain't ready!"

Hazel was growing furious. Yes, the horrendous bang had startled her but she knew there was a sane explanation. "Clonner, this crystal didn't cause that sound."

"Yeah? Then what did?"

Hazel shrugged. "It was a clap of thunder, or a transformer blowing out." It had to be . . .

She momentarily looked outside and found a clear night sky looking back. The closest transformer, mounted on the phone pole which housed a parking lot light, stood intact.

"Tell me what you know about this crystal and I'll let you live," Hazel said when she returned.

"Kill me," blurted the crumpled old man.

Hazel pointed to the bucket. "I will drown you in that bucket full of piss, puke, and cum!"

The old man actually smiled in spite of his terror. "Then do it, ya red-hairt little whore. Know what you are? A cream-pie with tits. And I'll bet'cher mama blows dogs."

Hazel smiled. "You must really want to die, Clonner. I'm off the hook right now, I feel *crazy,* so believe me, I'll do it. At least tell me. Tell me why you want to die."

"'Cos I fucked up is why!" Clonner hitched. "When the emissary come back, if I ain't dead . . . he'll take me to them *things . . ."*

"There are no Tentacle People," she said through gritted teeth. "I dreamed that . . ."

"Ya didn't dream it, ya asshole! They'se real! And what they done ta yer friend, well . . ."

How could Hazel forget what Sonia had insisted? *They switched my baby with a MONSTER baby!* "She was in a delusional state, Clonner."

Clonner managed a smile. "Let me ask you sumpthin', Twinkie. Was it your mama taught you how ta suck dick, or your daddy?" The broken old man winked. "My bet's it was your daddy. Bet he had his dick in yer mouth the minute your mama pumped ya out her pussy."

Hazel slumped. He was just trying to rankle her, she knew, to provoke her to kill him more expediently. *You shouldn't have mentioned my father . . .* She was very tired now, physically, and also tired of everything that pressed on her mind. She slapped a long piece of duct tape over Clonner's mouth, then lifted his legs and stood upright such that she was holding the old man upside-down by both of her arms wrapped around his thighs.

"One, two . . ."

She tightened her grip.

"Two and a half . . ."

The old man mewled beneath the duct tape.

Hazel forewent the "three" and lowered his head into the bucket.

God, that's gratifying . . .

She was happy to see the level come up well above his nostrils. Clonner didn't weigh much, but she was surprised he didn't put up much of a fight once submerged. After several long moments, the bucket's horrendous contents began to bubble. Clonner's stumps flailed, however lamely, and then the frail body bucked a few times. The bubbles grew violent, then—

They stopped.

Hazel hauled him out, threw him down, and tore off the tape. Detestable as the task may have been, she straddled him and pumped his chest several times till he hacked out a lungful of fluid. Then—*Wow, this is really gross!*—she cleared debris from his mouth with her fingers, and—*Here goes!*—brought her lips to his, blew, and re-inflated his lungs. Next, she compressed his chest until his heart re-started. A hacking fit ensued, then his eyes fluttered back open.

"Did you meet your maker?" Hazel asked.

Tainted spittle flew when he cracked, "Ya evil bitch! You was supposed to kill me!"

"I did." She smiled. "Then I resuscitated you."

His stumps rowed in the air. "Kill me, ya dirty 'ho! Ya cock-sucking, piss-swiggin', ass-lickin', dog-dick-blowing jizz pot!"

Hazel stood up and smiled, then, by complete surprise, she brought her heel down into Clonner's solar plexus, and when his toothless mouth shot open in a gasp—

Ahhhhh, she thought.

She upended the bucket over his face, filling his mouth.

She watched him squirm aghast-faced, and said "I feel so much better," to the destroyed tavern.

But what of the Shining Trapezohedron and its mysterious box? *We'll see about this.* She picked the odd objects up and stomped outside. Clonner cussed after her, feebly flopping on the floor.

In the parking lot, the sound of crickets and peepers throbbed in a delightful din. The full moon *beamed. Not a cloud in the sky,* she saw, but certainly the tumultuous sound she'd heard minutes ago *had* to have been a particularly vicious thunderclap.

She sat on a bench for a few minutes, to let her psyche calm down. The cricket-sounds tranquilized her. She looked uneasily at the crystal and the box. *I wish I'd never seen these things . . . whatever they really are . . .* She knew she should be trying to find Sonia instead of sitting here but . . .

She had to prove something to herself first.

Hazel set the crazily-angled crystal atop the band. Her fingers hovered. *Nothing's going to happen,* she thought. Then she closed the lid—

What she witnessed took only several minutes to transpire but it might as well have been hours. Sounds immediately deafened her, first the series of the same cacophonic *Bang!* she'd heard before, so loud she couldn't hear her own screams. Then came a great all-pervading *cracking* sound. Behind it all rose wheeling squeals so high-pitched it felt like lances in her eardrums. The squeals came from the sky, and that's where her terrified gaze shot next: to the sky . . .

The sky was *swelling;* it was *churning* itself inside-out, and with each churn it seemed to occlude more of the *real* sky she'd just been looking at. At first Hazel thought the sky was changing, but after the cacophony and chaos began to set to its own tempo, she realized it wasn't changing at all . . .

It was being blotted out.

But by what? What could account for this? Did she hear echoic laughter behind the squeals? Like something of titan proportions laughing into a mountain rift? When she looked again, the moon was now fully covered over, and so were all the stars. The only illumination came from the sodium light on the pole which swayed madly back and forth as if in hurricane winds, but, but—

The *was* no wind.

Hazel sat petrified, staring up with the closed box cradled in her lap. Now the sky began to twist in an impossible swirl, in motions like water going down a drain only in reverse. A thunderous groaning reverberated and pressured her eardrums, and whatever the sky had become, it had turned into sickly colors, a brownish-blackish-gray that seemed to throb. The colors merged into shapes, not accidental but deliberate shapes which left Hazel with no choice but to think of appendages of some kind. Then the appendages began to reach down and touch the land . . .

Each contact flattened what it touched: centuries' old trees, vehicles in the parking lot, and the entire strip mall across the street. The great crunching and crackling trebled, then she noticed rent-marks in the road that were *wider* than the road itself. Uprooted trees flew by in one direction, then a mangled panel truck flew by in the other, with the delirious driver still in it. Hazel watched the light pole bend to the ground as if stepped on by some invisible cyclops.

Desperately, then, she opened the metal box and removed the Shining Trapezohedron.

Nothing happened.

The revelation was met with more of the wheeling squeals, more of the same otherworldly laughter. Amid the chaos, all the electricity shut off, darkening the town beyond. Yet the dark, pulsing luminescence provided enough light to continue to see the destruction. Savaged rooftops blew by but it was nothing like wind that propelled them, more like something concussive or pressurized or perhaps even a perversion of gravity. People flew by, too, screaming people.

A plume of the brown-black murk funneled downward and crushed the town hall building to a pile of rubble.

The sky had become an *excrescence* that was alive, calculating, and premeditating. Hazel kept screaming when several more uprooted trees soared right toward her, then served away at the last second. Now all she could see was the roiled murk—murk within murk—and she thought she also saw shadows within shadows. She had the idea that the excrescence was *evolving* now, even vomiting things up from its midst. Shapes that seemed bipedal disgorged from more shadows and darted about almost too fast to see. Did the shapes have *tentacles* for arms and legs? Could the inky flaps about them be *robes?* Did a quick glimpse into one of the hoods show her a corroded face that was upside-down? Towering above her, though, was the most massive shape of all, a multi-appendaged, glob-headed *thing* that stood hundreds of feet high.

Pressed into the glob was a face that was somehow *no* face. It grinned insanely. Hazel drooled, detecting the suggestion of a monstrous eye up above, a burning, three-lobed eye.

Then the figure began to walk . . .

Down the way, she saw great perimeters of woodland crushed flat with each thunderous step. The smaller figures continued to dash about in the meat-smelling murk, some molesting people with their invading tentacles, others plowing down buildings by merely passing through them. When three of the shadow-boned shapes zipped toward Hazel, she screamed over the impossible din, but just as the things meant to seize her, they paused, and skirted away, right into the tavern. Seconds later, they hauled out the squirming forms of Clonner, Shot Glass, and Clayton just as a rive formed in the lowest part of the murk–not a rive, no, but an orifice. One at a time, they dragged their victims through the orifice and disappeared.

All of this chaotic sound, motion, and destruction took place all around Hazel. *The crystal,* she numbly thought. *It's protecting me while everything else is being destroyed* . . . Now the earth in the distance actually *beat* as if by the footfalls of a colossus.

When Hazel ran across the parking lot—

Wham!

—the entirety of Bosset Way's Woodland Tavern was first crushed flat, then upheaved into a million pieces.

What am I gonna do!

The earth continued to beat, the mad flutes piping, and the evil shadows soaring this way and that, and all the while that obscene colossus continued to pound the earth.

Hazel fell to her knees and curled up shrieking into a ball.

"Give me that!" snapped a meaty voice above her, and suddenly two hands were scrabbling at the Shining Trapezohedron and its carrier. Hazel's eyes flicked up—

"Frank!"

Indeed, it was Frank who'd prized the objects away from her: unkempt, dirty, hair sticking up. He still wore the preposterous sunglasses. "Hazel, you *idiot!*" he roared, black breath smoking.

"Frank, for God's sake, what is *happening?*"

"What's happening? You're destroying the town, that's what's happening," he fumed. Very quickly, he placed the Shining Trapezohedron back into the metal box, closed the lid, and muttered, "Meb gled'nl, e uh, ngai ygg . . ."

The words gusted out with his black-mist breath, and when he'd finished speaking them—

The sky *cracked*—

Hazel stared.

—and the excrescence and all in its midst convoluted in on itself and—

Bang!

—was gone.

Hazel stood reeling. Above, the stars twinkled, and the full moon's bright white light bathed both her and Frank as they stood in the destroyed parking lot.

"You're quite the little dickens," Frank said. He chuckled and shook his head.

"I just accidentally did what Henry Wilmarth did in St. Petersburg last Mother's Day," Hazel murmured.

"Yes, and it was damn foolish. But—" He held up the crystal. "Your foolishness provided me with *this*—the very first stone. It's ten million years old, Hazel. And now that we have it . . ."

"Now that you have it *what!*" Hazel shouted.

"Just forget it. I've got a lot of work to do." Frank turned around and began counting off steps. "One, two, three—"

Hazel jerked after him. "Where's Sonia!"

"Safe. With us—five, six, seven—"

"Bullshit, Frank! I want answers!"

Frank began to jog. "Eleven, twelve, thirteen—Go home, Hazel, and consider yourself lucky—sixteen, seventeen, eighteen—"

"Why?"

"Twenty, twenty-one—Because I'm letting you live—Twenty-five, twenty-six—"

Hazel broke into a sprint. "Thirty-three passports! Thirty-three people! And the thirty-three clay boxes you paid Horace Knowles to make!"

"Thirty, thirty-one—"

Hazel grabbed him and halted his progress. "Henry's notes said that the non-Euclidian theorem relied on an energy quotient of ten to the thirty-third power!"

Frank turned to face her. He smiled. "Your yearning to know is *remarkable,* Hazel. But won't you take my word for it that it's really something you *don't* want to know?"

"No." She shuddered in place. "Tell me."

Ever grinning, he took one step backward. "Thirty-two . . ."

"Don't leave me here not knowing, Frank!"

"Thirty-three—"

Frank disappeared in a puff of meaty black mist.

Figures . . . Hazel slumped in the moonlight. In the distance she heard shouts, shrieks, and moans. Dogs barked. Sirens of emergency vehicles began to bay . . .

Hazel turned to leave, then—

"Got'cha!"

—two hands reached out of the thin air, grabbed her by her top, and hauled her into oblivion . . .

***

"So," Frank whispered and rubbed his hands together. "Here we are."

Hazel lay crumpled on the stone floor. When Frank had pulled her into nothingness, they'd both been regurgitated into the middle of the Gray Cottage. The sheet of vellum fluttered on the door, then the door slammed shut.

Candle flames flickered all around. Frank meandered about the stone-lined interior, glancing idly out several windows. He carried the Shining Trapezohedron in both hands as though it were as fragile and valuable as a Faberge egg. "You've helped us more than you can ever know," he intoned in a slight echo. His breath gusted black.

"Because of the crystal," Hazel said.

"Finding this more than outweighs any detriments you may have caused."

"What detriments?"

"Killing Richard Pickman, for one, and"—he chuckled—"taking Walter Brown and Clayton Martin out of the picture. They'd all become indoctrinated—they were all *agents* for us. Of course, the three of them will have to be replaced, but we've got plenty of time for that."

Hazel frowned. "Three of the thirty-three, you mean."

"Yes."

"Frank, did you see the hell that broke loose down there? I wouldn't be surprised if half the people in town got killed, including most of your *agents.*"

"No, no, they were all protected, just like *you* were protected."

"What, the rings? They're made of the same stuff the crystal's made of, aren't they?"

Frank nodded, smiling downward. "And you were protected by merely being in possession of this"—he held up the Trapezohedron—"just as Henry Wilmarth was last Mother's Day in St. Petersburg."

"So what protects you?" Hazel asked.

Frank took off his sunglasses, showing that his excavated eye sockets had been re-filled with golf-ball-sized nuggets of crimson crystal.

"I should've known," she muttered. "But where's the metal box?"

"I left it down there. We don't need it anymore," and then he pointed to the opened suitcase in the corner, which sat filled with thirty-three of the new clay-versions of the box.

"I don't get it," Hazel blurted.

"And you probably *won't* get it all entirely, Hazel. It's incontemplatable. You're not *smart* enough to get it."

She smirked at him. "I know, I'm just a *lit-head.*"

"But, see, *we* were smart enough. Me, my father, and Henry—especially Henry. In a sense, when it came to non-Euclidian thesis, Henry was even smarter than *them.*"

"Who's *them,* exactly?"

Frank only pointed to the door. "The metal box you can think of as a power harness. Like the stone, it's over ten million years old. It was delivered here all those eons ago: an experiment to see what the creatures of this planet might one day learn to do with it. But when Henry broke the code, he realized that the glyphs engraved on it were actually geometric equations that could tap the power of the Shining Trapezohedron. But he realized something else as well."

"What?" Hazel asked, incredulous.

"He realized that those equations were obsolete. They didn't even come *close* to accentuating all of the crystal's energy." His scarlet eyes glittered at her. "So you know what he did?"

The answer clicked in Hazel's head like a pencil snapping. "He rewrote them—"

"And thereby *improved* them—yes! Very good! See, that's how smart Henry was, and that's why he had that bumpkin build him a prototype of a new carrier with the *improved* equations on it."

Hazel leaned up on her elbows, sickened. "I think I *am* beginning to get it now, Frank. He took the crystal and the metal box to St. Petersburg as kind of a test run, didn't he?"

Frank stilled. "Yes," he eventually answered. "Just to see if it really would work. That's why he chose Mother's Day. The city was a ghost town. Most businesses were closed, a good number of residents had left town for the holiday."

"So that if it really *did* work, then there'd be a minimal loss of life," Hazel deduced.

"Exactly. And that was Henry's downfall—he *wussed out* at the last minute." Frank sighed black mist. "When it got right down to it,

Henry wasn't evil enough to rise to his full potential, and neither was my father."

"But *you* are," Hazel said with venom in her voice. "Pure, grade-A fuckin' *evil.*"

A chuckle, then Frank shrugged. "It's all just rhetoric, Hazel. If you like, you can easily replace the word *evil* with the word *responsible.*"

"Oh, for shit's sake, Frank!"

"What?" He seemed surprised. "Was it *evil* for the United States to nuke Japan, or for Rome to destroy Carthage? Was it *evil* for the Mongols to decimate Eastern Europe? Or was it *responsible?* Weren't these more worthy races merely taking steps to keep themselves intact? Weren't they being *responsible* for their own preservation?" He looked more deeply at her with the scarlet eyes. "That's all I'm doing. I'm being *responsible* for my masters."

"You must really hate the world," she sputtered.

"The world? What's the world, really? It's a pile of shit that mankind has fucked up in every way possible. The human race is a *disgrace;* it no longer deserves to even exist. Survival of the fittest, as they say. And mankind ain't it."

"The Shining Trapezohedron somehow triggers devastating storms," Hazel apprized. "And you want to use it to create storms in the thirty-three biggest cities on earth."

Frank's lips pursed in annoyance. "Not storms, Hazel. You saw what happened down there. Was that a *storm?*"

Hazel's lip quivered.

"It was a *summoning*—"

"For some god or something"—she remembered what Pickman and Clonner had said, and she remembered the word from her visions. "Narloth-something."

"Nyarlathotep, Hazel. The Messenger. And his message is annihilation. That was him you saw down there, he and his attendants; his mere presence brings destruction all in the glory of Yog-Sothoth." Frank closed his eyes and for once appeared solemn. "Yog-Sothoth is the key. The Old Ones were, the Old Ones are, the Old Ones shall be. Not in the spaces we know, but *between* them. Yog-Sothoth is the gate whereby the spheres do meet, and Nyarlathotep is his messenger . . ."

Hazel wanted to get up but pain flared whenever she tried. "So *that's* what this is? You're shitting me, Frank. Occult spells?

Witchcraft?"

"Really now, Hazel. In older times—back when this cottage was built—the truth of Yog-Sothoth was indeed camouflaged by occultism. First, Indians? Then superstitious Colonists? Witchcraft was the only concept they could relate to. They were ignorant peasants; they *thought* they were worshiping the devil because the devil was all they could understand. But they were really paying homage to Yog-Sothoth. Their lopsided pentagrams were, unbeknownst to them, non-Euclidian formulae." Frank continued to step about the meat-scented room. "But in truth? It's not witchcraft, Hazel. It's not *spells.* It's simply math that gives one plane of existence access to another."

How could Hazel believe such a thing? And—now—how could she *not?*

Frank's voice darkened as he quoted, "'The earth gibbers with their Voices; the earth mutters with their Consciousness—'"

"Where's Sonia, Frank!" Hazel spat.

"'—where reverence of their Word lingers, and upon where their Totems are blessed, they come. They come and they roil the seas—'"

"Frank!"

"'They smash the forests.'"

"Frank, what's *happened* to you!"

"'They crush the cities . . . '"

Suddenly the wind could be heard howling outside. Frank turned to her again. "They made me an offer, and I accepted. *That's* what's happened to me. They made the same offer to my father who began to accept it but then reneged. For this he was blinded. They made the offer to Henry too, but he rejected them outright when he realized the totality of the theorem's potential. I've agreed to serve them, Hazel, but as a full-blooded human they'd find me detestable. So . . . they changed me a little, that's all." He grinned. "I've been transfected with mutagenic material of their own creation, from an entity of servility known as a Shoggoth. Sort of like DNA only much more complicated." He seemed to flinch, as if in momentary discomfort. "It takes a while, but once I've turned over, I'll be acceptable to them. I'll be able to serve them, here, once the earth is cleared off."

Hazel didn't want to hear it anymore. "Fine, Frank. Whatever. But where's Sonia?"

"I told you. She's safe."

"She said that something on the other side of that door took her someplace . . . and took her baby out—"

"That's quite true." He coughed. "The baby had to go . . ."

"Frank! That was *your child!*"

Black mist shot from his mouth as he chuckled. "Do I look like I care?"

"What did they do with it?"

"Oh, once aborted I'm sure they used it for amusement and food, after the fetal brain tissue was sucked out, of course. They use that for research."

Hazel cringed against her body's aches and pains. "And *then* what?"

"Think, Hazel. They took the baby out to make room."

"To make room for *another baby!*" Hazel shrieked. "I thought she was crazy when she told me that, but it's true, isn't it? They took her kid out and put one of *their* kids in!"

Frank's moldering face creased up in the sharpest frown. "Oh, Hazel, you're hopeless. We have thirty-three cities on the list, right? And thirty-three passports coming for thirty-three agents. You *know* this. Once the passports are processed, thirty-three plane tickets will be issued. The theorem works in sequences of thirty-three; this *has* to be obvious to you now. *Think*, Hazel. *Think*."

"I *am* thinking, you prick!" she yelled. "But what's all that got to do with them putting a monster in her belly?"

Frank walked over to the suitcase and pointed. "Thirty-three power-carriers, right?"

"Yes!"

"But only *one* of these," and he held up the Shining Trapezohedron. "*Now* do you understand?"

Hazel was about to yell an emphatic *No!* but instead she shrieked when a loud knock came to the door.

When Frank opened it, it was not the night sky nor the twilit town that she saw, it was dark, pulsing blood-red light. Tendrils of black mist slithered up from the floor, and then she heard a squishing sound—

No, no, no . . .

—as four robed and hooded aberrations walked into the room. Their hideous inverted cones for feet moved them inside, and in their tentacular arms they cradled Sonia.

She was nude, dull-eyed, and very, very pregnant. Her entire body shined as if shellacked, and for the most irreducible moment, her head lolled to one side and she made eye-contact with Hazel. Her lips tried to move but no sound came out.

Two of the things constricted their tentacles to part Sonia's thighs, then Frank stepped up. He leaned over, peering between his fiance's legs like a demented gynecologist. He raised the Shining Trapezohedron—

"No!" Hazel screamed.

—and inserted it into Sonia's vagina. He pushed, then his hand disappeared, then half of his forearm had been inserted as well. Then: *shhhhluck*...

He pulled his hand out, leaving the crystal in Sonia's womb.

"That's why they sucked out the baby, Hazel. Not to replace it with one of their own but simply to make room."

"For more Trapezohedrons," Hazel croaked.

"Now, for the first time in history, all thirty-three of them are together." He patted the bloated stomach. "Perfect hiding place, huh? And when the time is right, each agent will come to her, take their crystal and their power carrier, and then fly to their pre-assigned destination." He addressed the robed things. "Take this cow out of here. I'll arrange for her transport later."

They walked back the way they came, Sonia satcheled in their ropy arms. When they'd cleared the threshold, the door slammed.

Was Frank fidgeting now? He seemed to do so as if chilled. "The power is exponential, Hazel. With all thirty-three crystals on earth at the same time? Let me give you an example. Once activated, darkness is what summons Nyarlathotep. Together they're all thirty-three times more powerful than if used individually. Now, imagine the force that Henry unleashed in St. Petersburg being increased by thirty-three but instead of fifteen minutes of activation, it goes on *all night long.* Can you *conceive* of that? Hmm? When the agents use these, they will begin at the minute after sunset, and it won't stop until dawn. It starts in the middle and works outward. See, Nyarlathotep is like your God in a way. He is omnipresent. He can be thirty-three places at once, or thirty-three *million* places. I'll bet we kill a billion people the first night. And when the first thirty-three cities are annihilated, the agents will then proceed to the *next* largest city, and on and on until there's nothing left." A hush filled the room. "It will be glorious . . . Glory be to Yog-Sothoth and to his messenger Nyarlathotep, whose message is annihilation."

"When, Frank?" came Hazel's parched question.

His grin seemed multi-dimensional. "When the stars are right. When the sun is in the Fifth House and Saturn is in Trine. Then Yog-Sothoth will come again, once His messenger has made way for Him."

"And what about you?"

"Me? I will live to serve them and their retinue forever, here and everywhere, in other dimensions, in other phase-shifts." Frank's breath rattled when he sighed. "Forever and ever . . ." Was he limping when he went and opened the door? He looked out into the twilight as if marveling at preeminent sights. But when he turned—

Hazel winced.

Frank's pants were open, his genitals exposed. "For old time's sake, okay? You do it so well."

"Frank, do you have any idea of the *shit* I've been through?"

"But that's life, isn't it?" He stepped forward until his limp penis dangled before her face. "Please? Then you can go."

Hazel wished she could dematerialize.

"I said please." A chuckle. "And it's not like I have to."

Groaning, Hazel straightened up on her knees. His crotch couldn't have smelled more foul; obviously he hadn't washed in days. She kept her mind blank when she took the shriveled flesh into her mouth and began to work it with her lips. The malodorous balls started constricting at once, then the puny flesh lengthened to full hardness in only moments. She got up as much spit as she could, then moved her head back and forth till she found her rhythm.

"Yes," he seemed to gurgle.

Her head bobbed, lips tightly sliding, tongue curled beneath the veiny, hot shaft. When his hips began to quiver, he grabbed her head and started humping her face. But when he came—

Frank's throat boomed laughter.

—he violently filled Hazel's mouth with anything *but* normal semen. It was more like chunky slime, with a rotten and somehow tarry taste. The putrid slop filled her mouth one gust after another, until she pulled her lips off and shrieked, only to take another blast right in the face. Frank was jerking the rest out by hand, laughing in a deep sub-octave staccato, and when it was done, Hazel leaned back against the stone wall, sopped.

"There!" Frank exclaimed. "Yes—look! It's happening!"

The final stroke of his hand peeled the skin off his penis, and then the penis swelled as if from within. Frank tore the scrotum and testes off too, tossing them aside, then looked down with his scarlet eyes and watched as the skinless shaft expanded and then—

Pop!

Frank's old human penis split open, and from within sprang a new and incontestably *inhuman* one. What emerged, however, was something she'd seen before, in her visions: a grayish coil of meat, like the first two feet of an elephant's trunk.

Only then did Hazel look at the rest of him.

Black mist seemed to exude from his pores; he was *teeming* with it. Whatever this otherworldly ichor was, it melted off his clothing, his shoes, even his belt and then began to melt off his *flesh.*

Hazel simply stared, even as the last of the noxious ejaculation dripped from her mouth.

When the metamorphosis was complete, Frank's humanity had been sloughed away, and what stood now in its place was the *new* Frank . . .

Hazel began to crawl toward the wide-open door.

The thing was a twist of what could only be called tentacles: two for arms, two for legs, and a suckered column of many such appendages comprising his mid-section. Inverted cones of flesh sufficed for feet that *schucked* when he stepped forward.

By now Hazel was quite ready to die, but before she could roll herself over the threshold to plummet to the bottom of Whipple's Peak, the thing that used to be Frank snatched her up with its ropy arms and held her aloft.

In a slopping voice, he gushed, "Glood bye, Hlazel!" and then he flung her viciously out the door.

Silence. Stillness.

Hazel expected to plummet immediately to her death but instead she merely hung there in the air . . .

In the doorway, the monstrosity was donning a crimson robe with gold fringe. When it pulled the hood up over the nodule-like bump for a head, Hazel glimpsed its face.

If the pestiferous visage could even be *called* a face, its features were upside-down. A puff-lipped mouth formed an arc on the forehead, while irregular outbreaks for eyes extruded from the cheeks. Its complexion gave the face the overall semblance of an overcooked pie.

"Shub neb flurp n ey ftagn," it said to her and waved a mocking tentacle. "Naabl e uh bleb nuuurrlathotep—"

Hazel fell.

6

"God in Heaven," whispered Father Greene, pastor of the United Trinity Church of Christ, near Providence, Rhode Island. He stared through the car window with eyes held wide on what could only be called a *landscape* of destruction.

Sitting beside him behind the steering wheel was an equally shocked grad student by the name of Ashton Clark. When the state police had noticed Father Greene's roman collar, they'd allowed the vehicle to pass through the road blockade.

"This is horrendous," Ashton fretted. "Everything looks *flattened*."

Greene gripped the silver cross about his neck. "It's even worse than the news reports this morning."

The great pines and oaks that densely lined the road had, indeed, been crushed flat by a storm of incredible magnitude. The news had yet to properly identify what had happened here. Hurricanes brought rain, yet there'd been none, and they certainly couldn't form instantly. A multiple-vortex tornado system was the only speculation thus far.

"Just like the Mother's Day Storm in St. Petersburg," Ashton muttered. "And I don't like the common denominator."

"That man, yes," Greene replied. "The suicide."

"Professor Henry Wilmarth. Sir, it's just *too much* of a coincidence. The guy killed himself *here,* in *this* town, just last week." He paused as they cruised by a small trailer park: crushed flat. Ashton saw limbs sticking out of some of the folds of metal. "And now . . . *this.* Same thing all over again. You tell me."

"It's not for us to know, Ashton," the reverend said. "It's for us only to have faith. We *must.*" He crossed himself when they passed several mangled bodies. "I have faith in God on High that Hazel is still alive . . ."

Ashton was about to say something but then his lips stilled when he saw a woman whose body had been accordioned between two felled trees. Some of her internal organs hung out her mouth, shadowed by flies.

"I guess . . . this is the town," Greene remarked. An upside-down sign lay across still more snapped trees: WELCOME TO BOSSET'S WAY. POPULATION: TOO FEW TO COUNT. The demolished forest-scape gave way, then, to what had once been a small town square, crushed buildings and cars its most salient feature now. Several people in the road looked crushed flat as well, as if steam-rollered. What on earth could've *done* this?

Ambulances sat with lights athrob, while National Guardsmen stretchered out corpses they'd found in the rubble. A strange tarped pile lay near what looked like a demolished tavern: *More dead bodies,* Ashton thought, but then—

He jerked the car to a halt, jumped out, and ran.

"Ashton! Where are you—" Father Greene got out and chased him, hurtling over tree stumps, debris, and more bodies.

"That car!" Ashton yelled. "Look!"

Huffing, the older man peered and spotted a silver sedan sitting half squashed under rubble from the tavern. *Rhode Island plates,* he detected.

Ashton plowed into the mess, throwing planks, heaving rubble aside. "I'm pretty sure this car belongs to Professor Sonia Heald! It's the car she and Hazel drove up here in!"

Please, God, please, Greene prayed, prying planks away. *Don't let my daughter be in that car.* No one inside could've possibly lived.

"Thank God, it's empty," Ashton said, and slouched on his knees. "But it's got to be the right vehicle." He pointed to the Brown University sticker on the cracked windshield.

"This cabin they went to," Father Greene inquired. "We've got to find it."

"Wilmarth's cabin." Ashton dusted himself off. "We'll have to ask a local . . . if any are still alive."

They meandered back out to the parking lot. "Keep looking around," the pastor said. He hefted his prayer book. "I suppose I'd better do my job," and he approached the tarp-covered corpse pile and began to read the Intercessions for the Dead.

When Ashton saw a man coming down a side road, he ran up. It was an *old* man, bent-spined. He hobbled along bearing a suitcase.

"Sir, sir! I'm trying to find the Wilmarth cabin," Ashton begged. "Do you know where it is?"

"Waal, ee-yuh, I dew, young feller," the codger said, and wiped his brow. Advanced age and a life of hard work had wizened his face. "Jest up that road theer, but . . . I en't gonna lie to yew, son. I walk by theer this mornin' and it's . . . waal, it's destroyt."

Ashton slumped in place. "Have you seen a young woman,

early-twenties? Red hair, slim, nice figure? Or a woman with black hair, a *pregnant* woman?"

"New, son. Curn't say's I have." When he wiped his brow again, Ashton noticed a clunky crimson ring on one finger. "Good luck, young feller. I'se got to go. En't many heer survived last night, but they're drivin' me aout."

A car horn honked; Ashton saw an old pickup with several rustic types inside. He helped the oldster stow his suitcase in the back. Then the old man squeezed into the car. "Could'a ben wuss, I s'pose but, son, be keerful 'roaund heer. Be bettuh for yew to leave." The truck rattled away but not before Ashton noticed a similar scarlet ring on the finger of the weathered driver.

A stench was rising, an odd one . . . like fresh meat and rotting meat together. When squawking was heard overhead, Ashton looked up to see great swarms of crows circling, *hundreds* of them. *They want to eat,* the student thought. He jogged back to the pastor just as a military truck roared by, its rear load-bed *stacked* with occupied body bags.

Father Greene was making the sign of the cross over several more bodies. The corpses' limbs appeared burned somehow, charry, yet the bones showing were bent and oddly *yellowed.* One corpse, wearing a Boston College shirt, had a head that looked melted. "What could cause *that?*" Ashton asked.

"God knows," came Greene's solemn reply. "I've seen several bodies like that already." He reached down—

"Keep your hands away!" barked one of the soldiers. It was a sergeant who strode over.

"Sergeant, any idea what—"

"It could be some sort of corrosive," the poker-faced troop told them. "We don't know. Almost everyone from the residential section is dead, and most of them looked burned like that." He grabbed a stick and prodded a dead, fat woman's bowed shinbone. It jiggled as if something had turned it rubbery.

"Corrosive?" Ashton asked. "This was some kind of a freak storm. What could *corrosives* have to do with it?"

"Look, Father," the sergeant said, "I know you're concerned here, but it might be better for you to clear out till we can get things in better order."

"All right, Sergeant," the pastor agreed. He nudged Ashton by the arm and veered back toward the car. "This might be our last chance," he whispered. "What did the old man say?"

"That Wilmarth's cabin was destroyed," Ashton repeated.

"But we've got to look nonetheless."

"The road's up here . . ."

More trucks roared by, corpse-laden, while more ambulances moved in. Blanched-faced EMT's stood drained or knelt grimly before still more corpses. The stench was rising with the sun. It didn't take long in heat and humidity like this; Father Greene had seen as much in Bosnia.

"The road'll probably be blocked by fallen trees," Ashton observed as they approached their car.

"We'll drive as far as we can, then walk the rest." Greene gripped his cross till his knuckles whitened. *All this death—everywhere, but I KNOW Hazel's still alive. She's GOT to be.*

"Hey, Father, look at this . . ."

Ashton had picked something up and handed it to him:

"Jewelry box? Snuff box?" Greene turned the empty object around in his hand. "It seems to be deliberately lopsided—look, the angles are all off."

"Looks like gold maybe."

Greene squinted at the curious hieroglyph-like designs on it. He didn't know why but he didn't like the look of them. On the top was a faint engraving of—

Greene shuddered as if sickened.

"Gold or not it's . . . not for us." He only sensed something *awful* about it, something bankrupt of God, Christ, and the Holy Spirit. He dropped the peculiar box and stomped it flat under his sole.

What he could see of the road leading past the town looked clear. Father Greene took one last look around. *All those bodies. All these people dead.* His faith was tempering—he was *mad.* He ground his teeth as he looked to the sky. *In the name of CHRIST, God! After all I've done in Your service for my WHOLE LIFE, could you PLEASE let my daughter be alive, damn it!*

When he looked across the car's roof, Ashton had broken into a sprint, yelling, "Holy shit!" and commenced to running up the road.

Where's he going? Greene's brow furrowed. He looked up the road—

His heart quaked.

A waif-like woman staggered toward them, her eyes opened in a thousand-yard stare. Her hair looked filthy but its color could not be denied: oxblood red.

"Hazel!" Ashton croaked. "Thank God you're alive!" Ashton nearly collided with her. He wrapped her up in an embrace, tears welling in his eyes. "Oh, *shit,* we were so worried."

When Father Greene's disbelieving stare snapped, he ran toward them. *Impossible. A second ago I looked up that road and she was nowhere in sight . . .* He wasn't about to argue, though. But it looked like Father Greene had just run up a *big* marker with God . . .

"Ashton?" Hazel mumbled. She clung onto him, weak-kneed.

"Are you all right?"

"I . . . don't know . . ." Her shock-wide eyes flicked to her father. "Oh, dad!"

Greene hugged his daughter as he never had. "Honey, we thought . . . ," but he let the words dissolve. She was covered with some indescribably foul-smelling muck. "Hazel, were you sick?"

"What's all that gunk on you?" Ashton asked.

"You don't want to know," she whispered.

It didn't matter. Father Greene's prayer had been answered, his greatest wish. But Hazel seemed teetering now. *Probably dehydrated, probably hasn't eaten anything since last night.* "Let's get her back to the car, Ashton."

No sooner had Greene said the words, Hazel's knees went out. Ashton hoisted her up in his arms and carried her to the car.

They arranged her prone in the back seat. Father Greene grabbed a bottle of water, which she half-drained in one gulp once she'd re-composed herself.

"Honey, where are your friends?" Greene asked.

"Huh?"

Ashton knelt before her. "Sonia Heald and Frank Barlow–you know. Hazel, where are they? Are they—"

Hazel looked out into space. "Gone."

Father Greene knelt as well, and gripped her hand. "Honey, Ashton's going to take you away now. He'll get you checked out at the nearest hospital, then he's going to take you back to Providence—"

"No," Hazel blurted.

"Hazel, what are you talking about?" Ashton questioned.

She cleared her throat. "I have to stay here . . ."

"There's no *here,* Hazel!" Ashton exclaimed. "There was a storm last night—"

Did she smile sarcastically? "No storm, Ashton. It was . . . something a lot worse than a storm . . ."

"The point is, honey," he father cut in, "everyone here is dead. Come back home." He smiled at her. "Come back to God . . ."

Hazel looked back at him. "I'm not worthy of *home,* dad. I'm not worthy of Ashton, I'm not worthy of you, and I'm *especially* not worthy of God."

"Nonsense! Why do you say that?"

She glanced to Ashton, rolled her eyes, then glanced back to her father. "I'm *erotomanic,* dad. You probably don't even know what that means—"

"Hazel, just . . . forget all that," Ashton tried to stop her.

"I let myself be raped, dad. I submit to *gangbangs.*" Her eyes never blinked as she stared her father down. "I beg men to choke me while they're *fucking* me. I drink their *piss,* dad. So . . . I know damn well God could never forgive *that.*"

"Of course He can!" Father Greene said without even being taken aback. "He forgives worse than that every day." He squeezed her hand harder. "But you have to take the first step. Think about it, honey. Okay?"

Hazel gulped and nodded. When a car idled by, she jerked up and looked out. It was a long, beat-up sedan jammed with people. The trunk had been tied down over a stack of suitcases.

"Survivors," Ashton uttered. "Evacuating."

"Not survivors," Hazel said under her breath. "Agents . . ."

"What's that, honey?" Greene asked.

Did a man in the passenger window actually wink at Hazel? Another weathered, redneck type. Father Greene's stare narrowed on the man's hand as it hung out the window. He wore the oddest scarlet ring . . .

Hazel moaned and fainted.

"She's exhausted from all she's been through," Ashton observed. "The terror of the storm, witnessing all these people getting killed."

"And realizing that her friends are probably dead," the minister finished. He closed the door and came around. "Take my daughter out of here, Ashton. Check her into the hospital, make sure she's all right, then take her home."

"What about you?"

"I'll get a ride out tomorrow." He turned and saw a bevy of National Guardsmen bearing more corpse-laden stretchers out of the woods. "By the looks of things around here"—he held up his Book of Common Prayer—"I'll be able to make myself useful."

"Well, all right. If you're sure. I'll call you on your cell once I've gotten Hazel looked at."

"Thank you, Ashton."

They both stalled in place. More black birds swarmed overhead, and more sirens wailed in the distance. Farther off, they heard helicopters.

Father Greene's face became stamped with disdain. "This is an *evil* place, Ashton."

"I know. I can feel it . . ."

"It even *smells* evil." The stench grew miasmal. "It smells . . ."

"It smells like the devil took a giant shit here."

Greene's shoulders slumped. "Not exactly the words I would've chosen but..yes. You're quite right."

A few more words, then they parted. Ashton backed the car up, then turned onto the main road and drove out.

When two more wan-faced Guardsmen marched by with a stretcher, Greene blanched at the corpse on it: a man, whose entire ribcage seemed stripped of flesh. The bones beneath were cindery yet yellowed and bent wildly out of place, like melted plastic.

"Aw, fuck!"

"Shit, man!"

Greene looked to the commotion. Several soldiers thrashed out of the collapsed woods; they all looked disgusted. When the sergeant asked, one of them said, "We just found a dozen more bodies over there, under a wall. I can't hack this shit, sarge!"

Father Greene sighed. He opened his prayer book again and began to recite, "'Oh, God, whose mercies cannot be numbered, accept our prayers on behalf of the souls of thy servants departed . . . ,'" as he walked without encumberment toward the excruciating scene . . .

EPILOGUE

NEPTUNE, NEW JERSEY
TWO MONTHS LATER

Night-watchman Wally Gilman and bus-driver Joe Sargent stared intently between the curtain-gap at the window of Room 18 at the McNaughton-Regency Motel. Joe had his penis out, was slowly masturbating as the scene within progressed: three men and two women preparing to perform cunnilingus on the room's very nude and very pregnant tenant. She lay on the bed, buttocks at the mattress edge, knees pulled up to make the sensitive aperture between her legs as accessible as possible.

"Unmotherfuckingbelivable," Joe whispered, finessing his penis.

Yeah, Wally agreed. It disconcerted him, though, that Joe's dick was considerably larger than his. *What a ripoff*. . . But of the scene inside?

Wally didn't know what to make of it.

Right now a beer-gutted redneck in a wife-beater T-shirt was kneeling right between the pregnant chick's spread legs. Shiny black hairs spouted up around the pink cleft. The cleft glimmered.

"A pussy-eating party in a fleabag motel," Joe muttered. "And on a pregnant girl ta boot. Man, it doesn't get better than this." The sounds of his masturbation rose.

"Yeah, but Joe, it doesn't make much sense, does it?" Wally queried. "Those guys in there are backwoods rednecks and so are the two women. What's the deal with them coming here in the middle of the night just to go down on a hot preggo and leave?"

Joe frowned over his shoulder. "You're complaining? Who cares? It's probably some kinky swingers club or something."

Wally considered the idea, not terribly convinced.

The moon shimmered down. Wally felt antsy, heebie-jeebied, like someone was watching them from nearby. But when he looked at the scrubby bushes behind him, of course, no one was there.

"Oh, fuck, man!" Joe whispered fiercely. "Look at this shit!"

When Wally peered back into the gap, his mouth fell open.

So THAT'S what they're doing.

The guy in the wife beater, now, had his hand stuck up to the wrist in the pregnant woman's cooze . . .

Joe enthused, "Man, this ain't no pussy-eating party. It's a *fisting* party!"

And so it seemed.

Wife Beater traversed his hand in the pregnant's chick's vaginal vault. He *pushed*...

Next thing they knew, the dude's hand was two inches past the wrist, three, then *four*...

Neither Wally nor Joe uttered a sound as, just a moment later, the dude's arm was stuck up the woman all the way to the elbow.

"Can't believe what I'm seein'," Joe whispered.

"What's he trying to do? Give her an abortion?"

When Wife Beater withdrew his arm, there was a large scarlet crystal in his hand.

Then he stood up, put the stone in a bag, and made way for the next in line.

Joe had stopped masturbating by now. The spectacle had gone from being erotic to outright gross. And more than that, too: inexplicable.

It was a bun-haired fat women who was next to slide her arm into the pregnant's woman's sex and withdraw a scarlet crystal...

Joe had never looked so off-kilter when he turned and leaned against the wall, his face a mask of either fret or confoundment.

His whisper, now, was a fear-traced etch. "Wally. What the *hell* is going on in there?"

"I. Don't. Know."

"There's something really wrong here, man. That chick ain't pregnant. She's got a fuckin' uterus full of *red rocks.* They look like giant fuckin' rubies, man."

Wally stared. "I. Know."

"I've never seen anything so fucked up in my life..."

That statement would prove a fitting epitaph for Joe Sargent, for they were the last words he would ever speak. Wally had spoken his last as well, though he wasn't aware of it just yet. He was taking one more peek at the inconceivable scene on the other side of that dingy window:

A third visitor was extracting a crystal from the pregnant woman's plump vagina...

How many of those things has she GOT in her? came Wally's morbid question.

He turned to look at Joe again just as he received another queer inkling that someone was watching them. He had no time to scream, nor did any synaptic activity in his brain have time to even *consider* what he might be looking at. It had actually been standing there all along, though invisibly from another phase-shift: a slug-skinned, tentacular abomination in a scarlet robe and hood. Simultaneously, the thing had slipped a tentacle-arm about each man's neck, and with a quick constriction—

pop!

pop!

—both Joe Sargent and Wally Gilman's neck-bones were separated, severing the spinal columns. The final image to register in Wally's brain was the marauder's face: swollen lips on a bulbous forehead, eyes implanted on corroded cheeks, all set in the countenance of something rotten.

"Sneb ngal'n shubb," the thing uttered, and then a para-dimensional egress opened rather like a malformed zipper. Wally and Joe were shoved into the egress, then the egress disappeared.

This repulsive servitor—whose name it still thought of as Frank—peeked into the window.

The last agent of the night, a Bosset's Way resident named Jervas Dudley, was just now withdrawing a crystal from Sonia Heald's multipurpose womb.

At the window, Frank nodded in approval.

Minutes later, the agents inside had all left. Tomorrow night more would come, and more the night after that and the night after that, until all of the Shining Trapezohedrons had been dispensed. Then off each agent would go, plane tickets in hand, to their specified target cities. It would not be much longer before Nyarlathotep's message had been delivered, all in the glory of Yog-Sothoth.

Frank eyed Sonia and her robust breasts, her great white belly, the abundant pubic plot, and when he did so, the puffy turd-like lips on his forehead turned up into a smile.

Ah, yes.

Frank decided that once all the crystals were out of the cow, he'd be knocking her up again just for the hell of it.

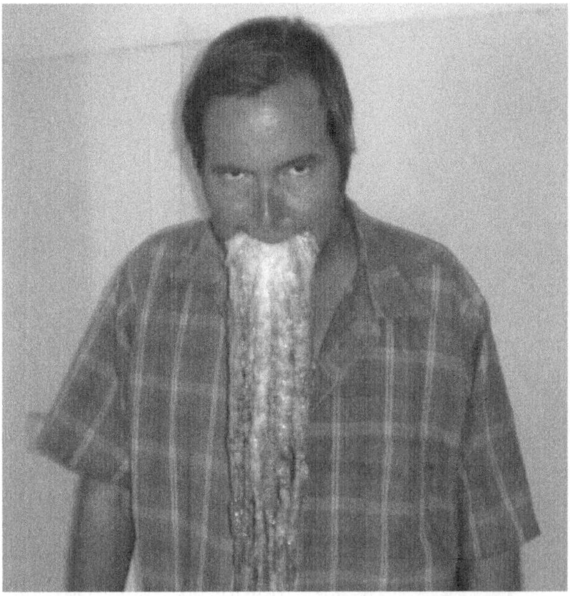

ABOUT THE AUTHOR

Edward Lee has authored close to 50 books in the field of horror; he specializes in hardcore fare. His most recent novels are LUCIFER'S LOTTERY and the Lovecraftian THE HAUNTER OF THE THRESHOLD. His movie HEADER was released on DVD by Synapse Film in June, 2009. Lee lives in Largo, Florida.

deadite press

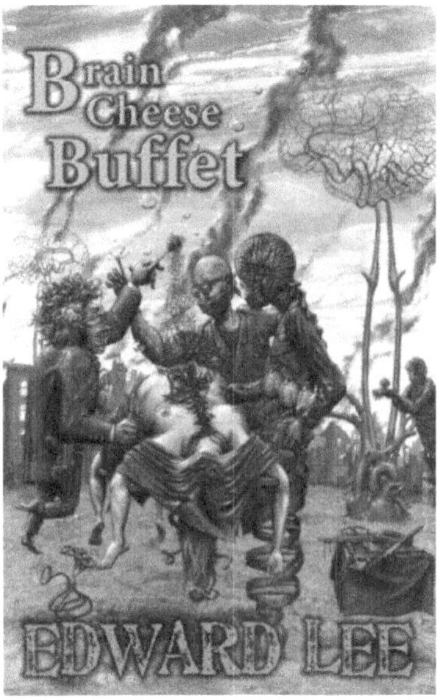

You've seen Cannibal Holocaust. You've seen Salo. You've seen Nekromantik. You ain't seen shit!

Brain Cheese Buffet collects nine of Lee's most sought after tales of violence and body fluids. Featuring the Stoker nominated "Mr. Torso," the legendary gross-out piece "The Dritiphilist," the notorious "The McCrath Model SS40-C, Series S," and six more stories to test your gag reflex.

No writer is more extreme, perverted, or gross than Edward Lee. His world is one of psychopathic redneck rapists, sex- addicted demons, and semen-stealing aliens. Brace yourself, the king of splatterspunk is guaranteed to shock, offend, and make you laugh until you vomit. *Bullet Through Your Face* collects three novellas demonstrating Lee's mind-blasting talent. Featuring "Ever Nat," "The Salt-Diviner," and "The Refrigerator Full of Sperm."

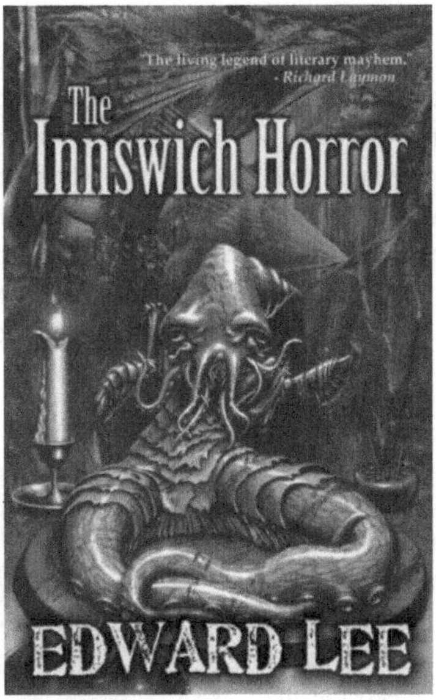

The sickest writer in horror takes on the Cthulhu Mythos!

In July, 1939, antiquarian and H.P. Lovecraft aficionado, Foster Morley, takes a scenic bus tour through the wilds of northern Massachusetts. He wants to go where Lovecraft went, and to see what he saw, to further distill his understanding of history's most impacting horror fantasist.

Join splatter king Edward Lee for a private tour of Innswich Point - a town founded on perversion, torture, and abominations from the sea.

All Aboard Trolley No. 1852!

Through the midnight bowels of New York City, the trolley travels. Admitting only a special sort of passenger, and taking them to a very select destination . . . The 1852 Club is a bordello unlike any other. Its women are the most beautiful in the whole city and they will do anything. But there is something else going on at this sex club. In the back rooms monsters are performing vile acts on each other and doors to other dimensions are opening . . .

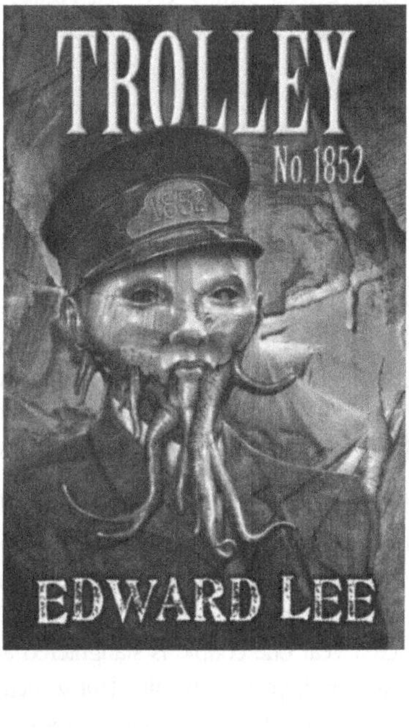

THE VERY BEST IN CULT HORROR

deadite
press

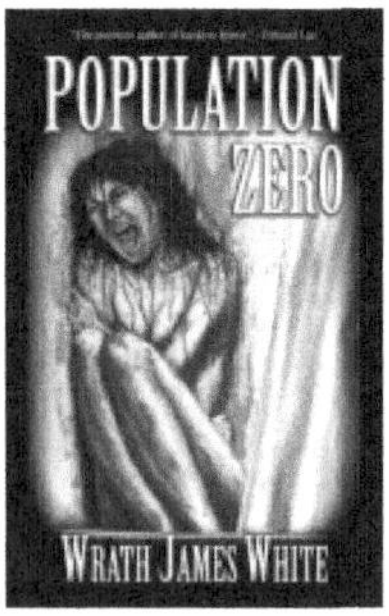

"Population Zero" Wrath James White - An intense sadistic tale of how one man will save the world through sterilization. *Population Zero* is the story of an environmental activist named Todd Hammerstein who is on a mission to save the planet. In just 50 years the population of the planet is expected to double. But not if Todd can help it. From Wrath James White, the celebrated master of sex and splatter, comes a tale of environmentalism, drugs, and genital mutilation.

"Whargoul" Dave Brockie - It is a beast born in bullets and shrapnel, feeding off of pain, misery, and hard drugs. Cursed to wander the Earth without the hope of death, it is reborn again and again to spread the gospel of hate, abuse, and genocide. But what if it's not the only monster out there? What if there's something worse? From Dave Brockie, the twisted genius behind GWAR, comes a novel about the darkest days of the twentieth century.

"Zombies and Shit" Carlton Mellick III - *Battle Royale* meets *Return of the Living Dead* in this post-apocalyptic action adventure. Twenty people wake to find themselves in a boarded-up building in the middle of the zombie wasteland. They soon realize they have been chosen as contestants on a popular reality show called Zombie Survival. Each contestant is given a backpack of supplies and a unique weapon. Their goal: be the first to make it through the zombie-plagued city to the pick-up zone alive. A campy, trashy, punk rock gore fest.

"Slaughterhouse High" Robert Devereaux - It's prom night in the Demented States of America. A place where schools are built with secret passageways, rebellious teens get zippers installed in their mouths and genitals, and once a year one couple is slaughtered and the bits of their bodies are kept as souvenirs. But something's gone terribly wrong when the secret killer starts claiming a far higher body count than usual . . .

"*A major talent!*" - Poppy Z. Brite

"The Book of a Thousand Sins" Wrath James White - Welcome to a world of Zombie nymphomaniacs, psychopathic deities, voodoo surgery, and murderous priests. Where mutilation sex clubs are in vogue and torture machines are sex toys. No one makes it out alive – not even God himself.

"If Wrath James White doesn't make you cringe, you must be riding in the wrong end of a hearse."
-Jack Ketchum

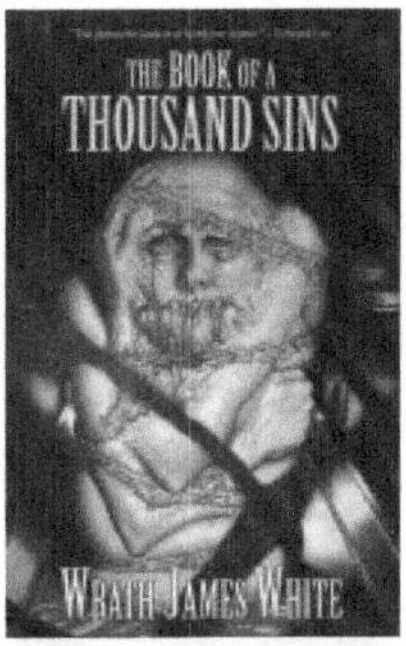

"Squid Pulp Blues" Jordan Krall - In these three bizarro-noir novellas, the reader is thrown into a world of murderers, drugs made from squid parts, deformed gun-toting veterans, and a mischievous apocalyptic donkey.

"*. . . with SQUID PULP BLUES, [Krall] created a wholly unique terrascape of Ibsen-like naturalism and morbidity; an extravaganza of white-trash urban/noir horror.*"
- Edward Lee

"Apeshit" Carlton Mellick III - Friday the 13th meets Visitor Q. Six hipster teens go to a cabin in the woods inhabited by a deformed killer. An incredibly fucked-up parody of B-horror movies with a bizarro slant

"*The new gold standard in unstoppable fetus-fucking kill-freakomania . . . Genuine all-meat hardcore horror meets unadulterated Bizarro brainwarp strangeness. The results are beyond jaw-dropping, and fill me with pure, unforgivable joy.*" - John Skipp

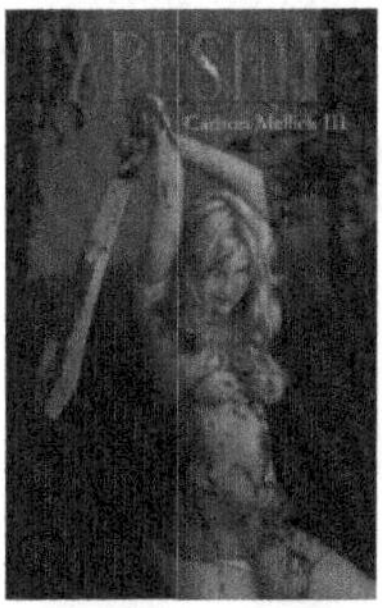

"Super Fetus" Adam Pepper - Try to abort this fetus and he'll kick your ass!

"*The story of a self-aware fetus whose morally bankrupt mother is desperately trying to abort him. This darkly humorous novella will surely appall and upset a sizable percentage of people who read it . . . In-your-face, allegorical social commentary.*"
- BarnesandNoble.com

THE VERY BEST IN CULT HORROR

deadite press

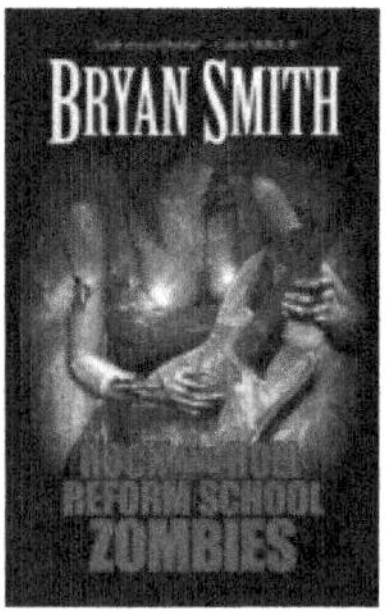

"Rock and Roll Reform School Zombies" Bryan Smith - Sex, Death, and Heavy Metal! The Southern Illinois Music Reeducation Center specializes in "de-metaling" – a treatment to cure teens of their metal loving, devil worshiping ways. A program that subjects its prisoners to sexual abuse, torture, and brain-washing. But tonight things get much worse. Tonight the flesh-eating zombies come . . . *Rock and Roll Reform School Zombies* is Bryan Smith's tribute to "Return of the Living Dead" and "The Decline of Western Civilization Part 2: the Metal Years."

"Necro Sex Machine" Andre Duza - America post apocalypse...a toxic wasteland populated by bloodthirsty scavengers, mutated animals, and roving bands of organized militias wing for control of civilized society's leftovers. Housed in small settlements that pepper the wasteland, the survivors of the third world war struggle to rebuild amidst the scourge of sickness and disease and the constant threat of attack from the horrors that roam beyond their borders. But something much worse has risen from the toxic fog.

"Piecemeal June" Jordan Krall - Kevin lives in a small apartment above a porn shop with his tarot-reading cat, Mithra.She brings him things from outside and one daybrings him an rubber-latex ankle... Later an eyeball, then a foot. After more latex body parts are brought upstairs, Kevin glues them together to form a piecemeal sex doll. But once the last piece is glued into place, the sex doll comes to life. She says her name is June. She comes from another world and is on the run from an evil pornographer and three crab-human hybrid assassins.

"The Vegan Revolution . . . with Zombies" David Agranoff - Thanks to a new miracle drug the cute little pig no longer feels a thing as she is led to the slaughter. The only problem? Once the drug enters the food supply anyone who eats it is infected. From fast food burgers to free-range organic eggs, eating animal products turns people into shambling brain-dead zombies – not even vegetarians are safe!

"*A perfect blend of horror, humor and animal activism.*"

- Gina Ranalli

"Dead Bitch Army" Andre Duza - Step into a world filled with racist teenagers, masked assassins, cannibals, a telekinetic hitman, 100 warped Uncle Sams, automobiles with razor-sharp teeth, living graffiti, cartoons that walk and talk, a steroid-addicted pro-athlete, an angry black chic, a washed-up Barbara Walters clone, the threat of a war to end all wars, and a pissed-off zombie bitch out for revenge.

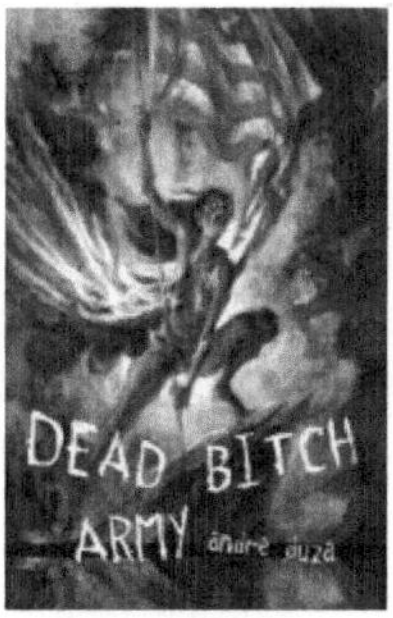

"Fistful of Feet" Jordan Krall - A bizarro tribute to Spaghetti westerns, H.P. Lovecraft, and foot fetish enthusiasts. Screwhorse, Nevada is legendary for its violent and unusual pleasures, but when a mysterious gunslinger drags a wooden donkey into the desert town, the stage is set for a bloodbath unlike anything the west has ever seen. Featuring Cthulhu-worshipping Indians, a woman with four feet, a Giallo-esque serial killer, Syphilis-ridden mutants, ass juice, burping pistols, sexually transmitted tattoos, and a house devoted to the freakiest fetishes, Jordan Krall's *Fistful of Feet* is the weirdest western ever written.

"Jesus Freaks" Andre Duza - For God so loved the world that he gave his only two begotten sons… and a few million zombies. Thugs, pushers, gangsters, rapists, murderers; Detective Philip Makane thought he'd seen it all until he awoke on the morning of Easter Sunday 2015, to a world filled with bleeding rain, ravenous zombies, a homicidal ghost, and the sudden arrival of two men with extraordinary powers who both claim to be Jesus Christ in the flesh.

AVAILABLE FROM AMAZON.COM

CPSIA information can be obtained at www.ICGtesting.com
Printed in the USA
LVOW01s0708080913

351478LV00008B/67/P

9 781936 383399